Island

Sistahs

By

Patrice Frith

PUBLISHED IN THE UNITED STATES OF AMERICA
BY
BLACK FOREST PRESS
539 TELEGRAPH CANYON ROAD
BOX 521
CHULA VISTA, CA 91910
(619) 656-8048

Island

Sistahs

By

Patrice Frith

BLACK FOREST PRESS
San Diego, California
March, 1999
First Edition

DEDICATED TO THE MEMORY OF
MY COUSIN AND FRIEND -

MY PUDDIN'
RODERICK KIRKPATRICK SIMONS
1946-1996

THANKS 'RA'

Bermuda Scenery Calender: Photographer, Mary C.
Dunning
Personal Slides: Photographer, Nigel Richardson
Hair Designer: Rawle Fraser
Make-up: Lauren Perinchief

Printed in the United States of America
Library of Congress
Cataloging-in-Publication

ISBN:1-881116-98-0

Acknowledgment

I began writing this book in October, 1993 while sitting in my Granaway Heights yard. Five years and many life changes later, I have finally finished it. I kept this project very close to me - few people were aware of its existence - and there were times I even began to doubt it would come to fruition. I will be forever grateful to my best friend, my confidant, my inspiration, my soulmate, my love, my future husband - Leroy 'Lee' Hayward, who demanded I pull out my notepads and finish my book. Thank you, baby, for your love and support, for believing in me and for always letting me be just that - me.

To my buddy, my editor, Terry 'Chris' Spencer, thank you, thank you, thank you, darlin', for your invaluable criticism, advice, suggestions and time. Through our disagreements, we did it.

To my parents, Allan and Wilma Frith - who didn't have a clue about *Island Sistahs*, until I completed it - thank you, simply for deciding to have me and always for your never-ending love and support. My siblings, Nell, Glenn, Patrick and Ian, thanks for all being a part of my family and also for your love.

My patrons, friends and supporters, thank you for your continued patronage. I trust you all will enjoy what I hope is the first of many books to come.

Last, but by no means least, I give thanks to my heavenly Father for giving me life and the gift, the fortitude and the tenacity to write.

THE CHARACTERS IN 'ISLAND SISTAHS', LISTED BELOW, ARE PURELY FICTION AND A PRODUCT OF THE AUTHOR'S IMAGI-NATION AND IN NO WAY REFER TO PERSONS LIVING OR DEAD WITH THE SAME NAME.

MAXINE 'MITZI' ROBINSON	CRYSTAL THELMA OUTERBRIDGE
EBONE` SIMONS	MELBA DEE VIVIAN IRENE SCOTT
SUNDAE KELLY TUCKER	MALIQ SIMMONS
MADGE SIMONS	OLEETA ROBINSON
MACKY ROBINSON	FRANKIE
MAXWORTH ROBINSON	GEORGE BEAN
ROBERT	RAOUL OUTERBRIDGE
MARCUS SIMMONS	ROBERTA
ATIBA SIMMONS	AFENI SIMMONS
RODERICK	MALCOLM SIMMONS
MARSHALLE	RANDY
CHARLES	SINCLAIR
SAMMY	NA'IMAH SIMMONS
MICHAE	MIKE
CEE CEE	DEE DEE
AL	SHERRY
SMOKEY	ALBERT
QUINCY 'Q' BUTTERFIELD	MARILYN HUNT
MIRANDA	SONIA
TERRY	RICKY TROTT
RODDY SMITH	RONALD
PEARL	ERIC SIMONS
WENDELL	BELINDA
MRS SEYMOUR	MRS RAWLINS
BEY	MALIQA
TYRONE RYAN BURROWS	SANDRA FRANCIS
ROBYN	GERALD 'G'

CHAPTER ONE

Oh no, I'm not ready for her to come home yet. Mitzi Robinson was sitting on her living room floor, painting her nails and listening to Gladys Knight and the Pips singing, "Neither One of Us." She loved old songs. They sorted her thoughts. Today she needed to decide whether or not she wanted to end whatever it was she had with Darren. They had been together for about seven months, and she just didn't feel he was 'right', whatever 'right' was. She sensed that he wasn't really happy either, but she could never be sure with him. She swore that down, old songs subliminally helped her make decisions. This was her 'quiet' time, the period between when she got home from work and when Ebone´, her roommate of five years came home. Today Ebone´ was early. *I wonder what mood she's in today.* Mitzi always had to prepare herself for Ebone´'s unpredictable moods. The door slammed. *I guess she's pissed off.*

"Hi, Ebone´." She decided to be cautious.

"Hey." She threw her bag on the couch and walked into the kitchen that was separated from the living room by a counter and four stools. A minute later the fridge slammed, and she walked back into the living room, drinking an Amstel beer.

"And who are we mad at today?" Mitzi really didn't want to know.

"That friggin' Ricky. All week we had plans for tonight. He was supposed to pick me up from work, take me for cocktails, dinner and movies." She sucked the beer bottle again. "Simple plans, but plans." She threw herself on the couch which annoyed Mitzi because it was new and Ebone´ knew she took pride in her things.

"So, what happened?" She knew another 'he makes me sick' story was coming.

"His mama called him and said she had pains in her chest and wanted to go to the hospital." She cut her eyes.

"And because of that you are angry?" Mitzi wasn't surprised. Ebone´ was very selfish. "Come on, girl, suppose she's having a heart attack or something?"

"I'd be lucky."

"You amaze me, Ebone´."

"Look, don't start, okay? That witch probably knew we had planned on going out, so she decided she wasn't feeling well. She makes me sick. And so does he." She got up and threw the empty bottle in the trash. "Do we have to listen to this ancient music?"

Mitzi turned the tape off and the radio on. "Of course not." Ebone´ didn't even realize she was being sarcastic. Sometimes she had a child-like innocence about her, a gentle harshness. She almost had a baby face which didn't give away her age. Ebone´ Simons was thirty-two, a year older than Mitzi and had a cute, short, cropped haircut with hair that old people considered 'good'. Her dark brown skin was flawless yet her make up was always overdone, unlike Mitzi, whose face was always perfectly made up. Ebone´'s light brown eyes looked sad most of the time - even when she laughed and exposed her straight, white teeth. Like Mitzi, her teeth were her pride and joy. She had a good heart, but she rarely allowed it to surface. She exuded anger and bitterness and was always on the defensive. "Come on, girl, give her the benefit of the doubt. Maybe she really is sick."

"Oh, she's sick alright. In the damn head. Mitzi, don't make excuses for that wicked woman, okay?"

"Okay." Resignation.

Ebone´'s expression suddenly changed. She almost looked like she cared. "You think she really is?"

"What?"

"Sick."

"Who am I to say?" Mitzi knew how to nip things in the bud with her.

"Come on, Mitzi, don't play games."

"Look, we don't know whether she's really sick or not, and we'll probably never know. But all you ever do is complain about Ricky. It seems to me that you should just leave him."

"I can't."

"Why not?"

"Because. He's all I have right now."

"You have yourself."

Ebone´ looked at her like she was crazy. "You know I can't be alone."

Sometimes Mitzi really felt sorry for her friend. There was an unending succession of men in her life because, as she often said, she couldn't be alone. Ebone´ had never been married and had a childhood a soap opera couldn't make look worse. They had been friends since they were five and six years old, having been in the same class at West Pembroke. Ebone´ had started a year late for reasons Mitzi never knew. They remained friends after primary school while they went to separate high schools and when Mitzi finally went to college and Ebone´ went to work at the post office. Even then, they wrote to each other every week. Ebone´'s letters were always twice as long as Mitzi's were because she always had a long story to tell. Either about a man, someone on her job or her mother, whom she despised. No one really knew why, but Mitzi knew that Ebone´ had an unnatural hatred for Madge Simons.

"Look, Ebone´, why don't you forget about Ricky and take some time to be by yourself, so you can see things clearer?"

"I just told you, I don't want to be alone."

"Why not?" Mitzi just couldn't understand, and Ebone´ was frustrating her now.

"Because, I feel... empty without a man."

"Listen, Ebone´, when you are not enough for yourself, you will never find anyone to fill the void."

Ebone' rolled her eyes. "Listen, Mitzi, I don't need your famous, holier-than-thou clichés right now. Got it?" She took a cigarette out of her bag, lit it and lit an incense at the same time. She inhaled deeply and let the smoke drift from her nostrils. She turned to Mitzi. "What about you and Darren?"

"What about us? Give me a cigarette."

"No."

"Why not?"

"Cause, you really don't want it, and you'll only waste it." Mitzi had quit smoking five months before - at Darren's insistence - but she still needed to at least fire up every now and again.

"What's the deal with you two anyway?"

Mitzi sighed. "He's too..."

"Too what? What? Too nothing. You've got a good thing and don't even know it."

"Look who's talking. I don't think he's good for me, Ebone'. He's too demanding, too suffocating, and he tries to tell me what's best for me."

"Oh please, talk about picky."

"Look, I don't need... or rather, I don't want a man under me twenty-four seven, questioning my every move." She got up and took the nail polish to her bedroom. Everything had its place with Mitzi. She believed in organisation and order. "Makes life easier," she always said. It irritated Ebone'. When she came back, Ebone' was sitting on the coffee table with the ashtray on her knee. Lord only knew what the reason for that was. Mitzi was immediately annoyed but said nothing.

"I would love for a man to be around me constantly," she said, looking at the floor.

"Why? Tell me exactly what it would do for you."

"It would make me feel wanted."

Please tell me she didn't say that. How old is this girl?

"Come on, Ebone', surely you don't mean that." Mitzi sat on the couch opposite her.

"I most certainly do." She nodded, looking real pleased with herself.

"Ebone´, just because a man is with you all the time, doesn't necessarily mean he's madly in love with you - he might not want anyone else to be with you." Ebone´ sucked her teeth. Her signature. "Darren is demanding, but in a subtle way. He tells me what I should be saying or doing, or how I should be acting or should be feeling." It irked her just to say it.

"Maybe he's just voicing his opinion."

"Well, I don't need a man to have a voice in my life right now." She crossed her legs as if to make her point.

"Oh, everybody knows that. Now or never, Miss 'I am my own woman but I want a man just in case'."

"I just have some soul searching to do about my relationship with that boy." She got up and started pacing which wasn't a good sign.

"Your soul must be searched beyond recognition by now."

I'll ignore that. "Tell me something, Ebone´, what about all those guys you've met at the restaurant?" Ebone´ was a waitress.

"Like who?" She stubbed out her cigarette and sat back on the couch.

"Like... Kent?"

"Ugly."

"Colin?"

"Too short."

"Mike?"

"Don't make enough money."

"Um, Tyrone?"

"Can't slow dance."

This is unbelievable. "Eddie?"

"Can't kiss."

"Ray?"

"Now, I actually gave him some play, but he's terrible in bed. Cute, but terrible in bed. Maybe I can teach him a few things, though," she added thoughtfully.

Mitzi shook her head in disbelief. "In the abundance of water, the fool is thirsty."

"Huh?"

Mitzi knelt beside Ebone´ and tapped on her head. "Doesn't what's inside account for anything?"

"I can't see inside, Mitzi." She over-pronounced her name. Beat that explanation.

"Aren't you getting a bit too old to be needing your man to be a cute, rich, good kissing, money-making dancer?"

"I do deserve the best." Ebone´ got up and walked toward the kitchen. "What smells good?" Must have hit a nerve. She always changed the subject when someone hit a nerve.

"I made vegetable lasagna."

"You got off early or something?"

"Yeah, my last client was at two." The oven timer buzzed, and Ebone´ turned the oven off and took another beer from the fridge. *I guess it would be a bit too much to ask her to take the lasagna out.* "Have you called your mama to thank her for the perfume yet?"

"No!" She opened the beer and threw the cap in the trash.

"Not going to call, are you?"

"Mitzi, you know I don't have a damn thing to say to that woman." She looked at her accusingly. "Did she call here today?"

"No, she didn't. But I think you should call her. This lasagna looks good if I say so myself."

"Call her for what? To thank her for the 'guilt' gift? Never."

"I will never understand how a grown woman can hate her own mother." Mitzi poked a fork in the lasagna.

"You had to be there." Ebone´ put the beer bottle on the counter and took two plates from the cabinet. The phone rang. "You get it. If it's Ricky, I don't want to talk to him."

"S'pose it's your mom?" Ebone´ cut her eyes as Mitzi answered the phone. It was Darren.

"I really need to talk to you, Darren. At your earliest convenience." She felt like she was talking to a client, a sign that he was really beginning to turn her off. "Would you like to come for dinner tomorrow?" Darren said that he would. "No, I don't think we'll be needing wine. Seven o'clock okay?" It was. "See you tomorrow."

"What you gonna tell him?" Ebone´ passed Mitzi a plate of hot lasagna.

"I really don't know." She closed her eyes and said her grace.

"I'm sure Diana or The Isleys or Teddy will help you think of something."

I hate sarcasm. Especially when it doesn't come from me.

"Remember, if Ricky calls, I don't want to talk to him."

"Until when?"

"Maybe forever. I hate him." She started eating without saying her grace. As usual. She was never thankful - for anything.

CHAPTER TWO
Friday Evening

"Where you goin'?"

"Out."

"With who?"

Ebone´ sighed. Mitzi already knew. "With Ricky, okay?"

"Fine. It's your life, sister." Mitzi was sitting at the dining table, reading the weekend papers. "Guess you don't hate him today, huh? What's that perfume you're wearing?" She already knew that, too.

"Red!" Ebone´ snapped.

"The same Red your mama sent you? The same Red that you haven't thanked her for yet? The same Red..."

"Yes! The very same Red. So what? She gave it to me to wear, I'm wearin' it." She rubbed lotion on her hands.

"This is simply amazing." Mitzi shook her head. "So when did you stop hating Ricky?"

"I didn't really hate him. Anyway, he and that woman had a big fight. He put some 'forks' in her ass." She put her cigarettes in her bag.

"His mother?!" Mitzi couldn't believe what she was hearing. "He cursed his own mother?" This upset her for several reasons. First of all, she couldn't think of anything she hated more than excess profanity. Only uneducated people used profanity, for lack of a sensible word, she maintained. If a person was justifiably angry, she could accept it, but in everyday conversation, never. And for someone to curse a parent was totally unheard of in her book. Her friends always teased her because she often substituted a curse word with something tamer, but they respected her and tried not to curse in her presence. They thought it was hilarious when she got mad, and a bad word slipped out.

"Yes, he cursed her." Ebone´ clapped her hands and bent over laughing. She obviously thought it was hysterical.

"You are going out with a man who curses his mother?" It sounded worse by the minute.

"So what?" Ebone´ stopped laughing. "She deserved it."

"So what about when you do something that makes you deserving of a good 'forking off'?"

"Look, he wouldn't do that to me, okay? I'm his baby." She started to get serious.

"Yeah, today. You don't get it, do you, Ebone´? You just don't get it."

"What's to get? If those two are off books, he'll have more time for me."

God, she's shallow. "Come on now, Ebone´, are you that desperate?" She ignored her and stopped to look at herself in the floor-length mirror in the short hallway leading to the front door. She looked like a prostitute, as usual. She had on a cute little red spandex dress, but it looked like it belonged on Barbie. Even though she only weighed about a hundred and fifteen pounds and had a body to die for, she had ugly varicose veins and should never wear anything above the knee. But you couldn't tell her that. The dress was so short, Mitzi could actually see the line in her stockings.

"No one will have to ask what you had for breakfast," Mitzi pointed out.

"Why not?" She added more lipstick to her already over-painted lips.

"Because, as soon as you sit down, they'll be able to see what you had."

"Good." She put her keys in her bag and swung her jacket over her shoulder.

"Good night, Maxine. Don't wait up." She gently closed the door behind her.

Mitzi felt like running after her and shaking some sense into her fluffy, empty head. "I cannot believe that woman is one of my best friends," Mitzi said out loud. She went back to reading the papers. "Well, that's her life. I have my own problems right now." She ran her fingers through her hair. *I need a touch-up.*

Mitzi put the papers down and looked around the house. She cherished the place for many reasons but most of all because it was hers. She had left school at sixteen without graduating and went right to work at the cleaners. She hated school and wanted to make money. A year later she also got a part-time job as a waitress. She worked five days and five nights a week for four years. Her parents hated it, but it was good money. One day she woke up - literally, and decided that she was going overseas to school. Her mama and daddy were ecstatic. They gave her half her tuition and sent her on her way. She knew she wanted to study hairdressing and cosmetology and a take a quick course in business. Then she wanted to return home and open her own business. Then her daddy died suddenly. She had been back in school three weeks after Christmas break when she got the call. She was on her way to class one morning when the phone rang, and as soon as she heard her mama's voice, she knew something was wrong. Mama was never sad, and she never cried unless she was real happy. Nothing could have prepared Mitzi for what her mom would tell her. The man who had been everything to her - mentor, role model, provider, friend, protector - everything, had suffered a heart attack at fifty years old. Death had come in with its brazen self and taken her daddy in the wee hours of the morning. With no warning. No preparation.

For months afterward, in the dark hours, while listening to songs like The Stylistics' "You're a Big Girl Now," Mitzi would question God and his judgment. Although she knew that this was something one should never do. Why her Daddy? Maxworth Robinson wouldn't have hurt any one of God's creatures even if he tried. He would open the door to let a fly out instead of killing it. He bought groceries for the elderly neighbours. He made her mama buy Christmas presents for every child in the neighbourhood. He was the one who implored Mitzi and her younger brother, Macky, never to make fun of anyone. To befriend the child at school whom everyone else had alienated because he or she was different. And he told them to carry with them through life the conviction that it was nice to be important but more important to be nice. Mitzi was born with his disposition and strove to do him proud at all times although he never demanded it. "Never be afraid to tell me you have failed," he had said. "I can accept failure, I can't accept not trying."

His funeral was a blur. She wept. Her heart and soul wept. All she knew was that her daddy was gone. His body was in the cold, hard ground, never to be seen or touched again. She had never seen her mama so pained and lost. For weeks they all functioned in a vacant state. And although time didn't exactly heal the wounds, it gradually diminished the pain. A week after the funeral, Mitzi returned to school with renewed determination and graduated ahead of time.

On her twenty-third birthday, she married Quincy Butterfield. Pretty Quincy. Mega-handsome Quincy. All baby skin, diamond in his tooth and well-kept hair Quincy. Rock hard body Quincy.

Uncle Frankie, her mother's brother, gave her away, against his better judgment. He claimed he had been 'out there' and knew all about 'Q', which was what he insisted people call him. But Mitzi knew that 'Q' had come into her life at a time when she needed someone most - right after her daddy died. Max had left his wife and children a small fortune, and Mitzi bought her house with her money. Even though she was in love with 'Q', she knew she didn't want any man's name on the deeds purchased with her beloved daddy's money, so she told him that it was her auntie's house, and they would rent it. What Uncle Frankie knew about 'Q' was that he used women, in every way - mentally, sexually, but most of all, financially. She had put up with his abuse, mind games, insecurities and immaturity for two years before she realized that she had come to this earth for greater reasons.

When she got up one morning after her husband hadn't come home, went outside and found him and a woman passed out in a car in her yard, Mitzi thought she had stepped out of her body and was watching someone else. She calmly went to the back of the house, got the garden hose and sprayed cold water into the open sunroof of the car. The scatteraction that ensued was priceless, and so were the looks on their faces. 'Q' and the woman, who he later insisted was his cousin, looked like the drowning rats they were. Apparently, 'Cousin Dearest' had driven him home - they were both drunk - and had passed out once the car stopped. That morning, within the hour, all of his worldly goods were packed in 'Piggly Wiggly' bags and out in the yard. "Go stay with your cousin!" Mitzi had screamed in his face. 'Q' had begged pathetically and pleaded his case, but she didn't hear him, couldn't hear him, wasn't trying to hear a damn thing he had to say. Nothing he could have said would have mattered. She had all she needed to finally convince herself that that was it. She could rid herself of the pretty little nothinarian.

The lawyer said the divorce would be straight forward. He would see to it that Mr. 'Q' got exactly what he deserved - nothing. For all he did to her, the lies, pain, manipulation, head games, disrespect, he would get just what he deserved - exactly what he was - all of nothing. He had always had to have the final say in all their decisions, and he was always right - or so he thought. He wasn't. He was a wrong, arrogant bastard. Two days before she was to go to court to terminate their farce of a marriage, Quincy had the audacity to get himself killed in an accident on North Shore. Mitzi was angry. Angry because he still had had the last word in how their marriage ended. He had made her a widow. In any case, he was out of her life for good. Notwithstanding, she was a little sad as she always was when the world lost a being. But at least now she could go on. She had promised her daddy many years before that she would never allow any man to undermine her integrity, but for a few years she had. But all that would change. And she somehow thought at the time that Max was somewhere giving Quincy hell for the way he had treated her. But now, as she stood at her picture window and looked out at the South Shore and thought about it, there was no way that Max and Quincy could possibly have ended up in the same place. Wherever it was.

The phone rang and interrupted her thoughts. It wasn't until then that she realized that her eyes had welled up. They often did when she thought about Max. Maybe this was Darren calling to say he couldn't make it.

"Hello." Maybe not. It was Crystal, another one of her best friends - probably the best. She had left a message earlier for Crystal to call her. "Hey Crys, how you doing? Good. Listen, I really can't talk right now, I got something to do, but can we have a girls' hair night tomorrow?" Of course she could have gotten it done at 'The Nubian' - her beauty shop - but this was one of the rituals she and her friends had - to get together and 'beautify' each other. "Thanks. I'll cook dinner. Call Melba to see if she can come, and I'll ask Sundae. Our 'ladies beauty and gossip night' is overdue, and so is my touch-up. Check you about six-thirtyish."

As soon as she hung up, the doorbell rang. She turned the oven off first. Darren could wait. Thinking about the late 'Q' had put her in a defensive mood. Darren had no idea what he was in for. She opened the door, and there was boyfriend, flowers, wine - hadn't she told him not to bring wine? - And a bloody, stupid grin. Or was it a smirk? Whatever it was, it irritated her. But just for the purpose, he looked good. Actually, he always looked good. There was no doubt about it, Darren Wilson was a together brother, physically. But at thirty-one, who needed just a good-looking man? Ebone´ might, but Mitzi certainly didn't. Darren had on a black sweat suit and white Nikes. His face was clean shaven except for his mustache.

He must be expecting something, Mitzi thought. *He is, he's wearing Lagerfeld cologne. Does he think I called him up here to propose marriage or something? Poor him.* She also noticed that 'Bermuda Rot fungus - or whatever it was called, on his neck. *Yuck!* He somehow looked different from when she had first met him eight months ago, on Labour Day at Bernard's Park. She was watching the Gombeys with Ebone´ and Sundae when she felt him staring at her. When she looked at him, he waved, and she smiled and waved back. He looked like a nice person, but she had been down that road before. Looking nice didn't cut it. And furthermore, now that she thought about it, why was such a good looking man single? Like a sandwich walking around in Somalia - something had to be wrong. But then again, she was single, too, so take that back. But when he came over, introduced himself and extended his hand, she knew he was 'nice'. And he was, until he tried to have a say in her life shortly after they started going together. He was fun most of the time. He was thirty-six, an architect, divorced and had two children who lived in the States with his ex-wife. He had just bought a piece of land and was working on the plans to build. They often worked out together at the gym.

"Hi." She tried to sound enthusiastic.

"Hi. How come you took so long to open the door?"

"Scuse me?" Instant attitude.

"Were you on the phone or something?"

"Or something." She left him standing in the doorway and went to the kitchen. He trailed behind her with those silly flowers and rested them and the wine on the counter.

"Am I late or something? You seem to have an attitude."

Very good, you noticed. "No, you're not late. And why would I have an attitude, Darren?" She looked him dead in the eye as she put emphasis on his name. Her eyes must have dug deep because he looked away. She had thought about cooking something special for this little tête-à-tête, but now she was glad she was warming up leftover lasagna. She had also made a salad.

"Would you like some wine now or later?" He offered.

"Now." *You might not be here much later.*

"These flowers are for you." As if she didn't know.

"Thank y..."

"Why don't you put them in water?"

Why don't you shove them up your backside?

"So how was your day?" He got the corkscrew and opened the bottle.

Let me act right. "It wasn't bad. Hectic, but not bad."

"It seems your days are always hectic lately. You should take some time off."

"Not yet." *I'll damn well take time off when I'm good and damn ready.*

"Did you go to the gym today?" He put the wineglasses on the table.

"No, I came straight home."

"Be careful." He sat on the couch and turned on the TV.

"What does that mean?" She put forks and knives on the table.

"You shouldn't skip too many days at the gym. You're fine now, but I don't particularly like my woman big."

"And I don't particularly like anyone telling me how they particularly like me to be." She slammed the plates on the table. A piece of lettuce came off one of them. "And furthermore, this body has brought you endless hours of pleasure." Mitzi took issue with that statement because she fought hard to keep her weight under control. She was five feet, six and weighed a hundred and thirty-seven pounds, but she had been much heavier, and no one knew better than she, what could happen if she let herself go.

"What's wrong with you, Mitzi?" He stood up as though he had to prepare to defend himself. Mitzi took a deep breath. She didn't want it to turn ugly. Yet.

"What's wrong with me is the reason I asked you to come here tonight." He rubbed her arm. She pulled away like a child would.

"I thought we were just having a nice dinner." He didn't have a clue.

"That's because you're too busy telling other... no, telling me what I should be doing, to hear what I'm trying to say." She sat at the table. "Didn't you hear me say I wanted you to come for dinner because I needed to talk to you?"

"No." He sat opposite her and put the fallen lettuce back on his plate.

"My point exactly."

"Mitzi, I thought everything between us was fine."

"No, Darren, it's not. It could be, but it's not."

"I don't understand..."

"Listen, I like you, I really do. You have... attributes that many women would kill to have in a man."

"So what's the problem?" He sipped his wine as he waited for her answer.

"You're overbearing." The words came out sharper than she meant for them to.

"Ow." He looked hurt.

"I don't mean to be rude, Darren, but you're... suffocating me. Excuse me a second." She closed her eyes and blessed her food. He followed suit. When they had both finished saying grace, they started eating.

"You shouldn't use so much salt." She shook more. "I didn't realize you felt that way, Mitzi." He looked at her, eyes suddenly filled with sadness. Or were they? She started to feel a little sorry for him. He looked so pitiful now. He was basically a nice guy.

"You know, I make it a habit never to compare any man I'm going with to my ex-husband, but I did learn a lot from my marriage. I never call the marriage a mistake because I am much more the wiser as far as relationships and men are concerned. As a result, I now know what I want and what I'm not going to accept - from anyone." She wasn't hungry anymore and was moving the food around on her plate.

Darren wasn't bothered. He was eating like it was the Last Supper. "Are you sure you aren't making other men, namely me, pay for what your ex did?" he asked with his mouth full.

Mitzi became irritated again. Both because he had talked with his mouth full and because of what he had just said.

"Do you ever listen?" She put her fork down and pushed the half full plate away. She picked up the wine glass and spoke slowly. "Maybe if you listened more, you'd be half as smart as you think you already are." She drank some wine and hoped she had cut 'Mr. Know It All' deeply.

"Look, Mitzi ," Darren said, slightly annoyed. "I'm a bit older than you, therefore I do know a bit more."

No, he didn't say that. "Not by age, but by knowledge, is wisdom acquired," she shot back confidently. She wished she had a cigarette. She would blow the smoke right in his face.

"Quite the woman of words, aren't we?"

"We are," she said, patronizingly.

"Nevertheless," he continued, "I'm a person who tries to help anyone I can. If I see you doing something that may not be good for you, I'm going to tell you." He put his fork down and wiped his mouth."

I can put that plate back in the cabinet without washing it. "Because you may or may not agree with something, doesn't mean it is or isn't so."

"Listen to me, Mitzi..."

"No, you listen to me, Darren," she cut him off and stood up. "There is no right or wrong here. And I am not a stupid woman. As a matter of fact, I am an extremely intelligent woman, and I cherish my integrity."

"And I respect you for that, honey. You know I have always held you in very high esteem."

"When I'm doing what you think I'm supposed to be doing." She cleared the table.

"I'm sorry you feel that way," he said, solemnly and went to sit on the couch.

Mitzi stacked the dishes in the dishwasher, and neither of them spoke for a while. He was thinking of what he could say to make her see things his way, and she was thinking that maybe he wasn't so bad after all. Maybe he would change... *Oops, don't even go there. They don't change, you know better than that,* she told herself. She turned the dishwasher on and went back into the dining room. Darren was leaning back on the couch, flipping through the weekend papers. Mitzi took a toothpick from the table, stuck it in her mouth and, with her foot under her, sat in a chair.

"You shouldn't pick your teeth with a toothpick," he said, as matter-of-factly as he could.

Mitzi just shook her head. *Is this boy thick, or what? Even though he's right, I certainly don't need him to tell me right from wrong.* She took the toothpick out of her mouth - because she wanted to - and rested her elbow on her knee. The phone rang, and she let the voice mail kick in. "You know, Darren, in thirty-one years, I have gone through a complete personal metamorphosis," she said, looking past him.

"Meaning?" he asked, unsure if he really wanted to hear it. He was a little intimidated by Mitzi. Not physically, but he knew she was strong-willed and didn't give in easily.

"Meaning," she said, after a minute, walking over to sit beside him, "that throughout my childhood, my daddy was always there, and I always felt protected. And so, the first serious boyfriend I had, I always wanted him around, to protect me. I was very insecure when he wasn't there." He listened intently. "When he messed around on me, I realized that no matter how much time he spent with me, unless it was twenty-four hours a day, he could still hurt me."

"At least you realized that. Some people go a whole lifetime never knowing that."

Oh, shut up. She kept talking, determined not to let him make her lose her script. "Over the years, I have gone from needing a man, to having to have a man because all of my friends had one, to simply wanting a man because I didn't want to be alone."

"And where are you now?" He ran his hand over his head.

Perfect question, my boy. She got up and poured more wine for both of them. "Now, I realize that while it's nice to have - as they say - a 'significant other' in your life, there is absolutely no sense in having someone in your life whom you can't feel good about." She gave him the wine.

"All this is really surprising to me, Mitzi. I mean, I feel good about you, I look forward to being with you, I enjoy your company, our conversations..., we seem to be compatible in bed..." he shrugged and looked lost.

Compatible in bed? Where did he dig up that phrase? "All that may be true, Darren, but don't you understand what I'm trying to say?"

"No." He was gulping his wine now. Poor sight.

"For instance, the other day we were walking in town, and I spoke to a couple of my male clients."

"Yeah."

"Do you remember what you said to me?"

"It escapes me right now." He rested his glass on the coffee table.

"Your exact words were, 'Is it really necessary for you to speak to every man you see on the street?'"

"Oh yeah, that's how I feel." He leaned forward and rubbed his hands.

"Well, Darren, I do intend to speak to every man that I know."

"Isn't that kind of disrespectful to me?" He turned to look at her as if that would get his point across.

"I'm speaking to them, not sleeping with them, for God's sake."

"Mitzi..."

"Let's get something straight, I will not, for any man, act as if I don't know another man just because someone is insecure."

"I'm hardly insecure, Maxine." Got him. He had called her Maxine.

"Whatever. But if these people are my clients, and most of them have been for years, I will treat them in public as I do in my salon, no matter who I'm with. I am not phony, and I have nothing to hide."

"Don't you think that some of them might be attracted to you? You're a beautiful woman..."

"I certainly hope some of them are attracted to me, I try my damnedest to look good. But so what if they are? So what? Who am I with?" She sat on the edge of the couch and faced him.

"I don't want to share you, Mitzi."

"You're not listening." *As usual.* "What is it with you men?" She hated to generalize, especially when it came to men, but she was reaching the end of her rope.

"I am not, 'you men'." He looked hurt again. She felt sorry for him again.

Am I on a roller coaster, or what? She leaned back on the couch. "I'm sorry. Tell me something," she said, trying not to sound irritated. "Don't you come in contact with females on a regular basis?"

"Of course I do, but I'm not interested in any of them."

"Exactly! So if you speak to them, I won't automatically assume that you want them. Hell, you could stop and have a conversation, ask them to dance, buy them a drink, things that friends would do. It wouldn't bother me, Darren."

"I would never do that, with or without you around."

Oh grow up. This conversation is wearing me out. "But you could if you wanted to. I mean, I wouldn't particularly be too pleased if you took another woman for a romantic dinner or a trip or something like that, but no one should ever treat their friends differently when they're with their mate."

He sighed. "I'm sorry, honey. Maybe I do come across a bit insecure. But I think it's because you are such a together lady. I really don't know how to handle you."

"I don't need to be handled, Darren. I need to be cared for. Respected. Appreciated."

"I do feel all those things for you, baby." He gently pulled her back by her shoulder. She moved reluctantly. She didn't come around quickly. Actually, she could hold a grudge, but she felt a little empathetic toward him now. And he suddenly looked a little cute again.

"I also need to maintain my independence right now. Darren, you run your business, and I run mine. We are both mature, responsible adults. I treat you as such, please afford me the same privilege."

He put his arm around her shoulder. "I'll try, Mitzi. You just mean so much to me, I guess more than you realize."

She softened and reached up and locked her fingers in his. She turned to look at him. *Is this going to work? Because I don't feel like dealing with all this confusion. Relationships are so difficult. Too damn difficult. I don't even love the man.*

"*S*o, can I stay for a while?" He asked, unsure of what should happen next.

"Sure." She closed her eyes and let the wine take over her mind.

"I give my all to this relationship, honey," he said suddenly, with an air. Or was it the wine? She kept her eyes closed and listened. "I give my all to whatever I do. And I am usually very successful in whatever I attempt to conquer."

Conquer? Am I a conquest? Where was the man who had gained her sympathy a minute ago? "Excuse me?" She let go of his fingers but kept her eyes closed. He slid his free hand down toward her breast, apparently quite comfortable with the direction this conversation was taking.

"Like I said, I'm older than you, so obviously I'm wiser and more mature than you are."

This man is an idiot. A deaf idiot.

"All I want is to guide you. Keep you on the right path." His hand moved south. Obviously the conversation aroused him. *That's it. He feels empowered when he's in control. Well, I'm about to disconnect his power.*

"Just exactly what is it you're trying to say, Darren?" she asked, trying to sound dumb. Her eyes were still closed, and his hand felt very heavy.

"It's simple. Where you are, I've been. What I am, you should aspire to be." He crossed his ankle over his knee, obviously very pleased with that little proclamation.

I must be drunk. Mitzi very deliberately removed his hand from her breast and rested her glass on the coffee table. Darren thought she was moving into position and rested his glass, too.

But Mitzi stood up and slowly walked to the door. She opened it and leaned against it.

"What you doin', baby?" He was smiling. A confused smile.

"It was nice having you, Darren." She looked outdoors. It was raining lightly. Good.

"What you sayin'...?" He looked at her in utter confusion.

"What am I saying?" She asked innocently. "I'm saying that what I am is pissed off. What you are is history." He walked to the door and reached for her arm.

She pulled away. "Drive safely." She folded her arms and looked at him. She often didn't need words. Her eyes said it all.

"I don't understand you, girl. What...?"

"Well, now there's absolutely no reason for you to try to understand me."

He felt for his keys in his pocket. "You know something?" he asked, one hand on the door, the other on his hip.

"I know a lot. Not half as much as you, of course, but a lot." She stared at him coldly.

"You probably wouldn't know a good man if he came down from heaven."

"Tell you what, when I do need to know, I'll call you, because you're mature. You know everything."

"Good luck, Maxine." He lingered on the step. Was he waiting for a kiss? Ha!

"Thanks. I'm sure I'll need it." She felt like slapping the Bermuda Rot right off his neck. It irritated her, and so did he. Darren put his jacket on, shook his head and looked at Mitzi. She looked out at the rain. "I would hate for the rain to ruin this carpet." She looked down at the floor. *That wasn't necessary but who cares?* Darren walked out of the house and deliberately avoided the cracks in the stepping stones. *Probably something I should have been doing all these years.* Mitzi gently closed the door, making certain not to slam it because experience had taught her that men loved it when a woman slammed the door. It made them feel as though they had accomplished something. "I can't believe that fool," she said out loud. "And he almost had me, too." She took the wine glasses from the coffee table and stacked them in the dishwasher along with the rest of the supper dishes.

"A man will never control me. No, now, I'm not havin' it, dammit!" She slammed the dishwasher shut and turned it on again. It was nine o'clock. She went into the living room and closed the blinds. It was still raining. Perfect night to be with a man. Friday. Cool. Raining. But at her age, she decided that it was better to be alone on a Friday night, than to spend it with a dictating, controlling fool. She checked to make sure the house was locked, turned the hallway light on for Ebone´ and turned the other lights out. She went into the bathroom, half filled the tub and poured in some avocado bath oil she had bought from Trimingham's while she plucked some hairs from her chin. She decided that Ebone´ probably wouldn't be back until morning and turned the hall light back off. She got her pajamas and turned on the TV. 'Family Matters' was on so she lay across the foot of her bed to watch it. When she woke up again, it was one twenty, ZFB was off, and the bath water was cold. She put her pajamas on and went to bed. She felt a sense of relief. She was no longer undecided about Darren. It was over. She was a woman in control again. There had been no tears, no shouting, no love lost. She had never loved Darren. She was physically attracted to him and had once really liked him. Things change.

CHAPTER THREE
Saturday

Mitzi couldn't believe it was eight twenty. She never slept this late, on any day. She knew something had happened last night, but it didn't click right away. A sign that she was at peace with herself over whatever it was. She remembered. No more Darren. She sat up and yawned. "Thank you, Lord, for a new day. Please help me to be a better person today than I was yesterday," she prayed. Then she remembered the water in the tub and opened the blinds. It was still raining. She had made up her mind when she opened her own business that she herself would not work on weekends. The other girls did, but she only worked from Monday to Friday except when she had a wedding party to do. Her staff was extremely efficient, especially her Assistant Manager, Ronald. He wasn't a stylist; he just ran the business, and Mitzi trusted him. He had been with her from day one.

On Saturdays Mitzi usually got up early - between six thirty and seven, went for a run, showered, then cleaned her house. Ebone´ helped her sometimes, but she preferred to do it herself. No one cleaned her house the way she did. When she was finished, she usually went to Paget to Granny's house, washed her hair and did her grocery shopping for her. She had been doing her shopping since Papa died three years ago. Granny was seventy-five and claimed to have a bad hip, so she didn't go out much, except to her neighbour's house. This morning Mitzi decided to do what she had to do for Granny first then come back and clean her house. It was too late to go for a run. She wanted to change the living room around today, too. She took the linen off her bed and went to get a clean set from the hallway closet.

She froze when she rounded the corner and saw a figure lying on the floor. Then she recognised the red spandex. Ebone´ was curled up in a ball on the hallway floor with her coat over her legs. "Oh my God! Ebone´! What happened to you?!" She knelt down beside Ebone´ who didn't move. *Is she dead?* She was soaking wet. She felt her face. It was cold and wet. "Ebone´?" She shook her gently.

"Huh?" She kept her eyes closed.

"What happened?" Mitzi got up and got a blanket from the linen closet and covered her with it.

"Leave me alone. I'm alright."

"No, I'm not leaving you alone. And if you're alright, why are you lying on the floor in wet clothes?" She tried to turn her over to face her. *Is she drunk? No, something's wrong.* "Come on, honey, let's go to your room and take these wet clothes off." Ebone´ was limp and started to cry. Despite her harsh exterior, she cried a lot. She let Mitzi help her up and into her room which was next to hers. She looked like hell.

"What happened to you, Ebone´?" Mitzi unzipped the spandex and peeled it off of her. It was soaked, and she had on no underwear. She gave her a towel to dry herself with and helped her put her robe on. Ebone´ wrapped the towel around her wet hair and got under her covers. Mitzi sat on the foot of the bed. "Do you wanna talk about it?" Mitzi asked, sympathetically. She knew she would tell her. She always wanted to talk about it, no matter how ridiculous her escapades.

"Ricky hit me!" She blurted out. She was still crying.

"For what?" When would this stop?

"I called his mama a bitch," she answered.

"No, Ebone´, you didn't call the boy's mama a bitch?" This girl could borrow trouble, as if she didn't have enough of it already.

"Well, there's more to it than that. A whole lot of stuff went on, and then when I called the bitch a bitch, he choked me and banged my head up against the car window."

"Ebone´, you can't go 'round calling people's mamas names."

"I thought since he cursed her, he really wouldn't care."

"It don't work like that, honey. If he and his mama had it out, that's their thing. But no one lets anyone else talk bad about their mother, no matter how bad she might be."

"I don't give a damn what anybody says about my mama. I hate her. Mamas are not all they're cracked up to be."

"That's you. Ricky didn't necessarily curse his mama because he hates her. He was angry with her at the time. Didn't I warn you about that, Ebone´?"

"Don't start," she said, blowing her nose.

"Yes, I am going to start. Get it in your head, girl, a man who disrespects his mother will never respect you!"

Ebone´ sighed. "My life is a friggin' mess." She put her face in her pillow.

Her life was always 'a mess' when she broke up with a man, which was often. She had had a myriad of them. "How you end up wet?" The whole story wasn't clear yet.

"Lemme tell you how it started."

This could take all day.

"When I left here, I got a lift down to Ricky's house. When I got there, this girl was in his bedroom." She sat up straight.

"A girl?" Mitzi tried to act surprised even though this type of story was the norm, and she was used to it.

"Yes. Some girl. He claimed she was a friend from a long time ago." She blew her nose again.

"What were they doing in his bedroom?"

"Talking."

Right.

"Anyway, he introduced us and asked me if I was ready to go."

"Where?"

"We were going to dinner and for a few drinks." She dried her hair with a towel.

"Where was 'Miss Thing' going?"

"With us, I found out eventually." She lit a cigarette.

"What you mean, with you?" *This is unbelievable.*

"Apparently, this girl used to go with Ricky years ago. They broke up, and she went away to live." She closed her eyes and let the smoke drift from her nostrils.

"So what? She's come back and wants him back?"

She dragged on the Marlboro again. "I don't know. He said that's not it, but she went out with us."

"You let her?" Mitzi couldn't believe her ears.

"What could I do?" She opened her eyes a little. Boy, she was pathetic sometimes.

"Ebone', Ebone', Ebone." Mitzi shook her foot. "What you could have done was tell Ricky that it was either her or you. What is the matter with you?" Ebone' sucked her teeth and stamped out the half-smoked cigarette. She drew her knees up and started to cry again.

"I don't know, Mitzi," she cried. "I'm such a loser. A damn loser." She started sobbing uncontrollably. Mitzi stood beside her and rocked her friend as a mother would her infant. For the next half-hour, between crying attacks, Ebone' told Mitzi how the night's events had led to Mitzi's finding her curled up on the floor.

After it was decided that Jackie - as it turned out was her name - would join them for the evening, they left Ricky's house after his mother wished Ricky and Jackie a good evening and told the two of them to have a good time. Strike one with Ebone'. At least Jackie had the good sense to sit in the back of Ricky's Golf convertible. They started at Captain's Lounge for cocktails, where Ebone' insisted that everybody in the whole place was staring at her, so she forced Ricky to slow-dance with her so she could silently announce that she was his woman. While they were dancing, she asked him why Jackie had to come with them.

"Look, she's an old friend. I knew her before I knew you, so if you don't like it, you know what you can do," was his reply. With that, she held him closer, staking her claim. The next couple of hours took them to dinner at Coconut Rock, which was Jackie's choice and where Ricky and Jackie sat next to each other, with Ebone' across the table moping. After dinner, the three of them went back up to Captain's, despite Ebone''s protests, where the crowd was much larger. They stayed for about two hours while Jackie and Ricky commenced to get totally drunk and talk loudly amongst themselves.

"It was like I wasn't even there!" She bawled. "I wanted to choke her with her weaved hair."

"What about Ricky, Ebone'?" Mitzi decided to ask a stupid question. Ebone' sucked her teeth. Again.

By the end of the night, all of the preceding had taken place, as well as the three of them leaving Captain's Lounge, after Ricky and Jackie had slow-danced and were then totally inebriated. Ricky put the top of the car down even though it was still raining lightly and told Ebone' to drive while he and Jackie squeezed themselves in front beside her. Ricky instructed her to drive out to P.C.C. where they parked and sat and talked for a few minutes until Ricky suggested that the three of them go down and sit by the water.

"And this is when you decided to leave and come home, right?" Mitzi asked, sure that that was what she would say.

"I wasn't leaving her alone with my man," she said defiantly.

My man? "Ebone', why you bring these things on yourself?" Mitzi asked, trying not to sound annoyed although she was visibly so.

"I didn't bring anything on myself, Mitzi." She was getting defensive. The gentle act hadn't worked.

"I am Ricky's woman!"

Well, why you let ex-girlfriend tag along, honey? "I know that, but does Jackie know?"

"Look, I don't know what type of game she was playing, but anyway, before we got out of the car she and Ricky decided they were going to blow a little coke."

"Whose coke was it?" Mitzi was concerned now. She hated drugs more than she hated cursing.

"To tell you the truth, I don't know who brought it out. All I know is they did a few lines, and then Ricky asked me if I wanted some."

What a punk. "Tell me you didn't do it, please."

Ebone´ lit another cigarette. Mitzi thought the room was getting dark and depressing, with the blinds still closed and the smoke floating around. Ebone´ closed her eyes and exhaled slowly.

"No, I didn't take any."

Thank you, Lord.

"But I wanted to, though. Because I felt left out. Here this girl was with my boyfriend, obviously in complete control, and they were getting high together. Doin' what Ricky liked."

"So what, Ebone´? It's not what you like anymore." Several years before, Ebone´ had 'used coke occasionally', as she put it, until one night she had a really bad experience. It must have been a dream or something because the way she explained it to Mitzi, she had died and was trying to get through a swamp. It had to be a dream because there were no real swamps in Bermuda. She was trying to get to a red spot, which apparently would bring her back to life, but it kept moving farther and farther away from the swamp. Some hour in the morning, Mitzi had heard her scream and then heard a loud thump. When she got to her room, Ebone´ was on the floor, having fallen out of the bed, soaked with perspiration and shaking uncontrollably. When she finally caught herself, she vowed she would never use drugs again. And to Mitzi's knowledge, she hadn't.

"It seems like no matter what I do, I can't seem to make Ricky happy."

"Have you ever stopped to think that he doesn't want you to make him happy? You're convenient, Ebone´, that's all. Taking Jackie out with you lot should have proven that."

"He was probably just using her, too, especially if she was the one who had the drugs."

Mitzi sighed as deeply as humanly possible. *Why do I even bother?*

"I still can't believe what happened." She blew her nose.

"And I still don't know what happened." Mitzi was growing tired of this interminable story and wished it would end.

"When those lot had finished snorting, we all got out of the car and walked down to the water. By now, it was raining hard, but I was the only one who knew it. I told Ricky that I wanted to go back to the car, and he told me to 'shut up and keep walking,' which was hard to do because of my shoes and my dress. They left me way behind."

"So, you just shut up and kept walking?" Ebone´ didn't answer - she didn't have to.

"By the time I caught up to them, they were taking off each other's clothes."

"What the devil...?"

"I guess they thought I had gone back to the car. When I asked Ricky what he was doing, he told me to watch and wait my turn."

"Oh come on, Ebone´... and you waited?" *I'm getting pissed off now.*

"No, I told him that I was leaving and started walking away, but he grabbed me, slapped me and pushed me to the ground."

"What the hell...?"

Ebone´ started to cry again but kept talking. "He went back to Jackie, who was lying on the grass, buck naked, and started..."

"Ebone´, please tell me that you didn't sit in the rain and watch your man have sex with another woman!" Mitzi was furious.

"I didn't exactly just sit and watch." Mitzi got up and threw the blinds open. The rain had stopped, and the sun was shining. Outside, at least. "I just lost it and started hitting the girl."

"You should have hit Ricky, girl!"

"He stopped a few licks, too, but I wanted her. When I kicked her in the face, Ricky got up and punched me in mine." Mitzi shook her head while her mouth hung open. "When I fell, he held me down, pulled my dress up and had sex with me while Jackie held my arms." Tears were running down her face.

"Ebone´! He raped you. Do you know that?"

She was lighting another cigarette. "How could it be rape? I'm his woman." She always had a good reason for something. The cigarette shook in her hand.

"Dammit, girl! What's wrong with you?!" Mitzi started to leave. She no longer felt sorry for her. She was angry.

"Don't leave me, Mitzi, please," Ebone´ pleaded. She looked so pitiful and weak.

Mitzi stopped and closed her eyes for a second to try to control herself. Never in her life could she ever imagine going through half the things Ebone´ already had. She put her hands over her eyes briefly, took a deep breath, then walked slowly back to Ebone´'s bed.

"I know you're mad," Ebone´ said slowly.

"You should be mad. I mean, the rocks in that boy's head must match the holes in yours." She was really frustrated.

"I don't need you to talk to me like that..."

"Yes you damn well do! You have made every excuse imaginable for every asinine, low-down, dirty thing Ricky did last night, and you expect sympathy from me? Hell no! You ain't gonna get it, Ebone´!"

"I must make you sick, Mitzi. I make myself sick."

"Then do something about it for Christ's sake!" She was bordering on the profane - in her book, anyway.

"I need help. Would you help me?"

"You need professional help, girl. You need a couch, the straight jacket, the man in the white coat, you need it all!" Mitzi was shouting now. "I'm sick and tired of bailing you out of every damn thing you get into, only to have you turn around and do some dumb shit again!" There it was. She cursed. It was time to leave. She walked out into the hallway and stopped. She couldn't leave the girl. She took another deep breath and turned around. Ebone´ was lying on her back with her eyes closed. Mitzi felt sorry for her again. She tried to calm down before she spoke again.

"Do you want to call the police?" she asked, almost in a whisper. She already knew she didn't.

"Would you be mad at me if I didn't?" Poor sight.

"No." Mitzi sat on her bed again.

Ebone´ opened her eyes. "I don't want to live like this anymore, Mitzi. Going through all these changes with men."

"Then don't, honey. Cut Ricky off. Let him go. You don't deserve all that. Nobody does."

Ebone´ sat up, and thick tears rolled down her cheeks. "After he..." she paused and sighed. "Raped me, he got up, kissed Jackie, and they both got dressed and started walking toward the car. Then he turned around and told me that I had five minutes to get my clothes on, if not, he would leave me."

"What a sick man."

"I walked to the car in the pouring rain, and when I got there, they were snorting the rest of the coke in the back seat. Ricky told me to drive here, and when we got down by Rangers, he told me the night had been 'real' and said we should do it again sometime. I told him that Jackie was a bitch just like his mama. That's when he made me stop the car, choked me and made me get out. When he drove off, Jackie waved to me."

"You walked home from Rangers?" She nodded. "What time was that?" It really didn't matter.

"The clock in the car was saying four-twelve. I walked up the road, came in the house and collapsed."

"You should have come in my room." But then again, she was kind of glad she hadn't.

"Mitzi, I feel so shitty. What did I do for him to treat me like this? What could I have done to make him treat me better?"

Okay, I give up. "Ebone´, you don't cut your foot to fit the shoe. You throw the shoe out if it doesn't fit." She looked blank. "You can't make a person like you. You be yourself and hope that the person likes you for what you already are. What you have to learn is that just because you meet a guy, go out with him a few times and have sex, doesn't mean you'll be together forever. It would be nice, but it doesn't always work that way."

"Don't I know."

"It might take a while to figure out, but when you do, you move on, but never, ever try to be what someone else wants you to be. Maybe the other person is the problem."

Ebone´ sighed. "If only it were that easy."

"It can be that easy." She paused. "I broke up with Darren last night."

"You did?"

"Yeah."

"What happened?"

"The shoe didn't fit." She smiled, and Ebone´ looked like she understood for the first time. Kind of. Mitzi looked at the clock on the VCR. "Hey, it's gettin' late. My granny must be wondering where I am." She walked to the door. "What time you making to work?"

"I can't work today. I need to get my head together. Would you call in sick for me?"

"Sure. But only if I can be sure you won't call Ricky."

"Oh, I won't be calling him." She sounded stronger than she looked.

Sure, Ebone´. "Incidentally, Crystal, Melba and Sundae are coming up here this evening so we can do our hair."

"Mmn." Ebone´ closed her eyes again. She couldn't stand Mitzi's 'other' friends. She was actually jealous of them and didn't really know them. Whenever they came around, she acted strangely, so consequently, they all thought she was strange.

The phone rang as Mitzi was about to call Ebone´'s job. It was her mama calling to tell her that her granny had called her to find out why Mitzi hadn't come to do her hair yet. Obviously she still thought Mitzi was a child. Whenever she wanted to know something about her, she called Oleeta as if Mitzi couldn't talk for herself. She called her granny, told her she would be there shortly and then called in sick for Ebone´. It was another half hour before she left home and already she felt as if half the day were over.

CHAPTER FOUR
Saturday Evening

Mitzi opened her door to find Crystal and Melba, two of her closest friends, the others being Ebone´ and Sundae, waiting to come in. They both had bags full of food. Crystal had insisted that it was too much trouble for Mitzi to cook.

"Hey guys, where's Sundae?" Mitzi asked as they walked past her.

"At a funeral, where else?" Melba answered as if it were a stupid question. Actually it was. They always teased Sundae about her funeral obsession. It seemed as if not a week went by that she didn't have a funeral to go to.

"Who died now?" Mitzi asked, poking in the bags they had rested on her table. She was playing 'The Best of Bob Marley' CD.

"Probably her next door neighbour's sister's husband's boss's mother-in-law," Crystal answered. Melba and Mitzi hollered.

"You know," Melba said, putting her hand on her hip as though a thought had just occurred to her, "that girl must be an orphan by now, the amount of funerals she goes to. Everybody she has ever known must be dead by now."

"The sister loves a planting ceremony. I hate 'em," Crystal said, cringing.

"I abhor them," Melba declared. Mitzi and Crystal looked at each other. Melba always used big words unnecessarily.

"Hey, you lot going to Sonia's shower?" Crystal asked, taking a Barcardi Breezer from one of the bags and drinking it from the bottle.

"No, I'm not," Mitzi said.

"Why not?" Melba wanted to know as she very lady likely poured her Breezer into a glass.

"Why not?" Mitzi repeated. "Because for the past month she has been goin' around asking everybody when they're going to have a shower for her. I hate that. When are people going to have the tact to realize that a shower is not compulsory? That is something your friends choose to do for you because they care about you, not because they have to." Mitzi was annoyed just talking about it.

"And furthermore," Crystal chimed in, "now that you say it, I heard she also typed up a guest list for the shower and gave it to her maid of honour. I'm not going, either."

"That's a tad tacky, isn't it?" Melba asked, like she wasn't sure. She would probably do the same thing herself.

"She's a tacky broad, what you expect?" Crystal asked. "Oh, and included with the guest list was a list of gifts she wants and where she wants them from."

"And what food she wants served, don't forget that," Mitzi added.

"When is the damn thing, anyway?" Melba asked.

"Next Saturday." Mitzi and Crystal answered together.

"Then she's gonna have the nerve to act surprised," Mitzi said, cutting her eyes.

"And start bawling!" Crystal added.

"You two have made me a bit dubious about going now," Melba said. Mitzi and Crystal looked at each other slyly again. Give Melba a couple of Breezers, and the big words would spill out.

"But were you ever invited, Melba?" Crystal asked. She never bit her words.

"What constitutes an invitation?" she asked innocently.

"A piece of paper or card addressed to you with a date, time and place," Crystal answered, taking a piece of fried fish from a bag and winking her eye at Mitzi.

The doorbell rang, and Sundae strode into the room. She always seemed to be in a hurry.

"Hey!" she sang out while she took her jacket off. She joined the others at the dining table where Mitzi was neatly arranging the food buffet style. "Where this food come from?" Sundae asked, taking off her shoes.

"That new restaurant that just opened in town," Crystal answered, mouth full of food. Mitzi glared at her. She ignored her and looked down at Sundae's shoes. "Incidentally, Sundae, nineteen eighty-four called and said they want those shoes back."

"Where you going in those things, Sundae?" Melba asked, frowning.

"I've been to a funeral. These are my 'don't let me fall down' shoes, girl. Good thing I wore 'em, too. We had to walk all over people's graves to get to ours." She bit a piece of fish.

"Ours? Tell me something, Sundae," Melba said. "Do you even know the first name of the deceased?"

"Don't be so stupid," Sundae said, grabbing a fork and plate. "Of course I do. You think I just go to anybody's funeral?" She regretted saying that as soon as she had.

"Yes!" the others answered.

"Look, this woman looked after me and my sister for years."

"She died?" Crystal asked, feeling a little bad about teasing her.

"No, her mother-in-law did," she said simply. They all looked at her as she bit a piece of fish. "What?" she asked blankly, looking from one to the other.

"The old baby-sitter's husband's mother?" Crystal calculated thoughtfully. "That should have gotten you three days' compassionate leave." They all laughed, including Sundae.

"Why don't you use a fork, Crystal?" Melba asked, pretending to be disgusted. Crystal was shoving food into her mouth with her fingers.

"What for?" she asked, licking her fingers. "Fingers were made before forks."

"You're acting like you're shipwrecked, Crystal," Mitzi teased.

"But who the hell am I botherin'?" Crystal was never really fussed about anything. Crystal Outerbridge was a beautiful person, inside and out. She would give you the heart out of her body if you needed it. At thirty-five, she too was a hairdresser who had gone to college with Mitzi. They had come home together and had both gone to work at Crystal's mother's salon until Mitzi had opened hers. Crystal was married to a man who actually adored her. What everybody admired about Raoul was that he respected his wife, even in absence. You never heard him say a bad thing about her, even when the other 'boys' dogged their wives. But Crystal demanded love and respect without having to ask for it from anyone. Raoul often said that he loved her heart, which said it all. At five feet, three inches tall, she weighed about a hundred and ten pounds, which was surprising because she ate constantly. They had a four year-old son, Raoul, Jr., or 'R.J.', as he was called and a six year-old daughter, Zindzi. Both were Mitzi's godchildren.

"So, what were you guys talking about before I got here?" Sundae asked, sitting on the floor. Heaven forbid she should miss a little gossip.

"You," Melba said. Sundae cut her eyes at her.

"Sonia's shower," Crystal said, wiping her fingers with a napkin.

"Oh, talkin' 'bout that," Sundae said, ready to kick in with her knowledge of the topic.

"Guess who's in the wedding?" They all waited for the answer. "Valerie."

"Valerie who?" Crystal asked, in slight disbelief of the inevitable answer.

"Valerie... your ace girl, Crystal," she said slowly, waiting for the reaction she knew they would have.

"Girl, no!" Mitzi said.

"What the dresses look like?" Crystal wanted to know. "'Cause dressing her up is gonna be like hangin' a lace curtain over a broken window," she said dryly. Sundae and Mitzi thought that was hilarious.

"Are we here to confabulate?" Melba asked.

"Yes! Whatever the hell that means, yes!" Sundae shot at her.

"You lot want your hair permed, or what?" Melba asked, hands on her hips.

"What confabrilate mean?" Sundae whispered to Mitzi.

"Confabulate," she corrected her. "It means to gossip."

"I'm ready for somebody to do my hair," Crystal answered Melba. "For a change. Come on, Melba, you can start roasting my nuts." She threw her empty bottle in a paper bag and took her earrings off.

"Got a towel, Mitzi?" Melba asked. Mitzi went to the linen closet to get one.

"But guess who else is in the wedding?" Sundae continued the conversation. "Come on, Mitzi, let me start your hair," she said before anyone answered her.

"Who?" Crystal asked, sitting in a chair.

"Tina."

"Is Sonia desperate for maids, or what?" Melba asked, putting on the cheap gloves that come with perm kits.

"You're confabulating, Melba," Crystal said. Melba knocked her shoulder.

"That Tina can be in a wedding, can't she?" Mitzi asked. "I certainly hope they have a miracle-working makeup artist for her."

"Damn right, 'cause that Tammy Faye Baker replica needs help with hers desperately," Crystal added.

"And she don't need an excuse to draw attention to herself," Melba said. "She'll be in her element, basking in the rays of her non-existent beauty."

"Go on, Melba girl," Crystal laughed. "Have another drink, honey."

"Talk about Tina if you like," Sundae said. "At least she's got a man."

"And what?" Crystal wanted to know.

"But guess who the man is, Crystal," Mitzi said. She didn't give Crystal a chance to guess. "David Richardson."

"David Richardson from down North Shore?" Crystal asked.

"Yep."

"Any port in a storm, I guess," Crystal laughed.

"You didn't know that, Crystal?" Melba asked. "She talks about the boy, ad nauseum."

"Melba, is it really necessary for you to use those damn big words when the sisters are just sittin' around shooting the breeze?" Crystal was getting tired of her and her vocabulary.

"Don't hate me because I'm an educated woman."

"It's not because you're educated, we just hate you." Crystal said, matter-of-factly.

"David's a nice guy, you know," Sundae continued. "I was talkin' to him for a while the other day. He never mentioned Tina, though."

"Would you?" Melba asked.

"Melba, you have perm in my ear, girl," Crystal said, slightly annoyed.

"Alright, I didn't do it on purpose. Keep still."

"David seems kinda educated," Sundae kept going. "He was talkin' 'bout how the black man is making it in the business world, and that it's about time we blacks started sticking together and supporting each other."

"I concur," Melba said, nodding.

"He was also saying that we women have to stop wearing ankle chains, too."

"Why?" Crystal asked. She wore two.

"Because, he believes that the chains were taken off of our ankles after the slave-masters had them on for so long, and we put them right back on. He thinks that wearing ankle chains is our way of holding on to our ties with the slave-masters. I took mine off."

"Wait a minute, wait a minute, wait one minute, Sundae!" Mitzi said, turning to face her. "You're listening to some fool tell you not to wear an ankle chain because it ties us to the slave-masters, but yet it's alright for him to allow cocaine to be his slave-master?"

"Hello," Crystal said. Sundae was speechless. "Wanna buy a vowel, Sundae?" Crystal asked, laughing and going to the kitchen sink to wash the perm out of her hair, which was short and curly.

"Sundae, you're sweet, but you're a little thick, aren't you?" Melba asked, condescendingly.

"What you mean?" Sundae asked, taking off the rubber gloves.

"What she means, dear girl," Mitzi said, standing up. "Is that sometimes you don't use your head and you just listen to anything anybody tells you. This coke-head talks some stuff to you about something as far-fetched as ankle chains, while he would probably sell his mama to get high on the drugs that have enslaved his mind, body and soul." She walked into the bathroom.

"I didn't know the boy was on drugs," Sundae said innocently.

"Well, now you do," Melba snapped. "So put your damn ankle chain back on and stop being silly." She got another Breezer from the fridge.

"Get me one, please," Sundae said sheepishly.

"How you making out, Miss Lady?" Melba asked Crystal.

"Fine. I'm finished." She turned off the water.

Melba sat at the table with Sundae and poured her drink. "So tell me, Sundae," she said, "not to change the subject, but how thick you planning on letting that mustache grow?"

"Leave her alone, girl," Crystal said, towel drying her hair.

"Well, it's not necessary, in this day and age, for her to go around looking like Victor Newman." Sundae thought that was funny. Crystal cut her eyes.

"What I s'posed to do with it?" Sundae asked, completely blank.

"Sundae, you work in a beauty salon, surely you must know that you can have it waxed." She lit a cigarette.

"That's painful."

"The pain only lasts a second. Please do something about it. Please. It's driving me crazy!"

"Alright!" Mitzi said, coming from the bathroom. "You're acting like she's a hairy beast. Sundae, if you want to take it off, do it. If you don't, don't."

Sundae acted like and was treated like a child sometimes. She was twenty-eight and a little naive. The others loved her dearly, but one of them was always trying to tell her what was best for her, usually Melba. But whoever wasn't picking on her was defending her. Sundae was divorced and worked for Mitzi. Although she was a bit simple, she was an excellent beautician, and except for Mitzi, she had the most clients at 'Salon Nubian'. She beat Mitzi when it came to cutting hair, though.

Melba was a travel agent and had been a client of Mitzi's since the day she'd opened. They hit it off right away for some reason, and Mitzi had introduced her to Sundae and Crystal, and the four of them had become a clique. Melba was thirty-three and had never married although she had been living with Roger Burchall for ten years. To her friends' knowledge, he had never even mentioned marriage to her.

Ebone''s bedroom door opened, and she went into the kitchen, looking absolutely awful.

"Hey," she mumbled. Mitzi's friends spoke to her, all of them surprised to see her. They knew she usually worked on Saturday nights.

"How you doin', Ebone'?" Crystal asked.

"Alright." She got a beer from the fridge and headed back toward her room.

"You want something to eat?" Mitzi asked, concerned about her.

"No, I'm cool." She went back to her room and closed the door.

"I didn't know she was home," Melba whispered.

"Me either," Crystal was whispering, too. "Don't she usually work on Saturdays?"

"Yeah, but something happened, so I called in sick for her."

"She looks like hell," Sundae said.

"Please don't let her hear you lot," Mitzi whispered. She had always tried to include Ebone´ in most of their plans, but Ebone´ always declined, saying that Mitzi's friends all thought they were better than she was, which wasn't true. Well, maybe Melba did, but what she thought didn't really count.

"So, what's her function?" Sundae wanted to know.

"It's personal."

"So, we're your personal friends," Sundae insisted.

"Sundae, you know I'm not going to tell you." Although Ebone´ annoyed Mitzi on a regular basis, she never bad-mouthed her. "Were you lot able to fit Pat in today?" she asked Sundae, trying to change the subject.

"Uh uh, she called back this morning to say 'never mind'," Sundae said, rolling Mitzi's hair.

"After all that fuss she made to get the appointment?" Mitzi asked, annoyed.

"No, she called to say she was going away today - it was a last minute thing."

"Oh," Mitzi said, a little calmer. "She and Philip must be going on a little lover's holiday."

"She and who?" Crystal asked, passing Melba a roller.

"Philip, her husband, Crystal."

"Oh no, honey, get your news. Love don't live there anymore."

"They broke up?" Mitzi was genuinely shocked.

"You need to get out more, Mitzi," Sundae said.

"I didn't know either," Melba said, "but, of course, the 'galloping gossiper of the ghetto' would know," she said, referring to Sundae.

"Thank you very much," Sundae said, hardly offended by the description.

"What happened to those two?" Mitzi asked. She was a little surprised she hadn't heard already, too. Pat was a regular client of theirs although Mitzi forbade gossip in her salon. In fact, there was a sign on the reception desk that read, 'Thank You for Not Gossiping'.

"Girl, he used to beat her senseless," Sundae said.

"How you know, Sundae?"

"Don't worry 'bout it."

"God, I hate when men do that," Crystal said. "And then you have the silly woman staying with him just because he was sorry afterward. Raoul should try that stuff, he'd be two olives short of a bladdy martini."

"At least Pat had the sense to leave, poor sight," Mitzi said. "Ow, Sundae, you dug that pick right in my scalp."

"Sorry. But it's hard when you love a man," Sundae said softly.

"What's hard?" Melba asked. "He hits you, you leave."

"Roger's never hit you?"

"Is Roger still alive?" Melba was known to have had her share of fist fights over the years. She was tame now, but Mitzi and Crystal had once seen her fight like a man. She said she had learned it watching her mother fight her father, and Roger knew just how far to go. She might act uppity and sophisticated, but offer her a good hook, and you'd swear she was somebody else.

"Hey Mitzi, you have a little silver up here, too," Sundae said, pulling at a gray hair.

"I know, I hate it. I'm too young to have gray hair."

"It's worse when you find one 'down there'," Crystal said.

"Down where?" Sundae asked, blankly.

"Down in hell! Where you think, Sundae?" Melba snapped.

"Oh, down there." She caught on.

"Oh no, I'd have to pull that Johnson out, honey," Mitzi said, frowning.

"That don't stop 'em," Crystal said.

"Must we talk about something so private?" Melba protested.

"Oh girl please, get over it," Crystal said, cutting her eyes.

"Melba, I don't know why you have to act so P. R. E.," Mitzi said. Her granny said that often, but she didn't know exactly what it meant. It seemed to fit in this case.

"Anyway, we were talking about Pat and her husband," Melba said.

"My ex-husband used to hit me sometimes," Sundae volunteered. Nobody was surprised. "But at the time I knew he was under a lot of pressure. He didn't mean it. He really loved me."

"I know what you mean, Sundae girl." Crystal stood up. "'Cause every time Raoul busts my behind, I thank God he loves me." She cut her eyes and went to get a drink.

"Come on, Sundae," Mitzi pleaded. "Surely, you don't think that the man loved you while he was beating you up?"

"I know he loved me. And plus, he didn't really beat me, he would just hit me sometimes." She sat in the chair Crystal had gotten out of.

Melba knocked on Sundae's head as if it were a door. "Sundae, Sundae, Sundae," she repeated. Then she sighed. "Never mind. I give up."

"Why you leave him?" Crystal asked, eating chips she had found on top of the fridge.

"He left me. For his pregnant girlfriend."

"Sounds like true love to me," Crystal said sarcastically, salt on her face.

"Sundae, it's time women stopped making excuses for the things men do," Mitzi said. "A man only does what a woman allows him to get away with."

Sundae sighed. "I know. It's too hard havin' a man."

"You won't always feel this way, Sundae," Crystal said sincerely. "I mean, this all starts when we're teenagers. But with time, some women learn how to handle men."

"Remember all the things we did for a boy when we were younger?" Mitzi reminisced.

"Like, he would say he would call at such and such a time. Remember when it was almost time, you'd be waiting, and Lord forbid your mama or somebody would be on the phone at that time," Melba continued.

"Right, 'cause it wasn't about call waiting then," Crystal said.

"You'd be watching the digital clock until it changed to the exact time," Mitzi said.

"You'd be watching TV and by the time the next commercial came on, you knew the phone would ring. No, the next commercial, no, definitely the next one." Crystal was laughing.

"Then it would happen!" Melba said, dramatically. "That beautiful sound."

"You snatched it before the first ring finished..."

"And it was your auntie!" Crystal shouted. They were all laughing now. Ebone´ was in her room, wishing they would leave.

"I remember, by that time all I could do was lie in my bed, curled up in a ball. I just couldn't function until the boy called," Crystal said.

"But how 'bout the lines they used in those days. I think the best one was when we were about to hang up the phone, he would say, 'Would you think about me?'" Mitzi couldn't stop laughing while the others nodded. They remembered.

"And we fools would say, 'I can't think about anything else, 'cause you're always on my mind!' " Crystal was bouncing on the couch and clapping her hands now.

"God, Crystal, you get completely and endlessly excited about absolutely nothing, don't you?" Melba asked.

"Shut up, bitch!" Crystal said, bursting into laughter again.

"How 'bout this line," Mitzi said. "This one guy I used to go with - I was about sixteen - called me and said, 'Baby, your feet must be tired.' And me and my simple self, mesmerised by the very sound of his voice, said, 'Why you say that?' And my boy said, 'Cause you've been running through my mind all day.' "

The four of them keeled over. Tears were streaming down Crystal's face, and Mitzi was slapping the floor. They laughed for a good two minutes. The phone rang.

"This is Roger," Mitzi said, pulling herself up off the floor to answer the phone.

"How you know?" Melba asked suspiciously.

"Because, Melba," Crystal said slowly, anxious to get her back. "Everybody knows that whenever you go out, Roger tracks you down."

"Phone, Melba," Mitzi said, smiling.

"Told you," Crystal said, crossing her legs, still wiping her eyes.

"What he want? Sundae asked loud enough for Melba to hear. She turned her back while she talked to Roger.

"Mitzi, what happened to the 'Want More'?" Crystal asked, referring to Mitzi's masterpiece dessert.

"Oh, I almost forgot about it. It's in the fridge."

"I'll get it." Crystal jumped up. "Hi, Roger," She said as she walked past Melba. She ignored her, and Crystal could tell they were arguing.

While Crystal went to the fridge, Mitzi took fifty dollars from her pocket and gave it to Sundae. "You can pay it back when you have it," she whispered. Sundae had asked her for the money earlier in the day. Mitzi couldn't understand why she was broke. It was Saturday, they got paid on Fridays. Then she decided that things came up from time to time. Crystal came back with the dessert, plates and spoons.

"You know, when I think back, I really did some crazy things for the love of a man," she said.

"You and me, too," Mitzi admitted, shaking her head.

"Remember when we used to cry over boys...? Hey, you still do, don't you, Sundae? Big boys!" Mitzi tried not to laugh, but Sundae did, so she did, too.

"Very funny, Crystal," she said, throwing a rolled up napkin at her.

Melba finally hung up on Roger and tried to act like everything was fine.

"Can't stay out and play any longer, Melba?" Sundae asked.

"I can stay out as long as I want to," she snapped. "I'm not married to Roger."

"Don't we know," Sundae said.

"Now, don't even try it, Melba," Crystal said seriously. "'Cause you're traveling with me, and I'm not ready to go yet."

"I don't have to... I mean, I'm not ready to go either." Mitzi glared at her and cut her eyes.

"I'm gonna tell you lot something I did once for a guy," Crystal said, continuing the conversation where they left off.

"Oh my God," Melba said.

"Don't you talk, Melba," Sundae said, "'Cause we'll make you tell one."

"Listen you lot," Crystal said, determined to tell her story. "When I first came back home from school, I got my own apartment." She ate a spoonful of dessert and kept talking. "So anyway, I was going with this boy, I really liked him, and I used to cook for him a lot. Well, things weren't working out, so he broke up with me. But guess what? I was so messed up by the boy leaving me that for about three weeks after he left me, I would cook dinner, set the table for two and take up two plates of food."

"No, Crys," Melba said, unable to believe what she was hearing.

"But that's not the best part. Then, I would stand an eight by ten picture of the boy on the table in front of his plate and have dinner with him!"

"No bye, Crystal, you had it bad," Sundae said, shaking her head.

"Where is the boy now?" Mitzi asked.

"Down my house. I married him," Crystal laughed. "It was Raoul, we got back together." They all laughed. "But don't ever tell him, you lot, 'kay?" She pleaded.

"He doesn't know?" Mitzi asked.

"You 'fullish'? I would never let a man know he had me messed up that bad."

"You shoulda never told me," Sundae said, licking her spoon. "You know I can't hold anything."

"I would kill you, Sundae." Crystal pointed her spoon at her. "Come on, I know I'm not the only one with a 'stupid things I did for a man' story."

"I have a few," Sundae said.

"Oh, I could just imagine, 'Rose Nylund'," Melba said.

"I'll tell you lot one of them." Sundae got comfortable on the couch, feet under her, cushion squashed in her arms. "One time, this guy asked me to go out with him, and he didn' t have transportation, so he asked me to pick him up. Well, I got to the house, knocked on the door and your boy came to the door staff naked."

"Stark naked," Melba corrected.

"Whatever. He didn't have clothes on anyway. So I swallowed that and went in the house."

"This was the first date, Sundae?" Melba asked.

"Yes, Melba. Come on now, stay with the tour," Mitzi said. Crystal sucked her teeth in Melba's direction.

"Anyway, he told me to wait in the living room while he got his shower. Two minutes later, he calls me to come in his bedroom, and when I get there, he has rose petals spread all over the bed and a dish of strawberries and Cool Whip in the middle of the bed.

"For what?" Melba asked, shocked.

"I don't know. Anyway, I'm standing in the middle of the room, and I look into the bathroom, 'cause the door's wide open, and the shower has a crystal glass door, so I could see him showering."

"I would have been kinda scared," Mitzi said, looking at Melba and Crystal who were both nodding.

"I wasn't scared, but I felt sort of uncomfortable. Anyhow, he came out of the bathroom with a towel wrapped around his waist and asked me if I wanted some strawberries and whipped cream."

"What a jerk," Melba said.

"He really was."

"Did you eat the stuff?" Crystal asked, fascinated with the story.

"Hell no! I told him I was allergic to strawberries. Anyway, we finally left his house about an hour later and had a really terrible time." She waved her hand to signal the end of the story.

"Could someone please tell me what makes the preceding a story about the stupid things one does for a man?" Melba asked.

"Oh, I forgot the bottom line," Sundae said. "I went out with him two more times after that."

"That beats my story," Crystal said dryly.

"That's a story to beat all stories," Mitzi said.

"I cannot believe you would do something so ludicrous," Melba threw in.

"What about you, Melba?" Sundae asked.

"I don't have a story," she said quickly.

"Of course you don't, because your story's still happenin'," Crystal said.

"Go to hell, 'Miss Set the Table for a Ghost'," Melba said. "My life is just fine, thank you, and never, have I ever, done anything stupid for a man."

"Come on, Mitzi, your turn." Sundae was hot to find out if anybody had a story worse than hers.

"Sorry, I'm fresh out of 'stupid' stories. 'Q' put me through a few changes, but I would hate to talk ill of the dead," she said, failing in her attempt to sound sincere.

"Right," Crystal said, nodding. Melba yawned. They all looked at her. She always yawned to signal that it was time for her to leave. Roger had probably told her to be home by a certain time, and that time was drawing near. Crystal ignored her.

"Whose is this wallet?" Sundae asked, picking up a brown, leather wallet from the coffee table.

"Sundae, it has the initials C.T.O. on it, now who could that be?" Crystal asked, sarcastic as usual.

Sundae ignored the sarcasm - probably didn't even notice. "What's your middle name, Crystal?"

"Nonya," Crystal answered.

"That begins with the letter 'N', this has a 'T'."

"Sundae, where have you been living?" Melba asked, annoyed. "Nonya means none of your business."

"Well what does the 'T' stand for?" she insisted.

"For heaven's sake, it stands for Thelma!" Crystal snapped, snatching the wallet from Sundae.

"Your mama named you Crystal Thelma?" Melba asked, surprised.

"I'm named after my grandmother, okay?" Crystal said, yawning. It was one-forty in the morning.

"I am, too," Mitzi said, proudly. "Both of them - Maxine Elfreda Helene."

"And you tell people?" Sundae asked, laughing.

"Girl, you're named after a day of the week, and you have the nerve to laugh at somebody else's name. What's your middle name, Sundae? Morning?" Crystal asked.

"No, it's Kelly."

They looked at Melba. "It's Dee, okay?" she answered without being asked.

"Not bad," Mitzi said.

"Irene Vivian," Melba continued. They all laughed.

"Your mama thought she was only having one child, didn't she?" Mitzi asked.

"They couldn't decide on one, so they gave me all of them."

"Now you lot," Crystal said, yawning again. "I'm goin' home - take off my ankle chains." Sundae glared at her. Crystal burst into laughter and held her hand up. "I'm sorry, Sundae," she said, still laughing. "I'm tired. Come on, Melba." She didn't have to call Melba twice; she had her bag on her shoulder, ready to go. Crystal walked toward the door with her shoes in her hand. Sundae was putting hers on.

"It's been real, you 'byes'," Mitzi said. "Thanks for doin' my hair, Sundae."

"Oh, just put it in my paycheque on Friday," Sundae joked.

"Right. Get out." Mitzi pushed her out of the door.

"Bye, chicky," Crystal said. Melba was outside.

"Good night, Melba," Mitzi shouted, leaning out of the door.

"Oh, night girlfriend," she shouted back. "Thanks for everything."

"Get her home 'fore she turns into a pumpkin," Mitzi whispered to Crystal.

"Don't let her get on my nerves, 'cause I'll drive her St. George's and then take her home."

"Let's do that!" Sundae said anxiously.

"You crazy? It's two o'clock in the mornin'. I'm going home to my husband. And I've had a few drinks, too. Raoul's in trouble."

"Don't bore me," Sundae said. "Check you later, Mitzi," they both said. Mitzi waved. Melba was in Crystal's car already. Sundae had her own car, and they drove off together, Crystal and Melba to Spanish Point and Sundae to Somerset.

Mitzi soaked a bag of codfish, turned the lights off and opened the door to Ebone''s room. The TV was still on. "Ebone'?" she whispered. Ebone' pretended to be asleep. Mitzi closed the door and went to her room.

Don't worry 'bout me. Why don't you go with your other friends?

In her room, Mitzi smiled as she put her pajamas on. She always had a good laugh when she got together with those three. They were really good friends, and she liked being around them. Then she thought about Ebone' and what she was going through. Mitzi felt for her, but it was definitely time for her to get her act together. She would help her. Only God knew how, but she had to help her. She whispered a prayer and got in her bed. Tomorrow she would seriously think about what she could do for Ebone'. She was her friend, and Mitzi loved her.

CHAPTER FIVE
Sunday Morning

Mitzi got out of bed at seven-thirty and went for a run. When she got back forty-five minutes later, Ebone´ had finally gotten out of bed and was sitting at the kitchen counter, looking through the TV guide.

"Hi, Blackie," Mitzi said, affectionately and slightly out of breath.

"Hi," Ebone´ said, not looking up.

"It's good to see you up - finally."

"Don't get excited, I just wanted to see what's on TV." She looked terrible, and to Mitzi's knowledge, she hadn't bathed since the night all the confusion had taken place. Her hair was all over her head.

Ebone´, you can't stay in your bed indefinitely," Mitzi said, wiping her face with a towel. She sat beside her. "When are you plannin' on going back to work?"

"Tomorrow, I guess."

"Well, tomorrow is also the day you start pulling yourself together," Mitzi said seriously. Ebone´ sucked her teeth. "Look, I know you're hurting, and I really feel for you, but you have to move on."

"That's easy for you to say."

"Maybe it is, but think about it. I broke up with Darren the same night you broke up with Ricky. I've put it behind me. And Darren didn't treat me half as bad as Ricky treated you."

"I loved Ricky. You said you didn't love Darren. There's a difference."

"True." *Bad example, but I tried.*

"Nevertheless," Mitzi continued, getting water from the fridge, "you can't keep going on like this. You've been in your bed since yesterday morning, and you look like hell."

"Thanks." Ebone´ walked toward her bedroom.

"Ebone´," Mitzi said, wiping her mouth. "I'm telling you now, I'm giving you 'til the end of the week to get over this. The boy is not worth all of this time."

"I don't know how to get over it, Mitzi," she said, leaning on the wall. "I love the man, I always wanna be with him."

"But you can't be with him now, Ebone´." Mitzi was almost pleading with her to understand. "This man is renting space in your mind and your heart, and he ain't even paying."

"You always know what to say, don't you?"

"I've just been paying attention to life lately, honey."

Ebone´ sighed. "I just can't see myself with anybody else. I hate startin' over." She sat back down. "You know, sometimes I believe that some women were born to take shit from men, and I think I'm one of them."

"That's bull, Ebone´. And you know it." Mitzi didn't want to shout at her again today. She wanted to shake her though, but she told herself to stay calm.

"I don't know, Mitzi," Ebone´ continued. "I want Ricky so bad, sometimes I think I just might as well put up with the way he treats me. We do have some good times. At least I would have him. I can't be happy without him."

"And you can't be happy with him. Do you know what you're telling me?" She didn't wait for an answer. "That you are worth no more than another person."

"Maybe I'm not."

"But you are." Mitzi was pleading with her eyes. "You are worth a whole lot more than Ricky Trott. Maybe you can't see past the pain you're feeling right now, but you don't need him, and he don't want you." She looked hurt. "I'm sorry, but I'd rather hurt you with the truth than encourage you to believe a lie."

"Thanks." Ebone´ played with the napkin holder on the counter. Mitzi put her arm around her. "Don't hurt yourself anymore, Ebone´. Please? For you." *And for me.*

"Okay." She stood up. Mitzi's hugging was a little too much for her. She didn't receive affection well. "I promise you that I'll try."

"That's all I ask." *Is this Max Robinson talking, or what?*

"I just wanna be happy, that's all."

"Then do it."

"Okay."

"Wanna have breakfast with me?"

"Codfish?"

"Yeah."

"Nah, I don't feel like eating."

"You're gonna make yourself sick if you just keep smoking cigarettes and not eating."

"I'll live." She smiled. It was a start.

Mitzi hugged her friend again. Ebone´ attempted to hug her back, but she didn't know how.

"I'm here for you, 'kay?"

"I know." She was fighting tears again.

"Ebone´?"

"What?"

"Get a bath."

She broke into a huge grin. "I'll think about it."

"I'm going to call my mama and see if she and George wanna come for breakfast."

"I'm gonna be in my room. I don't feel like socializing, okay?"

"Okay. I'll tell them you're still asleep. But remember what I said, Ebone´. Tomorrow you start working on the new you, and by the end of the week I want to see the new you."

Ebone closed her door, and Mitzi called her mother to invite her and her boyfriend to breakfast. Oleeta said she would love to come, but George was playing golf. "I have some things to talk to you about anyway," Mama said. When Mitzi hung up, she put the fish and potatoes on to cook and went to take a shower. By the time her mama arrived, breakfast was ready. Mitzi had also made a tomato sauce and muffins to go with the bananas and avocado pear.

Oleeta came at ten-thirty, wearing a fuschia sweat suit and white sneakers. She looked pretty. Her salt and pepper hair had been done by Mitzi the Friday before and still looked good. She was smiling as usual. The thin sliver of gold in her teeth sparkled slightly. Mitzi had inherited her mother's smooth brown skin and perfect teeth. She was about the same height as Mitzi and apart from her slightly large bust, she was petite - pert. No one believed she was fifty-two years old.

"Something smells good, sweetie," she said, stopping to kiss Mitzi on the cheek on her way in. Mitzi was listening to Blondell's 'Living Memories'.

"Thank you, Mama. I wish George could have come so he could see that I really can cook."

Oleeta laughed. "Don't pay him any mind, child." George always teased Mitzi, telling her she was just a pretty face and didn't have the faintest idea about domesticity. He was a really sweet man. He was fifty-five, and he and Oleeta had met five years before at his fiftieth birthday party. She had gone with Aunt Bey. At first it was hard for Mitzi and Macky to see their mama with another man, but when they saw how genuinely kind he was to her, it made him easier to digest. He had never tried to take Daddy's place. They laughed a lot, and sometimes they acted like teenagers. It made Mitzi happy to see her mama happy. She deserved it.

"I'm kinda glad he couldn't come because I wanted to talk to you about something." Oleeta took off her sneakers and sat on the couch. "You changed the furniture around. It looks much nicer this way. Check the new couch, it's pretty."

"Thanks. Mama, don't tell me you and George are having problems?" Mitzi looked horrified.

Oleeta waved her hand. "Oh no. This isn't about George. We're fine. It's that damn Macky. Can I have a cup of tea, please?"

"What he do?" Mitzi asked as she went to put the kettle on. She was surprised to hear her mama complain about Macky. That was something she never did. He was seventeen and was going to Bermuda College. He was doing very well in school and had just started working nights as a busboy at Princess. They were planning on sending him away to school next year. He wanted to be a P.E. teacher. Mitzi came back carrying a tray with two cups and saucers, tea bags, cream and Equal sweetener.

"Ever since he's been working, his whole attitude has changed." She played with the diamond and ruby ring George had given her on their fifth 'anniversary'.

"Like what?"

"Well, you know he has the little girlfriend, right?"

"Tatyana?"

"Yeah, I can never pronounce her name properly. I just call her 'honey'." She called everybody 'honey'.

"The other night, George and I went to Mrs. Jones' house to a dinner and when we got home... I mean, he took me home about two o'clock." Mitzi smiled at her. She knew that George usually stayed at Oleeta's house whenever Macky stayed at a friend's house, which was often. He and his 'boys' would stay at each other's houses after they hung out. But her mama never, as she put it, let the sun catch George at her house. Mitzi went to get the boiling water.

"Anyhow, there was 'Miss Lady' - Tanya, or whatever - and Macky, laying off in his bed."

"I hope he's using condoms," Mitzi said thoughtfully.

"Mitzi! That's not the issue here. I thought is was quite inappropriate for those children to be in Macky's bed like that."

"Were they dressed?"

"Yes. They were lying on top of the spread, but still... I told them that I thought it was time for her to leave. I said it politely."

"Hmm. Things have changed. When I was home courting, when you thought it was time for the fella to go, you or Daddy would turn on the living room light and say, "It was nice having you, so and so."

"I don't remember doing that." Oleeta sipped her tea.

"Of course not."

"Anyhow, Macky took her home - she just lives over the way - and came back with an attitude. I said 'good night' to him, and he just went in his room and closed the door. He barely said a word to me all weekend. I just left him alone."

"You should have gone upside his head."

"I should have. But Sunday now, I told him to get the trash ready for Monday morning and take it up the hill. He didn't answer, but I knew he heard me."

"You've gone soft, Leeta girl." Mitzi was blowing her tea.

"No I haven't. So when I got up Monday morning, he was still asleep. I get dressed and go to get in the car, and there's the trash, still in the garage. Now you know I wasn't taking anybody's trash out in my good clothes."

"Especially when you had an overgrown son in the house sleeping."

"Exactly. I went back inside and told him to get up and take it up the hill, and I left."

"Did he take it?"

"Well, I get home Monday evening and guess what meets me at the door?"

"No, Mama. You have to do something about him." Mitzi was angry.

"Well, I called him into the kitchen - he never did go to school that day - to find out what his problem was."

"He's not going school?"

"That day he claimed he didn't have to. So I asked him what was with the attitude he had, you know, why he was acting so simple."

"And?"

"He got all huffy and started going on about how I still treated him like a child when he's out working now. He thinks he should be treated like a man."

"Oh he thinks so, huh?"

"Mitzi, I give Macky his space. His friends come down the house anytime they want. Some of them just walk in."

"I don't like that."

"I don't mind. They all respect me, and I feed them sometimes, they use my car, I tolerate that loud rangae."

"Reggae."

"Whatever. And that rap junk. I listen to all of it, but I would rather listen to that than have them out on the street getting into trouble."

"That's all well and good, Mama, but that don't give Macky the right to disrespect you."

"Well, I'm not saying that, Mitzi, but just here recently he's starting to have this air about him, and I'm wonderin' what happened."

"Tatyana happened."

"What happened to her?"

"No, she happened to him. He's got a little sweetie now, so he thinks he's 'Mr. Man'. I think Master Robinson needs a little reality check."

"Macky don't wanna see me get ugly, you know, Mitzi."

"I know. I've seen it, and it's not a pretty sight." Mitzi laughed. "Don't worry about it, Mama, I'll deal with him."

"But don't tell him I told you about Tanya, okay?"

"Tat-ya-na. And yes, I am telling him you told me about her." Mitzi got up to get the breakfast. "What is it with you mamas and your sons?"

"It's not that..."

"It is that. You just sat here and complained to me about the boy, and now you don't want him to know."

"I have to live with him, you know."

"No, he has to live with you. That's your house, you pay the mortgage and make the rules. Macky's a guest in your home."

"Only the Lord knows why I waited so long after I had you to have him."

"Don't matter, he's here now, and you can't send him back."

"Sometimes I'd like to."

"It don't have to go there. Straighten his little black behind out now. Number one, make sure he knows who you are and what you're not going to stand for. Number two, don't make excuses for him, number three..."

"And just how many children do you have, Missy?"

"I might not have children, but you don't have to be a cow to know what milk is."

" 'Scuse me," Oleeta laughed.

"We children weren't brought up like that. I couldn't get 'huffy', as you say, without a slap upside my head from you or Daddy."

"Your daddy never hit you, Mitzi."

"He didn't have to, you did it for him."

"That's right." Oleeta sat at the table where Mitzi put a plate of codfish and potatoes in front of her. "This looks good, honey."

"Thank you, honey." They said grace and began eating.

"Mama, I'm warning you, don't let Macky think he can start getting over you because you'll regret it, and I'll kill him."

"Mitzi, you know I don't let anybody get over me, especially you children."

"If you don't pay attention, Macky will have gotten over you, and you won't even realize it."

"Where you get all this wisdom, child?" Oleeta asked, putting her fork down.

"My daddy." Mitzi smiled proudly.

"You're right. As long as you're around, Max Robinson will never be dead."

"If Daddy were alive, Macky wouldn't even try this stuff."

"Well, Daddy is gone."

"Right, so I have to sort Macky out. For Daddy." Oleeta smiled at her daughter and shook her head. "What you doing for Mother's Day?"

"When is it?" She was making another cup of tea.

"Two weeks from today."

"I haven't even thought about it."

"Wanna go away for a few days? There are a few specials on from Thursday to Sunday. We could go to Raleigh."

"Can you get the time off?"

"Mama! I own the place, 'member?"

"I know, but I was wondering if that would be a good time for you to take off." Oleeta wiped her mouth.

"According to Darren, this is the perfect time," Mitzi said, more to herself than to her mama.

"Why?"

"Huh? Oh that was kind of a private thing. But I can tell you. Darren and I broke up."

"Why, honey?" Oleeta was frowning, but she was happy - she had never really liked him.

Mitzi sucked her teeth. "Because he tried to run my life."

"In what way?"

"That's why I said what I did just now. He thought that I should take some time off."

"So?"

"He thought I should do everything he thought I should do."

Oh, one of those."

"To tell you the truth, Mama, sometimes I wonder if I've just hardened myself against all men. Maybe I'll just be alone for the rest of my life."

"Listen to me, Maxine," Oleeta said seriously but gently. "Don't settle for less than you deserve, even if it means you'll never get married again."

"I would like to one day."

"Fine, but don't compromise anything. I don't worry about you, you know, Mitzi, because I don't have to. You know what you want and what you don't want. Don't change just because you may want to get married again. What you want is to be happily married."

"If my marriage could be half as good as yours and Daddy's was, I would be satisfied."

"We had our little problems, too, Mitzi."

"Well, I don't want to hear about them."

Oleeta laughed. That's just what she and Max had had - little problems. "Mitzi, I would be a very happy woman if my children could have a marriage like I had."

"Maybe one day, Mama girl," Mitzi smiled.

"While we're on the subject of marriage," Oleeta said while Mitzi cleared the table and took the dishes into the kitchen. "George asked me to marry him."

"When?!" Mitzi screamed from the kitchen.

"Last weekend." Oleeta moved from the table to the couch.

"Mama! How come you're just telling me?" Mitzi had run back into the living room.

"Because I feel silly."

"You feel silly about a man like George asking you to marry him?

Why?"

"I'm a little too old to be getting engaged."

"Mama, you are fifty-two years old. You're a young woman. Marry the man, for goodness sake."

"You like George, don't you?"

"I love him, Mom. Because he's good to you, he respects you and he has never tried to take Daddy's place. He's a decent man. He's always been very kind to me and Macky, he has a good job..."

"Alright, Mitzi. I get the picture."

Mitzi sat on the couch beside her mother. "Do you love him, Mama?" she asked sincerely.

"Of course I love him..."

"And he loves you. You know he does. He told me he does. Marry him."

"I don't know, Mitz. I believe in my heart that it would work. Marriage is a wonderful institution between the right people. But I think if I marry George, first of all, I'll lose my independence."

I thought I was my father's daughter.

"And furthermore, I think if I get married again, it will somehow cancel what your daddy and I had."

"Mama, what you and Daddy had is in your heart. Who can take that away?"

"You really think it'll be okay for me to get married again?"

"Not that you need my approval, but of course it'll be okay. If that's what you and George want, that's all that matters. Are you worryin' about what people are gonna say?"

"Kind of."

"Well don't."

"You know what I'm worried about the most? What your nana's gonna think."

Nana was Max's seventy-eight year-old mother who lived in Florida with her second husband. She and Oleeta had remained very close over the years. Nana had always loved her and thought of her as a daughter.

"Don't you think Nana wants you to be happy? She got married again after Papa died. She'll understand. You don't have to change the relationship you have with her." She got up to get a toothpick. "What does Mr. Bean think?"

"Mr. Bean?"

"George's daddy."

"Oh, we haven't told him yet. But we're not worried about him."

"You told Granny yet?"

Oleeta rolled her eyes. "Yes! You know her. She had to say something smart first."

"What she say?" Mitzi was laughing already.

"When I told her, she said, "You might as well, so you can stop living in sin.""

"Why she say that?" Mitzi smiled.

"Obviously she knows George and I have sex."

"Mama!"

"Oh grow up, Mitzi. You think only you young people can do it?"

"No, but you don't have to say it. You think you sound cute?"

"We're both women, Mitzi, and yes, as a matter of fact, I do think I'm cute." She smiled at Mitzi. Mitzi cut her eyes.

"Then Granny said that since she couldn't have Max, she would settle for George. She really likes him."

"Oh, I know, 'cause if she didn't, we would have known a long time ago."

Granny Lambert was a saucy but loving woman and like her youngest daughter, her looks didn't give away her age. She didn't look a day over sixty, which was what she told people when asked. "Nobody has any business asking a lady her age," she often said. "It's the height of bad manners." When Mitzi reminded her that she was lying about her age, she always replied, "It's a little white lie, they don't count." Apart from her 'little white lies', she usually spoke the truth, even if it was what one didn't want to hear. If you had on something that didn't suit you, she would say, "Perhaps that would look better on someone else, darlin'." If you asked her opinion, or even if you didn't ask, that's exactly what you got - an honest opinion.

Oleeta had two sisters, Belinda and the oldest, Roberta, who was named for their father, Robert. They had two brothers, Robert, Jr., Roberta's twin who was lost at sea when Mitzi was a teenager, and Frankie. Mitzi was very close to her Aunt Belinda and often went to church with her. As far as Granny was concerned, the sun rose and set on her daughters and grandchildren - there were twelve altogether - including Uncle Robert's two, and she treated them all the same, even though everybody thought Mitzi was her favourite. Granny always had something cooked or baked, a story and some money. But nobody could get over her. She would lend anybody money. But, if by chance, one of the grandchildren 'forgot' to pay her back and tried to borrow more, she would say, " 'Cause I'm an old lady, you think I'm 'fullish'? You haven't paid back the last lot, so I know you can't pay back any more." She and Robert, Sr. had been married fifty-one years when he died.

"Mama, please, if you love George, marry him."

"He wants me to stop working if I do."

"He doesn't want you to stay home and have babies, does he?" Mitzi smiled.

"Hell no! Don't be ridiculous. And furthermore, if I do have any more children, I'll be able to retire a very wealthy woman."

"Why?"

"Because I'll sue for money the doctor never had."

"That's right, you had your tubes tied, didn't you?"

"No honey, I had a hysterectomy - had the whole baby carriage taken out." She smiled. "Still got the playpen, though." Mitzi looked at her out of the corner of her eye. "Nothing to get in George's way." She was laughing.

"All right, Mama!" Oleeta put her arm around Mitzi's shoulder and pulled her close to her.

"Come on, Mitzi," she said and kissed her on the cheek. "You're my friend."

"No I'm not. I'm your daughter, I don't want to be your friend," Mitzi said, laughing and struggling to get out of Oleeta's grip. "Go tell Aunt Bey or your sisters all that stuff." Aunt Bey had been Oleeta's best friend for the past thirty-five years and was just as sweet as she was.

"Seriously Ma, what you gonna do?"

"I'm just concerned about Macky right now."

"We'll work things out with Macky, but you have to live your life, too. Macky's gonna be grown and married with his own children, and George will be gone, and you'll be by yourself, still worrying about Macky."

Oleeta sighed. "Okay, Maxine. I'll tell George that I'll marry him."

"Thank you." Mitzi clapped her hands and looked heavenward.

"But I'm not gonna ignore what's happening with Macky."

"You don't have to. We'll deal with him together."

"Thanks, Mitzi. I don't know what I would have done without you these past years."

"Lord knows I've needed you more than you could have ever needed me." They smiled at each other for a few seconds.

Oleeta looked at her watch. "Now, lemme go. George should be off the golf course by now." She stood up. "By the time I get down Belmont, he should have had a few bangers at the bar and should be ready."

"Mama, don't forget now. I'll call Melba and make the reservations for Mother's Day weekend."

"Oh, right. What days are we going? Thursday to Sunday?"

"Yeah, we can still be home for Mother's Day so you can be with your baby boy." She smiled.

Oleeta cut her eyes. "I'd slap you down."

"I'll call you after I talk to Melba and let you know what's happening. We can stay at the Sheraton. I'll pay for your ticket, that's your Mother's Day gift."

"You're such a sweetheart..."

"Yeah, today right?"

"Mitzi, please find out what's happening with Macky."

"I promise you, Mama, I'll talk to him as soon as I can."

"Thanks for everything, honey. Breakfast was lovely."

"You're welcome, Ma." They hugged at the door. "I'll call you tomorrow."

"Bye, honey." Oleeta left in her Ford Laser, and Mitzi went to clean the kitchen. In her room Ebone´ wept. She envied Mitzi and Oleeta's relationship. Actually, she hated it.

CHAPTER SIX
Monday Morning

"Hey, Macky." Mitzi had stopped by her mother's house on the way to work.

" 'S up?" Macky held the kitchen door open.

"Pardon?"

"What's up, Mitzi?"

"Oh, that's what you said." Mitzi followed him into the house. "I'm okay. I need to talk to you, Mack." He kept walking.

"Where you going?"

"To pee," he said, turning to look her right in the eye. "Do you mind?" She saw what her mama was talking about.

"No, I don't mind." He turned and walked away. Mitzi sat at her mama's glass top table and read the morning paper which Macky had obviously been reading before she got there. He came back a few minutes later.

"I was reading that," he said defensively. Mitzi purposely ignored him. "I was sitting there, Mitzi," he said a bit louder.

"What's your problem, Macky?" Mitzi asked calmly without looking up from the paper.

"I ain't got no problem. I just wanna sit there and read the paper, that's all."

She folded the paper and put it to the side. "You can read it later," she said, looking at Macky who was now sitting in another chair. "I need to talk to you."

"Talk."

"Why you treating me like this, Macky? I thought we were tight."

"What about the way everybody's treating me?" he asked, going to the fridge and taking out a bottle of apple juice. He opened it and sat back at the table.

"Who's everybody? I haven't treated you differently."

"Mama acts like I'm a child. She's getting on my friggin' nerves." He drank from the bottle.

"Wait a minute, Macky." Mitzi was ticked off by that statement. "That's my mama you're talkin' about. And yours, but obviously she don't rate any respect with you!" Macky sucked his teeth. "How is she getting on your nerves?"

"Hey look, Mitzi, I'm almost eighteen. I'm workin', I give Mama money every week, and she still treats me like a child." He pounded his chest with his fist. "I'm a man, I should be able to do what I want..."

"Let me tell you something, Macky!" Mitzi was shouting already. She didn't think she was coming here to deal with something like this. "Working, making money and getting a little bit of leg, does not make you the man of this house!"

"Well, who is the man of the house? 'Cause George sure as shit ain't!"

"No, George isn't the man of this house, nor does he want to be, but Mama is the woman of the house, and what she says, goes!"

"Hmph."

"And if you don't like it, you can pack the li'l bit of clothes you own, take your chump change and get the hell out of Mama's house!" She stood up, and so did he.

"Well, tell her to give me the money Daddy left me, and I'll go!"

"No, Macky, you don't get that money until you're twenty-one, if Mama feels like giving it to you!"

"It's my money!"

"What you gonna do if she don't give it to you? Take her to court?!"

"I..."

"And incidentally, just 'cause you're built like a male, does not make you a man, got it?! A man does not disrespect his mother. A real man protects his mother! Especially a mother who has done the things Mama's done for you!"

"I do things for her, too!"

"Big deal, Macky! What you do for her don't come near the stuff she's done and is still doing for your black ass! She gave you life, boy! She could have jumped off the damn roof while she was carrying you!"

"Hey, she could have. Maybe she should have." He lowered his voice.

Mitzi walked to the door and stopped. She turned to look at him. She didn't understand him. "What's the real deal, Macky?"

He sighed. "What real deal?"

"Where all this come from? Is it George?" He sucked his teeth. "Do you two get along?"

"He's all right. But I hope he knows he ain't gonna be tellin' me what to do."

"He don't wanna tell you what to do. He's been around since you were twelve, he hasn't told you what to do all this time, has he?"

"Nah." He was sitting on the stool next to the fridge. She leaned on the fridge beside him.

"Why you putting Mama through changes, man?" *Oh Lord, I just finished telling him he's not a man.* "You know that's not right. She don't deserve it, and that's not what Daddy would have..."

"Well Daddy's not here now, is he?!" He was shouting again. "Daddy left us, remember Mitzi?" He stood up. His words shocked her.

She spoke in a whisper. "Daddy died, Macky." She couldn't believe he had said that.

"Whatever. But he wasn't there when I needed him, was he?!" He was screaming again, and tears were in Mitzi's eyes. "Was he there to watch me play football and cricket? No!" His hands were in the air. "Was he there when I went high school and when I graduated? No! He took me fishin' three times, that's all! He never saw me ride my bike when I went

sixteen. He never met my girlfriends. He wasn't there, Mitzi!"
They were both crying now.

"I'm sorry, Macky. I didn't know you felt like this." He
was crying hard. She felt really sorry for him. He was very
suddenly her baby brother again. She helped him sit in a chair
and held him while he cried. "Let it out, Macky, let it all out."
She hadn't seen him cry since their daddy's funeral, and he
obviously had been holding a lot in. It hurt her to see him cry
because she had gotten used to his being tough. He always said
that he was her big brother and that he had to look after her. He
had told several of her male friends that if they messed with
her, they would have to deal with him. He was about two
inches taller than she was, and they had always been very
close.

"I wish he was here. You don't know how bad I wish he
was here." He was still crying and shaking.

"Yes I do." She was still crying, too. "Daddy wasn't here to
see me do a lot of things either." She rubbed his head. He
hated it but said nothing. "But he's gone, honey. I know it's
hard, and you need him sometimes, but he's gone. Forever.
Just hold on to the memories, and do what you think Daddy
would want you to do." He had stopped shaking and was
crying softly. "Does Mama know you feel like this?" She
knew she didn't because she would have told her.

"Uh uh. I didn't want to upset her."

"Well, you have upset her because you've shown your
feelings in other ways. She thinks you're mad at her for some
reason."

"She's all caught up in George..."

"What? You think she don't have enough time for you?"

"Sometimes."

"Come on, Macky, you're not exactly a little boy." He had
stopped crying and wiped his face with his shirt.

"I know, but I just don't want her to forget me."

"You know she ain't gonna do that. Macky, Mama spoils us."

"In a way, I think I've always blamed her for Daddy dying."

"Why?" Mitzi sat down.

"'Cause, I didn't have nobody else to blame."

"I know. I blamed God."

"You can't do that." He looked horrified.

"I know. Don't tell anybody. I asked Him to forgive me." Macky had calmed down and felt a little better. "Listen, when I was seventeen, I thought I was a woman - I thought I was every woman, in fact. But I wasn't. And the more I thought I was, the more Mama reminded me that I wasn't. It took me a while to realize that I wasn't grown up yet and that I still needed Mama and Daddy. I still need Mama today. She's our friend, Macky." He sighed. "Look, I was gonna let her tell you this, but I think now's a good time to tell you."

"What?"

"George asked Mama to marry him."

"He did?" He looked a little surprised.

"Yeah, but she told him she would have to think about it for a few reasons. And one of the reasons is because she's worried about you and wanted to find out what your problem was first." She looked at her watch. It was nine twenty, and her first appointment was at nine thirty. She stood up. "Tell her what the problem is, Macky. Tell her how you've felt about Daddy and everything all this time. She's really worried. I'm sorry, man, but I have to go." She walked to the door.

"That's not the only problem, Mitzi." He rubbed his face and sighed.

"What's up?" She opened the kitchen curtains. It was beautiful outside.

He sighed again. "Tatyana's pregnant."

"Oh damn, Macky!?" She sat back at the table in shock. "What happened to using condoms? I know Mama buys 'em for you."

He sucked his teeth. "Sometimes I just get caught up and never get around to putting it on."

She stared blankly at him for a few seconds. Then she spoke slowly. "I cannot believe you just said that." This wasn't the time to get mad. He didn't need that right now - he had opened up to her. "Macky, at this stage in your life, you should always be getting around to putting a condom on. It's your responsibility."

"Well, what about her? Shouldn't she be taking the pill or somethin'?"

"Did you know she wasn't taking the pill, or somethin'?"

He stood up and walked to the sink and leaned on it. "Yeah, I knew she wasn't on nothin'."

"Then it was your responsibility to use protection. Don't rely on other people to decide what's going to happen for you. Now you have a baby that you're gonna have to be responsible for. She is going to have it, right?"

"I don't know." He looked at the floor and was only a child himself. "She wants to have it, her mama thinks she should get an abortion, and I don't know what I want."

"I guess Mama don't know yet."

"Hell no. I don't even know how to tell her."

"Well, you have to tell her, and I might as well tell you, she's going to be hurt, disappointed and upset. But I promise you, she won't kill you." She stood and faced him. "I'll tell her with you if you want me to." He stared at her for a second and suddenly grabbed her and pulled her to him.

"Thanks, Mitz. Sorry for acting so frigged up."

"Don't worry 'bout it," she said into his chest. He was messing up her makeup and making her late for work, but that didn't matter right now. He needed her, and she was here. She couldn't let him down now. He let her go. "Another thing, Macky. Only you and Tatyana should decide what to do about the baby. How old is she?"

"Seventeen."

"How far along is she?"

"Ten weeks."

Mitzi shook her head. "You guys are too young to be anybody's parents, but an abortion is a serious thing. Once it's done, that's it."

"I know. I can't believe this is happenin'."

"Believe it, 'cause it's happenin'." Mitzi took her cosmetic bag from her purse and fixed her makeup. "And just let me tell you something else. Don't you be blaming her for this. You both made this child, and both of you are to blame, if blame has to be laid anywhere. She don't need you to turn on her now."

"I'm not gonna do that. I was kind of pissed off at first, but she started cryin' and everything, so I left her alone."

Mitzi snapped her compact shut and rubbed her lips together. "If I live to be a hundred, I will never understand how a man can have sex with a woman, knowing full well that neither one is protected and then turn around and be angry when she gets pregnant."

Macky looked at her blankly. "I know Daddy wasn't there to tell you this, but I'm sure you've heard. When you put that li'l thing inside..."

"Big thing."

She glared at him. "Whatever. But when you put it inside a girl, and it feels all nice and everything, usually that's the time when your... little soldiers are marching, and if it's the right time - or the wrong time - they march right out of you and into her eggs. And from there comes the baby. So it's not just about feeling good and..."

"Little soldiers?" He looked at her like she was stupid.

She laughed. "I heard Jazz on 'The Fresh Prince' call 'em that. I thought it was cute. But anyway, you get the picture. So you sometimes pay a big price for feeling good."

"Don't I know."

"So, when you gonna tell Mama?" Mitzi's bag was on her shoulder, and she was at the door again.

Macky rubbed his hand over his face. "I don't know. Not yet."

"It's not gonna go away, Macky. We should tell her tonight."

"Tonight?"

"Yes, tonight. Get it over with."

"Should I tell Tatyana to come?"

"No." She didn't want her mama to make off in front of Tatyana.

"Mama can talk to her later. The three of us should sit down and talk about this."

"What time?"

"I'm going to the gym when I knock off, then I'll come about six-thirty. Be here, Macky. Don't play around."

"I'll be here."

She playfully hit him upside his head. "I can't believe you did this. You know better."

He sighed. "Stuff happens."

"Yeah, right. But it shouldn't sometimes." She shook her head. "I'm gone." She started to leave. "You going school today?"

He looked at the clock. "Yeah, I'm making ten."

"Well get crackin'. I'll check you this evening."

"Yeah, okay. Thanks, Mitz."

Mitzi sat in her Toyota Corolla for about a minute to collect her thoughts. Macky was making bones. Her mama was going to kill him. She had promised him that she wouldn't, but now that she thought about it... She looked at Oleeta's hibiscus hedge. It was full and beautiful. The whole exterior of the house was immaculate, as always, thanks to Mama and George. On the other side of the hedge was the moongate, covered with hibiscus, too. She had taken pictures under the moongate on her wedding day. That seemed like a century ago. Macky was only ten - the pageboy. What the hell was he doing getting somebody's child pregnant? It was so unnecessary in this day and age. "Dammit!" she said and started the car. She wanted a cigarette. Bad.

Pokey Mrs. Seymour was across the yard, pretending to clean her windows. She had probably heard her and Macky shouting. Mitzi acted like she didn't see her and drove to work.

* * * * *

It was a hellish morning. The new girl, Samantha, had started this morning. Mitzi had hired her to do the 'Goddess' braids on a temporary basis. If there was a great demand for the braids, she would keep her permanently. Mitzi finally got to work at nine fifty to find Mrs. Sampson waiting and looking a bit miffed. She apologised profusely and did her hair for free. The reception area was full of Sundae's clients. Ronald informed her that Sundae had called in sick, and they were trying to fit her clients in with the other two stylists. Mitzi apologised to everyone individually. It was the least they deserved for being inconvenienced. She herself wasn't very busy, so she was able to take some of the ladies while a few of them opted to make other appointments. It wasn't like Sundae to call in sick, and Mitzi wondered what had happened.

By lunch-time, things were back to normal, and the salon was no longer a madhouse. Mitzi called Sundae to see if she needed anything, and she said she didn't. She thought she had caught some kind of bug but was sure she would be in by Wednesday. Tuesday was her regular day off. Then Mitzi called Ebone´ at her job to see how she was making out. Wendell, the owner, answered the phone and told her she was busy and couldn't take the phone. He was glad she had called though because Ebone´ was walking around like a zombie, and he was concerned. Mitzi briefly explained what had happened as she had done several times before. She trusted Wendell and knew Ebone´ wouldn't mind her telling him. Wendell assured Mitzi that he would keep an eye on her, and she knew he would. After talking to him, Mitzi called Melba and arranged the trip for her and her mother. Melba got them a discount at the Sheraton in Raleigh. By the time she knocked off at five fifteen, she decided that it was best to wait until after the trip to tell her mama the news about Macky, Tatyana and the baby. Knowing Oleeta, she probably wouldn't want to go, and if she did,·she wouldn't enjoy herself. She called Macky and told him that it was best to wait. He agreed, of course. She went to the gym where she saw Darren. They spoke like polite strangers and for the hour she was there, he completely ignored her. *How childish,* she thought and wondered how she could ever have given him the time of day, let alone lie down beside him. By the time she got home, it was seven thirty, and Ebone´

was in bed. Still wearing her sweaty gym clothes, she went into Ebone´'s room and sat on the floor to talk to her.

"How was your day?"

"It was a day."

"I called for you today."

"I know. Wendell told me."

"He said you were busy."

Ebone´ looked at her for the first time since she had come in the room. "You told him what happened between me and Ricky?"

"Part of it. I just told him that something had happened, and you two broke up." Ebone´ looked away. "You're mad?"

She shook her head. "He asked me if I wanted a few days off."

"What you say?"

"I told him I didn't know. I think it's better if I work, though."

"I think so, too. The less time you're alone, the better."

"Probably."

"Wanna go out Saturday night?"

"I'm workin' Saturday night."

"After you knock off. I'll pick you up from work, and we can go to a barbecue up Horseshoe Bay."

"I'll think about it."

"No, you're going. You'll feel a lot better if you get out around people." She wanted to say that she also might find somebody new but decided against it. She needed to find herself first.

"Who's having the barbecue?"

"Smokey and his girlfriend. They got engaged last week, and they're having a little 'do'."

"I guess I'll go."

"Good. Have you had your supper?"

"Yeah, I ate at work."

Mitzi got a shower and then made a salad, just in time to watch 'Oprah'. When the first commercial came on, she called her mama to tell her the plans were made for them to go away.

"Did you talk to Macky?"

"Yes, he's just going through some changes with Tatyana." It wasn't a lie. "He also still has a problem with Daddy's death."

"He does?" Oleeta was surprised.

"He misses Daddy a lot, Mama."

"He's never said anything to me about it."

"I know. He said he didn't want to upset you, but he wishes Daddy were still here to do things with him."

"Poor baby." She paused thoughtfully. "Did he say anything about George?"

"Yeah, he likes him, but he's scared you'll be giving all your attention to George and forget about him."

"Did you tell him different?"

"Yes, Mama. I told him what he means to you. And I also told him you and George might be getting married soon."

"I wish you hadn't, Mitzi. What he say?"

"He was okay. He felt better though, when I told him you hadn't given George an answer yet because you were worried about him."

"Should I talk to him, or am I not supposed to know that you told him?"

"No, you can talk to him. Tell him I told you how he's feeling. He cried real bad, Mama girl."

"Macky cried?" Oleeta was shocked and upset.

"Yes, he was like a little boy."

"My poor baby." Her voice cracked.

"Yes, your poor baby," Mitzi teased, trying to make light of it.

"He's not here right now, but as soon as he comes home, I want to talk to him. I would have never imagined..." She trailed off.

"Anyway Mama, now you know what's happening." *At least part of it.* "Now, I'm gone."

"What you doin'?"

"I'm going to eat my supper and finish watching Oprah."

"Okay, honey, talk to you tomorrow."

"Try not to worry about Macky, Ma. He'll be okay. Tell your fiancé I said 'hi'."

Oleeta smiled. "I'll tell George you said 'hello'."

Mitzi hung up the phone and sighed. Was she doing the right thing by not telling her mama about the baby? Time would tell. She ate her salad, watched the rest of 'Oprah' and 'The Fresh Prince' and got in her bed. It felt like she'd been up for twenty-four hours.

CHAPTER SEVEN
Saturday Evening

Mitzi checked herself in the mirror. *Not bad, chicky.* She had on a long purple beach wrap with the opening up the left leg and a matching tank top. Underneath she had on her favorite purple, orange and lime green bathing suit. She also had on little orange sandals that she had bought from Calypso. She had gotten a pedicure on Friday, and her toes looked pretty, painted with bright orange polish. Not that anyone would notice her toes at night, but then one never knows. She had also gotten Samantha to put her hair in the 'Goddess' braids and was still trying to get used to them. Everybody at the salon had told her she looked like a Nubian princess, so she had taken their word. She drove down South Shore to Ebone´'s job. She was a bit early so she sat at the bar and talked to Wendell while she waited for Ebone´ to knock off. When she walked in, Ebone´ was coming from the kitchen with a tray of food, and her face was almost on the ground.

"Hi, Ebone´."

"Hi," she grunted.

"Let your smile be your umbrella," Mitzi said with an exaggerated grin. Ebone´ smiled slightly and cut her eyes. Wendell was behind the bar watching them.

"I asked her if she wanted a few days off," he quietly said to Mitzi while Ebone´ served a party of four. "She wasn't too good for business tonight." Ebone´'s hair was slapped back with gel, and she had on no makeup - not even lipstick. "I might have to insist that she take a few days," Wendell said, wiping the bar. "She's gonna make me lose customers with that attitude." As he spoke, Ebone´ was slamming dishes and ignoring customers. "I can get Sandra to do her shifts. I'll still pay her." Mitzi knew he would. He thought the world of Ebone´ and went out of his way to accommodate her. To Mitzi's knowledge, he didn't do half as much for the others as he did for Ebone´. He had actually called her and offered her the job a few years ago - he was a friend of her family. Naturally, she didn't appreciate it and never thanked him like she should. Ebone´ brought some dirty glasses to the bar. A man put a five dollar tip on her tray and thanked her as she passed. She didn't even look at him. Mitzi looked at Wendell, and he shook his head.

"Now Wendell, how late you think these people are gonna be?" she asked, referring to a couple that had just walked in. They were the last reservation for the night.

"I don't have a clue, Ebone´" Wendell said, trying not lose his patience. "Two?" she asked without having greeted them first.

"Yes, and do you have any non-smoking tables?" The man asked.

Ebone´ glared at him. "None of our tables smoke. Come this way."

Wendell practically hopped over the bar and took the menus from her. "I'll seat them."

"Good." She sat beside Mitzi at the bar and lit a cigarette.

"Is it really necessary for you to act like that, Ebone´?"

She sucked her teeth. "These people bore me. Always asking somethin' stupid."

"They're customers, Ebone´. If it weren't for them, you wouldn't have a job."

"I would find one somewhere. This is Bermuda, I'm a Bermudian." She left her cigarette burning, took the order from Wendell and took it into the kitchen.

"Do yourself a favor. Either give her a few days off or put her in the kitchen."

"I don't think she's ever been this bad," Wendell said, looking at Ebone´, who was now slamming two salad plates in front of the guests. Then she went and cleared the table of four next to it.

"Anything else?" she asked abruptly.

"Just the check, sweetheart," a man replied politely.

"I'm not your sweetheart!" she snapped and left to get the check. When she returned, the man explained that he wasn't trying to be fresh and that he used the word sweetheart often when he didn't know a person's name.

"I'm wearin' a name tag, so what's the problem?" The man apologised again, paid the bill and the party left. Ebone´ sat at the bar again. "Cheap friggers," she grumbled, lighting another cigarette.

"You actually expected a tip after the way you treated those people?" Mitzi asked. Ebone´ sucked her teeth again.

"Come on, Ebone´, I'm not going to have you treating my customers like that, okay?" Wendell was annoyed now. "And you know I don't like you lot sitting at the bar while we still have customers." If the others see you, they'll think they can do it." She looked at him and cut her eyes, ignoring what he had said, as usual.

"Ebone´, why do I pay you?" Wendell was really pissed off.

"Evidently to get rid of your small change." She took her cigarette and went into the ladies room. Forty-five minutes later the last table had finished dinner and was just sitting around drinking coffee and talking. After a few minutes, Ebone´ stormed over to the table and asked them if they wanted breakfast menus. Once again Wendell bolted to the table and with a big grin on his face explained to them that Ebone´ was a big joker. They were not amused. Wendell grabbed her by the shoulders, steered her toward Mitzi and said, "Leave! Now! And don't come back until next Friday!" His patience had run out. Mitzi waited while Ebone´ went to shower and change in the staff room, and Wendell dealt with the guests who were now ready to leave.

By the time they got to the beach party, it was eleven thirty, and there was a nice crowd on the beach. The area was decorated beautifully with bunches of gold balloons tied together, trailing from potted palm trees. There were also half a dozen giant candles lit, creating just enough light to see where they were going. There were two long, decorated tables lined with food, a bar and two big gas barbecues burning. They could hear people nearby in the water, and a female was desperately trying to get away from two guys who were in the process of carrying her to the ocean, fully clothed. By the time they reached the water's edge, she was laughing because there was nothing else she could do. The water looked like a huge mirror under the full moon. There was a slight breeze every so often, but it was extremely warm for the end of April.

"What everybody starin' at?" Ebone´ asked. Mitzi hadn't noticed anyone staring at them.

"Just ignore them, and have a good time."

"Hey Mitzi, hey Ebone´." It was Crystal. She, Raoul, Melba and Roger were sitting on a big bedspread. Ebone´ sighed as she followed Mitzi in their direction. Mitzi plopped down beside Raoul who leaned over and kissed her on the cheek. Crystal jokingly cleared her throat. Raoul laughed and kissed her, too.

"Oh please," Mitzi said, hitting Crystal with a towel. She looked back for Ebone´ who had stopped to talk to a guy. He was pointing to the left of them, apparently showing her someone. Ebone´ was nodding and lighting a cigarette. The guy left, and Ebone´ joined Mitzi and the others. She actually smiled when she spoke to them. *What had that guy said to her?* Mitzi wondered. Her whole attitude had suddenly changed.

"You girls want somethin' to drink?" Raoul asked.

"What do they have?" Mitzi asked.

"Everything," Crystal answered.

"Beer, Breezers, swizzle." Raoul stood up.

"Get me a Beck's," Ebone´ said.

"Can I have some swizzle, please?" Mitzi asked, looking at Ebone´ as she did. Ebone´ shrugged her shoulders. Raoul left.

"Hi, Melba girl," Mitzi said.

"Hey, girl."

"What's happenin', Roger?"

"Nothin' much."

"Doghouse," Crystal whispered, acting like she was getting something from her bag.

"Duh," Mitzi said.

Raoul came back with drinks for Mitzi, Ebone´, Crystal and himself. He had chosen to ignore Melba and Roger. Ebone´ said, "I'm comin' right back," took the drink from Raoul, got up and walked in the direction the guy had been pointing to earlier.

"I'm glad I got her to come out," Mitzi said to Crystal, taking off her sandals.

"She's still going through changes?"

"Yeah, it's a long story."

"I'm sure it is, knowing her."

"How are my babies?" Mitzi asked, referring to her god-children.

"Rude as hell," Crystal said.

"No, they're not," Raoul said. "Crystal just can't handle them."

"I cut R.J.'s little tail this morning." She looked at her husband. "He's getting rude, okay, Raoul?"

"I ain't said nothin'." He stuck his tongue out at her when she turned her head away. Mitzi laughed.

"What he do?" Crystal asked, turning to look at him.

"Nuffin'." Mitzi said, smiling. She loved Crystal and Raoul together.

"Wanna dance, Melba?" Raoul asked. Roger looked at her.

"No thanks."

"How about you, Mitzi?"

"Sure, honey."

"Are my legs broken or something?" Crystal asked.

"I have much bigger plans for you later, baby." Raoul winked at Crystal as he led Mitzi over to the make-shift dance floor. Crystal lay on her side and leaned back on her elbow with her hand behind her head. She was beginning to feel uncomfortable with Roger and Melba. It was obvious they weren't speaking. Hell, she wasn't going to let them spoil her night.

"You guys having a good time?" she asked, knowing damn well they were not.

"Yeah," Melba mumbled. Roger didn't answer. *Fool*, Crystal thought.

"It's such a pretty night," Crystal continued. "Perfect for lovers, hey?" She looked at the two of them. Melba glared at her. Roger got up.

"Comin' back," he mumbled and walked toward the cove.

"Where he going?" Crystal asked Melba.

She sucked her teeth. "Probably to smoke a joint."

Crystal sat up, eyes wide. "He still smokes weed?" she whispered loudly.

"Um."

"How old is he?"

"Forty-one."

"Get the hell outta here! Isn't he a bit old to be sneaking around smoking joints in the bushes?"

"It pisses me off."

"Why, for Christ's sake, Melba, do you put up with it? And incidentally, what's you two's problem tonight anyway?"

"We had an argument when we first got here."

"That's all you lot do - get dressed up to argue. You might as well stay the devil home."

Melba was drawing in the sand with a stick. "When we left home, he was fine. Soon as we got here, he started grumbling. He's so damn moody."

"It's that stuff he's smoking. People talking 'bout herb or whatever they call it these days, don't have side effects - it damn well does. These lot smoke that stuff - more moody than a woman. Bladdy fools."

Melba looked around. "Don't let him come back and hear you."

"Melba, I'm not scared of Roger."

"I'm not scared of him either, but if I don't start none, there won't be none."

"That's really how you wanna live, girl? Scared to say what you wanna say, 'cause he might make off? He would, huh?"

Melba started to say something, but Mitzi and Raoul came back, laughing.

"Crystal, this boy is not well," Mitzi said, sitting down beside Melba.

"I know, I tried to have him committed, but nobody was qualified to deal with him."

Raoul sat beside Crystal and stared at her, then started smiling. "You're just jealous 'cause I didn't ask you to dance." He put his arms around her shoulder.

"Oh Raoul, please." Crystal laughed.

"Come on, baby, let's go throw stones at the moon." He pulled her to her feet.

"We'll be back, you lot." Crystal took her sneakers off.

"You know you're going somewhere to do the nasty, Raoul," Mitzi was laughing. "They call it throwing stones at the moon now?" Raoul winked at her as he and Crystal walked away.

"You must be fullish," Crystal said. "No crabs are gonna be crawling up my..." Raoul put his hand over her mouth and pushed her ahead of him.

"Those two have a good time wherever they go," Mitzi said to Melba, sipping the rum swizzle she had left behind.

"Lucky them," Melba said.

Mitzi looked at her. "Melba, you don't need to be going through what it is you're going through, right?"

"Yeah, right. I already heard it from Crystal."

So I guess I should shut up. "Well, I guess you don't need to hear anything I have to say."

"Bingo."

Silly girl. "I wonder where Ebone´ went," Mitzi said, more to herself than to Melba.

"I was shocked to see her out. She looks so miserable."

"And you're the picture of happiness," Mitzi said, staring her in the face. In the glow from both the moon and the candles, Melba's eyes looked sad, and Mitzi knew they depicted what she actually was. She was an extremely unhappy woman. At that moment, Roger returned and sat beside Melba.

"You all right?" he asked. He looked a little less disagreeable than he had earlier, and Mitzi noticed his eyes looked a little red. She wished Crystal would come back so she wouldn't have to be alone with the two of them.

"Mitzi!" Sundae was running toward them. *Thank God,* she was saved.

"Hey, chicky, where you been?" It was after one in the morning.

"To a wake. It was jammin'!"

"Who died now?" Melba asked.

"Good mornin' to you, too, Melba. Hey, Roger."

"Hi, Sundae," Roger said. Melba still didn't speak to her.

"Who died, Sundae?" Mitzi asked her.

Sundae sighed. "You don't know her."

"And you probably don't either." Mitzi laughed and looked at Melba who actually smiled. Roger was sitting with his eyes closed.

"Feelin' nice, Roger?" Sundae asked sarcastically. Roger smiled with his eyes closed. Melba cut her eyes at Sundae who ignored her. "Where's Crystal?" Sundae asked.

"She and her husband have gone to throw rocks at the moon or some nonsense," Melba said, looking at Roger who still had his eyes closed.

"Leave it to them," Sundae said, spreading her towel, then sitting on it.

"How long you been here?" Sundae asked Mitzi.

"About two hours, I guess. I waited for Ebone´ to knock off."

Sundae looked around. "Where's she?"

"I don't know. She went off somewhere a little while after we..." Sundae knocked her arm.

"Look! Look!"

"What?"

"Check your boy Darren with Cindy." Darren was walking past them, holding hands with a white girl.

"Who's Cindy?" Mitzi was hardly interested and was finishing her drink.

"Cindy - you know her. Where the hell he going with her? I didn't know he had jungle fever." Mitzi was waving to one of her clients. Sundae sucked her teeth. "Mitzi! You're not even listenin' to me, girl."

"Sundae, you worry about Darren - 'cause I'm not. Hey Bev, how you doin', girl?" Bev waved back. They heard Crystal's laugh and turned to see her on Raoul's back as he struggled to walk in the sand. He dropped her on the spread.

"Where you been, Sundae? Funeral?" Crystal asked. Sundae acted like she didn't hear her and spoke to Raoul. Mitzi looked at Crystal and nodded her head. Crystal shook her head and laughed. "Oh, we saw Ebone´," Crystal said.

"Where?"

"Down that way." She pointed in the direction she and Raoul had just come from. "Talking to Ricky Trott."

Mitzi's face fell. "She was?"

"Yeah." She acted like she didn't see us." She was wiping sand from her feet.

"I'm sure she did." Mitzi was annoyed. *Why didn't she just stay away from the boy?*

"Let's go for a walk, Mitzi," Sundae said. "I might be able to find something to take home tonight." She stood.

"Yeah, right. Let's go." Mitzi put her towel around her neck and got up.

"Your hair really does look nice like that, Mitzi," Sundae said.

"Oh, yeah," Melba said. "It looks nice." She hadn't mentioned it all night, but now that Sundae had, she thought she had to. She was so strange sometimes.

Mitzi and Sundae walked along the beach, stopping to talk to friends along the way. The beach was crowded. Smokey and Paula were either real popular or the word just got around. Robyn Baxter invited the two of them to a breakfast at her house after the beach party. She had told everybody to come about four o'clock. Then they ran into Ebone´ or rather, she spotted them first and ran over to them. She had obviously been talking to someone whom she didn't want them to see, so she came to them and attempted to block their view. It didn't work. Mitzi could pick out Ricky's big head with blindfolds on. And his silly gold teeth were shining in the moonlight.

"Hey you two. Where you off to?" Ebone´ asked nervously.

"Just walking. Checking the sights," Mitzi said. *I'll play the game.*

"You're not leaving yet, are you?" Ebone´ turned her whole body so Mitzi and Sundae would look the other way.

Mitzi looked at her watch. "Not yet, but we're going to a breakfast at Robyn's house around four."

"The breakfast starts at four?"

"Yeah, give everybody chance to leave the beach. Wanna go?"

"Nah. I don't feel like it. I'll get a lift home."

I'm sure you will. "Okay, I'll check you later."

"See you, Ebone´," Sundae said as she and Mitzi headed back toward Crystal and Melba.

"She seemed happy for a change," Sundae said, looking back at Ebone´.

"Mmn." Mitzi was looking out at the ocean. How could Ebone´ be so stupid? Things like this really pissed her off. This was exactly why she didn't want to help the silly girl.

"Mitzi, I'm not really going to the breakfast, you know. I just told Robyn that we would come."

"How come you're not going?" It really didn't matter to Mitzi. She suddenly didn't feel like going.

" 'Cause, her house is filthy, and I ain't eating out of nobody's dirty house."

"Robyn dresses like a million dollars, don't wear nothin' twice, drives a nice, clean car and her house is dirty?" Mitzi was surprised.

"Yep. Always looks immacurate, makes sure she gets her hair and nails done every week, but would she clean her house? No."

"Well, that ain't playin'. I'm not going either. And the word is immaculate."

"You're not going where?" Crystal asked. They had reached their spot and sat with the others. Roger wasn't there, and Raoul was asleep with his arm draped over Crystal's leg.

"To Robyn's house for breakfast," Sundae said.

"Oh no, do not eat in that pig sty," Crystal said, messing up her face.

"How come everybody knows about this except me?" Mitzi asked.

"I didn't know either," Melba said solemnly. She was more miserable because Roger had disappeared again.

"You lot need to get your news," Sundae said matter-of-factly.

"Of course we do, Sundae," Melba said sarcastically, cutting her eyes.

"Hey girl, just 'cause you're having man troub..." Mitzi put her hand over Sundae's mouth as Melba glared at her and lit a cigarette.

"What time is it, you lot?" Crystal asked, yawning.

"It's ten after three," Mitzi answered, yawning too. "I'm goin' home."

"Let's go somewhere else, you guys," Sundae said.

"Sundae, I am going home. There's nowhere else to go, girl."

"Go down Robyn's to the breakfast, Sundae," Crystal said, packing up.

"She'd be lucky."

"Come on, Raoul." Crystal was trying to wake up her husband. He didn't move.

"Where're the children, Crystal?" Mitzi asked.

"Down his mama's house." Crystal nodded her head in Raoul's direction and rolled her eyes. She couldn't stand her mother-in-law. Mrs. Outerbridge thought she should tell Crystal and Raoul how they should run their lives. Everything from what type of house they should buy, to what Crystal should cook for Raoul, to how they should raise their children.

She hated it when Crystal spanked her children. "If we let her, she would tell us how often we should be having sex or in what positions we should be doing it," Crystal once told Mitzi when she was really mad with Mrs. Outerbridge. But Crystal wasn't the only one. Raoul had three brothers who were all married, and Mrs. Outerbridge treated all the wives the same way she treated Crystal. From time to time, the four Mrs. Outerbridge's got together to vent their 'mother-in-law from hell' frustrations. Raoul also had a sister who was their mother's clone, that's why no man had ever married her. She and Crystal spoke to each other, and that was the extent of their relationship. Fortunately, Raoul and two of his brothers didn't side with their mother like Dennis, the youngest, did. Dennis and his wife had major arguments because of his mother. Raoul and the others knew what she was about. She had to be in control, that's why Pa Outerbridge had left her after twenty-eight years of marriage.

"You have to pick them up before you go home?"

"Hell no. You think I feel like hearing her tell me that I shouldn't be keeping Raoul out this late?" She stood up.

"Crystal, don't talk about your favourite mother-in-law like that," Raoul said, sitting up and stretching.

"I thought you were sleep!" Raoul had caught Crystal off guard, but she knew he didn't care when she said things like that. They were true. And there was really no love lost between Raoul and his mother.

"I hear everything. Even in my sleep - remember that." He stood up and playfully hit her on the behind.

"You lot ready?" Crystal asked.

"Yeah, let's go." Mitzi was getting tired.

"Hey, what about Roger, Melba?" Crystal asked.

"Look, I'm ready to go, I'm going. He'll have to get home the best way he can."

"That a girl," Sundae said, sticking her tongue out behind Melba's head.

They all stopped at Crystal's car in the parking lot. "What you doing tomorrow - or later today, Mitzi?" Crystal asked.

"Oh Lord." Mitzi put her hand over her mouth. "I just remembered, I promised my Aunt Belinda I would go church with her today. I'm never gonna be able to get up."

"Well, call her up and tell her you can't make it," Sundae said, searching her bag for her keys.

"No, I don't like doing that. Let me go home, I must be out of my mind. See you lot later."

Melba got in her car, slammed the door and drove off. "When she gonna get a life?" Crystal asked as Raoul got in the passenger side of their Sentra and laid the seat back.

"Look at him. Half hot, that's his problem. Hey, who told you I feel like driving?"

"Shut up, woman, and let's go. See you girls later."

"Had a good time, Raoul," Mitzi said, laughing.

"Yeah, yeah. Come on Crys."

Mitzi laughed again, and Crystal shook her head. "Raoul don't wear me out. Check you girls later."

"Hey Mitzi, call Melba in the morning and find out what happened. Then call me." Sundae was excited to think she might be getting some gossip.

"No, pokey - you call her. Bye."

On the way home, Mitzi was annoyed to think that Ebone´ had even spoken to Ricky, let alone spent the evening on the beach with him. She was sure she would be spending the night with him, too. As she drove into her yard, she noticed a strange car parked outside her gate. The driver could have been at Mrs. Seymour's house. She locked her car and looked around out of habit. Even though the yard was well lit, she still liked to check. As she began walking up to the house, she heard shouting, but she wasn't sure where it was coming from. As she got closer to her door, she realized the shouting was coming from inside her house, and it was Ebone´'s voice. Mitzi stopped and listened for a minute then tried the door. It wasn't locked, so she eased it open and quietly slipped into the hallway. She smelled marijuana, cigarette smoke and incense. She heard 'Reasons' from her Earth Wind and Fire CD.

Thought she couldn't stand my old music. Only the lamp was on low.

"Ricky, I said no, and I mean it!" Ebone´ was shouting again. Mitzi couldn't see what was happening, so she sat on the floor against the opposite wall in the hallway where she could.

Ricky was standing over Ebone´ who was on the couch. "Why you playing me like this, Ebone´? It ain't like we haven't done it before."

"Look, I don't want to do it, okay?" She tried to get up but couldn't get past him.

"Oh, you could sit on the beach and talk to me all night, make me bring you home, and now you're treating me like dirt? Come on, Ebone´." He tried to kiss her, but she turned away.

"Ricky, I just wanted to find out what happened between us, that's all." She was struggling to get up from the couch. Mitzi was disgusted.

"And I told you, I made a big mistake breaking up with you. I want you back. Come on, baby, you know you want me..." He tried to take her top off.

"Stop it, Ricky!" Ebone´ was fighting now.

"Look bitch...!" He pulled his arm back to slap her. Mitzi couldn't take anymore - not in her house. She turned on the light. Ricky spun around.

"Get out of my house, Ricky." She was too tired and fed up to even raise her voice as she leaned against the wall. The sudden light and the sound of her voice shocked both of them. Ricky stood up, and Ebone´ started crying.

"This is Ebone´'s house, too."

"No, Ricky, it's Ebone´'s home, but it's my house. And furthermore, I do believe she wants you to leave, too." She was still calm, but furious.

Ricky looked at Ebone´. She looked away. "I thought you said she wouldn't be home 'til mornin'."

"Well, it's mornin', Jack, and I'm home. But does that really matter, Ricky? When you gonna leave Ebone´ alone? You treat her like dirt, you hit her, you lie to her..."

"All that was in the past, sister. Can't a man change?" He slapped his chest. "I'm a changed man!"

"Yeah, right." Mitzi put her hands on her hips and looked at him.

"What? You don't believe me?" He shook his head. "Why can't you women let sleeping dogs lie?"

"Why can't you dogs stop lying?!" Mitzi shouted in his face. "You were gonna hit her before I turned on the light."

"No I..."

"You're a punk, boy! You ain't nothin' unless you're beatin' and lyin' to a woman. You have taken this girl to the brink of destruction!" She held her arm out in Ebone´'s direction. "Look at her! She's a bloody mess! Leave her the hell alone! Why don't you just go somewhere and overdose on that cocaine you love so much?"

He looked at Ebone´ like he wanted to kill her. "Hey, I don't appreciate no bi..."

"Just get the hell out, boy!" Mitzi was shouting now.

"Boy? Boy? How big do men grow in your country, girl?!" Mitzi moved closer to him. "Let me tell you something...!"

"Bitch, fuck you!"

"You can't. I've heard you don't have adequate equipment." She was calm again.

Ricky looked at Ebone´ accusingly. *Just gave yourself away.* He came toward Mitzi. She raised her eyebrows. "You planning on hitting me, Ricky? 'Cause you put a hand on me, and you'll draw back a damn stump! I don't fear you, got it? Now get out, or I'll put your ass out!"

Ricky walked up to her, looked her in the eye for a second and walked toward the door. "Bitch!"

"Yeah, yeah, I know the story. Go away, little boy, and don't forget to slam the door." He walked out and left the door open. Mitzi closed her eyes, let out a deep breath, closed the door and leaned on it.

"Mitzi..."

She held up her hand. "I don't even want to hear it. It's late, I'm tired and I have to get up early to go to church."

Ebone´ looked at her watch. "You're going to church?"

Mitzi stared at her. "Somebody around here needs to go." She walked past her, got a glass of water and went to her room. She got in her bed - fully clothed -and fell asleep in the middle of saying her prayers.

CHAPTER EIGHT
Sunday Morning

Mitzi hated being late, especially for church. She had woken up at nine but dozed back off and jumped up at nine thirty. Her aunt was picking her up at ten fifteen. They were going down to North Shore to The First Church of God. Mitzi grabbed her black dress which didn't need ironing, threw it on her bed and ran into the bathroom to get a shower. She turned the water as hot as she could stand it - she usually preferred her water lukewarm - but she thought if she had it a little hotter, she might feel better. This would have to be a quick one. No second soaping and no shower gel. "Oh man, I don't think I have any stockings that aren't stranded," she said aloud. She talked to herself often in the shower. She could have gone without stockings because the weather was nice and warm, but her feet were still a bit pale to go without stockings during the day. Maybe this afternoon she would sit outside for an hour or so, read a book and brown up her legs, feet and arms. She got out of the shower, wrapped a big towel around her and ran out to answer her phone. It was Sundae, asking her if she had called Melba to find out what had happened to Roger.

"Sundae, I told you I'm not calling her, and I don't have time for you right now. I'm gonna be late for church." She was trying to dry herself while she held the phone between her ear and shoulder. "Now bye. I'll call you later." *Why is she up so early, other than to get a scoop?* She put on her underwear and went to the kitchen to put the kettle on for tea. She looked in the living room, and Ebone' was sitting on the couch in a shabby tee shirt. She was holding a pillow in her lap. "Mornin'," Mitzi said and walked to the stove.

"Mornin', Mitzi."

"You sleep there?"

"No, I just came out here."

"What you doing up so early?"

"My mama called me and woke me up a few minutes ago."

Mitzi turned around and looked at her. "Your mama? What she want this early?"

"She wants me to come over to her house today. Said she needs to talk to me about something important."

"You goin'?" Mitzi was putting bread in the toaster.

"I don't know. I guess so. Sounded like it was real important, and she didn't sound too good either."

Mitzi turned and leaned over the counter. "Just go and find out what she wants. It won't hurt." She was still pissed off with her.

"How you goin' church?"

"My auntie's picking me up."

"Can I use your car? Please?"

She said 'please', she knows I'm pissed with her. "Yeah, but come back as soon as you leave your mama's house 'cause I'm going to need my car later."

"I won't be long."

Mitzi took her tea and toast into her bedroom to finish getting ready. It was ten o'clock. All she needed to do was put on her makeup and her dress. Thank God for her braids. She wondered what Mrs. Simons wanted to talk to Ebone´ about. She probably just wanted to make peace and put whatever it was they had to behind them. Mitzi made her face up lightly - she didn't think it was right to wear a lot of makeup to church. Then she sprayed some 'Narcisse' on her neck and between her breasts - not that anyone would be going there anytime soon - and rubbed some lotion on her hands. She finished her tea, put on her shoes, grabbed her earrings and her bag and went back to the kitchen. Aunt Belinda was outside, blowing her horn. She put her cup in the sink and took her extra keys out of her shoulder bag. "Here're the keys. Not all day, Ebone´. See you later."

"Thanks. Mitzi?" Mitzi turned around. "Would you pray for me?"

Mitzi stared at her for a second. "I don't have all day, Ebone´." She walked out the door.

Mitzi could never understand why, but every time she went to church, she had the urge to cry. She didn't remember when it started, but she always wanted to weep as soon as the music started playing. As soon as she sat down, she bowed her head and said a long prayer, asking God for forgiveness for a lot of things and for help with even more. Now, they were singing, 'I Surrender All', and her eyes had welled up. She looked at her Aunt Belinda who was crying. Maybe it was a family thing. She suddenly thought of Macky and his situation, and the tears started to roll. She dug into her bag, got out a Kleenex and wiped her eyes and nose. Belinda reached over and touched her hand.

"Did you enjoy the service?" Belinda asked her. They were driving along Blackwatch Pass.

"Yeah, it was a bit long, but I enjoyed it. I always enjoy his preaching. And that choir is really good."

"What were you cryin' for?"

She shrugged her shoulders. "Just reflecting."

"I know what you mean."

"Tell me something, why is it that no matter where I go to church, all the women who are dressed to kill - gloves, hat and handbag - always walk in late and have to walk right up front and sit down?"

Belinda laughed. "You noticed it, too, huh?"

"Can't help but notice it. And it's always the same women. Is that all they come to church for?"

"Afraid so. Those are the posers."

"And then they're the first ones to stand up and start clapping. I mean, I don't have anything against anyone getting a little Holy Spirit and being moved to their feet or nothing, but I think it's phony when those people get up."

"It's sad really. But you see, they aren't fooling anyone but themselves. The Lord sees them."

"Indeed He does. Even I know that. One sister I saw today - one of the first on her feet, saw her last night at a beach party with a drink in her hand, talking to somebody's husband. Now, she could have been drinking a soda, discussing the 'Word' with him, but I don't know. And I'm not sure, but I think I saw them leave together, too." She looked at her aunt and smiled.

Belinda smiled back. "I know exactly what you're talking about. And I don't have the right to judge anyone, but people like her are going to hell with gasoline underwear on."

Mitzi clapped her hands and laughed. "That's a good one. There're quite a few going down that way. Could we stop at People's Pharmacy please? I need to get some Tampax."

"Sure. I need the weekend papers anyway."

When Belinda dropped Mitzi off half an hour later, she was surprised to see that Ebone´ was back with her car. Or had she even gone to her mother's house? Thanks, Auntie girl. We must do this again sometime."

"We could go again next Sunday."

"Now, don't overdo it. Anyway, me and Mama are going away this Thursday - we don't come back 'til Sunday afternoon."

"Oh, that's right, I forgot. Hope you girls have a good time."

"We will. Next time, you'll have to go with us."

"I'd love that. Too bad we didn't think about it before, I could have gone with you this week."

"There'll definitely be other trips. Check you later." She probably should have invited her in the house, but she wanted to talk to Ebone´ and find out what, if anything, happened. She realized that Ebone´ had been somewhere in her car because the seat was pushed back and, of course, she couldn't put it back the way she found it. The house was quiet. Was she home? "Ebone´?" The house stank of cigarette smoke, and the blinds were still closed, something else that was too much to ask of Ebone´. She rested her bag on the couch and opened the curtain at the picture window and the blinds at the other two. She left the windows wide open and closed the screens. Ebone´ must have gone out again. Mitzi went into the kitchen to get something to drink and noticed the trash can full of empty beer bottles. She could see at least four. It was impossible that Ebone´ had drunk all that beer this early in the day. And on a Sunday? She wouldn't put it past her, though. She always said it was twelve o'clock somewhere in the world when she drank early in the morning. Mitzi grabbed her bag and walked toward her room to change her clothes. She instinctively looked in Ebone´'s room, not expecting to find her there, but she was. She was lying face down in her bed. Was she crying? *Not again.* "Ebone´?"

"Yeah?"

"What's going on?"

"A lot."

"Ricky?"

"Who?"

Good. "I'm coming right back." She went to her room to change her clothes. She put on a tee shirt and some knee length leggings in preparation for her sit-out in the yard. She went back to Ebone´'s room and sat on her bed. She was sitting up, holding her pillow. Her eyes were glassy and red. "Are you drunk?"

Ebone´ shrugged her shoulders. "I hope so."

"Did you go to see your mama?"

"I sure did." She put her hands over her face. When she moved them, Mitzi could see she was crying. "My whole world is fallin' apart." She looked at Mitzi. "You'll never guess what she wanted to tell me." Mitzi said nothing - she couldn't guess. Ebone´ drew her knees up, hugged them and sighed. "She's dying, Mitzi." It took a few seconds for what she said to register with Mitzi.

"What?"

"She's dying. She's got ovarian cancer - had it for about a year, and now it's as bad as it's gonna get." She sighed again. "They've only given her a few more months."

"Oh God, Ebone´, I'm sorry." Mitzi was stunned. She thought of all the times she had told her to make peace with her mother. She could never say it now, though. One never knew.

She really didn't know what to say to her now. "How did it go, you know, with you two?"

Ebone´ sucked her teeth and ran her fingers through her hair. "Oh girl, it was a trip. I don't even know where to begin."

"You did put the past behind you, didn't you? I mean surely..."

"I had no choice but to put it behind me. It wasn't the past I thought it was."

"What you talkin' 'bout girl?"

"Mitzi, my mama told me some things that still haven't sunk in."

"You want some tea?" Ebone´ was clearly devastated. And a little drunk.

"No, I want a beer."

"Come on, you should have some tea so you can have a clear head to deal with what you have to deal with."

"I don't want no tea. Girl, I feel so messed up. Where do I start? Okay. You obviously know that my mama hasn't been my favorite person for years. But you never knew why."

"No, I didn't. I know I could never understand what could be so bad."

"Well, what you also don't know is, when I was seventeen, shortly after we finished school, I got pregnant."

"No, I never knew that."

"I know. Hardly anybody knew - just my sisters and my mama really. Well, a few days after I told my mama that I was pregnant, we had a big argument - I can't even remember what it was about - but my mama pushed me down the steps. The next day I was in the hospital havin' a miscarriage. I had started bleeding the night before, but I was too scared to go to the hospital or tell anybody. Finally, I was bleeding so much, my sisters took me to the hospital."

Mitzi sat silent. *Poor sight.*

"Before the day was out, I had lost the baby, and they had to give me a hysterectomy because there was so much damage done." She closed her eyes.

Mitzi's eyes widened. "You had a hysterectomy at seventeen?" Ebone´ nodded. "Man, I can kind of understand your having some animosity toward your mama. Why did she have to push you down the steps, knowing you were pregnant? That seems so cruel."

"That's what I could never understand. As you know, I went to live with my granny for a while, and when I went eighteen, I got my own apartment."

"I never did know the reason for your going to live with your granny."

"Well, that's why. Anyhow, shortly after that, my daddy died, and I was told that he had committed suicide. They found him in his bed - with a gun - with a shot to his head. There was a note beside him saying that he couldn't take the pressure of life anymore."

"I remember that."

"I always blamed my mama for being such a bitch to him because all she ever did was argue with him." She sighed. "Little did I know that she really was to blame."

"How?" Mitzi was confused.

Ebone´ closed her eyes. "She killed him, Mitzi. My mama shot my daddy, and nobody ever knew it." Mitzi was speechless, and her mouth hung open. "She told me today that she held the gun to his groin and told him if he didn't write the note, she would shoot his di... penis off and leave him bleeding all night and tell people that he was raping his daughters, and that's why she shot him there. So he wrote the note, and then she shot him in the head. She obviously was a pro, 'cause nobody ever found out she did it. As far as everybody was, and still is concerned, he took his own life."

"Damn." Mitzi had never heard such in her life.

"So, all these years I have hated my mama for killing my baby and for making my daddy kill himself."

"I'm confused. Why did she kill your daddy?"

" 'Cause he was rapin' his daughters. He molested all four of us."

"What the hell...? You, too?" Ebone´ nodded. "Well what, you don't remember him doing that?"

"Yeah, but I loved my daddy, and it was all I ever knew. It went on from the time I can remember until I was about sixteen. But he was never mean to me or made me feel afraid. I thought it was what I had to do to make him happy because he always bought us girls nice things. And my mama was always grumbling about something he did or didn't do."

"Jesus, Ebone´. You know now that it wasn't right, don't you?"

"Of course. You know, all these years, I've just put it out of my mind - I've been too busy being pissed off at my mama to even remember that it happened. I guess, in a way, I finally realized that it was wrong, but I didn't want to have any bad thoughts about my daddy, so I blocked it out. But, as the years have gone by, I've felt more and more resentment toward him - even though he's dead. The more I've seen it on talk shows, the more I realized what a bad bastard he was for doing that to us. Just because I wasn't afraid of him, doesn't mean it wasn't wrong." She looked at Mitzi. "How can a man do something like that to his own child?"

Mitzi just shook her head in answer. She didn't have the answer. "Did your mama tell you why she pushed you down the steps?"

"Yes. Because she thought my daddy had gotten me pregnant and that was her way of lashing out - more at him than at me. But I told her today that it wasn't my daddy's baby. He had stopped messing with me then - I guess it was Dee Dee's turn. Dee Dee was her youngest sister. "The baby belonged to a boy I really liked." She thought for a minute. "You remember Maceo?" She looked at Mitzi.

"You were pregnant for Maceo? I never knew that."

"Well, I guess it was all for the best anyway. Maceo wanted me to get an abortion from the day I told him I was pregnant. He never wanted the baby. But I always have been bitter about the fact that I could never have children after that.

"You had every right to be. Ebone´, I'm really sorry." Mitzi rubbed her hand.

"But you haven't heard the ultimate yet."

"Oh, I have heard the ultimate - it can't get any worse, Ebone´, surely."

"It does. Well, I don't know if it's worse, but it's deep." She sucked her teeth, stood up and walked to her dresser. "My mama told me today that Eric Simons," she paused, "wasn't my real daddy."

Mitzi's mouth hung open once again. "What? Get out of here, girl. What in the world is going on in your family?"

"She and my daddy... Eric, broke up for a short while years ago, and she had an affair for a few months. Then she and my daddy got back together, and a few weeks later she found out she was pregnant - with me. They all knew it was the other man's baby, but my daddy said that he wanted her back and that he would raise the child as his own. They had already had my two older sisters, and eleven months after I was born they had Dee Dee. So we all came up thinking we all had the same daddy." She turned and looked at Mitzi. "Wendell is my daddy."

"Wendell, your boss?" Mitzi asked in disbelief.

Ebone´ nodded her head. "We were always told that he was a family friend and come to find out, Eric threatened to do something to him if he ever told anybody the truth."

"Ebone´ girl, this is unbelievable. I don't even have the mental capacity for it all to sink in."

"Well, how you think I feel? It's my life and after all these years, I'm finding out all this stuff in one day."

"I'm glad your mama got to tell you the truth. Before anything happened to her." Mitzi wasn't sure if she should have said that last part.

"I wish she had told me all this a long time ago so we could have gotten on with our lives. But I guess that's something she wanted to deal with herself. She said now she wishes she had told me before. I guess she only told me now because she didn't wanna take it to her grave. 'Cause that's where she'll be soon." She sat on her bed and started to cry. Mitzi sat beside her and hugged her. Ebone''s shoulders shook as she sobbed. "She's dying, Mitzi, and I've acted so frigged up to her all these years!"

"Ebone´, after what happened, or what you thought happened, you were kind of justified in feeling and acting the way you did. I'm just sorry she waited this long to tell you. Now all you can do is spend as much time with her as you can. Go and stay with her at night."

"I don't even know what to say to her!" She wept.

"Trust me, you'll find the words. You all have a lot to talk about. She knows you've been consumed with hatred. Let her know you've forgiven her and that you love her."

"I don't even know how to say that."

"Just say it, every day. It's important that you say everything you want to say to her. It'll be too late when she's gone. Saying, 'I love you', never hurt anybody. What your sisters saying about all this?"

"She told them about the cancer last month, but nobody told me. She told them not to."

"Do they all know that she told you everything?"

"Yeah, they were there. She told us all together. And you know what? Not one of them felt any way about the fact that she killed our... their daddy."

"They were probably relieved, in a way. Especially since he was interfering with all of you."

"I guess they didn't feel the same way about him - and what he was doing - as I did."

"Didn't you girls ever talk about it?"

"No way. We all knew it was going on, but it was never talked about. So I guess we did know that it was wrong, but like I said, that was all we knew."

"If your mama knew what he was doing, why didn't she put him out or leave him?" It always made Mitzi mad when a mother allowed her man to molest her children. As far as she was concerned, silence was consent.

Ebone´ shrugged her shoulders. "She loved him - I guess - and didn't want to be without a man in the house or in her life."

Fruit doesn't fall too far from the tree. If that were the case, then Ebone´ came by her man 'dependency' honestly. She needed a lot of therapy and perhaps psychiatric help. This was a hell of a lot to deal with: the way her step-father died, finding out her true paternity, her mother's illness and impending death. She also needed to deal with the fact that she had been molested as a child, even though she thinks it hasn't been a problem all this time. Mitzi would help her get all the help she needed later. Right now she just thought it best that Ebone´ spend as much time with her mama as possible - saying all the things that needed to be said. Mitzi stood and hugged Ebone´ who was no longer crying but looked absolutely drained and years older.

"I'm here, you know that, right?"

She forced a little smile. "Aren't you always?"

Mitzi smiled. "What you doin' today?"

"I'm goin' back over to my mama's. I came home to bring your car back and 'cause I needed to be by myself for a little while. My sisters are cooking, and we're all going to have dinner with my mama today." Ebone´ had a half-way decent relationship with her sisters, although they hardly did anything together, mostly because of the way Ebone´ had treated their mother. They all understood why she felt the way she did about her, but they didn't really appreciate her behaviour. They were the ones who had persuaded Madge to tell Ebone´ everything. Her sister Cee Cee still lived at home and was the closest to their mother. She was devastated, as they all were, by everything that was happening.

"You gonna stay over there tonight?"

She looked at Mitzi doubtfully. "I don't know, should I?"

"I think you should. You don't know how much time is left."

Ebone´ sighed. "Lemme pack some clothes. Would you take me back over there?"

"Of course I would. You going to take your work clothes...
Oh my God! What you gonna tell Wendell? You gonna tell
him that you know?"

"I've been thinking about that ever since. I don't know what
to do. What you think?"

"Tell him that you know, Ebone´. You've lost years with
your mama and in essence, you've lost years with your real
father, too, because although he's known all this time, you
haven't, and the relationship with Wendell hasn't been a father-
daughter relationship."

"When should I tell him?"

"As soon as possible. Don't waste time." Mitzi thought for
a minute. "Now I understand why Wendell's let you get away
with murder all these years. You've been daddy's spoiled little
girl!" Mitzi laughed, and Ebone´ cut her eyes and smiled.

"I wonder if he's ever wanted to say anything to me... Oh
hell! Guess what?!" She sat on her bed and put her hand over
her mouth. "This is crazy - it gets worse!"

"What?"

She grabbed Mitzi's arm. "You know my sister Sherry is
married to Wendell's son, Robert. My sister... is married to my
brother! I didn't even think of that all this time."

Mitzi's eyes widened. "How could you *not* think about it?"

"Well, you know Wendell and Robert don't really set, he
don't come around the restaurant or nothing, so I just never
think of the two of them as being related. Did that make
sense?"

"Yeah, I guess so. This is too wild. By the way, how come
Robert and Wendell don't get along?"

"I was told a long time ago that Wendell messed around on
Robert's mama years ago, and it really destroyed her and
Robert. She almost went off her head - they were gonna put
her in St. Brendan's... Oh shit! He must have been messing
with my mama! He told me that he and his wife broke up
about thirty years ago."

Mitzi held both her hands up. "Ebone´, I'm going in my
room, okay? I really don't think I need to hear any more. I

really don't think I can take any more. Get ready so I can take you over your mama's." She walked out of Ebone''s room into hers, sat on her bed and held her head. This was simply unbelievable! Who else but Ebone'? She went to her closet and pulled out her Louis Vuitton steamer bag. She needed to start packing - she was leaving in four days' time. "Holler when you're ready!" she shouted to Ebone'.

She felt a nagging pain in her stomach. Her period was due today, and it was never late, so no doubt, this pain was the dreaded cramp. She didn't suffer too badly, but the cramp was enough to make her miserable, unlike Crystal who was always bedridden for two or three days and totally miserable. Crystal was totally different at that time of the month. She had endometriosis and suffered terribly. She had wanted a hysterectomy for a few years, but Raoul kept talking about having another baby. Mitzi took the box of Tampax from her dresser and went into the bathroom. "Yep. I thought so," she said out loud. As her granny would say, her 'friend' had come to visit. Only God knew why it was referred to as a friend. As long as it was finished before she got on the plane on Thursday. She went back and started pulling clothes from her closet to pack in her bag. She didn't need much - they would only be gone for three days, but she knew she would pack more than she needed - she always did and ended up not wearing half of it. She took out a pair of jeans, a pair of dress pants and a pair of cotton pants which had a matching top. She threw in a couple of tops to wear with her jeans, then Ebone' told her she was ready to go. She would finish packing when she came back. Although she didn't have to pack much, she had a lot of clothes, and what to take was always such a hard decision. She grabbed her bag and keys and went into the living room to find Ebone' with a stuffed duffel bag.

"You coming back home sometime this year?"

Ebone' smiled. "You told me to stay a while."

"You're actually going to do something I suggested? Don't go changing on me, you know, Ebone'. I couldn't take too much at one time."

Ebone´ sucked her teeth and smiled. "Come on, girl."

Mitzi felt bad for Ebone´ when she dropped her off at her mother's house. She looked so scared, confused and uncomfortable. This was truly a difficult time for her. In time - probably a long time, everything would be fine. She had a lot to think about and digest, and it wasn't going to be easy. Ironically, this was what it might take to get her to forget about Ricky. What was the lesser of the two evils? Mitzi went right back home, finished her basic packing - the little things could go in later - got a bath and lay across her bed. It was almost five o'clock, and she was hungry. She didn't feel like fixing anything to eat, but she wanted to take a couple of Advil, so she made a cup of tea, took the Advil and called Crystal. She had to talk to somebody. She knew she could trust Crystal. Of course, she couldn't tell her everything, but she just wanted to tell her that Mrs. Simons was terminally ill, and that she and Ebone´ had buried the hatchet. Crystal was in bed when Mitzi called. She thought she was hung over from the night before so Raoul had taken the children down to St. John's field to the cricket game, and she was getting a little rest.

"You sound terrible, Mitzi. What's your problem?"

Mitzi hadn't realized that she sounded terrible, but she felt drained and tired. She had hardly had any sleep. "Nothin', except my stupid period came today."

"Oh please, don't say that word too loud. Mine is due next week. Lord, my head hurts. So, what's up?"

"A lot's up. I called you 'cause I needed to talk to somebody."

"What's wrong?"

"Nothing's wrong with me but, Ebone´..."

"Oh no. What now?"

"No, this time it's real. Her mama's real sick, girl. She doesn't have much longer to live."

"What's wrong with her?" Crystal sounded like she wanted to cry already. That was the type of person she was. She played hard, but she would cry in a minute.

Mitzi told Crystal that Mrs. Simons had told Ebone´ about the ovarian cancer and that they had reconciled.

"I hope it's not too late."

"Maybe, but I hope not. She went back over there to stay for a few days."

"Poor Ebone´. Her life always seems to be full of... something. Always some confusion."

More than you could ever imagine, honey. "Yeah, don't I know. But I had to call you 'cause I feel so helpless. What should I do?"

"What can you do, Mitzi? Just be there when she wants to talk and do whatever you can for her - whatever she asks you to do, I guess. I don't know."

Mitzi sucked her teeth and rubbed some lotion on her feet. "Anyway, I'm going to lie down for a while. I'm hungry, but I'm too tired to cook."

"Well if your period's on, you should eat something. Want me to bring you something when those lot get back with the car?"

"No girl, I don't want you to drive all the way up here. I can get something later. Thanks anyway. I should call Ebone´ and see how she's doing. I'll talk to you tomorrow."

"Okay. Let me know if I can do anything, see?"

"Thanks. Check you later, chicky." Mitzi turned the TV on. 'The Bodyguard' was on HBO, so she left it on that channel and closed her eyes. "What a day this has been. Roll on Thursday." A few minutes later she called Ebone´. Cee Cee answered the phone, and Mitzi told her that Ebone´ had told her that their mother was sick and that she was really sorry. Ebone´ sounded a little solemn but told her she would be all right. They were all getting ready to sit down and have dinner, so Mitzi told her to call if she needed anything and hung up. As soon as she did, the phone rang again. She looked at her caller I.D. box - it was Sundae. She hardly felt like talking to her right now. She felt like a dish rag. She let her voice mail get it. She wished she had a man in her life - one she could talk to and get advice from. Also because she wasn't feeling that well. Was it too much to ask to simply have a man hold her while she was feeling down? She didn't think so. Something would have to be done about this immediately. But what?

CHAPTER NINE
Monday Morning

It was eight o'clock, and Sundae had called in sick again before Mitzi got to work.

"What did she say this time, Ronald?" Mitzi was a little more than annoyed.

Ronald shrugged his shoulders. "She said she was sick," he said with his lisp. Mitzi would usually laugh at him, but she was too angry with Sundae, and she still had cramp, which was odd.

"What is her problem?" She put her bag in her desk drawer and plopped down in her chair. She pulled out the big cosmetic bag that held all her curling irons, combs and blow dryer. "How many clients does she have today?"

"Ten. I already called three of them. Two will come in for anybody to do their hair, but Mrs. Richards wanted to make another appointment. I'm calling the others now."

"Damn!" She banged the desk. "I will never again hire a friend or befriend another employee. They take my friendship and kindness for weakness."

Ronald looked at her like she was crazy. "PMS?" he asked casually.

She glared at him. "How you know?"

" 'Cause you're being a bit dramatic, Miss Thing."

Maybe she was. But so what? She had a lot on her mind. "Look, Ronald, you know I hate confusion. Sundae called in sick last week, and she's called in sick again today. I have a business to run, okay?" She walked out and slammed the door. Ronald shook his head. He had been living and working with women for years and knew what they were like. She would come around.

Mitzi's first lady came in at eight thirty, along with one of Sundae's ladies, and so the chaos had begun. It dawned on Mitzi that this was Mother's Day week, and they would probably have a lot of walk-ins. Was Sundae trying to drive her crazy? She couldn't take her mind off of Ebone´ and wondered if she had gone to work and told Wendell what she knew. She burned two of her clients' ears with the curling iron and blow dried one woman's hair when she had wanted it set. And the silly woman sat, let her do it, then complained after she had finished. Mitzi felt like telling her to go to hell, but she apologised and took five dollars off. Then, to top it off, Macky came in to talk to her. She had practically forgotten about his situation.

"Mitzi, when we gonna tell Mama?" he asked her when they went into her office.

"Macky, I'm sorry, but I really can't talk to you right now. I'm short-staffed." She picked up the new mail. "Tell you what, you know me and Mama are going away on Thursday, and Mother's Day is Sunday. I really don't wanna tell her before we go, and I don't want to upset her on Mother's Day, so Monday evening I'll come over the house, and we can tell her."

"Good, 'cause I want to get this over with."

"You should have thought about all that before you did this, Macky." She looked him in the eye.

He backed away from her and frowned. "What's wrong with you, girl?"

She closed her eyes. She had to calm down. "I'm sorry, I'm just real stressed out right now." She sighed. "I have to go back to work, Macky." She put her hand on the door knob and turned to look at him. "I'm sorry, honey."

He shrugged. "Yeah, peace. I'll catch up with you later."

One good thing about today was that Samantha was fully booked with clients wanting braids. She was fast and got the ladies in and out. Mitzi didn't finish until seven, and Melba came by to bring her plane tickets.

"Sundae's gone already?" Melba sat at the reception desk while Mitzi looked at tomorrow's appointments. Ronald was in the office, and the others had left.

Mitzi sucked her teeth. "She never came in. Called in sick again."

"What you mean, again?"

"She called in sick last week, too."

"What's her function?" Melba was trying to read the appointment book upside down.

"I don't know, girl. So much is going on right now. I don't know if I'm comin' or goin'." She put her hand over her forehead, sighed and yanked it down again. She leaned toward Melba. Sundae had borrowed money from Mitzi several times since the first time at her house. "You think she's on drugs, Melba? She keeps borrowing money..." She regretted saying the words as soon as they left her tongue.

"Oh?" Melba's eyes widened as she crossed her legs, waiting to hear more.

Damn, why did I say that? Melba loved things like this. Well, she wasn't gonna hear any more. "Never mind, um, what happened with Roger on Saturday night?" She wanted to change the subject. Of course, Melba didn't.

"Oh no, honey. We're not talking about Roger. We're talking about Sundae."

"I'm not saying any more, Melba, so can we change the subject?"

"How come she's always borrowing money? Who she borrow it from - you?" Guess she didn't want to change the subject.

"Yes, okay? Now come on, Melba, let it go."

"Why you acting like you don't want to tell me? Aren't we all friends?"

"Exactly. That's why I shouldn't have told you. If Sundae wanted you to know, she would have asked you to lend her the money."

"Ha! Do I look like a woman of immeasurable wealth? You're the one who owns your own business. She knows better than to ask me. But Mitzi, you have to be careful, you know, because if she is on drugs... have you noticed any inconsistencies in her money?"

"Don't go there, Melba. And furthermore, the only money she handles is her tips."

"Well, make sure it stays that way because it'll get worse. She won't ask you for the money eventually - she'll just take it herself. As far as I'm concerned, drug addicts are incorrigible."

"Oh for God's sake, Melba, let it go, I said. I don't really believe she's on drugs, okay?" She closed the book and headed toward her office.

"Yes you do! Why you say it if you don't think it?"

Mitzi spun around. She had had enough. "Look, I don't want to talk about it anymore, okay Melba?! I have had a bad day - in fact, I've had a few bad days, and I'm not in the mood for this right now - or ever, for that matter. I have a lot on my mind, my period is on, I have cramp and I am irritated! Got it?!"

"Fine." Melba snatched her bag and headed for the door. "Call me when you're in a better mood." She left, and Mitzi threw open the office door where Ronald was leaning back in his chair waiting for her.

"What you lookin' at?!" She walked past him, opened her drawer and took her bag out. Ronald smiled and shook his head. It wasn't often that she flew off the handle like this. In fact, it had been quite a while, so he knew that something was drastically wrong. Experience told him that she would be in a much better mood tomorrow.

"I'm gone. You got a lift home?"

"Yes. Pearl's coming for me." At least she wasn't too mad to care. He looked at his watch. "She should be outside now. Wait for me."

"Let's go!" She was like a stark raving lunatic, and she couldn't control herself. As a matter of fact, she didn't want to control herself. It felt good to act like this for a change.

The minute she started driving along East Broadway, the tears started. She felt so upset. She was upset about Ebone'. She was upset about Mrs. Simons. She was upset about Macky. She was upset about Sundae. She was upset about telling Melba about Sundae. She was upset because she had shouted at Ronald. She was upset about her period. She was upset because she didn't have a man. She was upset... By the time she reached home, she had cried all the tears she thought she could. She checked her voice mail. Her mama had called to see if she had gotten their tickets. She didn't want to call her back because she would know right away that something was wrong. Ebone' had called and wanted her to call her back. And Ronald had called - knowing she wouldn't be home yet - to tell her that he didn't know what was wrong, but he hoped she would have a good night and that she would feel better in the morning. She lay in her bed and dialed Ebone''s number. Ebone' answered. "Hey, what's up?"

"I just wanted to let you know that I told Wendell that I know the truth today."

Mitzi was surprised. "You did? What he say?"

"At first, he just stared at me. Then he hugged me and told me that he was sorry and that he hoped I didn't hate him, but he was just doing what my mama and her husband wanted him to do."

"I'm so glad you didn't wait to tell him. It'll be so much easier now. Did you tell him about your mama's illness?"

"Yeah. He's kind of upset about that. I think he still loved her after she and my daddy... you know who I mean - got back together."

"Why? What else he say?" Mitzi felt hot and stood up to take her clothes off while she talked on the phone.

"I don't know - he just got upset when I told him she was dying. We didn't talk too much about it because we were at work. And plus, I'm not really ready to talk about anything like that yet. I'm just worried about my mama right now. Wendell and I can talk about it later."

"How is you mama, anyway?"

"She wasn't too good today. She was in a lot of pain and those lot had to take her to the doctor. We hired a nurse for her. She's being strong, though - hardly ever complains."

"Well, you all have to be strong, too."

"We're hanging in there. What's wrong with you?"

"Why?" *Am I that bad?*

"You sound miserable. Who got on your nerves?"

"Nobody. I just had a bad day." Mitzi didn't want to tell her that she was really concerned about her - among other things. Ebone' wouldn't know how to deal with Mitzi's saying that anyway.

"Now, I'm gonna see if my mama needs anything. I'll talk to you tomorrow."

"When you coming home?"

"I don't know. Why?"

" 'Cause, I was thinking, I'm going away on Thursday so you might as well stay at your mama's while I'm gone, so you won't be here by yourself."

"I'll see. Check you later."

Mitzi hung up and lay on her back, looking at the ceiling for a while. Life was too difficult sometimes. She was usually very much in control, but occasionally she felt overwhelmed. Perhaps it was because she was always in control and had too much to deal with. She needed someone to take care of her and look out for her - when she wanted him to, but not all the time. Why couldn't she just design the type of man she wanted and then order him? Maybe she was too choicy, but she was determined not to settle for any less than she deserved and dammit, there was a man out there for her, and she was going to find him! Soon! She ran some water in the tub and put on Earth, Wind and Fire's 'Wild Flower'. She went back into the bathroom, undressed, dropped a foaming tablet into the water, got in, lay back and closed her eyes. She started crying again as she listened to EWF sing, 'Let her cry, for she's a lady. Let her dream...' She stayed in the tub for about half an hour until she felt relaxed enough to get out. The CD had finished, and she hated a quiet house. She put her pajamas on and went into the kitchen and made a cup of Lipton's Cup of Soup. She played a Barry White CD and read the *Royal Gazette* while she listened to Barry sing, 'I Got So Much to Give.' She had so much to give, why couldn't she find somebody to give it to?

Oh God, don't let me start crying again. This is getting pathetic. Why am I so consumed with these 'man' thoughts?

She hadn't felt like this for a long time. Then again, maybe she had been feeling like this but had just blocked it out until everything all happened to her at the same time, and she couldn't deal with it. This menstrual thing was serious - it could really temporarily change a woman. Men didn't know how lucky they were. Of course they didn't, they were too busy being a part of the damn problem.

Lemme get in my bed, because I can't take too much more of this day. Tomorrow has got to be better. If I wake up feeling this way, I'm stayin' home. Of course, she knew she really couldn't do that. Mitzi had always heard that exercise helped cramp, so she turned on the TV, got on the floor and did some stretches, leg raises and then forced herself to do some sit-ups. Then she got in bed alone. Again.

She had fallen into a peaceful sleep when the phone rang. She looked at the I.D. box - it was her mother. "Hi, Ma." She answered the phone with the deep voice she had when she had been sleeping.

"What's the matter, baby?"

"Nothing."

"Well it sounds like it to me."

"I was asleep." *Don't let me get irritated again.*

"Oh, I'm sorry, honey. I called you earlier to see if you got the tickets. Didn't you get my message?"

"Yeah, I'm sorry. I forgot to call you back. Melba brought me the tickets this evening."

"How come you're in your bed so early?" It was nine thirty.

"Mama! I'm tired, that's why."

"Okay, call me tomorrow. And when you do, let me know what your problem is tonight." She hung up.

Mitzi smiled. Oleeta always knew when something was bothering her. She would tell her tomorrow. She could talk to her about everything. She wanted to tell her about Ebone''s mama, too, but only about her illness. She would wait until after Mrs. Simons died to tell her mama everything. The fewer people that knew the whole story, the better right now. She asked God to help her to be a better person tomorrow than she was today - her standard prayer, set the sleep timer on the TV and dozed back off.

At the same time, Oleeta and Macky were arguing - again. Macky wanted to go out, and Oleeta thought it was too late. Once again Macky told her that he thought he was too old for a curfew. And once again she didn't want to hear it. He wasn't going and that was that. He wanted to tell her that he was old enough to make babies, too, so he could do what he wanted - but he wasn't that stupid. He tried his mama from time to time, but right now he didn't want to push her too far, especially with the news he and Mitzi had to tell her in a few days' time. Oleeta wondered what in the hell was going on with her children. Both of them were acting up tonight. She was getting too old for this nonsense. She couldn't wait until Thursday - her brain was tired, and she needed to get away from Macky for a while. She had planned for him to stay at Granny's house while she and Mitzi were gone, but he had almost had a heart attack over that news. So she asked Belinda to say at her house and keep an eye on him. Naturally, he didn't see why anybody had to stay anywhere and keep an eye on him. After all, he was a man - the man of the house. Oleeta knew better. Little 'Miss Thing' would think she could move in for the duration of the trip and be the woman of the house. Well, there was one woman of her house, and she was it. Macky finally gave up the argument and went into his room. Oleeta was waiting for him to slam the door so she could go behind him and straighten him out, but he closed it gently.

Something was definitely wrong. He didn't even argue with her for as long as he usually did. She knew her children, and something was going on.

Mitzi felt ninety percent better when she got up at six-thirty the next morning. The rest had done her a world of good. The only thing wrong was that she still had cramp. She would have to call the doctor as soon as she got back from North Carolina. She called her mama before she left home, apologised to her and explained that she hadn't been feeling well when her mama had called the night before. She also told her about Mrs. Simons. Oleeta told her that she had known something was wrong and also told her that she was looking forward to the trip because Macky was driving her crazy.

Now why in the world is he acting up now? He would want to stay on her good side. Only a few days and everything would be out. She went in to work and found a hibiscus in a glass of water on her desk. A minute later Ronald opened the door and peeped in.

"Do I have to throw my hat in first?" he asked, looking a little unsure.

Mitzi smiled. "No. Come in here, you silly man." He opened the door up and came in, carrying two cups of tea. He put one on her desk, stood back and looked at her. She smiled and so did he. "Thanks." She stood and hugged him. He was a good friend, and she could depend on him always. "Thanks for the phone call, thanks for the flower and... I'm sorry."

"I just hope you're feeling better today. I can't take a repeat of yesterday."

"Nah. All that won't be happenin' today. I had a lot going on yesterday - actually, it's still going on, but I realised I can only deal with things one at a time."

"Remember, Mitzi, there's no such thing as a problem - just a situation, and situations have a way of working out." He was the eternal optimist even when he didn't know what the situation was.

"Yes, Ronald," she said, mocking his lisp.

He laughed, as usual. "Go 'head see, your tongue's gonna get stuck like that one day."

*   *   *   *   *

The next couple of days flew by, and before she knew it, it was five o'clock on Thursday, and Mitzi and Oleeta were on the plane, headed for North Carolina. They sat back in their seats, both exhausted and excited. They talked about things in general - nothing in particular and had a couple of cocktails after they ate. Mitzi had two Bacardi's, and Oleeta had two glasses of wine. The wine made Oleeta sleepy, so she pushed her seat back and slept while Mitzi read a book. She was reading Terry McMillan's *Disappearing Acts* again. How appropriate at this juncture in her life. They arrived at the Sheraton at eight fifteen, dropped their bags in the room and walked over to the Crab-Tree Mall to shop for half an hour. They always had a ball when they traveled together - which was once a year or so - because they were both shop-aholics. They spent the little time they had in Casual Corner then walked back across the parking lot to the hotel. They saw a Bermudian couple in the lobby - they could pick them out a mile away - but they really didn't know them, thank God. They said 'hi' and went up to their room to order room service. They sat up talking until one o'clock - they both had a lot to say.

"I can't believe how fast the time went. We're on our way home already," Oleeta said, a little disappointed. They were in the hotel lobby, waiting for the limo to take them to the airport. They needed one just for all their luggage. They both had shopped so much they'd had to buy extra bags. Over the past few days, they had talked about Macky's behaviour - Oleeta would know the truth tomorrow - Mrs. Simons' illness, Oleeta and George's tentative wedding plans, the fact that Mitzi needed a decent man in her life - that was Oleeta's topic - and life, in general. They had a very special bond, partly because Oleeta was not a mother who thought she had to tell her adult 'child' what to do. If Mitzi ever asked for advice, most of the time Oleeta told her what she would do if in the same situation unless it was something really serious, which rarely happened. Especially now, Mitzi appreciated the closeness she and her mother shared. She wished Ebone´ could have experienced this type of relationship with her mama. It was much too late now. It was true that people should always treat their loved ones as if it were their last days. Once they were gone, it was too late, and that type of guilt was a difficult thing to handle.

"Mitzi, if you have a wrong to right with somebody or somebody needs your forgiveness, do it. Forgiveness is a gift you give yourself," Oleeta said.

"Where you get that one from, a student's companion?" Mitzi laughed.

"I probably got it from you, the cliché queen!" Oleeta's hands were on her hips. They both laughed. "Thanks for a beautiful trip, honey."

"You're welcome. Happy Mother's Day, honey."

When they got to the airport, they realised they weren't sitting together. Now why hadn't Melba told her? When she thought about it, Melba never really had a chance to tell her. She had given her the tickets the same night they had the argument. She would call her this evening. Oleeta was in row fifteen, and she was in row twenty-six. She would try to change her seat once everybody had boarded. When she got to her row, someone was in the window seat - she had the aisle. She put her carry-on bag in the overhead compartment, took down a pillow and blanket and sat.

"Hi," she said to the man sitting at the window.

"Hi, how you doing?" He smiled a little, and Mitzi thought she saw dimples. He was wearing Lagerfeld - her favourite men's cologne. He smelled real good.

She took her book from her bag and shoved the bag under the seat in front of her.

"Would you like to sit by the window?" Mr. 'Lagerfeld' asked.

"No thanks. I don't like to see what's happening out there while I'm flying." Mitzi smiled at him, and he smiled back, exposing the deepest dimples and the straightest, whitest teeth Mitzi had ever seen. He looked real cool in a denim shirt with the sleeves rolled up, jeans and sneakers. *Lord he's cute! I know he's somebody's man.* Mitzi hated sitting by the window, in fact, she hated flying, period. She also wanted to sit in the aisle seat because she had been drinking a lot of water on the trip and would probably have to make a couple of trips to the bathroom. She certainly didn't want to keep bothering the nice man sitting beside her. She opened her book and glanced over at the guy beside her. He was looking out of the window as the plane taxied down the runway. He seemed lost in thought and looked a little sad. She wanted to make conversation with him, but at that moment he didn't look like he wanted to be bothered, so she read her book. A minute later when the plane took off and made that noise that everybody says is the wheels being closed up, she jumped and gripped the arm of her chair.

"You alright?" her new-found friend asked, smiling again. She could almost see herself in his teeth.

Mitzi cut her eyes. "I will be as soon as I get off this plane. I hate flying. I always think something's going to happen - every little noise makes me think the plane's gonna crash."

"It's not that bad, is it?" he asked amused by her fear. "Nothin's gonna happen. It's just mind over matter."

"Well, my mind can't get over this matter." She closed the book and her eyes and pushed her head back against her seat. She prayed silently.

"Incidentally, my name's Maliq. Maliq Simmons." He had interrupted her prayer. She was never sure what to do in a situation like that, but this time she opened her eyes and held out her hand.

"It's good to meet you. I'm Maxine Robinson." They shook hands. His was soft, and she hoped hers was, too.

"I don't wanna sound forward, but your braids accentuate your beautiful blackness," he said, looking at her hair.

And you smell good. "Thank you, you're very kind."

"You must spend a lot of time in a beauty shop."

She smiled and looked at him. "A real lot of time. I work in one - actually, I own one." She didn't want to sound like she was showing off. Maliq seemed sweet. And humble.

"You do? Well ain't that nice? An ambitious sister. Bermuda needs more black women like you. You must be a very independent lady."

"I like to think I am. What about you? Can I be forward and ask what you do?" She really was interested, and he seemed interesting.

"I work for an airline. Accounts." *Does he work in accounts or is he an accountant?* He must have read her mind. "Actually, I'm an accountant." He smiled again, and for the first time she noticed his slightly receding hairline and the gray in his thick mustache. He looked like he would have a thick beard if he let it grow. He had very smooth skin, a dark complexion and light brown eyes. She realized she must have been staring at him, so she looked past him out of the window.

"Be careful. You might see something out there you don't want to see."

She looked back at him. "I don't think I was actually looking out there. I think my mind was somewhere else." She realised she might have sounded a little flaky in making that statement, but the truth was, her mind was somewhere else. She was thinking about how much she was enjoying this conversation with this stranger and about the fact that when the plane landed, they would both tell each other how nice it was to have met, get their luggage and go their separate ways. His wife would probably be waiting for him at the airport. She looked out of the corner of her eye to see if he had on a wedding band. He didn't, but what did that prove? Men these days hardly wore them - they couldn't be slick with a wedding band on. He had on a beautiful gold bracelet, though. Looked expensive. She looked down the aisle and saw Oleeta coming toward her. She had almost forgotten about her!

"Mitzi, I thought you were going to try and change your seat." Oleeta stood in front of her.

"The plane's full, mama. Maliq, this is my mother, Mrs. Robinson. Mama, this is Maliq Simmons." Oleeta smiled a big, 'Oh, so you've met a man' smile.

"Hello, Maliq. How are you?" She knocked Mitzi's foot.

"I'm good, thank you, Mrs. Robinson, and you?"

"Oh, I'm just fine." Oleeta was beaming, and Mitzi could have died.

"Happy Mother's Day to you. And to you, too, Maxine." He looked her in the eye. Or did he?

"Oh, I'm not a mother."

"But she would love to be one day," Oleeta said and walked in the direction of the lavatories.

Mitzi and Maliq looked at each other and laughed. "I'm sorry," she said, shaking her head.

"For what?" He shifted to face her. "You're mother's beautiful, Maxine."

"Please don't tell her that. And by the way, nobody calls me Maxine. It's Mitzi."

"That's cute." He looked at her book. "What you reading?"

"*Disappearing Acts* by Terry McMillan. It's really a good book. In fact, this is the second time I'm reading it." She turned it over. "I'm almost finished."

"You probably would have been finished if I hadn't interrupted you, right?"

"Probably." She smiled at him. "But you haven't interrupted me. I'm enjoying talking to you."

"And I, you."

Ouch, lyrics. "How would you have passed the time if we hadn't started talking?"

He sighed. "Usually I would be reading, too, but I had a lot on my mind when I got on the plane and thought I was going to spend the time looking out the window collecting my thoughts."

"I noticed you looking out there earlier, and you looked a little sad." Oleeta walked past and knocked Mitzi's arm.

"You're very observant." He looked out the window again for a few seconds, then back at Mitzi. "I do have a lot on my mind right now. I had a difficult, painful, but necessary decision to make, and I made it. You know how sometimes you just know when it's time to do something that you know will be all right later?"

"I know exactly what that's like." For a man with a lot on his mind, he didn't stay down for long. He seemed like a very upbeat, positive brother.

He smiled and gently hit her hand. "Get out of here. You look like a lady who's never had a problem in the world."

"Ha! Don't I wish. I've had my share of, as they say - ups and downs." At that moment the flight attendant brought their snacks.

Mitzi bowed her head, closed her eyes and said her grace. When she opened her eyes, Maliq was smiling at her. "I'm impressed," he said.

"You don't say your grace?" she asked teasingly.

"I have to be honest and say that I don't say it as often as I should. I need to start again, though, it's a good practice."

Am I making an impression, or what? "How's your lunch? This isn't bad." He had a vegetarian meal.

"This is terrible. You want something to drink?" Her mouth was full, and she nodded. "What would you like?"

Now she didn't know what to do. She really wanted a Bacardi, but she didn't want to look like a lush by ordering liquor if he was only having a soda. "I don't know. What you havin'?"

"Would you mind if I had a cocktail?"

Good. "Not if you wouldn't mind if I had one with you." Mitzi wondered how much and how often he drank. She was trying to figure out his m.o. She ordered a scotch and coke for him and a Bacardi and gingerale for herself. She also asked the attendant to give her mother a glass of wine when she got down to her seat. Mitzi reached under the seat for her bag.

"What are you doing?" Maliq asked, frowning.

"Getting some money," Mitzi answered, pulling her wallet out.

He rested his fork. "I am highly offended. I offered you a drink, and you want to pay for it?" He passed the attendant a twenty-dollar bill and told her the wine was to be included.

"I didn't mean to offend you, but I don't like to take things or people for granted, especially since I ordered a drink for my mama."

"I admire you 'new-age' women, but you make it hard for a brother to be nice. Cheers." They toasted with plastic cups.

She turned her head to the side and looked at him. "I'm sorry, brother. Didn't mean to block your niceness."

"Don't let it happen again." He looked serious for a second then looked at her and laughed. His whole face lit up when he did.

"Where you get those dimples?"

"Man made, sister. What's the book about?"

"In a word - relationships. In the nineties."

"That's four words, girl. What's wrong with you?" Mitzi rolled her eyes and laughed. She had been smiling and laughing non-stop since she had started talking with him. This was exactly what she needed, even if it would be short-lived. She had a lot to deal with when she got off the plane. It would be back to reality. "I think this would be a good time for me to buy that book and read it."

Hello! Tell me more. "Why you say that?" She was trying not to finish her drink before he finished his.

"Oh sister, I need a little help in that department right about now. I'm usually a private person, and maybe I'm gonna tell you this because I've had a few cocktails today, but I'll tell you anyway." He looked at her. "I've really enjoyed talking to you - you appear to have it together." He touched her hand.

Hey, don't do that after I've had a drink, you cute thing. "Thanks."

"Stop me if you get bored, okay?" He sighed and poured the rest of the scotch in his glass. Mitzi followed suit with her drink. "I've been going with a lady for about a year and a half..."

Dammit! Are there any seats next to my mama?

"... and I had to end it. It just would have never worked."

There is a God! "It took you a year and a half to decide that?" Everybody didn't move as quickly as she did.

"Yeah. Sometimes a person knows when something isn't going to work, but when love and feelings are involved, it's a little harder to get out. You know what I mean?"

"Yeah, I guess I do. But if you love her, don't you think whatever the problem is can be worked out. Doesn't love conquer all?"

"No. Not when the love isn't mutual. I don't think she loved me. She might have cared for me, but I seriously doubt she loved me. We argued almost daily because her family kept coming between us. Actually, her father came between us." The attendant collected their trays.

"Wait a minute. How old is this person?"

"Twenty-eight."

"And her father came between you? How could he?"

"The man is different. She lives with him - it's just the two of them - and he still has her living by house rules. I can't go to her house at night, and if she comes to mine, he expects her home by a 'decent' hour. If she gets home at a time he thinks is unacceptable, he rants and raves. Once or twice I convinced her to spend the night at my house, and when she got home, all hell broke loose. He called her a whore and told her that if she did it again, he was going to cut her out of his will and all this bullsh... Oops, excuse me." Mitzi smiled. He was such a gentleman, but she could see he was angry right now. "Needless to say, he hates me."

Mitzi held her hands up. "Is the obvious not so obvious here? Why doesn't she just move out of his house?" *What am I saying? Don't give him a solution, dummy.*

"That's what I have a serious problem with. I have asked her repeatedly - begged her - to get her own apartment. It's not like she doesn't have a good job, but she doesn't want to be cut out of the will, and she doesn't want her daddy to stop speaking to her. And if it isn't her daddy, she can't do this with me because she has to do something for her mama, or she can't do that with me 'cause she has to do something with her sister..."

"Obviously I don't know who you're talkin' about, but it seems to me that your 'girl' don't wanna grow up. Either that, or something else is going on."

He rubbed his hand over his face. "I don't know what the real deal is, but at my age, I don't need to be competing with nobody's daddy."

"And what exactly is your age?" She sipped her drink.

"Thirty-five. How old are you?"

"It is the height of rudeness to ask a lady her age." She looked at him angrily. He looked as if he wanted to die. She smiled. He closed his eyes and laughed. "How old do you think I am?" She drained her cup. She definitely did not need another drink.

"Oh no, sister. You ain't doin' that to me. I might say something wrong, and I don't think I want to get on your bad side. To be safe, I'll say that you don't look a day over twenty-one."

And you look like you need a good woman. Like me. Did I say that out loud? I hope not. "Bless your heart, Maliq. You'll be my friend forever."

"I hope so." He looked her in the eye. She felt a little uncomfortable and looked away.

"So, did you really break up with girlfriend, or do you *think* you broke up with her?" She hoped she didn't sound anxious.

He sighed. "She was supposed to come on this trip with me. We planned it about a month ago. I thought if we got away together, we could work something out... she's a sweet person, and I really thought this was the answer."

"So what happened?"

He smiled. "Two days before I left, she told me she didn't feel right about going 'cause her daddy would probably be mad at her, and she didn't know how to tell him."

Mitzi's eyes widened. "Get the hell out of here! What is her problem?"

"I don't know, but I went right off. I told her that was the last straw. I can't live like that anymore. I told her that she should just go and have a relationship with her father."

"Sounds like she already is." Mitzi was putting on lipstick.

"As terrible as that sounds, maybe it's true." He looked out the window again. Poor sight. He looked so hurt. Mitzi wanted to touch his arm and tell him not to worry, but she didn't.

"You gonna be all right?"

He shrugged his shoulders. "Do I have a choice? Life goes on."

"You heard from her since?"

"Yeah, she called me in Raleigh. She, her mama and her sister were in Atlanta. They decided to leave the day after I did." Mitzi shook her head. "You know she asked me to drive from North Carolina to Atlanta and get a room in the hotel they were staying in so that 'at least we could be together during the day'. I guess she didn't think I was serious about breaking up. I told her I meant what I said and didn't want her to call me anymore."

Mitzi looked at him doubtfully. "Are you telling me the truth, Maliq, or are you making this up 'cause..."

He held his hand up. "May I never leave this spot if I'm lying. I won't lie to you - I don't even know you."

Well, we can change that, honey. "Boy, I didn't realize things like that actually happened in Bermuda." The pilot announced that they had begun their descent onto the island.

He touched her hand. "I apologise, Mitzi, I have monopolized the entire conversation with my sorry story. Didn't I tell you to stop me when you got bored?"

She yawned then looked at him and laughed - again. "That was no reflection of you, honest." Maliq pretended to be hurt. "I wouldn't lie to you," she mocked him. "I don't know you."

"Thanks for listenin'. I really appreciate it." He looked at his watch. "In the few minutes we have left why don't you tell me about yourself. I would feel a lot better about talking your ear off about me."

"What you wanna know?"

"Is Mr. Robinson coming to pick you up today?"

She shook her head. "Oh please, Maliq. You have to come better than that. Didn't I tell you my mama's name is Mrs. Robinson? I am Ms. Robinson, and no, Mr. Robinson is not coming to pick me up."

"So, you have no husband, no children, a beautiful mother, pretty eyes, a wonderful sense of humour, a good listening ear, drink Bacardi, own your own business and seem to have it together. What else do you wanna tell me about Maxine 'Mitzi' Robinson?"

She likes you. "Nothing else to tell. That's me. What you see is what I am." She started to put her book in her bag and stopped. "Here, I think you might need to read this right about now."

"You haven't finished it, though."

"I told you, I read it before. I know how it ends." She unfastened her seatbelt and stood up to go to the lavatory. "But I want it back, though. I don't usually lend my books out, but I trust you to give it back to me. 'Scuse me, I'll be right back."

Was the plane rocking, or had she had too much to drink? She hoped she hadn't said anything stupid to Maliq. She had been so caught up in talking to him that she hadn't realised how bad she had to pee. She checked her hair and her makeup. Both looked fine. She hurried back to her seat to find Maliq reading the book.

"I think the stewardess forgot to bring my change from the drinks." He looked around for her. "Do you think your mother's upset 'cause you haven't been to talk to her?"

"Of course not. My mama's my girl, she don't get uptight about things like that."

"You have any brothers or sisters?" He put the book in his carry-on bag.

She hadn't thought about Macky since she'd been on the plane. "Yeah, I have a brother - he's seventeen and a major pain in the butt."

"See, I knew you weren't much older than twenty-one."

"You're basing this on the fact that I have a seventeen year-old sibling?"

"Yeah. It stands to reason that there wouldn't be that much more than five, maybe six years age difference between you two." He nodded his head and tried to look sure of himself. The attendant walked by. " 'Scuse me ma'am, I don't believe I got my change earlier." She looked in her pocket, and sure enough, there was his change. She apologised and gave him the money. It was really nice to see somebody remain calm about something like that. Darren would have performed - not to mention Quincy.

A few minutes later the plane hit the runway and lurched forward. Mitzi tensed up. "You think that was the pilot's first flight?" she asked Maliq. Her top lip was sweating, and she felt unnerved. She had been fine talking to Maliq the whole time they were flying, but a plane always sounded like it was about to explode whenever it landed. It was taxiing slowly now, and some foreign person was welcoming them to Bermuda over the P.A. system. "Well, Mr. Simmons, it has been my pleasure talking to you, and I hope things work out as you would have them." Mitzi unfastened her seatbelt even though the sign was still on.

"The pleasure has been all mine, Ms. Robinson." He emphasized 'Ms'. The seatbelt sign went off, and Mitzi got up to get her other bag from the overhead. Maliq stood, too. "How am I gonna get your book back to you?"

"Call me when you're finished. My number's in the book - that book," she said. *Did that sound forward? If it did, too bad, somebody has to make a move here. Time's a wastin'.*

"I'll do that. Thanks a lot. It was really nice talking to you, lady." She smiled. "You need help with your bag?" He stood up. He was a little thick, but firm. He looked like he was about six feet tall.

"No thanks, I'm fine. *And so are you.* Mitzi couldn't believe the way she was acting. She was a woman on a mission - she was on it, doggone it. By telling Maliq to call her when he was ready to return the book, she had put the ball in his court. She had done her part. She wanted to get to know this guy. He seemed like somebody she wanted to sip coffee with in the morning. "Enjoy the book." They were at the bottom of the steps where Oleeta was waiting for her. They waved and smiled at Maliq as he walked by. For the first time Mitzi really checked him out. He had the nicest, firmest butt, and his shoulders were broad. Who the hell in their right mind would let him go?! She was sure he wasn't perfect - none of them were, but she hoped whatever his shortcoming was, didn't come too short.

George was waiting for them to get through the dreaded customs experience. Mitzi always got a customs officer with an attitude. Why did some of them have to be so arrogant? This had been a bone of contention ever since she had begun traveling, and she was getting sick of it. One of them had once actually opened her wallet and counted her money. Then he deducted it from the amount she had on her foreign currency paper to compare it to her declaration total. Didn't the idiot think she had eaten and paid for transportation while abroad? Today this one searched her luggage, pulled all her things out and expected her to put them back. She would, huh?

"Could you kindly put my things back in my bag where you found them?" She looked at her with those Robinson eyes and put her hand on her hip. The officer glared at her, cut her eyes and stuffed her things back. It seemed like the people with the expensive luggage got roughed up. Now Mitzi had declared everything; the woman hadn't found anything illegal in her possession yet she had an attitude. Explain that. It was as if they were only happy when they busted somebody. Probably had an orgasm when they did. She was going to report this woman - but then again, who would do anything about it?

Nobody. She finally paid the duty and left the terminal. George and Oleeta were hugging and kissing like they hadn't seen each other in months. Mitzi smiled and looked around to see who was picking up Maliq. She didn't see him.

Mitzi was surprised to find her car in the yard when George drove up to her house. She had loaned it to Ebone´ while she was gone, and she expected her to be at her mama's house, today - Mother's Day - of all days. Maybe she had come home for something. George lifted her bags to the house, and Mitzi knocked on the door. She couldn't be bothered to look for her keys. When Ebone´ didn't open the door after a few minutes, she sucked her teeth, dug in her bag and fished her keys out. The three of them walked in and found Ebone´ sitting on the couch, drinking a beer and smoking a cigarette. She was clutching something to her chest.

"Hey, girl, you didn't hear me knocking?" Ebone´ looked at the floor and shook her head. "Ebone´?" Mitzi sat on the couch beside her. Oleeta and George stood in the doorway. Ebone´ had been crying. "What's the matter? How come you're not at your mama's?" Ebone´ looked at her blankly. "What happened?" Mitzi was almost whispering, afraid of what was coming.

"She's gone. My mama died this mornin'." She was holding a picture of her mother.

Mitzi closed her eyes and sighed. *Why today?* She hugged her friend. "I'm sorry, honey." Ebone´ started to cry, softly at first until eventually she was sobbing uncontrollably. Oleeta hugged them both. All three of them were crying. George went out on the porch and lit a cigarette.

"She's gone!" Ebone´ wailed over and over. Her whole body shook.

"Let it out, honey," Oleeta said softly, rubbing her back. "Let it out." Mitzi was glad her mama was there. When Ebone´ calmed down several minutes later, Oleeta went to put on some water for tea.

"I need to talk to her," Ebone´ said to Mitzi. Mitzi was confused. "I have some things to say to my mama." Mitzi looked at Oleeta who stood in the kitchen and shook her head.

"It's too late, she's gone."

"Is it really too late? I just want a couple of minutes... to tell her I'm sorry and I love her. I have to tell her - I want her to hear me... she told me she was sorry." She was starting to ramble on, but Mitzi let her talk. It was painful to hear. "You think she's goin' to heaven?" Mitzi nodded - she really wasn't sure. "When she gets there, she can look for my baby and take care of it." She looked at Mitzi and frowned. "My daddy won't be there, will he?"

"No." Of that Mitzi was sure.

"Good, 'cause I hate him, and I don't want him near my baby or my mama." Mitzi looked at Oleeta for help. Oleeta put her finger to her lips. She wanted Mitzi to let her talk. She obviously had some deep-rooted problems. Mitzi wondered if Ebone´ was going off her head and if they should call a doctor or somebody. Eventually she stopped talking, and the tears just flowed. She was in terrible pain. Oleeta brought her some tea.

"Did you ever have the chance to tell her anything?" Mitzi hoped she had, but she shook her head.

"I didn't think she would die this soon. They said a couple of months." She sipped her tea.

"No one can really tell exactly when it's time, Ebone´."

"I watched her take her last breath. Just before she died, she looked at me like she wanted to tell me something... and then she was gone. I said, 'Mama, I love you', but she didn't hear me, but she was still holding my hand."

"She heard you, honey," Oleeta said, holding Ebone´'s hand. Ebone´ looked at her. "Trust me, she heard you."

CHAPTER TEN
Monday Morning

Mitzi dragged herself in to work. She had hardly slept all night. Ebone´ had cried half the night and had even screamed a couple of times, keeping Mitzi awake. She had dropped her off at her mama's house on the way to work so she could help with the funeral arrangements. Mitzi walked into her office and found Ronald in a bad mood, which was rare.

"Mornin' Mitzi, welcome back, hope you had a good trip, sorry to hear about Ebone´'s mother, but you have to do something about Sundae. She came in at one o'clock on Saturday." He said it all in one breath - a very annoyed breath.

Mitzi looked at him in total shock. "One o'clock, Ronald?!"

"Yes, one p.m. She called at eight to say she wasn't feeling well and if she felt better, she would be in later. One o'clock, the day before Mother's day, she sashays in here and has the nerve to look harassed."

"Damn Ronald, I don't need this today!"

"Neither do I." He threw a folder on her desk. "Pearl informed me this morning that she is eleven weeks pregnant - with our fourth child! I wanted one child! I will never lie next to that woman again as long as I live!" He stormed out. Mitzi held her head. What else could happen? She didn't have the strength for this. How much could she take without going 'fullish'? Was there a conspiracy against her? Because if there was, why didn't they just kill her? She pressed the intercom button.

"Sundae, come and see me the first opportunity you get, and somebody please let me know the minute Mrs. James gets here." There was a knock on the door. She was ready for

Sundae. It was Michae, one of the shampoo girls, asking if she wanted tea. She needed more than damn tea. Two minutes later Michae passed Mitzi's tea to Sundae to take in when she went. Mitzi didn't beat around the bush. "Sundae, what the hell is going on around here?"

Sundae was shocked. "What you talking 'bout, Mitzi?" She sat in the chair beside Mitzi's desk.

"Sundae, if I look stupid, it's not my fault, okay? But this is not particularly a good time to play games, all right? And may I remind you at this juncture, that although we are friends, you work for me, and I want to know what's happening with you."

"Nothin's happenin' with me. What - Ronald told you I came in half a day on Saturday?"

"Of course he did, Sundae. That's his job. I'm sure the other girls were extremely inconvenienced on Saturday."

"Yeah, especially since you were on vacation..."

"I own this bladdy place, Sundae!" Mitzi pounded her fist on the desk and leaned forward. "I covered my ass weeks ago when I decided to go away! Not that it's any of your business!"

Sundae knew when Mitzi cursed it wasn't a good time to get on her nerves. "I guess it's not," she said softly.

"Let me tell you something, if you're having problems working here, then maybe it's time for you to move on."

"I don't have any problems working here."

"Then what's going on? You have missed God knows how many days from work over the past... three weeks."

"I was sick, Mitzi. Everybody gets sick from time to time."

"Not every week - especially not you, Sundae. You have been 'sick' more times in the past couple of weeks than you have in the whole time you've worked here. And furthermore, if you were really sick that much, you would have come to me and talked to me about it." She leaned back in her chair then sat forward again. "And then you stroll in here at one on Saturday - after being 'sick' that morning."

"I felt better." She was really nonchalant about this, and it was getting on Mitzi's nerves.

"Sundae, I have a business to run, okay? I can't be having all this type of stuff going on."

"It won't happen again," she said solemnly. Had Mitzi been too hard on her? No, she had to put their friendship aside and act in her capacity as employer. If not, her business would fail.

"How do you know it won't?"

" 'Cause I just know." She closed her eyes, and Mitzi knew something was wrong.

"Listen, I'm no fool, I know somethin's happening. I notice how tired you are when you come in here lately." She leaned back in the chair. "Tell me something, why you always have to borrow money these days?"

Sundae slowly opened her eyes. After a few seconds she said, "Melba thinks I always borrow money 'cause I'm on drugs. But how would Melba know that I borrow money from you?" She looked at Mitzi and waited for her to answer.

Melba is a wicked woman. She told Sundae what I told her last week. Mitzi closed her eyes and hung her head. She couldn't deny anything. "Look, the other night she came here to bring me a message and wanted to know where you were, and I told her you had called in sick again. I was totally frustrated, and I told her that I was concerned about you because you were missing a lot of time from work and borrowing money. I realized the minute I said it that I had made a mistake, and I asked her not to say anything to anybody, but of course, with Melba, that's impossible." Mitzi looked at Sundae. "I'm sorry, Sundae, you know I have never betrayed your confidence, but like I said, I was frustrated, and it came out. That's no excuse, but that's the truth."

The intercom buzzed, and Ronald announced that Mrs. James had arrived.

"I trusted you, Mitzi..."

"And you still can, Sundae. I made a mistake. That happens sometimes, but I've learned my lesson."

Sundae stood up. "I wasn't going to tell you or anybody this until I had my results, but since you all think I'm a drug addict,

I'll tell you - it's a short story. As you know, I never graduated from high school, and that has always bothered me. You girls are always laughing at the things I say or correcting my grammar - which doesn't bother me, but I decided that I wanted to improve myself. So I've been going to an English tutor four nights a week for the past month and have been studying for my GED. I sat the GED exam on Saturday morning." She held the door knob. "That's why I've missed time from work, always tired and have been borrowing money. I was up until three and four in the morning, and sometimes I just couldn't get up to come in. Then the tutor was costing me a lot of money - money I just didn't have.

Mitzi was speechless. "Sundae... why didn't you just come out and tell me instead of creating all this confusion and misunderstanding?"

"Because I didn't wanna tell anybody until I got the results back, in case I failed. The only person who knew was my tutor."

Mitzi shook her head. "You wouldn't be a bad person if you failed, Sundae. I'm your friend, you could have told me."

"See how you shallow Bermudians are so quick to judge people?" She stared at Mitzi then smiled slowly and shook her head. "Had me 'round the block, gunnin' dope. Please!"

Mitzi laughed. "I'm sorry, sister. I had no right to assume anything like that about you. It's just that it's happening so much - you don't know who's doin' what these days."

The intercom buzzed again. "Would you like us to wash Mrs. James' hair? Again?"

They both laughed. "What's with him?" Sundae asked, opening the door.

"He's in a bad mood. His... he is just stressed out, I guess." She had learned her lesson. She stood beside Sundae at the door.

"Congratulations. I know you passed your GED."

"You do? How you know? They called?" She looked excited.

"Well, I don't know for sure, Sundae." All the tutoring in the world couldn't change some things. "But in my heart I know you did. But just in case I'm wrong and you don't pass, keep the money you borrowed and get some more tutoring. But if you pass, I want my damn money back!"

"Thanks, Mitzi. You're my girl, you know? When you keep your mouth shut." She hugged her.

"Come on before Ronald comes in here and kills us. We'll talk later."

*   *   *   *   *   *

St. Paul's was packed. Ebone´ had asked Mitzi to walk with her family, but she didn't feel comfortable doing that so she, Crystal and, of course, Sundae, went together. Oleeta met them at the church. The service was due to start at five o'clock - it was now five ten, and they had just about managed to get seats together. She had spoken to Ebone´ earlier that afternoon, and she was really upset. She and her sisters had been arguing about the funeral arrangements since Mrs. Simons had closed her eyes. It was so sad that whenever someone died, there always had to be some confusion about the funeral. Mitzi always said she was going to put her wishes in writing. Perhaps she should get started - tomorrow was obviously not promised to anyone. Ebone´ and her sister, Sherry, had wanted the funeral in the morning, but Cee Cee and Dee Dee wanted it late so 'everybody' would be able to get time off from work. Who cared if people couldn't get time off? The people who mattered would be there. But since Cee Cee was the eldest, she got her way. There had been a lot of arguing about the way the funeral notice should be done. Cee Cee wanted to name her father as a survivor. A deceased person cannot be survived by a dead person. It always annoyed Mitzi and Oleeta when they read that in the paper. It was ridiculous really, and the undertaker - although he had to abide by his instructions - should put his foot down. Naturally Ebone´ didn't want Eric Simons' name in the paper at all, but Mitzi told her that he was the other girls' father and maybe it could be in there somewhere - even though Madge had killed the S.O.B. Then Sherry wanted to name every single friend her mother had ever had in her lifetime, and the others thought that was tearing it and only put two of her closest friends' names in the notice. People thrived on that - having their name in the paper as 'special friend', which was fine if that was truly what you were. Half of her 'friends' probably never even went to see her while she was sick - probably never even baked her a pan of macaroni and cheese or made her a cup of tea or took her to the doctor. But they would be right up front - chief mourners - crying and screaming and consumed with more grief than the woman's children. Mitzi often found that there was always some person - a fifth cousin or somebody - who wanted to take over. "Oh, I know your mama would have wanted this or preferred that," or "I think it would be better if you did this or that." And don't talk about when the procession got to the graveyard and the attention-seekers started that screaming and fainting. She and Sundae had been to a funeral once where a guy was burying his wife, and he got to the grave and started screaming, "I wanna go, too! I'm jumping in with her! Baby, I love you, don't leave me!" Then the fool jumped over to the other side of the grave, fell down and started pounding the ground. Somebody should have given him a good swift kick in the behind. That night he had another woman at the wake. She understood grief and grieving, and she knew how she felt when her daddy and her grandfather had died. It hurt, and no one could control crying - even weeping and perhaps even fainting, but there it was something so 'un-sacred' about being phony at a funeral. She thought it showed total disrespect for the departed, and everybody could see right through the facade, so she wished people would just quit doing it. Ebone´ and her sisters had also argued about what they should bury their mother in. The really sad thing about that was that Mrs. Simons had picked out her dress, but Cee Cee thought she didn't look good in that colour, so she picked out something else. Mitzi had never heard of such lunacy. She should have enough respect for her mother to doggone-well bury her in what she wanted. And furthermore, what did it matter whether she looked good in it or not? She would be so stiff and proud, she wouldn't care if she had her pajamas on - but bury the woman in what she requested. Cee Cee also wanted - it seemed Cee Cee wanted a lot - for her to be buried in all her jewelry, but Ebone´ thought they should take it off and share it amongst themselves, which made sense. Why send good gold to the grave? As materialistic as that may sound, it was senseless to bury valuables, which could have sentimental value. Ebone´ must have gotten her way, because when they went up to view the body, Mrs. Simons didn't have one piece of jewelry on. She had a million pictures in the casket though, pictures of her daughters and her grandchildren. And her glasses were in there. Mitzi could never understand that either. Maybe they thought she would need them wherever she was going. But she figured that if a person were going to heaven, the good Lord would restore the eyesight, and if they were going to hell, why would they want to see what was happening down there? She was going to talk to an undertaker one day and get a few things straight once and for all. She needed to know these things.

As they stood for the procession, she saw Wendell over to her right. He was looking at her, and she nodded. He nodded back. He probably knew that Ebone´ had told her that he was her father and would talk to her about it later. She wondered how he was feeling right now. Sad, she was sure and probably full of regrets. Ebone´ told her that he had come to see her mama while she was away, and she seemed at peace after he left. Their story was probably such a sad one.

"I am the salvation and the light..." the minister's voice rang out. Ebone´ looked absolutely awful. She had on a brown baby-doll dress that just hung, her hair was slapped back, and she had no makeup on. Poor sight - her eyes were red, but she wasn't crying. She was walking with her eighteen year-old nephew who looked high. Cee Cee was crying so hard her boyfriend had to practically drag her into church. Sherry and

Dee Dee were crying softly as were some of Ebone´'s nieces
and nephews. One of Mrs. Simons' friends read the obituary
and pronounced everybody's name wrong. It was embar-
rassing. Why didn't these people get all this stuff straight
beforehand? No, she probably called the girls, begging to read
it, to get her share of attention and wasn't close enough to
know the names of the woman's family. Ebone's nieces sang a
song that reduced everybody to tears - even the minister. They
sang 'Don't Cry for Me'. Mitzi had never heard it before, but it
was heart-wrenching. The girls were twelve and fourteen, and
the more they sang, the more they cried, and the more they
cried, the harder they sang. It upset the family terribly, and by
the end of the song, Cee Cee had run out of church and Ebone´
was weeping. Mitzi knew she wouldn't be able to hold up too
long and just prayed she would be all right. They still had to
get through the burial.

Mitzi's heart bled for her friend at the graveyard. They were
at St. Anne's in Southampton. Someone let out a loud, animal
wail, and Ebone´ sank to her knees at the grave and sobbed.
Cee Cee was screaming for her mama not to go, and Dee Dee
ran from the graveyard. Sherry was the strongest and was
trying to hold everybody together, which was impossible.
Oleeta hugged Mitzi who was crying softly, not so much for
Mrs. Simons, but for Ebone´ and the anguish she must have
been feeling. As they left the graveyard, Mitzi spotted Wendell
from behind and stopped to talk to him. A tear rolled down his
face as he turned around, which took Mitzi by surprise. "I'm
sorry, Wendell," she said as she hugged him. He hugged her
back and fought to hold back tears.

The minister had announced in church that there would be
no wake following the burial, but that meant absolutely nothing
to Bermudians. It was supposed to be just a family dinner, but
Ebone´ had told Mitzi to come to the house afterward. Oleeta
said she was going home, but naturally Sundae wanted to go,
so Crystal agreed to go for a while. She had told Raoul to
come and pick her up from Mitzi's house later. They could
hardly find a place to park at the house. There were just as

many people at the house as were in church. Mitzi went in to find Ebone´, and the kitchen was full of food. They had everything - big foil pans of chicken, peas and rice, Spanish rice, ox tails, macaroni and cheese, beans, potato salad, beets, cole slaw, rolls - it was a big buffet. And, of course, there was plenty of rum.

Mitzi went down the hall and found Ebone´ in her mama's bedroom talking to one of her aunts, telling her how her mother had taken her last breath in the same spot she was sitting. Her aunt responded by telling her that she should come in her mama's room every day so she could feel her spirit and that was the only way she would get over it. Mitzi felt like slapping the woman for saying something so ridiculously morbid. Mitzi had always thought the woman was illiterate anyway, and she also always thought it was better to be silent and thought a fool than to open your mouth and remove all doubt. She told Ebone´ that she just wanted to make sure she was all right, and she wasn't staying long. Ebone´ asked her to stay in the room with them, but Mitzi didn't feel like listening to any senseless rhetoric - if that wasn't a contradiction in terms. She had never seen Ebone´ look so distraught. Given the circumstances, she couldn't say she would have looked any better in her shoes. She was just glad the hardest part was over.

Mitzi went back into the kitchen and found Crystal with a plate of food and Sundae with a drink. A little old man - probably one of Ebone´'s relatives, was talking to Crystal and practically spitting on her. He looked drunk, and Crystal was holding her plate to the side so her food wouldn't be showered.

"I know what you mean," she was saying to the little drunk and cutting her eyes at Sundae who was standing behind the man, laughing. By now he was just about resting his head on her shoulder and looking up at her, smiling. " 'Scuse me, ace-boy," she said when she had had enough. She turned to look at Mitzi who was laughing, too.

"I'm scared of you, Crystal."

"I should be scared of him," Crystal said, nodding at the old timer. "He stinks, his breath stinks and his teeth look like a canteen of broken bottles. All these women here, why the hell did he have to pick on me? On second thought, why the hell isn't he somewhere pushing up daisies? You think it would be tacky if I put some foil over this plate and had a take-out?"

"Very tacky," Sundae said. "Just like the statement you just made - you're at a wake, you couldn't think of anything else to say? And furthermore, your boyfriend's waiting for you." She was looking at 'toothless', who was staring at Crystal's butt and smiling.

Crystal cut her eyes at him. "What a pervert. I bet you he wouldn't be smiling like that if I put my foot up his backside. I'm going outside. You lot coming?" She didn't wait for an answer. There was a mob of people in the yard.

"What time is Raoul coming for you?" Mitzi asked Crystal.

She looked at her watch. "He told me to call him when I was ready, and I'm ready. I'll call him from your house."

"I'm just going to get a drink, then we can leave."

"Bring me one, Mitzi, a rum and coke." Crystal shouted to her.

"No. Ask your boyfriend to get it. He's coming now."

"Oh hell!" Crystal was ready to tell him to get lost, but he walked past and ignored her.

Sundae thought it was hilarious. "Your stuff's gone bad already, Crys, and you haven't even taken him home yet!"

"Shut up."

On the drive to Mitzi's house, Crystal told her that she and Raoul were in the process of buying a house, and they expected everything to be finalized by the end of the month.

"Where is it?"

"Cobbs Hill. It's really nice, three bedrooms and two baths."

"Congratulations, sister. I'm really happy for you guys." Mitzi was genuinely happy for Crystal and her husband. They were good people and had a good thing going together. They both worked hard and deserved happiness. "Let me know when you're ready to start moving, and I'll give you a hand."

"It should be early next month. The house is empty now, so we can really move in whenever we're ready. Some guy built it and decided he couldn't afford to pay for it, so that's how we came to get it."

"At least you'll be a little closer to my house now."

"Please don't tell Raoul that. He thinks you and I are married now when we talk on the phone."

"Oh Lord, he probably hasn't even thought about this. I will be more than happy to inform him that he should be seeing a lot more of me after you move." They both laughed as Mitzi parked in her yard and the security light came on. "I tried to find Ebone´ to tell her we were leaving, but I don't know where she was."

"You would have never found her with all those people there."

"She'll probably stay over there tonight. I'll call her in the morning before I go work." She opened the door and turned the hall light on.

"Mitzi, can I borrow your black top? You know, the one you got from 'True Reflections'."

"I suppose so. Just bring it back, please. You borrow things, keep them for months, then swear down they were yours all along."

Crystal laughed. She knew she was guilty. "I'm calling Raoul."

"Go 'head. I'll get the top." She went into her room and looked in her closet for the top. It wasn't there. She came back down the hall. "Ebone´ must have borrowed it." She opened the door to Ebone´'s room and smelled cigarette smoke. She turned the light on and found Ebone´ sitting on her bed in total darkness with her legs crossed. She was holding something in her hand. "Ebone´! I'm sorry, I didn't know you were here. What you doin' home? I thought you were still at your mama's."

Ebone´ looked at her. She had a strange look on her face. "I had something to do. And plus, I don't have a mama any more, remember? She died." She spoke very slowly. Mitzi could sense that something was really wrong.

Mitzi sat on the bed. "What did you have to come home to do?" She was starting to get worried. She looked over on the night stand and saw a half bottle of vodka. She hadn't noticed it when she first came in. "You didn't drink all that yourself, did you, Ebone'? Ebone' nodded. "Why?"

"Because, I told you, I have something to do." She closed her eyes.

Mitzi's heart was racing. "What's in your hand?" Ebone' didn't answer. "What's in your hand, Ebone'?" She raised her voice a little, trying to sound authoritative.

Ebone' shook her head. "Nothing. Leave me alone." Mitzi grabbed her hand and tried to pry it open. Ebone' tried to get away from her, but Mitzi stood up and used both hands.

"Oh my God!! Crystal!!" Ebone' had half a bottle of prescription pills in her hand. What the hell are you doing, girl?!" She grabbed the bottle from her, the top came off, and they scattered over the room. Crystal rushed in.

"What happened? ... Ebone', I didn't know you were here."

"Crystal, call the ambulance. I think she took some pills and drank... did you take any, Ebone'?" She just sat with her eyes closed. "Answer me!! Did you take any?!"

"Maybe I did, maybe I didn't." Mitzi began shaking her. "Tell me, girl!!" Mitzi was crying. She held her by the shoulders. "Look at me. Look at me!" Ebone' opened her eyes and looked up at her. "Don't do this to me, Ebone'. This isn't fair. Did you drink all that vodka?" Ebone' nodded slowly. "Did you take the pills?" She held her breath and waited for her to answer. She said nothing. Mitzi looked at the bottle. It had Madge Simons' name on it. "Ebone', why do you have your mama's medication?" Tears streamed down her face, and Crystal stood by the door, crying too.

" 'Cause, I wanna be with her. I don't wanna be here no more."

"Oh Jesus. Ebone' please... how many did you take? Tell me... please God, make her tell me."

"I didn't take any. Yet." She started to cry.

Thank you, Lord. "Are you sure?" She nodded with her eyes closed. She looked so helpless and pathetic. Her hair was a mess, her dress was wet, and she stank of liquor.

"You want me to call and cancel the ambulance?"

"No, let them come. They'll decide if she should go to the hospital when they come. I think she should."

"I don't wanna go to the hospital. I don't need to go. I just want to die."

"You don't want to die, honey. Everything's gonna be all right." Mitzi held her - once again - and rocked her. They were both still crying, and so was Crystal.

"What can I do?" Crystal asked, feeling helpless.

"Would you get me a wet face cloth, please?" Ebone´'s face was covered in perspiration, and she felt hot. It was probably the vodka. "Talk to me, Ebone´. Why you doin' this?"

" 'Cause, I don't have nothin' to live for. I have nothin', and I am nothin'. Nobody loves me. Nobody gives a damn about me." She looked up at Mitzi like a lost child. Her eyes were swollen. Crystal brought the face cloth, and Mitzi gently wiped her face.

"Ebone´, I love you. I care about you. You know that - you're my girl. I know you're hurting right now, but time will heal all of this."

"No it won't. Everything just keeps getting worse. Every man I have ever loved has hurt me and left me. Ricky didn't even come to my mama's funeral. I was sure he would be there for me."

Will she just forget about that confounded boy? "Do yourself a favour and pretend that Ricky was buried today, too. He doesn't exist, Ebone´. Start over." She wasn't sure if that was the right thing to say, but that's how she felt. They heard sirens.

"The ambulance is here," Crystal said, running out to meet them.

"Ebone´, please don't do this." Mitzi was desperately pleading with her. "Taking your life is a very selfish act."

"So what? I'm a selfish person. You always tell me that." Ebone´ was shaking and rocking herself.

Oh hell, Ebone´. Now is not the time to start listening to what I tell you. I should keep my mouth shut sometimes. Mitzi felt a run in her stocking as she tried to think of what to say next. Crystal came back, followed by the ambulance crew. She had briefly told them what had happened, and Mitzi explained that she said she hadn't taken any pills but had drunk almost half a bottle of vodka. The nurse looked at the prescription bottle and asked Ebone´ if she was sure she hadn't taken any.

"I said no, didn't I?" She was very agitated and more than a little drunk.

"Ebone´, they're only trying to help you." She sucked her teeth and closed her eyes. She was still sitting in the middle of her bed, and the nurse was holding her hand. She was adamant about not going to the hospital, so the nurse took her pressure, checked her other vital signs and suggested Mitzi get in touch with a psychiatrist as soon as possible. Ebone´ definitely needed help - she had needed it before this episode. The paramedics left after giving Mitzi a number to call if anything else happened. Crystal walked out with them and met Raoul coming in the house. He looked horrified and held her as she cried and told him the story. She had never experienced anything like that, and it really shook her up. Crystal told him she didn't want to leave them yet, so she and Raoul sat on the couch and turned on the television.

"Damn, baby, I didn't know what to think when I saw the ambulance. I prayed nothing was wrong with you." He was caressing her arm, and she was still crying. He kissed her forehead. "That's some deep stuff Ebone´'s going through. I'm glad you girls came when you did."

"I don't even want to think about that, honey." She laid her head on his chest, and he stroked it.

"Crys?"

"Huh?"

"Don't ever do that to me, sweetheart. If ever anything's bothering you, just know that you can talk to me."

"I know that." Her eyes were closed.

He looked down at her. "I love you."

"I know that, too." Raoul smiled and knew that his wife was indeed sure of his love.

Mitzi came out into the living room. "Hey, Raoul. Crystal, would you call Wendell for me? Ask him to come up here, please. If he's not at the restaurant, his number's in the book."

Crystal sat up. "You want me to tell him what happened?"

"Just tell him something happened to Ebone´, and I really need him to come." She got a glass of water for Ebone´ and went back into her room.

"You think I'm weak, don't you Mitzi?" She drank the water.

"No. But if you had taken those pills, then I would have thought so." Mitzi sat on the floor and leaned against the dresser.

"It just hurts so bad. I feel so numb and... desperate."

"Ebone´, I'm gonna tell you a few things, and you're probably going to think I'm preaching. But I need to preach right now." Probably for the first time ever, Ebone´ neither sucked her teeth nor rolled her eyes. She just leaned against her headboard, held her water glass and stared straight ahead. She was no longer crying. "I realize you feel like you have nowhere to turn - that, as you say - you feel desperate. My granny always says, 'With despair comes hope, and you won't see the dawn if you can't make it through the night.' There is always a way, Ebone´ Always. You have to believe that. Suicide is never the answer."

"At least I wouldn't have to be here to suffer anymore."

"But taking your life is a sin. The unforgivable sin. And the price you pay for committing it might be a hell worse than the hell you've lived. God gave you life - you don't have the authority to take it."

"Mitzi, I don't know nothin' 'bout all that stuff."

"Well get to know it. Look, I'm not a born again Christian or anything, and Lord knows I do my share of sinning, but I am spiritually led. You must believe that there's a power higher than yourself. Turn to that power and pray. Ask God to help you and then believe that He will."

"God?" She looked at Mitzi. "God? I think God has forgotten about me."

"God hasn't forgotten about you, Ebone'. He woke you up this morning." Mitzi was filled with conviction and needed Ebone' to feel it, too."

"He hasn't done much else for me, though."

"You didn't ask." She knelt beside Ebone''s bed. "When was the last time you prayed?"

"I don't know how to pray." Poor girl hadn't really been taught a thing about life. She was a terrible victim of circumstance - in many ways.

"If you know how to speak, you know how to pray." Ebone' sighed. "But before you go asking for anything, you must give thanks for what you've already been given - like life."

"Have you ever felt alone? Like you have nobody in the whole world?" She started to cry again and so did Mitzi. In the living room, Crystal couldn't stop her tears, and Raoul was still holding her.

"No, Ebone', I can't say that I have felt like that. But you don't have to feel that way either." She held her hand as tears rolled down her face. "Just believe, honey. Put your hand in God's hand - God's got your back, and so do I." Mitzi could barely talk. She had been so afraid when she thought her friend had overdosed. She was usually the strong one, but now she broke down.

"I just want to feel like something - somebody. I want to be of some value to the world."

Mitzi tried hard to stop crying. "By virtue of your being, you are of some value to the world. As Crystal's son says, 'God didn't make no junk'."

"Help me, Mitzi. Please help me." Ebone' sat on the edge of her bed and hugged Mitzi as she knelt at Ebone''s knees and hugged her, too. "I'm sorry, girl. You didn't deserve this..." Crystal knocked on the door and opened it.

"Wendell's here." Wendell stood beside her.

Ebone´ looked surprised. "You called Wendell?"

"Yeah. I think you might be needin' to talk to him right about now." Mitzi stood up, and Crystal held her hand and wiped her eyes. "Thanks for coming, Wendell," she said. "Talk to him, Ebone´. Let him know everything." Wendell touched her arm and slowly shook his head. Crystal took the vodka bottle from the night stand and hugged Mitzi as they left the room.

"You all right, honey?" Raoul asked Mitzi. She nodded, and the tears started again. Raoul hugged her as Crystal rubbed her back. "You want Crystal to stay here with you tonight?" He asked, still hugging her. She shook her head and stood back.

"I'll be okay."

"You sure, Mitzi? 'Cause Raoul can come for me in the morning."

"No. Wendell's here. I just need to get a bath and get in my bed."

"Well if you can't sleep and need to talk, call me."

"Thanks, you guys. I don't know what I would have done if I had been by myself." She hugged them together.

When they reached the car, Raoul stopped and held Crystal's shoulders. "Don't ever do that to me, baby. Don't ever leave me."

"I'm not going anywhere..."

"I don't love you because I need you, Crystal. I need you because I love you. And as long as there is breath in my body, there will never be a problem too big for you to deal with."

Crystal started to cry again. "I feel the same way, Raoul." They stood in Mitzi's yard and held each other under the half moon for a long time. Neither one of them wanted to let go.

Mitzi took her portable CD player in the bathroom and sat in a tub full of water, listening to Bee Bee and Cee Cee sing 'It's Okay'. She played it over and over until she got out of the tub.

She knelt at her bed to say her prayers. It seemed appropriate to be a little formal tonight. She had a lot to be thankful for. She prayed for Ebone´ - she needed help, and right now it looked like the Almighty was the only one who could help her. She prayed for the fortitude and tenacity to help her in every way she possibly could. While she was praying the phone rang twice. She was not about to interrupt this prayer for anybody. When she finished, she went into the kitchen and made a cup of 'Soothing Moments' tea. 'New York Undercover' was on, so she sat on the couch to watch it. Wendell was still in Ebone´'s room. Mitzi closed her eyes and laid her head back on the couch. What a week this had been. It seemed like months had passed since she had been back from her trip, and it hadn't even been a week. She suddenly realised that she and Macky still hadn't told their mother about the baby. He was probably in a panic - she would call him first thing in the morning and tell him that she would come to the house on Saturday morning, and they could tell her.

Mitzi felt someone shaking her foot and woke up to find Wendell standing over her. It was one o'clock, and she had fallen asleep on the couch. "Is she all right?" Mitzi was dog tired.

"Yeah." He smiled weakly and took his keys from his pocket. Now that she looked at Wendell, Ebone´ resembled him a little. Or did she? Was it just because she knew he was her father? No. They had the same eyes. Mitzi guessed Wendell was about fifty-four, fifty-five and good looking. He looked like he could have broken a few hearts in his day. He was only about five feet, seven inches tall and maybe about 180 pounds. He had dark brown hair, which was gray around the edges, with a patch of gray on top. "She'll be all right. We need to keep an eye on her for a while, and she wants to get help."

"There's a lady I know - Mrs. Swan - she's some type of clinical social worker. I'll call her tomorrow and ask her what we can do..."

"I would like to go to counseling or therapy or whatever, with her." He looked really concerned, and Mitzi knew he was.

Mitzi sighed. "I hope some good will come out of all this. Hopefully, all that has happened has been a means to an end of the pain she's endured all these years."

"Mitzi, I hope neither you nor Ebone´ hold me responsible for all this."

She shook her head. "Hey, you did what you had to do. I'm sure if it were up to you, it would have been different. I don't think any less of you, Wendell." She stood and pulled her robe tighter.

"Thanks for calling me, Mitzi. She really bared her soul in there - we both did. I want a relationship with her - I always have - and she said she needs me. It's not like I'm a stranger, so it shouldn't be too difficult." He walked to the door, and Mitzi followed. He stood at the door with his back to her and hung his head. When he turned around a few seconds later, there were tears in his eyes. He held Mitzi's hand. "I have wanted this for a long time, that's why I gave her a job, so I could at least be around her. I love her."

"Did you tell her that?"

He nodded. "Yes, I did." He kissed her cheek. "Thanks for looking out for my daughter, Mitzi. You're a good person."

She smiled. "Thanks, I try."

"Come by the restaurant and have dinner sometime. Bring your boyfriend."

"Ha! You don't want me to come any time soon, do you, Wendell?"

He laughed. "Night, Mitzi." She closed the door and went to check on Ebone´. She was changing her clothes.

"How you feel, Blackie?"

"A lot better. Thanks for calling Wendell. We talked about everything." Mitzi sat on the bed while she got under the cover.

"Ebone´, it's gonna be hard for you for a while, and you won't get over this right away, but just take one day at a time and look to tomorrow. I promise you, it'll get better." She paused. "You hear me, Ebone´?" She didn't answer. She was asleep. "I guess I do talk too much."

"I heard you, but I was praying, and I'm sure it's bad manners to interrupt a prayer."

"I'm sorry." *Well excuse me. Lord, you really do work fast, don't you?* Mitzi was still a little wary of leaving Ebone' alone, so she got under the cover. She needed to be near her.

"Hey, hey, just don't forget who you're lying next to when you turn over in the middle of the night, see? I know it's been a while since you've had anybody in your bed." She laughed a little. It was a start.

"I could go and get in my own bed, you know. I'm worried about your behind."

"Don't go, Mitzi. I'm just joking." She took a deep breath. "Thanks. For everything."

"Just don't do it again."

CHAPTER ELEVEN
Friday

Mitzi was tired - again. She got to work and found Ronald still grumbling. Not as bad as the day before, but grumbling anyway. As soon as she sat down, Sundae pounded on the door and ran into the office. "Mitzi!" She was jumping up and down.

"Knocking does not automatically entitle you to enter, Miss Tucker," Ronald complained.

"Oh Ronald, get over or go under whatever it is that's troubling you." Ronald got up and walked out. "Mitzi, I called you last night after I got home from the wake. Where were you?"

"It's a long story."

"Well, I'm really not interested anyway because, guess what?! The results of my G.E.D. were in my mailbox when I got home. I passed!!" She started jumping again, and Mitzi leapt from her chair and jumped with her.

"I knew you would, Sundae! Congratulations, girl!!" They were still hugging and jumping. Ronald came back in complaining about them acting like they were at a meat market. They ignored the comment. "Ronald, Sundae got her G.E.D.."

"That has made my day," he said, pounding on the computer keyboard. "Meanwhile, you have a lady waiting."

Sundae bent down and kissed him. "I love you, Ronald!" He gently pushed her away, and she and Mitzi laughed. "Let me go take care of my lady. I just wanted to let you know the news." She ran out.

"What's your problem, Ronald? Besides the fact that your wife is having another baby." Mitzi was still smiling. She needed some good news after the week she had had.

"Mitzi, I told you, I only wanted one child. We already have three. Pearl knew that. " He was still working on the computer.

"So when does Pearl go to court?"

He stopped typing and turned to look at her. "For what?" He was frowning.

"For raping you. Ronald, does your wife force you to have sex with her?" He sucked his teeth and turned back to the computer. "I'm really surprised at you. You guys have been married all these years, you aren't paying rent, and it ain't like all your children are grown up already. You lot are young, Ronald. Think of it as a blessing."

He looked at her again. "And just how many children have you been blessed with?"

"None. But I wish I had at least one. I know that having children is a wonderful thing." She walked to the door. "And if it wasn't meant for you to have all these children, you all wouldn't be having them. She walked out and closed the door. Ronald wondered if he was being a little silly. Maybe Mitzi was right, and he should be happy.

Sundae had her certificate framed and on her work station. She had told everybody. "Ladies, I think a celebration for Sundae is in order." Mitzi announced. "What you doin' after work, Sundae?"

"Probably going to a funeral," Ronald said, coming from the office. Then he smiled. "Congratulations, Sundae. I'm proud of you." She started to say something, but she was too excited to be bothered.

"Thank you, darlin'. I'm not doing anything this evening, Mitzi. Why?"

"I think a party is in order. We could call somewhere and see if somebody could make us some..."

"Horses' ovaries," Sundae said. Mitzi looked horrified.

"Hors d'oeuvres, Sundae." Mitzi corrected. "We can get a coupla bottles of wine too and have a little set here after work."

"Oh yes we can! I love a party!" Michae - the shampoo girl - said, clapping her hands. Everybody looked at her. "You better go and fold those towels," Sundae said, hitting her with a towel.

"All right you lot, we have clients, so let's get back to work." Mitzi went to cut her lady's hair. "Ronald, when you get a minute, would you call and arrange some refreshments for this evening? And call Pearl and ask her if she would like to come." He glared at her and then smiled. She smiled back as she pumped the chair up. She knew he would come to his senses eventually. One of these days somebody would listen to her problems for a change. She had just started cutting when Ronald buzzed her and told her she had a call and that it was important. *What now?* She hoped nothing had happened to Ebone'. It was Melba.

"Hi, I called you last night to find out what the ambulance was doing at your house."

"How you know?" She was still pissed at Melba for opening her big mouth to Sundae, and she still hadn't had the opportunity to tell her off.

"Mrs. Rawlins called my mama and told her that it was some excitement in the neighbourhood and the ambulance was at your house. What happened?" How much did she really care? She hadn't bothered to come and see if something had happened to her, nor had she called before now.

"Mrs. Rawlins is too pokey - she don't miss a thing. Ask her if she knows her daughter is on drugs and selling herself."

"What's with you, Mitzi?" Melba was shocked by her harsh attitude.

"I have a bone to pick with you, okay Melba? But I'm busy right now, so I'll have to talk to you later."

"Whatever. But who did the ambulance come for last night?" She was amazing. Mitzi was not about to tell her what happened.

"Me. But I'm all right now. Not that you really care."

"I do care, Mitzi. Why you think I'm calling you?"

"Melba, if you really cared, you would have found out from somebody last night if something had happened to me. Why didn't you call Sundae? Like you did last weekend."

Melba was silent. "She told you?" She asked solemnly.

"Look, I have people waiting for me. I'll catch up with you later. I have a few things to say to you."

"Why don't you come up to my house when you knock off, and we can talk? 'Cause it's not the way you think it is."

Right. It's never the way anybody thinks it is when it comes to you. "No, I can't do that because we're having a party for Sundae here after work."

"For what?"

"Ask her the next time you talk to her."

"Oh, so you lot's having a party after work?" She was bucking for an invitation, but she wasn't getting one.

"Yep. I have to go, Melba. Talk to you... whenever." Mitzi hung up. *Don't mess with me!* She smiled to herself because she knew right now Melba was fuming - because Mitzi knew what she had done and because she wasn't invited to the party. She hated to be left out. Too damn bad. "Ronald, would you also call Crystal for me and tell her to come by later?"

Mitzi had never seen her girls work so fast. Promise them a party, and they break their necks getting clients out. They were all finished by six fifteen. Ronald's brother-in-law brought the food at quarter to six - a big spread. Codfish balls, chicken wings, a raw vegetable platter and a cheese, crackers and fruit platter. "He got this together real quick, didn't he, Ronald? I better line him up for my mama's reception." She picked at the vegetables.

Crystal walked in, and Mitzi explained what the celebration was about. "Sundae got her G.E.D."

"Sundae who?" Crystal looked around while everybody laughed, including Sundae.

"Girl, nothing will upset me tonight," Sundae said, clapping.

"You know I'm proud of you, sister. How come I didn't know anything about all this before?"

" 'Cause, contrary to your belief, there are just some things in life that are not for you to know, Crystal." Sundae was in her face.

"Ohh, contrary - a new dictionary word already. Go on with your bad self, girl." Crystal piled fish balls and meat balls on a plate and then started eating with her fingers as if she were famished.

"I want to make a toast," Mitzi announced. "Here's to my girl, Sundae, who took off her ankle chains and got educated." She and Crystal laughed, and Crystal almost choked on the food in her mouth.

"See, I am not amused. You lot are doggin' me behind my back, and my back ain't even turned."

"And she read Diana Ross' book. I am impressed." Crystal was getting more food.

"We are all very proud of you, Sundae," Mitzi said seriously. "And to show you how proud we are, here is a little token of our love and admiration." She gave her a giftwrapped box. She had sent Angela out earlier to buy her a Cross pen and pencil set and perfume. Sundae hugged and kissed everybody, thrilled with her gifts.

"Thanks, everybody. This stuff looks real expensive. Which one is the pencil? Or is it two pens?" She examined the gift.

"Not used to anything, are you, Sundae?" Ronald asked, sipping wine with Pearl at his side.

"You know she's not," Crystal chimed in.

"You know I have papers on you, don't you, Crystal?" Sundae took delight in watching her face fall.

"Okay, Sundae. I'm not saying nothing else, except that I think you are an exceptionally intelligent person who will go far in life." Sundae held her hand up to Crystal's face.

"Save it. 'Cause I'll still expose you. This is my night, dammit! And I'll do what I want, so don't step on my corns." She was laughing, and Crystal shook her head. "I want to say a little something." Sundae got serious. "I really have to thank

Mitzi for this. She is not only an employer, but a very good friend - although she makes sure that I don't forget that she is my employer." Mitzi smiled. "Anyway, she has always pushed me to do better than I was doing. I started here as a shampoo girl, and she pushed me to get my license and become a stylist. Now I do more business than her." They all laughed. Sundae was in her element. "But seriously, Mitzi has played a big part in what I have achieved today. It's not a master's degree or anything, but to me it's like a Ph.D. She always told me not to settle for anything less than I was capable of. I owe her a lot - she gave me a chance to prove myself, and this is just the beginning of what's to come."

"And the end of this damn speech, I hope," Crystal said, pouring more wine.

"Just give me a few more minutes." Everybody groaned.

"Psych. I'm finished. Thank you, Mitzi. And you, too, Crystal. I couldn't have done it without the two of you for friends." She hugged Mitzi.

"If I knew you were gonna mention me in your acceptance speech, I wouldn't have said all that stuff. I feel bad." Crystal said, looking sincere. Sundae went to hug her. "Oh well, I'll get over it." She turned her back, and Sundae put her arms around her and laughed.

Ronald packed the leftover food in the fridge for lunch the next day. Mitzi had put some in a container to take home for Ebone'. She had called her earlier, and she was in her room, watching TV. Wendell had sent her flowers and told her to take as much time off from work as she needed. Mitzi hoped she wouldn't become a recluse. She would find some things for her to do to get out of the house.

"I really enjoyed that, you lot," Sundae said. "Why don't we go out for drinks and a little dinner sometime soon?" They were walking to their cars. Mitzi was taking Crystal home.

"Just mention food, and you know I'll be there," Crystal said. She had taken some of the leftover food - for Raoul, she had said - but Mitzi and Sundae knew that Raoul would never put his chops on it. It would probably be gone before they reached Cox's Hill.

"How 'bout tomorrow night?" Sundae said, trying to make plans for a night out.

"I don't know about tomorrow night," Mitzi said. "Ebone´'s still a bit down, and I don't want to leave her home by herself. Maybe next weekend."

"We definitely have to go before I move," Crystal said. "Because I'll be too busy around that time. And broke, so let's go soon."

I didn't know you were moving, Crystal." Sundae wasn't pleased about not knowing this news.

"That's because, my dear graduate, contrary to your belief, there are some things..."

"Don't worry with all that, Crystal! You're childish, girl."

"Both of you are, if you ask me," Mitzi said, opening the car door.

"Who asked?" they both asked together.

"Oh, you wanna walk home, Mrs. Outerbridge?"

Crystal ran around to get in the car. "I'm just joking. You can't take a joke? Bye, Sundae. And now that you have your Ph.D., change your name - named after a day of the week. What's your mama's number? And furthermore, you're not sacred enough to be named Sundae, slut." She slammed the door, and Sundae got in her car.

"You shouldn't drink, you know, Crystal. You are a perfect idiot when you've had a few." Mitzi was laughing and shaking her head.

"I know, I keep telling myself that. And I know Raoul's gonna take advantage of me when I get home. I wonder if he's sleep."

"Just say no."

She looked at Mitzi. "You fullish? I ain't that drunk."

When Mitzi got home, Ebone´ was in the living room watching TV and eating ice cream. Her hair was combed, and she had on shorts and a tee shirt. Mitzi had expected to find her in her bed in pajamas. This was a good sign. She had put the flowers in a vase and rested it on the dining table. They were beautiful carnations with one rose in the middle. Wendell had told her that the rose represented her.

"He called you?"

"No. I called him to thank him for the flowers."

Come on now, where is the real Ebone'? 'Cause this sure ain't the one I know. "That was nice of you, Ebone'. He must have felt good."

"Why you say that?"

"No reason. He was just probably glad to hear from you." She didn't want to knock the dust and mess with progress. "You hungry?"

"Nah. Wendell sent David up here with some supper for me."

"He's taking care of his girl, isn't he?"

Ebone' smiled. "I guess so."

"Feels good, doesn't it?" She nodded. "I called and made an appointment for you to see a psychiatrist today."

"Do you have to use that word?"

"It's what he is, Ebone', and that's what you need right now."

"It sounds like I'm crazy."

"Ebone', there is no longer a stigma attached to seeing a psychiatrist. In fact, he told me that I would be surprised at the amount of people in Bermuda who come to see him. In this day and age almost everybody has a problem that they can't deal with alone, so they seek professional help."

"You don't seem to have any problems. Everything seems to work out for you."

"Believe me, Ebone' I have my share of problems, too. They may not be the same as yours or the next person's, but everybody has a cross to bear. And I get... down some days, but I focus on what life really means to me, why I'm here and what I want to accomplish in life, and that gets me through. I cry just like everybody else, but I keep going and try to see the lesson in what's happening. And I pray." She put the food in the fridge and took her shoes off. She was going to get a bath and get in her bed. As usual.

"I've been praying all day," Ebone´ said.

Mitzi raised her eyebrows. "You have? Do you feel any better?"

She shrugged her shoulders. "I don't know. I guess so."

"It's not gonna happen overnight. Just have faith in the Almighty, and like the minister said, 'He isn't gonna give you any more than you can handle'."

"He's sure takin' it to the hilt, though."

Mitzi smiled. "You can handle it."

"Not without you," Ebone´ said so low Mitzi could hardly hear her.

"What you say?"

Ebone´ cut her eyes. "You heard me."

Mitzi smiled and shook her head. "You're some child, Ebone´. I'm going to get a bath. Get your grocery list ready for tomorrow. You going shopping with me?"

Ebone´ shrugged her shoulders. "I think you should. Oh, let me call Macky... maybe I should go shopping by myself' cause I have to go down to my mama's and tell her 'bout Macky."

"What about him?"

"Between you, me and the door post, his girlfriend is pregnant."

Ebone´ looked at her. "Little Macky? Your mama's gonna kill him."

"That, she is."

"How come you have to tell her?"

"Well, he's gonna tell her, but he wants me to be there when he does."

"You weren't there when he made the baby." She lit a cigarette.

"I know, but he wants my support, and I don't like turning my back on people."

Ebone´ smiled. "Yeah, that's true. Don't worry, your day will come."

"When? When? Before the year two thousand, you think? I can't take much more."

"Don't be dramatic, Mitzi."

Mitzi cut her eyes. "Night girl. I'm moving early tomorrow, so would you open the house if you're going to be here?" Ebone' nodded while she flicked the channels with the remote control.

Mitzi started running her bath water and called Macky to tell him she would definitely be there in the morning. He told her that if she didn't come this time, he would tell Mama without her. Was he threatening her? *Make my day.* After her bath, she got a Tahitian Tangerine Bacardi Breezer, closed her door and listened to her Isley Brothers CD while she read the weekend papers. About half an hour later, there was a knock on her door.

"Open." She didn't look up because she was sure it was Ebone'. It wasn't, it was Melba, and Mitzi's face fell.

"Hey." Melba stood at the door, unsure if she should come in.

"You can come in." Mitzi kept reading the papers. She was sitting in the middle of her bed, legs crossed, in her pajamas. She could be found like this on any Friday night that she was at home - which was quite often these days. She drank some of her Breezer. Melba sat in the green chair beside Mitzi's bed and picked up the *Mid Ocean* newspaper.

"Want a Breezer?" Mitzi asked, still not looking at her.

"No thanks. I can't stay long."

Of course you can't. You have to get your butt home to Roger.

"So, what's up?" Melba asked, obviously uncomfortable.

"Tell me."

"Listen Mitzi, I just came to apologise..."

"Are you sorry for what you did or because you got busted?" Mitzi interrupted and turned to face her.

Melba sighed. "I had no right to tell Sundae what you told me."

"So why did you, Melba?"

" 'Cause if Sundae had a problem, I wanted to help her."

"Come on, Melba, you don't give a damn about Sundae's problems. You just wanted to have something on her, that's all."

"No I..."

"Yes you did. That's your m.o., Melba. You're always looking down on people, especially Sundae. I mean, we girls are sisters and tight and everything, but you seem to take pleasure in belittling Sundae and whoever else would let you."

"Oh, you all don't make fun of her?" She got defensive.

"Yes, we all do, but that's what we do, make fun of her. She knows we lot are joking with her, but you dig deep. And I am pissed that you went back and told her what I said. You must have known it would hurt her." Mitzi had been waiting a while to say this, and she spoke with acrimony. "You are no better than any one of us, Melba. But no, you walk 'round like Miss Omnipotent herself." She liked big words, let her figure that one out. Melba was quiet. She was probably trying to click into her mental thesaurus. *Deal with that, miss know-it-all.*

"Look, I know I have my ways, but I don't mean anything by it. And I don't think I'm omnipotent. I know I'm no higher or mightier than any of you, but that's probably just the way I come across."

Damn, she knows what it means. "Well, sometimes you're just a bit overbearing." She toned her voice down a bit and leaned back against her pillows. "What you might need to do is clean up your own back yard first."

"Meaning what?" She looked at Mitzi.

"I ain't saying nothin'." She folded her arms across her chest.

"Talking about me and Roger?"

"I never said that." She reached for her Breezer.

"Well, I know that's what you're talking about." She paused. "I have started to clean up my backyard. I told Roger to leave. He should be out of the house tomorrow."

Mitzi almost choked on her drink. "What happened to you two?"

"Come on, Mitzi, I should have done this a long time ago - we both know that. It was inevitable. Roger makes me miserable and has for the last ten years."

"I'm shocked, Melba. " She truly was. "I just thought you were content living like that."

"I take so much, then I act."

"It took you ten years to decide that you needed to act?" *Shut up, Mitzi, she didn't ask your advice so don't act like her.*

"Well, I loved Roger. I still love him, so I just kept hoping things would change. I thought if he saw how much I loved him and was willing to stay with him, he would change."

"People don't change Melba, they just become the person they always were."

"True. And Roger is moody, jealous and possessive. And he has a bad temper."

"He hits you?"

"No. Never, but when we argue, he says some real nasty things, and sometimes they hurt more than licks would."

"I know that story. But you know why he's moody, don't you?"

"Yeah. I used to think it was me until Crystal opened my eyes."

"You think he uses more than herb?"

"I don't know. He says that he hates coke 'cause his brother put his mama through hell by being on it. But I wouldn't be surprised if he uses it. He has some shady characters coming to the house sometimes."

"So what is he sayin' about moving out?"

"He don't want to go, but I told him he has no choice. I want him out and that's that. It's my daddy's house. As soon as I told him that he had to leave, he started making off, saying that I thought I could control him because we lived in my daddy's house and that I think he's not good enough for my family, but I could never make it a week without him and... blah, blah, blah. When he realized I wasn't paying him any mind, he changed his song and started telling me that he loves me, and he can't make it without me, and he would change and prove himself to me..." She waved her hand. "He should have thought about that a long time ago.

"Your daddy will be pleased."

"Right. 'Cause you know he was never fussy about me and Roger living like that anyway. And he's gotten worse over the years since we haven't gotten married all this time."

"And that's another thing, Melba. Maybe it's not my place to say, but why haven't you two gotten married all these years? I mean, not that you have to, but why have you been good enough for him to shack up with all this time but not good enough to marry?"

Melba sighed. "Roger asked me to marry him once about seven years ago, and I told him I wasn't ready, and he never asked me again. I think I hurt him by turning him down. Then, about four years ago, I asked him if he wanted to get married, and he said he wasn't ready."

"Payback."

Melba nodded. "I guess so. But I guess it was for the best. We would have never made it. And, quite frankly, I feel I have outgrown Roger." She looked at Mitzi. "Not to sound like I'm better than him, or omnipotent or anything."

"All right, don't kill it." They both smiled. "Melba, I'm sorry you're going through what you are, but obviously you know what time it is."

"Yeah. It's time to live for Melba Scott."

"Tell me something. You two never wanted to have children? I mean, you've been together all these years - you're not still on the pill, are you? I know it's not really any of my business but..."

"I really don't think Roger can make babies," Melba said quietly.

"I'm sorry. I shouldn't have asked you that."

"I don't mind. That's been bothering me, too. I met Roger when Melvin was six. He's sixteen now, and I always wanted him to have a brother or sister. Now, he's out of my house and all but his own man."

Melba had had her son when she was seventeen, and he was going to school in Atlanta now. Mitzi always thought that Melba just wanted him out of her hair so she could devote all her time and attention to Roger. Now she didn't even have him.

"I have been off the pill for six years and have never gotten caught. Roger and I may have had our differences, but we have always had a very active sex life. And he has no other children that I know of. I had a hysterosalpingogram about three..."

"A who?"

"A test to determine if I could conceive or not, and I was fine. I've had all my parts tested. Roger always said that our timing was off, but I think he knows he's sterile."

"I don't know if you know this..."

"Yes, marijuana. They say it diminishes a man's sperm count." She stood up. "Anyway, those apples have fallen already, and I don't feel like talking about this anymore. I just want to tell you again that I'm sorry, and I hope I didn't cause any serious damage between you and Sundae."

"No, we're cool. Sundae's a real forgiving sister. Good thing she is 'cause I don't think she'd be speaking to me today if she weren't."

"So what were you all celebrating tonight?" She was looking a Mitzi's collection of nail polish on her dresser."

"She got her G.E.D. yesterday. She had been borrowing money to pay a tutor. She was up studying 'til all hours in the morning, and some days she was just too tired to come to work. So I was wrong about her being on drugs."

"I don't even have a G.E.D., and I never even graduated from high school either." She looked at Mitzi and picked up her bag. "I guess that makes her a better person than I am."

Mitzi shook her head. "She's not a better person than you because she got a G.E.D. - anybody with a brain can do that. She may be a bigger person than both of us though, because she let our friendship come before some petty gossip. I was prepared to go a real long time without speaking to you, Melba. But that don't make sense. I've had a couple of days to be snotty to you, and it felt good at the time but..."

"Maybe we could learn a few things from Sundae." She smiled.

"Yeah. She may not use the right words or big words and she may be a little flaky and slow, but she's a beautiful person. We will always tease Sundae about the things she does, but it has never been, nor will it ever be, my intention to do it in a way that hurts her. Sure, she talks about other people - she lives to gossip, we all do, but she would never hurt one of us. She can take a joke, and she doesn't care if we laugh in her face, but she hurts sometimes, just like we do."

Melba sighed. "I know and maybe that's why I treat her the way I do - because she's such a free spirit, and I have subconsciously envied her, I guess. I should call her and apologise."

"And I bet you she'll act as if all this never happened."

"Anyway, I'm outta here. Gotta go home and face whatever's waiting for me." Mitzi got up to walk her out. "Sisters?" Melba asked, tilting her head to the side, waiting for an answer.

Mitzi smiled and nodded her head. "Sisters." They hugged. "Hang tough, everything will be all right. It'll be hard, but you'll make it if you remember that you come first."

"I know. I've had all I can take, so I know I'll be strong. Roger's done danced on my nerves for the last time."

Mitzi lit an incense and lay in her bed as The Isleys sang, 'Voyage to Atlantis' and thought about Melba. Miss High and Mighty was being brought down a few buttonholes. But as mad as Melba made her sometimes, she felt for her now. She knew that Melba wouldn't back down and give in to Roger. When she made up her mind, her mind was made up. Mitzi was kind of happy because Roger was such a loser, and even Melba, with her stuck up self, deserved better. Was this the reason Mitzi didn't have a man? Was she being punished for being too judgmental, or was she just not about to go through unnecessary changes over any man? Was there such a life? A man who didn't put a woman through changes. If there was, it sure wasn't hitting her upside the head. Mitzi fell asleep watching 'Hangin' with Mr. Cooper'. She dreamt that Roger came to her house and started beating her up because he thought she had made Melba leave him. At that moment, Roger was at Melba's house, packing the last of her belongings into a truck. The house was practically bare. Roger would soon find out that that would probably be the biggest mistake he would ever make in life.

CHAPTER TWELVE
Saturday Morning

Mitzi had just started to iron when the phone rang. She didn't recognise the number on the I.D. box.

"Hello?"

"Good morning, may I speak to Ma... Mitzi, please?"

Who in the world is this man with this sweet voice? "Speaking."

"Hi, it's Maliq."

"Who..? Oh, hi Maliq." So much had happened this week, she had completely forgotten about Maliq.

"What, you forgot about me already?"

"Of course not. I'm just surprised to hear from you."

"You told me to call you when I finished the book. I finished it, so I'm calling to return it."

"You finished it already?" It hadn't even been a week since she met him on the plane.

"Yeah. I stayed home last night and finished it about two this morning."

You should have called me then. "Did you enjoy it?"

"Very much. It was deep. And funny at the same time. I could relate to a lot of things in there."

"You couldn't relate to Frankie too much, could you?" Mitzi asked. She was laughing and hoping he was nothing like Frankie.

"In some cases. I'm nothing like him, though - if that's what you want to know."

We are in sync, honey. "Yes, that's what I want to know." She remembered how cute Maliq was, and hearing his voice took her back to the day on the plane. She had truly enjoyed talking to him and was right now hoping he would be returning the book soon. Like today.

"So, when can I get your book back to you? Are you gonna be home today?"

"Actually, I'm on my way to my shop now."

"What time are you making to work?"

"I'm not. I'm off on weekends, but I'm going in to have my hair done."

"In those beautiful braids, I hope."

Sorry baby. "Sorry, I just took them out, but I think I'll put them back in early next week. But after that, I have a few things to do, and I probably won't be back home until about..." She looked at the clock on her night stand. It was eight-fifteen. "Four, maybe five o'clock this afternoon."

"Oh well, I have to go to Somerset this evening, would it be presumptuous of me to drop the book off at your house on my way?"

"Not at all. I live off of St. Anne's Road, on the South Shore side. Call me when you're on your way, and I'll give you directions. Would that be all right?"

"It's all right with me but I don't want your man to attack me when I get there. I'm a peaceful brother, and I don't fight."

She smiled. "Trust me, there will be no fighting." She wanted to say that that was because she didn't have a man, but she didn't. And furthermore, that was what he was fishing for, so he would just have to find that out when he got here. She hung up the phone and started getting ready. She had another long day ahead of her, but hopefully this one would end pleasantly. She crossed her fingers as she thought about it. Mitzi had her hair done and got to her mama's house at ten thirty. Oleeta was planting flowers in the garden and was surprised to see her.

"Hi, honey. You been to do granny's hair already?" She stood and brushed her pants off.

"Not yet. I'll call her now and tell her I'll be a bit later than usual - you know how she acts when I'm late."

"We all know that. What you doin' here?" They walked into the house, and Oleeta took her gardening gloves off.

"Nothin'. Just stopped by to talk." She called her granny who sarcastically grumbled that because she was getting old, nobody had time for her anymore. She had been saying that for about fifteen years, and nobody paid her any mind. Mitzi promised to be at her house within the hour. That should be enough time for them to tell Oleeta the news and for her to rant and rave to Macky and tell Mitzi off for not telling her sooner. Then she would go to her room, close the door and not come out until tomorrow morning. Macky could deal with her after that.

"I haven't had a chance to really talk to you this week, with Ebone''s mother dying and all. Thanks again for the trip, honey."

"The trip was from me and Macky. Where is he, anyway?" She picked up Oleeta's mail and began looking through it. She was nervous.

"Child, is that mail addressed to you? 'Cause if it is, you can pay the bills that are in there." She took it from Mitzi and put it in the mail basket. "Macky's in his room, I guess. I haven't seen him all morning. He's still acting a bit strange, so I'll just leave him."

Mitzi noticed flowers on the coffee table in the living room. "Your Mother's Day gift from George?" She was stalling.

"I'm not George's mother, nor am I the mother of his children. He gave them to me just because I'm me." Mitzi rolled her eyes, and Oleeta laughed. "Want some tea?"

No, but a stiff drink would do. Pour one for yourself, too - and Macky. She shook her head. "No thanks." She went down the hall to Macky's room and knocked on the door.

"Yeah?" he shouted. She opened the door and poked her head in.

"Hey."

"Hey. 'Bout time." He got up from his bed and came to the door. His room looked like a pig sty.

"Macky, don't be smart, 'cause I'll leave you on your own, okay?" Mitzi walked back toward the kitchen.

"Chill, girl." He was trailing behind her.

"What you children arguing about? Mornin', Macky." Oleeta was sitting at the table, reading the *Royal Gazette* and drinking a glass of water.

"This boy is too smart." Mitzi was getting tired of Macky's attitude and wanted to get this over with.

"What's your problem, Macky?"

"Mornin', Mama." He sighed and stood beside Mitzi. He was now quite a bit taller than she was and looking more and more like his daddy.

"Mama asked you what your problem is, Macky." Mitzi looked him in the eye, willing him to get to the point.

He looked at the floor. "I just have a lot on my mind right now, that's all."

"Well, instead of taking it out on everybody, why don't you just talk about it? You know that in this house, we talk about things."

Say it, Macky. "Tatyana's pregnant." *Not that bluntly. But at least it's out.* Oleeta looked at him then at Mitzi. Mitzi nodded, and Oleeta looked back at Macky.

"I beg your pardon."

Macky sat down - he probably felt faint. "Tatyana's having a baby."

Oleeta stared at him in horror. Then she spoke slowly. "And you broke up with her, right? Because it can't be your baby, Macky. Not after all the talking we've done about condoms and AIDS. And your education!" This was it. She had gone up a tone. But what she said had surprised Mitzi.

"Mama! Of course it's his."

"How you know?" She cut her eyes at Mitzi. "Is it yours, Macky? Because that little girl seems a bit fast for me. I don't know..."

"It's mine, Mama," Macky whispered.

"Dammit, Macky! How could you let that child trap you like that?!"

"Mama, what are you saying?" Mitzi was shocked. She had not expected this.

"I'm saying that her mama should have had her on the pill. What type of woman is she? Allowing her daughter to be sexually active with no birth control!"

"Her daughter is sexually active with your son, Mama."

"Well, what was I supposed to do?"

"Nothing. Macky was supposed to use the condoms that you've been buying him." Oleeta cut her eyes at Mitzi again. *Am I to blame here? I'm just the mediator.*

"How did she get pregnant, Macky?" He looked at her and frowned. She sucked her teeth. "I know *how* it happened, dammit, but *why* did it happen?"

"We..."

"What is wrong with you children?"

"Mama, that's neither here nor there, the fact remains that it happened."

"Maxine, when you have your own children, then you can talk. Until then, this is my child!"

It must be time for me to leave.

"Mama, I'm not a child."

"You damn well are a child, boy! And I cannot believe that girl has ruined your future like this!"

"Well she did tell me she was on the pill."

Oh no, he didn't say that. Mitzi looked at her brother in total disbelief. He was changing up on her. "Macky, you did not tell me anything about that. In fact, you told me..."

"And how long have you known about this, Mitzi?"

"Ask your child." She was getting angry with both of them. "Macky, don't do this. You knew very well that Tatyana was not on the pill. Or at least that's what you told me, anyway. It's a different story now? 'Cause Mama's taking your side?"

"I wasn't sure if she was on the pill or not." What a punk.

"Well, isn't that all the more reason you should be accepting at least half the blame for this?" He sucked his teeth. "Macky, I cannot believe you... and what's with you, Mama? Why are you blaming Tatyana?"

"Because, Mitzi, I can't see Macky doing something this crazy - not with the plans we had for him to go to school next year." She looked at Macky. "And you *will* be going away to school next year, Macky."

"I know that." He looked real smug now. Mitzi felt like slapping his face. If she had known all this would happen, she would have let him do this alone. He obviously didn't need her - his mama was covering his behind.

"And who, pray tell, is going to be supporting the baby? You mama?"

"Not me. Oleeta Robinson had to raise her own children. I don't want no parts of that baby. And Miss Tayana, or whatever the hell her name is, better never dream of asking me to babysit." She stood up, and Mitzi could see she was angry. But at who? She was acting like Macky had nothing to do with the baby. She was showing her true colours. Colours that Mitzi knew nothing about. She was not the mama she knew. "Macky, you tell that child that I want to talk to her as soon as possible. And she can bring her mama with her if she wants to. I'll just be giving them a piece of my mind. And tell her that I can get the numbers of a couple of abortion clinics in the States." She walked toward her room.

"Mama...? You have always been against abortions." Mitzi was in total shock.

Oleeta spun around. "I was, until some little whore tried to trap my son! This is not the future I had planned for your brother, Maxine!"

"But it was obviously the future he had planned for himself when he screwed the girl without using at least one condom out of the case he has in his room!" This was getting ugly. Mitzi and Oleeta had never, ever had words like this before. Mitzi had just totally lost respect for her mother. But she wasn't even worried about that right now. This was wrong. It took two to make a baby, and that poor girl should not be blamed.

Oleeta walked right up to Mitzi, and for a second she thought she was going to hit her. "Don't ever think that you can come in my house and talk to me as you please, girl!" She spoke with asperity. "I didn't ask for your advice this time. This is my child and my problem, you understand?"

"Yes Mama, this is your house and your child, but this is not your problem. Your child chose to make a baby." Oleeta closed her eyes. "As hard as that may be to hear, it is what it is. And I cannot believe that you, the woman I have admired and have had nothing but the utmost respect for all my life, the woman who taught me and my brother to take responsibility for our actions, is blaming that poor girl for this pregnancy. No, maybe it wasn't planned and no, it's not what any of us wanted, but why should your child be exempt from blame? There is no such thing as accidental pregnancies in the nineties, *Mother*. You know that. Macky was man enough to have sex with Tatyana - without condoms - he should be man enough to take care of his child." She looked at Macky - she could have killed him - then looked back at her mama. "Apparently, you can't see the forest for the trees when it comes to your son, but I promise you, Mama, when the trees are gone and you can see clearly, Macky will have kicked your butt so bad, you won't even be able to function."

Oleeta shook her head and spoke to Mitzi as if she were a five year-old. "Why are you so against Macky? He's your brother, you should be on his side." She appeared to have calmed down a bit.

Mitzi shook her head. "Macky does not need anybody on his side, Mama. Yes, you can support him - we both can - but why did it have to be all this? I'm not against him, but right is right and wrong is wrong. Come on, Mama..."

"Well, I just don't believe that Macky is wrong in this case. He's not..."

"So, you're just gonna let your mama fight your battles for you?" She cut Oleeta off and looked at Macky who hadn't said a word for a while. Why should he? "This is exactly what I meant when I said that Mama does a lot for you. I guess more than I thought and more than you deserve. You're 'round here acting all big and bad, dissin' her - as you would say - slamming doors and things, but yet..." She grabbed her bag and held up one hand. "Look, I'm gone 'cause like you said, Mama, 'This isn't my house, and it sure isn't my problem.' You asked for my help, *little brother*, but it's obvious that you two can deal with this yourselves and don't need my help." She walked to the door and turned around. "I want to thank you, Macky, for coming between me and my mama." She left.

Mitzi couldn't believe what had just happened. It couldn't have happened. But it had. That punk, Macky. He had turned on her. And his girlfriend. And his baby. Well, he was cut off - for life. It was a beautiful spring morning, but it could have been raining at midnight for all Mitzi cared. She was furious, and as she drove down Middle Road, she got more furious by the minute. What was going on with her mama? She had been making a lot of excuses for Macky lately, but this was beyond that. It was as if she didn't want to face the truth. She was either in serious denial, or she felt like she owed Macky something. Mitzi should probably have never told her how he felt about their daddy's death because now she would probably try to overcompensate, as was quite obvious by today's events.

She didn't even feel like going to her granny's house because she would have to smile and act like nothing was wrong. She had been looking forward to seeing Granny, too, because she had been away the previous weekend. She wished she could tell her what had happened, but she knew her mama would be mad if she did, and she didn't want to make things any worse than they were. Granny would have acted differently - or would she have? She couldn't tell about people any more. Oleeta's reaction had surprised her, maybe Granny's would, too. Maybe she was wrong. She didn't think so, though. Not this time.

"Look, I can't be bothered," she said aloud as she parked her car in Granny's yard and closed the sunroof. She patted Butch - the German shepherd - as she passed him. She usually stopped and talked to him for a few minutes, but she didn't feel like it today. Granny was in the kitchen cooking peas and rice - as usual - she cooked peas and rice every single Saturday. And she had carrot cake in the oven. Her house was spotless and had that faint, musty smell that Mitzi could remember it having since she was a child. The 'old people's house' smell, Crystal called it.

"Mornin' Gran." She pushed her shades up on her head and kissed Granny on the cheek.

"Good afternoon." She kept stirring the pot. Mitzi was not in the mood for her sarcasm today, so she ignored it.

"Nice day, innit Granny?" She opened the fridge.

Granny stopped cooking and turned to look at her. "What's wrong, Puddin'?"

Mitzi frowned. "Why you ask me that?" She rested her shades on the table.

"I've been around longer than three score and ten. The Bible says I should be dead, so give me credit for knowing something. I can tell when something's the matter with you children."

"It's a long story. I'll tell you another time. Your fridge looks full."

"Your Aunt Belinda got my groceries for me 'cause I didn't know what time you'd get here."

Good. "Ready to get your hair done?" Mitzi leaned over her and looked in the pot.

"Mind my hip, child."

"Granny, your bad hip is on the other side."

"Oh, that's right." Mitzi smiled and shook her head.

"I notice you changed the subject, but whenever you're ready to talk, I'm here - but not for much longer, though."

Mitzi smiled again. "You're not going anywhere yet, Granny."

"Even if I wanted to, I couldn't go yet because I have to go to your mama's wedding. She told you she was getting married, didn't she?"

"Of course she did. But she didn't say when, though." She really didn't feel like talking about her mama right now, but at least she didn't have to pretend nothing was wrong. Granny was sitting at the kitchen table, and Mitzi was picking the 'bun' out of her hair. She had a lot of hair which had been thick at one time but was thinning out now. "I guess it'll be some time this year."

"The sooner, the better - maybe then you'll get the hint."

"What hint?" Mitzi acted dumb. Granny started humming. She usually did when she started something and didn't want to say any more. "What about you? Think you'll ever get married again?"

"Lord no. Even though I know there are men out there lined up to marry me."

Mitzi stopped doing her hair and laughed. "Can you still cut the mustard, Granny?"

"No. But I can certainly spread it, though." She cut her eyes and went over to the sink where she had put her shampoo. She bent over so Mitzi could wash her hair. She refused to go to the salon because she hated lying back in the shampoo chair. "Feels like they're trying to drown me," she grumbled whenever Mitzi tried to get her to go. "And furthermore, some of those shampoo girls need deodorant. Can't stand smelly pits in my face." She always tried to give Mitzi 'a little something' for doing her hair every week, but she would never take it.

"No, Mitzi, I was married to your papa for too many years for me to marry somebody else now. In my heart, your papa is eternally immortal."

"Don't you think you'd be happier if you had a husband now?"

"I'd be a lot happier if you didn't scrub my scalp so hard." Mitzi scrubbed softer. "No, I could never be happier than I was when your grandpa was alive. I swear I loved that man from the womb to the grave. And beyond." They were both quiet for a few minutes. Mitzi knew Granny was thinking about Papa, and she didn't speak again until Mitzi was wrapping the towel around her head. She sat back at the table and put on her glasses. "I hope your mama and George will be happy."

"I think they will."

"You know, people today don't know the real meaning of happiness or what a good marriage is. What Robert and I had was a good marriage." Mitzi turned on the blow dryer. "Don't turn that thing on. How the devil you s'posed to hear what I'm saying?"

"Granny, I have to dry your hair." Mitzi shook her head.

"Well, you know I hate to have my story interrupted." Mitzi sighed, put down the blow dryer and sat at the table. "You have to give and take, Puddin'. All you young people know how to do these days is take, take, take, take, take - don't wanna give nothing. You have to give a little to get a little. Your grandpa was out working all day, and I was here working - raising our children." Mitzi nodded. Granny liked to know that you were paying attention when she was talking. "And you better believe that when my husband got home, the house was clean, the children were clean and his supper was cooked - and hot." She hit the table to emphasize her point. "Not like you young brides today. Have your husbands waiting 'til 'The Young and the Restless' goes off to start cooking. Damn ridiculous."

"Granny, most young wives are out working just like their husbands are."

"Doesn't matter, take care of your man, and he won't have to go elsewhere."

"What if he's going elsewhere 'cause that's just what he wants to do? Why should the wife bend over backward for him?"

"That's another thing, see." She pointed at Mitzi. "If these women would stop being so uppity and pert and take care of their men - in the Biblical sense - then why would he have to go elsewhere?"

"It happens though, Granny." She was still living in the fifties obviously.

"But it don't have to happen. These women need to stop having so many headaches when it comes to doing their wifely duty. Give the man some good lovin'. You people need to learn how to communicate - in and out of bed."

"That's true." Might as well go along with her.

Granny felt her hair. "You planning on drying my hair today, or you want me to catch a death of a cold?" Mitzi shook her head and smiled. She was used to her being contrary.

They were all used to it. Mitzi went into Granny's bedroom to get a brush. Granny swore she had the same bedroom set she and Papa had bought when they got married. The bed had the sliding doors in the headboard. Being in this room today, for some reason, made Mitzi think back to when Macky was a baby. Granny used to keep him days while Mama and Daddy worked. She would hop on the first bus from Berkeley after school and race up Granny's to play with her baby brother. Granny usually had him lying in this same bed while she got Papa's supper ready. Seemed like yesterday...

Granny's bureau - as she still called it - had a lace scarf on it that Mitzi remembered from childhood. She probably had a dozen of them. And there was her vanity, the kind where the ends were higher than the middle. On it was that old comb, brush and mirror set that everybody's granny had - the set that was never used, it was just for show.

"Granny, where's the hair dryer brush I gave you?" Mitzi shouted to her in the kitchen. She came into the bedroom.

"You know I can't understand what the devil you're saying in here."

"Where's the blow dryer brush I gave you?"

"That hard thing? I don't know." She went back into the kitchen. That meant she had thrown it away. She told Mitzi it was too hard and would pull her hair out. Mitzi took her brush out of her bag.

"Things aren't the way they were when you and Papa got married, you know, Granny."

"Well they dang-well should be!" She was turning the carrot cake out of the pan. "Nobody told you youngsters to go and change things - marriages today don't last as long as a tube of gas. I don't buy wedding gifts 'til I see that first anniversary picture and thank you note in the paper. And that's another thing, this community thank you notice is impolite. People go to the trouble of buying you a gift, you should send them a personal thank you card in the mail. They can still put the picture in the paper." She often went off on a tangent, especially when something annoyed her.

"My girlfriend Crystal and her husband seem to have a good marriage, but I don't know too many others..."

"Which one is Crystal, the cute little one with the good hair?"

"Everybody has good hair, Granny."

She turned to look at her and frowned. "And you graduated from beauty school? Do you need glasses, child?"

"Hair that doesn't drop out is good hair."

" 'Cause you're a hairdresser, you think you can tell me all about hair? Some of these people have ha..., not even hair, it's so doggone nappy. They could save a few shillings on Brillo pads." She cut the carrot cake. "Need a good straightening comb, some of them do."

"Everybody's going natural these days, so it don't really matter. Now come on Granny, 'cause I have to go."

"You're the one doing all the talking."

Mitzi turned the blow dryer on and talked over it. "Crystal and her husband seem to get along real well, and she always says she thinks it's because they're friends before anything else. And her husband really respects her, Gran. It's unbelievable."

"Mutual respect will do it every time. A man who doesn't respect his woman might as well be dead. A woman who doesn't respect her man... needs to learn how."

"It warms my heart to see how they treat each other. I mean, they argue and stop speaking and all, but it never seems to be something they can't resolve."

"Hmph. That boy you married could have taken a few lessons, but then, I don't want to talk about your beloved husband."

"Please don't."

"Mitzi, any relationship will have its ups and downs because no two people are alike. You each have to deal with each other's idiosyncrasies, but a mate is what he is when you meet him, just as you are what you are."

"I know, but it's hard starting over - trying to get to know a person."

"You get to know the person first. Decide whether or not you like him. If you think he has potential, stay. If you don't think so, go. You work at it and when you truly fall in love, you love him *although...* and you like him *because...*"

"What you sayin', Granny?" She turned the dryer off.

"You got a college education, and you can't pick the bones out of that?" She turned to face Mitzi. "You know you truly love a person when you love him *although* he leaves his dirty socks on the floor or the toilet seat up, and you like him *because* you can be yourself with him, and he respects you."

"I guess that's why you and Papa had over fifty years in."

"No. I had fifty-one years in 'cause your papa was scared to leave me. He was even scared to die 'cause he knew how 'fullish' I was." They both laughed. Mitzi loved talking to her granny, and she was glad she came today after all. She felt a lot better than she had earlier. At least Granny had taken her mind off of Macky and Mama for a few minutes. She would talk to her about that situation another day. She finished Granny's braid and wrapped it into a bun, just as she liked it. Just as she had worn it for about twenty years. She sprayed her hair then washed her hands.

"Now, Gran girl, I'm gone." She was wrapping carrot cake in waxed paper for Mitzi to take home. "I'm going over to Mrs. Bascome's and catch up on some 'garpseed'. Thank God her husband's still in the hospital, 'cause he's as crazy as the day is long. Well, I'm not glad he's in the hospital, but you know what I mean." She and the Bascomes had been neighbours for over fifty years. Mitzi kissed her cheek.

"Mr. Bascome's not seriously ill, is he?"

"No. He's just seriously old - you know he's older than water. They can't find anything wrong with the decrepit, old crow."

Mitzi laughed. "Bye, pertness," she said. Even though she was seventy-four, Granny still had pretty, smooth brown skin and all her own teeth.

"Going to the grocery store?"

"Yep. You need something else?"

"Yes. See if you can find a man while you're there. One who don't have diapers - or Pampers or whatever you lot call them, for his baby or sanitary napkins for his wife - in his shopping basket. Come on, out. Bascome's probably wonderin' where I am." She didn't lock the door, as usual. "Is somebody going to walk into a house where the door's open?" She always asked her children and grandchildren when they admonished her for not locking up. "People break into locked places," she said confidently.

Mitzi stopped at White's grocery store and bumped into Sundae, who almost knocked down a stack of canned goods to get to her to tell her that Roger had cleaned out all of Melba's belongings. She had called the police, and they had arrested him for stealing. Sundae had said she felt sorry for Melba and was going to call her to see if she needed anything. When Mitzi got to the check-out, she found twenty dollars in her bag. Granny had obviously put it in there.

Serves him right, Mitzi thought of Roger as she drove home. Melba could handle it. She wondered if she had tried to call her and how Sundae had found out already. But then again... Mitzi pushed Luther into the tape deck and listened to him sing, 'A House is Not a Home.' Ain't that the truth? She should know. It was four twenty-three by the clock in her car, and she wanted to get home and do her housework. She hated starting this late. She wondered if Maliq had called and hoped she hadn't missed him. With the week she'd had, she probably had missed the call.

Ebone´ was out and had left a note. She was at her mama's house - or her sister's house now. She and her sisters were sorting out their mama's things. She checked her voice mail. Maliq hadn't called yet, but Melba had - three times. So had Sundae. Crystal had called twice. They were all calling to tell her about Roger. Mitzi didn't feel like getting caught up in all that right now. She had things to do.

By six thirty she had finished her housework. She had washed two loads of clothes, and they were out on the line. She was getting underwear from her drawer to take into the bathroom when she decided to call Melba. She got the answering machine. At least Roger had left that. She told her to call her back, and just as she was about to hang up, her call-waiting clicked. Her heart raced. What was the matter with her? She answered, and it was Maliq.

"I'm not too late, am I?"

No, you're right on time, honey. This had to stop. "No, in fact, I haven't been home that long." She didn't want him to think she had been waiting for him. It wasn't a lie - an hour and a half wasn't really that long. She heard a saxophone playing in the background - it sounded like... Earth, Wind and Fire's 'Reasons'. It was! Did he like that music, too? Was he at home? "You at home?"

"Yes. I'm ready to leave to come west. I'm calling to get directions." Mitzi told him how to get to her house, and he said he would be about fifteen minutes - he was coming from Burnt House Hill but had to get gas first. He told her to look out for him in a black Escort. She hung up and ran into the bathroom. She ran through the shower but made sure to use her White Musk shower gel. She came out of the bathroom and grabbed her black leggings from her drawer and ran the iron over her denim shirt. She put White Musk body oil in every place imaginable, making sure to rub it all in. She hated when people walked around with oil spots all over their skin. It looked ridiculous. She put on the black flats she bought on her trip and went into the living room. She wanted to burn incense, but she didn't want Maliq to think she had lit it just for him, so she broke one in half and lit it. She put on a Chi Lites CD and spread the newspapers out on the couch to make it look like she had been reading them for a while and was not waiting for him. She hated this and had butterflies. Maybe he wouldn't even come in - he might just give her the book at the door and dig off. "Oh my God! I forgot to put lipstick on!" That would have been a pure disaster. She ran down the hall into her room and put some pumpkin lipstick on and powdered her face. She didn't want to look too made-up. She heard a car in the yard and looked out the window. It was a black Escort. He was here. She went back to the couch so that when he rang the bell, she would be able to take her time opening the door. The bell rang.

Okay, calm down, Robinson. You know this is not you - acting like a damn teenager. She opened the door to the biggest smile and those beautiful dimples. *Damn, this boy is sweet!*

"Hey Maliq. I see you found the house without getting lost."

He leaned against the wall. "Yeah, it was easy." He had on a black tee shirt, a pair of jeans and sneakers. He looked so good. For the first time she noticed that he had really long eyelashes.

"I'm sorry, come in." What was her problem? She was hoping he wouldn't just give her the book at the door and leave, and now she had forgotten to invite him in!

He came in and looked at her kind of sheepishly, then he smiled. "I feel real silly. I forgot the book - which is why I was supposed to be coming here. I can go back for it."

"No, don't be ridiculous. I can always get it another time." *Maybe I'm not the only one who's excited. He came and he didn't even bring the book!* He followed her to the living room.

"I didn't realize I'd left it until I turned into your gate, but I didn't want to turn around then because I didn't wanna keep you waiting - in case you had somewhere to go."

I'm here for the night, darlin'. I'm glad you didn't go back because then I would have thought you were lost, and I would have felt bad. Have a seat."

"I had an idea where I was going - my aunt - Sandra Francis - lives just down the hill." They both sat on the couch.

"Oh, I know Mrs. Francis. Drives the little red car, has two daughters..."

"Yeah, that's my daddy's sister. I'm really sorry about the book."

"Please - don't worry about it. I can get it another time. It's not like I haven't read it already - twice."

He smiled at her. "I could always bring it back."

"Exactly, so stop apologising. Would you like something to drink?" She hoped he did. "I have soda, beer, wine." She smiled at him. "Scotch. And coke."

He laughed. "No, no, I'm not drinking that this week. I've put myself back in serious training. I have ten days to be ready to run the marathon."

"Twenty-fourth of May? Bermuda Day marathon?" He nodded. "I'm impressed."

"Thanks. But I'm not training so much that I can't have a glass of wine - with you."

"It's Green Label. You like that?" She stood.

"Yeah. That's nice. I haven't had it for a while." She hadn't either, but she just happened to buy some at the grocery store today - just in case someone stopped by her house this evening. She went into the kitchen as he watched her.

"This is a beautiful house, Mitzi," Maliq said, looking around.

"Thanks." Her hand was shaking as she tried to open the wine bottle. *Oh catch yourself, girl. He's only a man. My point exactly!*

"You live here alone?"

Was that a trick question? Was he going to turn out to be a cold blooded killer who would rape and strangle her? What the heck was she doing letting a strange man into her house? She quickly looked outside to see if his car was parked in Mrs. Rawlins' view. It was. If anything happened, at least he wouldn't get away with it. Mrs. Rawlins would undoubtedly take delight in spilling her guts. "My neighbour is so pokey. She's standing at her window, and I'm sure she's noticed the make, model and license number of your car. She drives me crazy. What were you asking me?" She poured two glasses of wine.

"You live in this big house alone?" he repeated.

"No." He looked disappointed. "My roommate is out." She passed him a glass. "She should be back in a while."

He smiled. "Thank you." He turned to face her as she sat at the opposite end of the couch. "So, you like the Chi Lites?" They made an unspoken toast with their glasses.

"I like anything that was recorded between the mid-seventies and mid-eighties."

He flashed his pretty teeth - and dimples. "You're givin' away your age."

She playfully glared at him. "Now, we ain't even gonna go there, are we? Did we not already have a conversation on this subject?"

Maliq opened his mouth to say something, closed it, then laughed. "I have a short memory, I guess." He rested his glass on the coaster on the coffee table. He was sitting up straight - like a gentleman visiting a lady for the first time should. Mitzi's back was against the arm of the couch, and she had one leg under her. She hoped it didn't look vulgar. "I like music from that era, too. I can relate to it, especially the reggae back then. I don't know what these people today are saying."

Mitzi laughed. "I feel the same way. And I already know your age."

He looked at her slyly. "I lied." Her face fell. *He better not have. I hate liars.* "No girl, I'm just joking. I am thirty-five - wanna see my license?" He reached for his back pocket.

She shook her head. "That won't be necessary. I believe you." It didn't matter if he was lying or not - she didn't even know him. He was nice though - or he seemed nice, anyway. And he wasn't arrogantly lying all over her couch. She liked that. He was still sitting up straight, but he looked a little more relaxed.

"I like anything by The Isleys, New Birth, Harold Melvin and the Blue Notes, Marvin Gaye, The Delfonics, The Commodores..."

"Oh please, that's all I listen to. It takes me back to my worry-free days."

He leaned forward with his elbows on his knees. "Yeah. And reggae was really reggae when Inner Circle, Third World, Bob Marley and Jacob Miller were hittin'."

"Session down 'The Barn' days," she reminisced. He looked at her with his mouth open. 'The Barn' was where Western Stars Sports Club is now. There was a reggae session almost every weekend when Mitzi was a teenager. It was called 'The Barn' or 'De Barn' because at the time it was wooden. She giggled. "I'm thirty-one, all right?!" She hit him with the TV guide. He flinched.

"Hey, I didn't ask you nothin', sister. You volunteered that." They both laughed. "I don't remember seeing you down there back in the day."

"Now, why would a guy who was four years older than me, be looking at a young girl like me? I was only fifteen - sixteen. You were twenty - a man."

He picked the wine glass up and leaned back, crossing his ankle over his knee. "I'm sure you were just as pretty then," He held the glass to his lips, looked at her for a second, looked away, then slowly drank some wine. She gulped some of hers.

"Nah. I was just a skinny little girl with knock knees and bushy, uncontrollable hair."

"Well, time was certainly on your side." He was looking at her again, and she felt uncomfortable - but he quickly fixed that. "I know time was certainly on my side. I was skinny, too, real skinny and had this big afro." He held his hands out on the sides of his head to demonstrate how big the afro was.

Mitzi slapped her leg and laughed. "You must have had that Linc Hayes from Mod Squad look."

He laughed and nodded his head. "That I did." He looked at her again. "You make me laugh." She smiled. "I thought I was bad back then, too." he said. "Remember when 'The Barn' floor used to bounce?"

"Who could forget? You didn't have to dance - the floor moved you." She sighed. "Those were the days."

"They sure were. I long to have them back."

"Not in this lifetime." Mitzi stood. "Can I get you some more wine?"

Maliq passed his glass to her. "Half a glass, please. I hope I'm not keeping you from doing anything."

"No, I don't have anything to do tonight." *Or any other night, for that matter.* "But I don't want to keep you from going up Somerset, though."

"Oh, I don't have to go now. Plans changed." She gave him a half a glass of wine, and she had one, too. She wondered if he ever really had to go Somerset in the first place as she put on her Bob Marley CD. She didn't think it was appropriate to continue playing these slow jams. "That's what I'm talkin' 'bout," Maliq said, referring to the new music. Marley was singing, 'I Shot the Sheriff'.

"So, how many Bermuda Day marathons have you run?" She was trying to keep the conversation going because she was enjoying his company and didn't want him to leave yet. It felt good to be having a decent conversation with a seemingly intelligent man. She wanted to ask him what happened with his girlfriend - or ex-girlfriend, but she thought if he wanted to talk about it, he would bring it up. Who wanted to talk about her anyway? Whoever she was.

"This will be my second marathon."

"You waited this late in life to start running marathons?" She raised her eyebrows.

"Hey, watch that. I'm not exactly ancient, you know. Just 'cause I listen to old music..."

"No, I mean, people usually start running all those miles in their twenties."

"I've been away in school for the past five years. I graduated last May."

"Oh, I see. You went back to school at thirty? You have guts."

"That's what it took, too. I thought I was crazy when I first got there, but I knew what I wanted to accomplish, so I persevered. It was worth it."

"Smart man."

"Thank you. I like to think I am."

"So that's why I've never seen you before."

"Yep. I was buried in books at 'The House' in Atlanta. I'd never seen you before last weekend either. Strange for both of us to be living in Bermuda and not know each other, isn't it?"

"I guess we haven't been running in the same circles."

"Just what circles do you run in, by the way?" She frowned. "I mean how come a beautiful lady like you doesn't have anything to do on a Saturday night? Where's your man? Away or something?"

"Do you think I would be sitting here, drinking wine with you if I had a man? What I look like to you?" She pretended to be offended.

"Oh Lord. I didn't mean to insult you, I just wondered..."

"If I have a man?" She twirled her wine glass with her fingers.

He nodded. "Yeah. I was just... wondering." He shrugged his shoulders and held his hands up. He looked like an innocent little boy.

Mitzi smiled and sipped her wine. "No, Maliq. I don't have a man."

He looked at her out of the corner of his eye. "How 'bout a husband?" He was playing with her.

"I'm a widow."

He got serious when he saw she was serious. "I'm sorry, Maxine. I was just joking. I'm sorry." He was a little embarrassed.

Mitzi waved her hand. "You don't have to be sorry. I was in the process of divorcing Quincy when he got killed."

Maliq frowned. "Quincy who?"

"Quincy Butterfield. He died the day before the divorce..."

"You were married to Quincy Butterfield?"

"You knew him?"

"Yeah. We used to play football together - for P.H.C.'

"I was away in school then."

He stared at her. "You hardly look like the type of woman to marry somebody like 'Q' Butterfield." He hoped he had worded that right.

"And what type of woman should have married 'Q' Butterfield?"

"A woman who didn't know any better."

"I was young. And in my infinite wisdom, you couldn't tell me anything. I didn't know any better."

"You're excused then. And you guys never had any children, huh?"

"No, thank the Lord. We weren't married that long. As my granny would say, it didn't even last as long as a tube of gas - or in our case - a thousand kilowatts."

Maliq was laughing. "So that's where you get your sense of humour from - your granny."

Mitzi nodded. "She's some darlin'. People say I'm a bit like her."

"She must be a beautiful person and a pleasure to talk to." He was playing with his watchband.

"Am I supposed to acknowledge your subtle compliments?" She was playing with her charm bracelet.

He looked at her. "No. But I know you hear me." He looked at his watch. It was nine twenty-five. He drained his wine glass. "Now, Mitzi, I better go. I want to get up early tomorrow to go for a run."

"I went for a run this morning."

He was surprised. "You run, too?"

"Sometimes. I usually go to the gym during the week and run on weekends. Sometimes I renege, but I try."

"You're a woman of many surprises, aren't you? I never would have guessed that you would get out on the street and run. You seem too... sophisticated."

She smiled. "You need to stop. I haven't had a man pay me this many compliments in my life, let alone one night."

"Well, these brothers ain't been paying attention. But I'm serious. Maybe we could go running together sometime."

How 'bout tomorrow? "I could never keep up with you, Mr. Marathon Runner."

"Judging from the little I've learned about you, I'm sure you could. You're a strong sister - I don't think there's anything you couldn't do. Wanna go running on the beach with me tomorrow morning? I mean, I don't wanna be forward or nothin'."

"Of course, you don't. Which beach?"

"Warwick Long Bay."

"Wow, that's a long run - but I think I could handle it."

"I go early, though - six thirty."

"That's the time I like to go, too. It's so nice outside that time of the morning."

"You wanna meet me there, or you want me to pick you up?"

Now we can't move too fast. "I'll meet you at the beach. I might not be able to keep up with you so I can get in my car and leave when I'm ready."

He stood up and smiled at her. "I have a feeling we'll be leaving the beach together. You can hang." Mitzi stood, too. "Now, Ms. Robinson, I want to thank you for your hospitality, the wine, the music. They were all almost as enjoyable as your company and conversation."

A man of words. I love that! "Thank you, Maliq. I have enjoyed your company as well. I look forward to running with you tomorrow. Or behind you." They were both being so polite. That's usually how it was when two people were trying to impress each other.

"You don't need a wake-up call, do you?" He was at the door.

She shook her head and smiled. "No, my biological clock usually goes off at six, mornings. I'll be on time."

"If you're not..." He opened the door. "I'll wait." He smiled. He was too cute and considerate.

"Thanks. See you in the morning - drive safely.

She wanted to stand at the door and watch him drive off, but she didn't want to appear desperate. She sat back on the couch and turned the TV on. She had truly had a lovely evening. Maliq was so sweet, and kind, and a lot of fun, and intelligent. She had really enjoyed talking to him. She didn't know what would happen next, but she was looking forward to the morning. Perhaps nothing would happen next. But...

CHAPTER THIRTEEN
Sunday Morning

Mitzi was up at five; she had woken up every hour and wondered why. The last time she woke up, the clock was saying four fifty-two, so she lay with her eyes closed and said a prayer. At five o'clock, she got up and got a quick shower. She often showered before running or going to the gym, especially if she was going with somebody. She perspired a lot when she worked out and didn't want to have body odour - especially today. After her shower, she brushed her hair back in a ponytail and put on lipstick, tights, a leotard and a tee shirt. Even though she had the body to work out without the tee shirt, she didn't feel comfortable yet. That went back to the days when she was a little heavy and very conscious of her body. Thanks to a serious year long exercise commitment and a change in her eating habits, she was now what was considered a 'brick house'. And she was determined to stay that way. Perhaps that wouldn't be such a difficult task considering her new found friend was into exercise, too. She plucked a couple of hairs from her chin - she always wanted to have them waxed, but there weren't enough of them to do so - there were enough to annoy her, though.

She got to the beach at six twenty-five - couldn't appear too eager. It was a beautiful May morning. The sun was peaking over the horizon, and the beach was spotless. There were about five or six other joggers out and a couple in the water. It was as clear and calm as she had seen it for a while. Maliq was waiting for her and smiled when he saw her. She was able to get a really good look at him in the early morning sunlight. And he looked good - even this early in the morning. He was wearing gray sweat pants and a white tank top. He had a 'Bulls' cap on - and he smelled good.

"Mornin', beautiful." He was still smiling.

"Mornin', Maliq." She smiled back. "How you doin'?"

"I'm good. How about you? Tired?"

"I look that bad?"

He laughed and held her arm. "No, you look fine. I was just asking - it *is* only six thirty. They both started walking along the beach, and Mitzi tied her windbreaker around her waist. "I told you, I'm an early morning girl. You miss out on life if you spend the day in bed - sleeping."

"True. And beauty such as this deserves to be admired and enjoyed." She thought he was talking about the beach, but he was staring at her. She pretended not to notice.

"You like the outdoors, huh?" she asked.

"I love few things more. Ready to start jogging?"

"Whenever you are." They started. "Let me know if I'm going too fast for you," he said. He was so considerate.

"Ha! How do you know I won't be going too fast for you?"

He pointed at her and smiled as they ran. "You know, one of these days I'm gonna learn not to say things like that to you - one of these days."

Sounds promising. "You think 'cause you're a man, that automatically means you'll out run me - 'cause I'm a woman?"

He started whistling, and she bent over laughing as she ran. They were running on the hard sand - near the water's edge.

"How long you been running?" he asked her as they turned around at the end of the beach.

"I started exercising seriously just over a year ago. I was a bit overweight, and I didn't want it to get out of control, so I cut out red meat, cut in fresh fruit, vegetables and exercise. Jogging was just something I got into after a while - about seven months ago." Actually, Darren had gotten her into jogging. He was good for something after all. She just hoped that every man she jogged with didn't turn out to be a perfect idiot - like Darren. Somehow, she didn't think Maliq was anything like him, but then again, she had just met him. Time would tell - if things went the way she wanted them to.

"You have a good pace - for a novice." He kept his head straight and smiled. She did, too. They didn't talk too much after that. They were concentrating on building up their pace. By the time they were on their fifth lap, they had picked up a good pace, and Mitzi was sweating profusely. She was glad she had taken a shower. She looked at Maliq - his thick body was shining with perspiration in the morning sun. They overtook a man who looked like he was on his last breath, looked at each other and laughed. By the time they had reached the end of the beach and turned around, the struggling man had given up and was leaving.

"You should be ashamed of yourself, you ran that poor old man right off the beach," Maliq said. *He probably got exhausted looking at your body,* he thought. Mitzi was running on the inside - closest to the water and suddenly started to notice that either the tide was coming in real fast or... "

Maliq! You're pushing me in the water!" He was trying not to laugh. He had been running closer to her, making her unconsciously run closer to the water's edge.

"I thought you might wanna cool down."

"No, you can't keep up with me, that's why you're trying to push me overboard." They were both laughing. Mitzi looked at him. His shirt was soaked and clinging to his body. He had a nice hairy chest, and the hair was soaked. She couldn't help staring. Maliq caught her, and she looked away, embarrassed. He smiled to himself and thought that she was the prettiest black woman he had ever seen. Her top lip was perspiring, her face was moist and her neck, chest and arms were soaked.

Damn, you look good! he thought.

"Maliq, if you're tired and want to stop, just say... ow!" She stopped running and bent over in pain.

"What happened?" He stopped to help her as she sat in the sand.

"I have cramp in my foot. Ow!" Maliq knelt in front of her, untied her sneaker and took it off. She hoped her feet didn't stink. Her sock was wet and sweaty and stuck to her foot, but he didn't care. He started pushing her toes back and forth, but the cramp wouldn't stop. He reached up to the top of her sock and pulled it off. Good thing she had painted her toenails.

She even has pretty feet. Maliq massaged her foot. "You okay?" he asked, genuinely concerned.

"I still feel it, but it's a lot better." *Don't stop yet.* He smiled at her, then hung his head and laughed. "What's funny?" Mitzi asked, throwing sand at him.

"'Maliq, if you're tired and want to stop'..." he said, mocking her. She threw her head back and laughed.

"If you didn't try to push me in the water, I wouldn't have gotten cramp. Let go of my foot," she said, pulling her leg up in mock anger.

He sat beside her, still smiling. "You're something else, you know that, lady? Wanna keep going or you had enough?"

"I hate to admit it, but I think I've had enough. But I don't want to mess up your training." She felt good sitting in the sand and the sun, talking to Maliq. It was seven fifteen, and the day was getting nicer by the minute.

"Nah, don't worry 'bout me, I can always come back this evening." Mitzi started to put her sock back on. "Since you have your sneaker off, we might as well go swimming."

She looked at him and raised her eyebrows. "Are you crazy? It's not hot enough to go swimming yet."

"Don't tell me you're one of those people who doesn't go swimming 'til the sun crosses the line."

"No, I'm not that ridiculous, but this is a bit too early. I at least wait until after the twenty-fourth of May."

Maliq looked out at the ocean. "You coming to watch me run on the twenty-fourth of May?" He looked at her and hoped he wasn't being forward.

"Sure. We lot always watch the runners up by Heron Bay School. We sit on the wall across from that house called 'Ran-Jan'."

"Oh, I know where that is. I remember last year, those people on that wall made some noise." He frowned. "You were one of that loud crowd?" He pretended to be appalled.

"Of course not," Mitzi said. "I sit in a chair and act very lady-like." She put her sneaker on and tied it.

"Right," Maliq said, nodding his head. "That's what I thought." Mitzi put her windbreaker on, and they sat on the beach and talked for about forty-five minutes. Maliq told her that his ex-girlfriend had called him on Friday night after he hadn't heard from her for about a week. She wanted to talk about their relationship. He said he told her that there was no such thing anymore, and there was nothing for them to talk about. She had apparently kept pleading with him to at least hear her out. He finally told her to come to his house and she could say what she had to say, but she couldn't come because she was looking after her sister's children *and* her daddy didn't want her to take them out of the house. "Case closed," he had said.

Around one o'clock she knocked on his door, but he didn't let her in. He told Mitzi that he just didn't feel like going through all the arguing and headaches anymore. Finally she left, and he finished reading Mitzi's book. 'Miss Girlfriend' had called him on Saturday morning and told him she would leave him alone and give him some time to think, and he would realize that he really didn't want to end the relationship. He said he told her not to call him again and he would be changing his number on Monday. In the end she told him she never wanted him anyway and commenced to 'f' him off. He had hung up on her, and she hadn't called since. Mitzi didn't really comment or pass her opinion because he didn't ask for it. She had just listened. It seemed like he just needed to talk.

"How's the cramp?" Maliq asked her.

"It's gone, thank you, Dr. Simmons." She smiled. "Now, I better go, and you better put something on. You should have put a shirt or jacket on a long time ago."

"I couldn't take care of you and get my shirt, too," he said, pulling her to her feet.

"Oh please, everybody gets cramp from time to time." She brushed the sand from her clothes.

"The way you were acting, I thought I was gonna have to call the ambulance." He smiled and turned his cap backwards. She took it off his head and hit him with it. He ducked. "And you're violent, too. There is a lot I don't know about you, sister."

"And all I know about you is that your ex-girlfriend is still in love with you, and you can't keep up with me - while jogging on the beach."

"Don't even..."

"We'll have to do something about that, won't we?" she asked seriously as they reached the parking lot. She had parked beside him. He got his sweatshirt from the back seat of his car.

"So, what you doin' today?" he asked, pulling the shirt over his head.

"I promised to help my girlfriend pack. She and her husband are moving into their new house at the end of the month. So I'll probably go home, get a shower and go down to her house for breakfast, then stay most of the day." He nodded. "What you doin'?"

"I'm going to clean my car when I get home, then I'll probably go down my mama's for a while - today's her birthday, and my family usually has dinner with her - or brunch. So I'll be surrounded by a house full of children for the afternoon."

"Yours, too?" She had wondered if he had children but hadn't asked before now.

"My daughter will probably come, but she won't be running around - she's too old."

"How old is she?"

"Seventeen." He looked for her expression.

"What was your problem - making babies at eighteen? You should be ashamed of yourself," she said, jokingly.

"I was and so was my family. Her old man had me thrown in jail for two days. She was a couple of months away from her sixteenth birthday when she got pregnant."

"You must tell me the story one day." Mitzi was really interested in finding out more about Maliq Simmons.

"So, I guess that means I can see you again?" he asked cautiously.

"You still have to return my book, don't you?" She was smiling at him.

He put his hand on his head. "Oh man, I meant to bring it this morning, but I completely forgot - again. If my head wasn't on my shoulders, I probably would have left that over Burnt House Hill, too."

"Nothing's wrong with your memory. But we can play this game as long as you want to."

He shook his head and smiled. "Perceptive lady. So, when can I bring your book?"

She took her keys from her jacket pocket and unlocked the car door. "I'll leave that to you. Just call me and let me know when you have time to bring it. " She got in her car. "And I'll let you know if I'm available." She smiled, and he raised his eyebrows.

"You're tough, aren't you?"

"No, darlin'. Just wise. Thanks - I really enjoyed this morning. Thanks for having me tag along."

"Anytime. And I mean that literally. Next time just don't slow me down." He was standing at her side of the car, and she glared at him. He held up his hand. "I'm just joking - you know that."

"How would I know that? I don't know you."

"Well, you shouldn't be out running on the beach early in the morning with a stranger, so we'll have to fix that, now won't we?"

She started her car. "Have a nice day, Maliq. Hope your mom enjoys her birthday." She paused. "You really coming back up here this evening?"

"Yeah, I'll come back about six and run for an hour, you coming?" She shook her head. "Okay," he shrugged. "Thanks, Mitzi - it was good to have company for a change - beautiful company." He walked to his car as she put hers in reverse. "I'll call you - if you don't mind - you know, to bring the book back." Mitzi nodded and drove off. As she drove up South Shore, she wondered if Maliq was telling the truth about his 'ex'. There was really no need for him to lie to her - unless he was interested in her. She smiled and opened her sunroof.

Maliq drove down South Shore with his top down and thought about Mitzi. She was a beautiful woman - inside and out, or so it seemed. He wanted to get to know her - she was so mature and strong - he could tell she wasn't easy to get over - not that he would ever want to get over a woman. All he wanted was a decent woman in his life right now. He wasn't necessarily looking to get married yet, but he had busted his backside getting his degree, and now he worked hard and just wanted somebody to share his ambitions with - somebody to have fun and enjoy life with. He would be returning that book real soon. He didn't want to appear overbearing though, so he would wait a few days. He wondered what she thought about him and suddenly realized that he hadn't even given her his phone number, so even if she was interested and wanted to call him, she couldn't. He was having it changed tomorrow anyway, just in case Marilyn had plans to call him. He would call Mitzi and give it to her - that would be a good excuse.

When Mitzi got home, Ebone' was in her bed. She said she didn't feel like doing anything today. Mitzi knew she would have days like this, so she left her alone. Oleeta had left a message telling her they needed to talk, but she didn't feel like dealing with that today. She had had a good start to the day, and she didn't want to ruin it by talking to her mama about that little, ungrateful Macky. She would call her later this evening or tomorrow. Crystal had also called, wondered where she was so early, and reminded her to come to her house. Melba and Sundae would be there, too. She wondered how Melba was making out. She hadn't talked to her since she had Roger locked up - she had been busy with Maliq. That was all right, she would understand. She was always there for those lot - this morning she had taken time for herself. She had had a lot happen in the past couple of weeks and needed this diversion - whatever it was worth. She wanted to tell Crystal about Maliq - not that there was much to tell, but she wasn't sure if she wanted Sundae and Melba to know anything about him. Sundae probably knew him already.

CHAPTER FOURTEEN
Sunday Morning

By the time Mitzi reached Crystal's house, it was nine thirty, and Crystal looked like a stark raving lunatic. The house was an organized confusion - boxes were in every room, half packed, and her children were running around. They were excited to see their Godma Mitzi. A minute later Crystal sent them to their room to read.

"If Raoul don't come back soon and take these children out of my hair, I'm gonna beat 'em to death."

"Crystal!! You can't say that!"

"It's a metaphor, child. When you have children, you'll understand exactly how I feel. I was gonna drown RJ in the dishwater this morning." Mitzi shook her head and laughed.

"Where is Raoul?"

"He went to take some things to the dump. Ask me why he couldn't put these children in the car and take them with him." She was wrapping her wedding china in newspaper.

"You hungry now? I was waiting to eat with you."

"You wanna wait for Melba and Sundae?"

"Sundae called me a few minutes ago - said she just woke up, and you know how long-winded she is. She probably won't get here 'til about noon. Melba said she won't be here 'til ten thirty; she had a few things to do. And you know your girlfriend is hungry, so I ain't waiting for those two." She took two plates from the cupboard.

"How did Melba make out with her furniture and Roger and everything? I haven't even talked to her since it all happened."

"She got it all back last night, girl. That's what she's doing this morning - putting everything back in place, she said it won't take her long. Ain't Roger nothin'?"

Mitzi shook her head. "Don't worry, his day is coming. Idiot."

"But that was a little brush with reality for sister Melba, wasn't it? I mean, I'm not saying it serves her right or anything, but..."

"I know exactly what you're saying. Maybe she'll come down a few buttonholes now. But then again, knowing Melba..."

Crystal was at the stove, heating up codfish and potatoes for their breakfast. Mitzi was making tea. "Girl Crystal, I have to tell you something, but I don't want to say anything to Melba and Sundae yet."

"It's gotta be about a man then. I'm listening."

"Promise not to say anything to those lot."

"I promise. What is this - Girl Scouts? Now don't keep me waiting, I might have a heart attack."

"Well..." RJ ran into the kitchen, asking Crystal to come and play with him.

"Boy, your Godma is getting ready to tell me something... never mind, you don't know how important things like that are." Mitzi shook her head. RJ was the image of his father - a handsome little boy. He was going to be tall like his daddy, too. "RJ, I told Zindzi to read a story to you, didn't I?"

"The story's stupid." He picked up a glass that was wrapped in newspaper. "What's this?"

"Will you put that doggone thing down?!" Crystal snatched it from him. "RJ, please go inside and finish listening to the story - it's not that long."

"I don't..."

"I am not asking you, I am telling you. Now go and do as you're told! When the story's finished, you can go outside and play." RJ ran off. Crystal cut her eyes. "If I ever get pregnant again, I'll chop my damn head off. Raoul Outerbridge wants another child - he better go somewhere else 'cause this shop is closed. I'll be glad when these children are old enough to call me and ask me to look after their brats so I can tell them 'no'."

"And I haven't even started yet," Mitzi said as Crystal put their breakfast on the table.

"Now, stop beating 'round the bush - get to the juice. What you gotta tell me?"

"Just a minute." Mitzi said her grace.

"Oh for..." Crystal closed her eyes, too.

"You know a guy named Maliq Simmons?"

Crystal frowned. "Maliq Simmons...? That name sounds familiar. Where he from?"

"He lives up Burnt House Hill, but I don't know where he's from originally."

Crystal shrugged. "Anyway, what about him? With a name like Maliq, he sounds young."

"No, he's thirty-five." Mitzi was eating.

"Well, what about him?"

"Nothing."

Crystal hit the table with her hand. "Well, why the hell did you bring his name up?!"

Mitzi laughed. "I met him on the plane the other day - we talked the whole flight home, I lent him a book, he came to my house last night - supposedly to return it, but he forgot it, and we went running on the beach this morning," she said all in one breath.

Crystal's eyes almost came out of her head. "And all that is nothing? Sure sounds like something to me."

"Well, it's not really - I don't even know him."

"That's usually how things start, girlfriend. How the devil you think people get to know people? You think everybody knows everybody they get involved with from birth?"

"All right! Sometimes you just go on and on." Mitzi cut her eyes at Crystal who was devouring her food. "Anyway, he's real nice..."

"Nice don't cut it. Darren was nice - hell, 'Q' was nice. What else do you know about him? Is he educated?"

"Yeah, he graduated from Morehouse College last year. He's an accountant."

Crystal raised her eyebrows. "Point one. He married?" Mitzi just looked at her. "I'll take that as a 'no', point two. He live with his mama?"

"Nope."

"Point three. Got transportation?" Mitzi nodded. "Point... four. Strictly heterosexual?"

"He appears to be."

"Well, check that out but give him the benefit of the doubt. Point five. He do drugs?"

"I didn't ask, but he works out regularly and seems a bit too educated for that."

"Six. Educated, huh? Can he hold a decent conversation?"

"Definitely."

"Seven. Got an ex-wife who might be a threat or drop their children on your doorstep?"

"Never been married, and his daughter is a teenager. He does have an ex-girlfriend who still wants him, though."

"She ain't important. She'll get over him - as long as he don't want her. Where was I? Um... point eight. He been up the Sallyport Hilton?"

"Where?"

"Casemates."

Mitzi laughed. "Not that I know of." Two days, eighteen years ago didn't count.

"That's nine. If he's never hit a woman, he's got ten points - at least. As far as I'm concerned, he's got it goin' on, and you need to get him and get it goin' on with him.

Crystal was getting a second plate of food. "You want some more?"

"No, I'm full."

"I was hoping you'd say no, 'cause if you didn't, I'd be cut short." She looked at Mitzi and smiled. Crystal's kitchen table was at a window which looked at the North Shore, and Mitzi was enjoying the view - it reminded her of this morning on the beach with Maliq.

"You didn't ask me what he looks like."

"I don't care if he's a cave-dweller, Mitzi. He could be a kangabat; does it matter?"

"You know it don't matter to me, but I thought you would have asked."

She patted her chest. "Crystal. Not Ebone´ or Melba. I mean Raoul's cute and everything, but he ain't the best lookin' man around."

"That's not what you said last night." Raoul walked in and pretended to be hurt.

"Oh Raoul, a woman will say anything in the throes of ecstasy," Crystal said, and Mitzi hollered.

"What you laughin' at?" Raoul asked jokingly.

Mitzi acted serious. "Nothin'." She looked at Crystal, and they burst into laughter.

Raoul sat at the table. "I just saw a woman down the road who said she thought I was cute. I think she wanted me, too." He folded his arms, pleased with himself.

"You went to the dump, Raoul! Am I supposed to feel threatened?"

"You don't know what type of women go to the dump."

"Well, that's true, honey, and if somebody out there wants you, then I feel damn lucky and privileged to be your wife," she said patronizingly.

He sucked his teeth. "You got something else for me to do?" He stood up.

"There's a lot for you to do. Inside."

He looked at both of them. "That a hint for me to leave you two alone?"

"Yes, honey, we're talking about something private."

"Oh, you're gossiping."

"It's about Mitzi, so it's not gossip."

"What? She finally got a new man? I hope so, then maybe I can have more time with my wife," he said jokingly. He really liked Mitzi.

"That won't stop me, Ace-Boy. And furthermore, when you move, you'll be living closer to me, so you'll be seeing a lot more of me. Hey, I might just move in."

"No, that won't be happenin'. You move in, I'll move out."

"Go inside, Raoul. I'm trying to get a scoop here." She lowered her voice. "You know I'll tell you later."

Mitzi's mouth fell open. "Crystal?"

"Don't worry 'bout it, we tell each other everything unless it's real personal. Incidentally Raoul, you know those children you gave me?" He looked at her. "You can have 'em back. They're driving me crazy."

"I'll take 'em down to Western Stars field to the cricket game so you girls can pack in peace."

"I knew I loved you for a reason. And you are kinda cute." She stood and squeezed his behind. "And that also means you don't have to do any more work, right?"

"You got it, baby." He left. Mitzi had cleared the table and was running water in the sink to wash the dishes.

"So what you gonna do, Mitzi? This guy seems like somebody you wanna write home to Mama about."

"I know, girl. He is so nice to talk to. I mean, first we only talked on the plane. Then last night he came to my house and stayed for about two hours - it was like we had known each other for years. I didn't feel shy or anything. We drank wine and talked - he's just so... interesting and, and... nice. I know you hate that word, but he's so... sweet. Then this morning, we ran together on the beach and talked some more, and it's just so nice to have a conversation with a man who doesn't dwell on himself and who has a decent vocabulary."

"How come he's still single?" Crystal was seasoning chicken to cook for dinner, and Mitzi was washing the dishes. Mitzi sighed. "Oh, Lord, I knew he sounded too good to be true," Crystal said, rolling her eyes.

"No, it's not that. First of all, he went away to school when he was thirty and just graduated last year and..."

"Let's have it. What's his downfall?" She looked up. "Lord, don't let it be something I can't handle." She put the chicken in the oven.

"It's just that he had just broken up with his girlfriend when I met him on the plane - like, that same week."

"Didn't I tell you don't worry about her? What did he say about her? Does he still want her? Is he unsure? What?"

"He said it's over. They've had too many problems and complications, and it's just not going to work."

"Who ended it?"

"He did, but she didn't take him seriously at first, but he made it clear that he was serious - now, all this is what he's telling me, anyway. I don't know how true it is."

"Take the man at his word. You like him?"

"I don't even know him."

"Oh come on, Mitzi, I told you already, this is me you're talking to. Do you like the boy or not? And don't tell me you just met him, and you just wanna be friends and all that crap, 'cause it ain't playin'. Even though you did just meet him, you know whether you're attracted to him or not. You wanna get something goin' with him, or what?"

"Yes."

"Thank you. Playin' all cute - I know you, girl. But what's the worst that can happen?"

"I could find out he's lying about the 'ex', or he might change his mind and go back to her."

"So what? It ain't like you're a person who falls in love fast. I mean, we both know that if the brother wants you, he's gonna have to work for you. Real hard. So if it don't work out, you'll get over it. Or go under it, but either way, you'll get past it."

"I don't know how he feels about me, though. I'm just assuming..."

"You know what they say about assuming, right? Whose idea was it for him to come to your house last night?"

"I told him he could come and return a book I lent him on the plane. But he forgot to bring it when he came."

"Wait a minute... He came to your house for the sole purpose of returning a book and forgot to bring it? Hello! Whose idea was it for you two to run on the beach this morning?"

"He said he was going and I..."

"Who suggested it, dammit?!"

"He did."

"Oh sister, you're in. What now?"

"Well, he did say that there was a lot to learn about me and that, I quote, 'shouldn't be running on the beach with a stranger so we would have to fix that', end quote."

"Hey now. So have you made plans to see each other again? I mean this sounds like it was meant to be - you met on a plane, for goodness sake. You, a single woman, just happened to be seated next to a single man on a plane. Come on, sister, make a move - and as Zindzi would say, 'you snooze, you lose.'"

Mitzi smiled. This did sound good - maybe it was too good. "He promised to bring the book back, so I told him to call me when he had the time to bring it."

"Okay..."

"And I told him I would let him know if I was available when he was ready to come."

Crystal sucked her teeth. "Now see, you had to throw that in, didn't you? It is exactly that attitude that has had you sleepin' alone all these nights."

"Well, it'll still be a while before anybody will be in my bed."

"Oh, that's right, I forgot how proper you are."

"And furthermore, it hasn't been that long; I just broke up with Darren a few weeks ago."

"Who? Can't say I recall a Darren. He couldn't have been important." They both laughed as Melba knocked on the door and walked in.

"Hey, what's so funny?" She put her bag in a chair.

"Raoul was just saying how some woman at the dump was checkin' him out." Crystal had always been a fast thinker. She could cover up real good, and Mitzi always told her that was because she was a good liar.

"Hey, Melba. How you doin'?" Mitzi asked.

"I'm making it." She sat at the table. She looked exhausted and like she needed some sleep.

"I'm sorry I haven't had a chance to call you, but I've had a lot going on. I've been thinking about you, though. You all right?"

"I will be. I just can't believe Roger did what he did."

"Well, believe it, 'cause he did it," Crystal said. "And Melba, I don't want to talk bad about a man that you invested ten years with, but do you think you're better off without him?"

Melba sighed. "I know I'm better off without him, especially since he showed me what he's really about, but every time I think about starting over..."

Just deal with one day at a time, Melba," Mitzi said. She had started wrapping some of Crystal's plates.

"Yeah, I guess I'll have to." She paused for a second. "I never thought I would say this or would have to say this, but... I envy you, Crystal."

Crystal looked surprised. "Why?"

"You and Raoul seem so happy together. You don't have a problem in the world. You have two beautiful children, you're moving into your own home, and your husband is in love with you. I don't think a man has ever been in love with me."

"Hold on a minute, Melba. My life is far from perfect. Yes, I do have two beautiful children who I love more than life itself, but some days I feel like strangling them. And yes, we are moving in our own home, but nobody gave us that house, Melba. Raoul and I have busted our butts working for that house. My husband has worked day and night for the past six years. We've had to sacrifice valuable family time while he worked nights, and I had to help my children with their homework and get them ready for the next day all by myself." She put a glass of apple juice in front of Melba. "And yes, Raoul and I are very much in love, but we have problems just like anybody else."

"It don't seem like it."

"Look, I love Raoul almost as much as I love my children, but there are some ways he has and some things he does that I absolutely hate. Sometimes we have vicious arguments, but beneath the arguments, there's still love. We have, on many occasions, agreed to disagree on things just so we could keep the peace and move on. And Lord knows, I have ways that Raoul hates, but we have a friendship first, and friends are willing to deal with friends' faults. We've worked at our marriage, our family, our house, everything." She lowered her voice. "I can't stand his mama, and she can't stand me, but I tolerate her, for my husband's sake. The things she does create little problems in our marriage sometimes, but that's his mother and I'm his wife, and he respects both of us for what we are to him."

"Melba, I know it's hard right now, but it won't last forever. Nothing does," Mitzi said.

"I have a feeling that this is going to last for a while, 'cause Roger's really acting up. You know about him taking all my things and all. Well, yesterday, after he got out of jail, he came right back to the house and wouldn't leave until I threatened to call the police. Then he called me eight times in an hour, begging me to give him another chance."

"You think you will?" Crystal asked.

She shook her head. "You know when I make a decision, that's it. He's called me three times this morning, too. I hope this don't go on for too long 'cause I don't have the emotional fortitude to deal with this. After all these years, he should realize the ramifications of messing with me." She paused. "I think I'll get a restraining order."

"You know, it's amazing to me that when a man has a good woman, he thinks he can treat her like dirt, put her through changes, and when she's had enough and is strong enough to leave him, he suddenly 'needs' her," Mitzi said, irritated.

"That's exactly what he said this morning - he needs me. But you lot don't know the whole story. I happened to stop by his friend Perry's house on Thursday night to talk to him about having a surprise party for Roger. His birthday is next month - and don't ask me why I would want to have a party for him - but anyway, who should open the door, but Roger, with no shirt on. He was supposed to be at work, and Perry wasn't home. I asked him what he was doing there, and he acted like he was trying to keep me outside, so I just gave him one hard push and went inside. Sitting on the couch in just a tee shirt was some girl, looked young enough to be his daughter."

"What?" Crystal was shocked, and so was Mitzi. "Melba? Are you serious?" Crystal asked.

She nodded. "Anyway, then and there I realized that it was time. And you know what? This hasn't been as hard as I thought it would be because to be truthful, I haven't loved Roger for quite some time now. I've just been with him and tolerated him and just needed a real reason to get out. And he gave it to me." She smiled. "I guess I should thank him for that."

"Yeah, send him some flowers," Crystal said, cutting her eyes. Melba laughed. She really was a tough woman. She had had to be all her life.

"Melba, I'm sorry," Mitzi said. "We lot didn't know all that happened. I didn't anyway."

"No need to be sorry. I'll be all right - you know that. Now, I'm hungry, any breakfast left?" She went over to the stove.

"Yo, yo, yo!" Sundae ran in the door. "My sistahs, what's up?"

"I can't believe you're here," Crystal said, looking at the clock. It was eleven ten

"I know. I'm tired, too. But you know I can't miss a session like this."

"Your hair looks nice, Sundae, you put a colour in it?" Mitzi asked.

"Yeah, yesterday. It's auburn brown. I think it looks quite nice myself. Brings out my natural beauty." She laughed, and the others looked at her like she was crazy. Mitzi shook her head. "Now, is breakfast ready? I'm starved - I had a few last night, so you know I'm hungry."

"Where did you go last night - to a wake?" Crystal asked.

"Not this time. Got one on Tuesday, though. Good thing it's my day off, 'cause my boss wouldn't be too happy about me takin' time off." She smiled at Mitzi. Mitzi cut her eyes. "So Melba," she said, hitting Melba on the hand. "You have one less bell to answer, huh? One less egg to fry?"

"Sundae!" Mitzi couldn't believe she had said that, but she was probably getting back at Melba in what was supposed to be a subtle way.

"It's all right," Melba said. "I told her everything. She even knows about Roger and the girl at Perry's house." Sundae looked at Crystal and Mitzi and nodded her head, smiling. She loved to know that she had found out something like that first. "She came down to my house yesterday morning to see if I was all right, and she was there last night when they brought the furniture back. I really appreciate your support, Sundae."

"Hey, that's what sisters are for. But tell me somethin', what you gonna do now that you're a SBF?"

"A what?" Melba asked, confused.

"A Single Black Female. You've never seen that in the *Bermuda Sun,* when people are advertising for men? Get with it girl, 'cause you're like Patti LaBelle now, 'On Your Own'." They all laughed.

"I can't be worried about that right now," Melba said, eating her breakfast. "I'll just have to get used to living alone. I think I just might enjoy it after all this time. Maybe I can try and find my true self now."

"You would want to do that, 'cause only God knows who you've been all this time." Sundae said. "But you know something, Melba? I don't like to talk about people but..."

"You don't what?" Crystal and Mitzi asked together. They all laughed.

"Anyway, not that I think I'm better than anybody else or anything, but I always thought you were too... good for Roger, anyway. I mean, what is he? Seriously Melba, you might be a bitch - and I'm sayin' that as a true friend - but at least you have a bit of class. He just wasn't... right for you. And he keeps some undesirable company..."

"Go on Sundae - with that dictionary word," Crystal said.

"You like that?" Sundae asked, smiling. Crystal nodded. "Anyhow, I always thought he was a shady character, and I never understood what you saw in him."

"At one time Roger had potential, but that was way back then. And his family didn't help any."

"As my granny would say, you have to keep the whole from the broken," Mitzi said. "He really isn't a nice guy, Melba - he never treated us girls nice. You notice we don't come down your house - 'cause he's so miserable, and we didn't feel comfortable."

"She never invites us to her house, that's why I don't go," Sundae said.

"That's 'cause her man was miserable," Crystal said.

"Why are you lot just telling me this now?"

"We've been saying it for years, Melba, you just didn't wanna hear it. You watch, now you'll realize a lot of things about Roger that've been there all along, but when one has tunnel vision, one can't see what's happening on the side," Mitzi said. They were all wrapping dishes now.

"Mitzi, do you feel like a... *real* woman or a complete woman without a man?" Melba asked.

"What am I - a nun?" Mitzi was slightly offended. "Sundae doesn't have a man either, how come you didn't ask her?"

"Okay, do you feel that way, Sundae?"

"Hell no. I know I'm a real woman. You lot go 'head and keep listenin' to Whitney Houston telling some man she has nothing, nothing, nothing, without him. A man doesn't complete my life, Melba. I would *kill* for a man, but I don't need one to feel like a whole woman."

"Melba, I'm sure you know that a man does not make a woman happy just by *being.* A woman has to learn to make herself happy first. If you don't have inner happiness, then no man will ever be enough," Mitzi said.

"That's exactly what I was gonna say," Sundae said.

"Right," Crystal said. "Come on, Melba, you're stronger than that."

"I know, but I keep thinking about what people are going to say."

"If you must worry what people are saying, think about what they've been saying all these years," Mitzi said. "You think we're the only ones who have noticed how bad Roger has treated you? And do you think for one minute, that nobody else knows about the girl you found him with? We lot didn't know, but I'm sure somebody knows."

"Who was it anyway?" Sundae asked.

"That's not important, Sundae!" Crystal snapped.

"I figure since she was telling all, she might wanna tell us her name."

"I don't know her. Never seen her before."

Sundae shook her head. "You people need to get out more. I bet you I would have known who she was. What kind of car was she driving? What's the number of the car?"

"I didn't see a car."

"Melba, why are you answering Sundae?" Mitzi asked.

"Hey, I'm just trying to be helpful. She might wanna go and have a word with the sister." Sundae was such an instigator - she loved a scandal.

"No, she can have him. He obviously wants her. And believe me, if I wanted to do something to both of them, I would have done it that night. But that girl wasn't the problem, Roger was. And he is no longer a problem to me, so let's change the subject."

" 'Bout time. I've been dyin' to talk about somethin' else, but I didn't wanna seem insensitive," Sundae said, taking her sneakers off.

"Wait a minute, let me see what these lot are doing. They're mighty quiet in there." Crystal went to check on her husband and children.

"Well, hurry up," Sundae said. "How much of this stuff do we have to wrap?" she whispered.

"All of it, Sundae. They're moving out. You think they're leaving some of it here?" Melba asked. She was obviously coming around.

Crystal came back in the kitchen. Raoul and the children were asleep. "Anyway, what you wanna report, Miss Chong?"

She looked at Mitzi suspiciously. "What was Maliq Simmons' car doin' in your yard last night?"

Mitzi's eyes widened. "How do you know that?"

"Oh come on, girl - this is Bermuda. You know we people can't make a move without somebody finding out."

"You know him?" Crystal asked Sundae.

"Yeah, from way back." She drank some of Melba's juice.

"Sundae, don't bibble in my glass, girl, I don't know where your lips have been." Melba wiped the glass with a napkin.

"Trust me, nowhere. Anyway, I haven't talked to Maliq for ages. He, his brother and sister used to come up my granny's house after school - she had an after-school type thing going on, all the neighbourhood children came there. That's how far back we go. His brother, Marcus was my 'play' husband when we were small."

Melba sighed. "I really don't have the tolerance level for one of her interminable stories."

"Hey, you lot asked. All right, we don't have to go way back to the seventies - just tell me what his car was doing in your yard last night."

"You tell me who told you, and I'll tell you why the car was there."

"It's not important how I know. I just know, okay?" Mitzi looked at her and said nothing. "All right, I came up your house, saw the car and left. I didn't wanna disturb your groove - if there was a groove, you know what I'm sayin'?"

"Oh Sundae, please..." Crystal said.

"Sundae, you would have broken the door down getting in Mitzi's house," Melba said.

"You know him, Melba?" Crystal asked. Melba shook her head.

Sundae waved her hand. "You know she don't know nobody." She thought for a second. "I don't think I have talked to Maliq since..." She shook her head. "It's been so long. Mitzi sat at the table beside Sundae. "You haven't talked to him, but what do you know about him?"

"Ohh, so you wanna negotiate now?"

Crystal hit Sundae across her arm with a dish towel. "Oh for God's sake, Sundae, let's have it! Should Mitzi knock boots with this guy, or what?"

"Crystal!!" Mitzi spun around and looked at her.

"Well, I can't take this anymore! It's driving me crazy."

Sundae looked at Mitzi and shrugged her shoulders. "PMS, I guess. You want him, Mitzi?"

"I don't want him, Sundae, I met him and I think he's... nice." She looked at Crystal and cut her eyes.

"Maliq? Sounds like a young person to me," Melba said.

"Thirty-five," Crystal said. "Come on, Sundae."

"He comes from a good family. They used to live over Princess Estate - I think his mama and daddy still live over there. When we were small..."

"Now, Sundae! Now! What's happenin' in the nineties?!" Crystal was shaking Sundae's shoulders.

"Why are you so volatile today, Crystal?" Melba asked.

"It must be time for my period 'cause I feel like I'm losin' my mind today, for some reason."

"You look like you've lost it in that costume," Sundae said. Crystal took a butcher's knife out of a drawer and rested it on the table. "Okay, all I know about Maliq right now is that he used to work for Telephone Company, then he went away to school for a while... hey, he was going with that girl Marilyn Hunt the last I heard." She looked at Mitzi. "You know that?"

"She's history," Crystal said. "But then again, wouldn't you know that?"

Sundae frowned. "This must be a new development. Anyway, he's a real nice guy - or he used to be anyway, and I can't see him changing. I could find out the scoop on him if you want me to.

"No thanks, Sundae. I'll find out myself - from him."

Sundae lit up. "So what, you two are an item already?"

"No, he was at my house last night - as you know - but nothing's happening. Yet."

"Well, go for it, girl. If you want something bad enough, don't wait for it to come to you - go and get it. You told me that," Sundae said.

"I'm glad I did, Sundae. Trust me, I'm glad I did." Mitzi looked at Crystal and shook her head.

"Hey, does he still have a deep voice like Kyle on 'Living Single'?"

"That's who he sounds like!" Mitzi slapped her leg. "I've been trying to figure out who that sweet voice reminded me of."

"Well Mitzi, don't show off, 'cause I've got a li'l somethin' goin' on myself. I'm going out with this guy today," Sundae said.

"Who?" They all asked, shocked.

Sundae crossed her legs and shook her foot. She picked up a muffin and began eating it. "This guy named Tyrone." She smiled at them.

"Tyrone who?" Melba asked.

"Like you would know him," Sundae said.

"Well, we might," Crystal said. "Tyrone who?"

"Can I have something to drink?" She was being evasive for some reason.

"This is exactly why I fly off the handle. Sundae, why the hell can't you ever just answer a question?" Crystal asked.

"Because... she don't know the answer," Melba said slowly. "Sundae, you don't know his last name, do you?"

Sundae sucked her teeth. "Look, I don't need a name, I need a man right now, okay." Melba's mouth fell open.

"Sundae, are you out of your mind? Did you take a 'stupid pill' this morning, or somethin'?" Mitzi asked, hitting her over the head.

"You are going out with some man, and you don't even know his last name?" Melba couldn't believe her.

"What's the big deal? I met him at my cousin's house - she knows his last name - and he asked me to go to a christening with him today." She held her hands up and shrugged her shoulders. "It's not like I'm gettin' married or anything."

"Of course you're not. 'Cause if you were, you wouldn't know what your last name would be," Mitzi said.

They all sat, talked and packed for the next few hours. Melba and Crystal spent half the day eating. It was normal for Crystal, but Melba never ate that much. Sundae left at two o'clock to go out with her mystery man, and Mitzi and Melba left after six. On the way out of town, Mitzi stopped and bought a bottle of cold water, then drove up to Warwick Long Bay. Just as he had said, Maliq was there. She didn't see him, but his car was parked in the parking lot. She rested the water on the ground beside his car with a note which read, "thought you might want to cool off." She smiled as she drove home. She wondered what he would think when he saw it. Would he even know she had left it? Maybe he had several women he ran on the beach with and wouldn't be able to figure out who'd left it. Oh well, time would tell.

Mitzi got home to find Ebone´ sitting on the couch in her pajamas, eating dinner, which Wendell and his daughter, Terry - the sister Ebone´ didn't know was her sister - had brought her. She looked a bit better than yesterday although she told Mitzi that she had been crying half the day. She also told her that she and Wendell had an appointment with the psychiatrist in the morning, and then she would be returning to work for the first time since her mama died. This was definitely progress. Mitzi felt a bit guilty because she hadn't spent much time with her these past few days, but at least Wendell had been there. And Ebone´ said she and her sisters were getting along much better.

Even though she was tired, Mitzi sat and talked with her for a while until Oleeta called. She wanted to inform Mitzi that she was going to stay out of the 'baby situation' and let Macky deal with it himself. Tatyana and her mother had been to talk to Macky and Oleeta; Macky wants her to have an abortion, she wants to keep the baby, her mother is willing to support her in whatever her decision is, and Oleeta told them she doesn't want anything to do with it because Tatyana should have been on the pill. Didn't sound like she was staying out of the situation to Mitzi - simply by making that statement to the girl and her mother. Mitzi told her that she didn't want to get involved any more and at the same time, made a mental note to call Tatyana and tell her she would be there if she needed her. She wasn't angry with Oleeta anymore - very disappointed in her, but she figured that that was Oleeta's way of dealing with something she didn't know how to deal with.

Oleeta also told her that she and George had set a definite wedding date for Saturday, September tenth. They planned to get married at The Hamilton Cathedral at eleven in the morning and would have a small reception at Belmont Hotel from one until four. She asked Mitzi to be her Maid of Honour, and she was more than honoured to oblige. She asked her what Macky had said, but Oleeta hadn't told him yet because, as she said, they had had an argument on Friday night, Macky had *cursed* her, and they hadn't spoken since. She said she left him alone because he was "going through a lot and was under a lot of pressure". The whole world was under pressure, but that didn't give everybody the right to act any way they chose - especially a seventeen year old. And as much as it angered her, Mitzi didn't say one word about it - he was Oleeta's son, and if she allowed him to curse her - and live, then more power to Macky. Mama would learn one day, probably when it was too late. Mitzi turned on the iron to get her clothes ready for work the next morning when the phone rang again. Without looking at her caller I.D box, she picked it up. She heard the music first - The Isley Brothers singing 'Voyage to Atlantis'. It was Maliq.

"Thanks, pretty lady, for the water," he said, sounding more 'Kyle-like' than ever.

What water?" She held the phone between her ear and shoulder as she ironed.

He laughed. "Only someone as sweet and thoughtful as you would do something so sweet and thoughtful. And by the way, I did need to cool off."

She laughed. "Guilty, I guess. I thought I would let you know I was thinking of you while you ran your butt off."

"You should have been with me. It wasn't the same without you."

"Nah, I didn't want to tire you out again."

"Yah, right. Why didn't you come down on the beach and look for me? I would have been glad to see you again."

I *was* going to surprise you, but I didn't want to be surprised - to see another woman running with you."

He chuckled. "There wouldn't have been another woman, I promise you that. I was all alone - and lonely."

Damn, you silly girl. "I doubt you're ever a lonely man."

"We must sit down and talk, so I can tell you all about my quiet, uncomplicated life. I'm a straight-forward guy."

"We'll see."

"When?"

She smiled and couldn't speak for a minute. She wanted to say, *Whenever you're ready,* but she didn't. "I don't know..."

He wanted to say, *What about tonight?* But he didn't. "What are you doing next Sunday morning, same time?" He really didn't want to wait that long, but it was the best he could think of right now - he didn't want to scare her away.

"I'll have to check my book," she said, joking.

"Well, *if* you're free, would you like to join me on the beach? I don't wanna run because it's too close to the race. I just like to do a lot of walking and stretching before a race."

"I'll call you through the week and let you know." She already knew she would be there.

"And, if your book isn't too full, would you have breakfast with me afterwards? At my house." He sounded almost afraid to say the last part. He was such a gentleman.

"And just what is the name of the chef, or the place we'll be ordering from?" She was teasing him.

"Chef Maliq will be at your service," he said, laughing. "I don't like to blow my own horn, but I can cook, sister. My mama taught me how to cook, clean house and wash and iron clothes very early - I think it was her way of ensuring I didn't stay in her house too long."

"Smart lady. I believe every man should be able to take care of himself - in the event he doesn't always have a woman in his life."

"And I believe that every man should know how to take care of himself *and* his woman, so he can make sure he always has her," Maliq said - with conviction.

Hello! This man is too good to be true! "I can't argue with that."

Mitzi agreed to call Maliq before the end of the week to let him know if she could make it on Sunday. Crystal would kill her if she knew she hadn't agreed right away. But that wasn't her style. She hated to always sound or be available. Maybe she would lose out one day, but she would cross that bridge when she got to it. She finished ironing her clothes, got a shower and before going to bed, she pulled out her Isley Brothers CD and started it on 'For the Love of You'. She went to sleep with a smile on her face.

CHAPTER FIFTEEN
Tuesday, May 24th

Twenty-fourth of May was here, finally - Bermuda Day. Every Bermudian looked forward to this day from the time the year started. It was an absolutely beautiful day - as always. There was never bad weather on Bermuda Day. They had arrived at Heron Bay at eight thirty. Out of their crew, Crystal, Raoul and their children got there first, followed by Melba who looked like she would have rather been elsewhere. Shortly after, Mitzi arrived and parked her car in the school yard next to a broken-down looking, blue Toyota Tercel with the words 'Struggle Buggy' on the side. The regular crowd was already in place and everybody was ready to enjoy the day - except Melba. Mitzi had gotten up early and taken Maliq up to Somerset to start the race.

They had spent a bit of time together during the past week. She had accepted his offer to walk on the beach on Sunday morning, then they had gone to his house to have breakfast. She was a little nervous, which wasn't like her at all, but she was glad she had gone. They had left the beach just before eight o'clock and gone to his house where he had fresh fruit and juice waiting for them. He had asked her if she wanted to take a shower, but she didn't feel too comfortable about showering in a man's house - especially one who she barely knew. She wanted a shower in the worst way. Maliq hadn't showered either, just so she wouldn't feel uncomfortable. He lived downstairs from his landlord in a quiet neighbourhood and had a beautiful apartment.

It was the cleanest man's apartment she had ever been in, and she wondered if he had cleaned it because she was coming or if it was always spotless. The apartment was kind of split-level; three steps spread in a semi-circle from one end of the apartment to the other and led down into a huge, open living room. The kitchen was on the upper level to the right, and Mitzi assumed his bedroom and bathroom were on the left. There were French doors leading from the living room out into a huge yard. The walls were decorated with beautiful African art, the furniture was black and included a floor to ceiling wall unit, which served as a library and which was full of books. Mitzi was impressed. On the other side of the 'library', in the middle of the living room wall, was a brick fireplace, and on the other side of that was a huge fish tank with every colour fish imaginable.

They had sat at his kitchen table and eaten breakfast while listening to music. He also had the TV on mute. He said he always had both on at the same time. He had cooked codfish and potatoes but offered to cook something else for her if she didn't want that, telling her that she could have anything she wanted. She had chosen the codfish. After breakfast they sat out on his porch and talked. They talked about everything, including his daughter. He told her the story of being locked up and how he was allowed to get out because his parents had promised to see to it that he took care of the baby, and he had. Mitzi told him about Macky because she was sure he could relate. He told her to just support Macky as much as she could because it was a lot for him to deal with. She told him how he had been treating her mother, and Maliq didn't think that was right. He told her that his daughter had just graduated from Warwick Academy and was a bit spoiled. She thought she was too grown to be told what to do, but he did what he could, and he and her mother had a decent relationship. She was married, and her husband didn't treat Maliq's daughter that nicely. Mitzi told him briefly about Ebone´ and what it had been like living with her. He said he thought he knew her and he definitely remembered Sundae from years ago. She told him about

Crystal and Melba and what she was going through. They had talked about their families. His parents were still living at Princess Estate, as Sundae had thought, and were about to celebrate their fortieth wedding anniversary. He had four brothers and two sisters; he was the fifth child. Mitzi told him she had always wanted a sister and more brothers, and he coyly told her she could be a part of his family. She wondered what they were like and hoped she would find out soon. She told him about her father's early death and her mother's upcoming marriage plans. He was looking forward to meeting Oleeta again and Macky and Mitzi's friends. It sounded like he had plans to stay around for a while. By the time she was ready to leave, she hoped she would be spending a lot of time with him, too. He told her he was a Virgo, his birthday being August twenty-ninth. She told him that she was a Cancer - July sixteenth. She left at two o'clock after having spent the better part of the day laughing and getting to know Maliq. She loved being around him - she had been able to be herself because he made her feel very comfortable. She also finally got her book back. He had asked her then if she would do him a favour and pick him up the morning of the race and take him to Somerset. She had gladly told him she would.

"Look for me on the street," he had said as she drove off. She promised him she would, shook his hand and wished him good luck. When she'd dropped him off, she wanted to kiss him for good luck and felt comfortable enough to do it, but for some reason, she didn't. She didn't want to seem... what? He had acted like he was kind of waiting for her to kiss him, too.

Now, as she sat on the wall and waited for, first the bike racers to come past and then the runners, she felt excited. And happy. She was a little worried about Maliq and hoped he would be all right. He had finished in the first hundred and fifty last year so she decided he would be all right. He had asked her to have water ready for him in case he needed it when he passed their spot

"Where's Sundae?" Mitzi asked Crystal. "She should have been here before me - I've been Somerset and back."

"How come you went Somerset?" Crystal asked. She was brushing Zindzi's hair.

"To take Maliq," Mitzi said, not looking at her. She felt Crystal looking at her and smiled.

"Oh, you didn't tell me all this. What's wrong with you? You know you can't keep things like that from me!" She hit Mitzi with the hairbrush.

"Who's Maliq?" Zindzi asked.

"Now, Zindzi, what did I tell you about when grown-ups are talking?"

"That children should stay outta grown-ups' con...va...sations."

"Well, in case you're not aware, you're still a child, so kindly keep out. So what's going on with you two?" Crystal was determined to find out. She and Melba were sitting in lawn chairs, and Mitzi was sitting on the wall. Raoul was sitting on the sidewalk with RJ and a few other spectators. Melba turned to find out what was going on, too.

"I don't know what's goin' on yet. We walked on the beach on Sunday, then I went to his house for breakfast."

"Mmm." Crystal said, digging in her bag for a mango - she had finished her daughter's hair. "Keep talkin'."

"He asked me if I would take him Somerset this morning, and I did."

"Did you kiss him? You know, to wish him good luck," Crystal asked.

"No. I didn't think it was appropriate. Anyway, we've hardly gotten to all that yet."

"A kiss? What's to get to?"

"Come on, Crystal," Melba said. "It is a bit early to be doing that."

"According to whose rules? It's just a kiss - friends kiss, don't they?" Crystal was sticking by her feelings. They turned to see Ebone' and Sundae walking toward them. Ebone' had told Mitzi she *might* come out, and now Mitzi was glad she had. She looked nice, too; she had on denim shorts and a denim top with white sneakers and socks. Mitzi hadn't seen her dressed that casually for a while. She was usually over- dressed in some get-up. Today her hair was combed nicely, and she had on lipstick with hardly any other makeup. She and Wendell had been to two counseling sessions already, and both times she had come home in very good spirits. She would make it - Mitzi was sure of that and told her as much. She was due to go with her to the psychiatrist this Thursday. Ebone´ spoke pleasantly to Mitzi's friends and sat beside her on the wall.

"Where's your car, Sundae?" Mitzi asked.

Sundae sighed, rolled her eyes and said, "Up Tyrone's house, all right?"

"Tyrone who?" Crystal asked, looking at Mitzi and laughing.

"Tyrone Ryan Burrows. Deal with that." She sat on the wall beside Melba. They all clapped and laughed.

"You lot are too childish." Sundae said. "So Mitzi, you find out any more about Maliq?" The girl could not make it through a morning without getting a story about somebody.

"Yeah, she found out his last name," Crystal said, dryly.

"Crystal, you have to tear the tail out of things, don't you? Anyway, Mitzi, what's happening? I'm 'jonesin'."

"I would hate to deprive you, Sundae. Actually, I've found out a lot about Maliq. I was at his house for breakfast on Sunday."

"Nobody told you that, Sundae?" Melba asked. Although she was joining in the conversation, she still seemed a little down. She had every right to be. Roger had been making her life hell. He had started stalking her - following her at night and hanging around her house. He had also been calling her and threatening her, telling her that if he saw her with another man, he would kill her and him. And just the past weekend, she had to call the police to get him off her property again. She had taken out a restraining order against him yesterday, but she was really upset. She usually wasn't afraid of him, but when a man started making threats like that, he should be taken seriously.

"No, I didn't hear about Mitzi being at Maliq's house on Sunday. That one got past me, I guess." She laughed.

"Have you met Maliq, Ebone´?" Crystal asked, trying to include her in the conversation.

"No, but I've heard all about him." Mitzi had told her about him the night before she went to walk with him on the beach.

"What did she tell you?" Sundae asked. She didn't expect Ebone´ to tell her, but she was trying to include her, too.

They were all surprised when she answered. "Just that he's a real nice guy, and she thinks she likes him. But the way she's been acting, I know she likes him." Mitzi didn't think she had been acting any differently. "She walks through the house, singing those old songs she loves." She looked at Mitzi and laughed. Mitzi cut her eyes. "Well, you do. You think I don't hear you. I have you checked."

"I must give you a call sometime, Ebone´," Sundae said. "Here come the bikes." They looked westward, and a pack of bikes was coming toward them. They always went by so fast. By the time the first runner was in sight, it had gotten a few degrees warmer, but there was a light breeze, and the cedar tree they were sitting under provided just enough cover for them to enjoy both the sunshine and the breeze. It was so exciting watching the lead runners - there were so much pomp and pageantry with the police bike escorts and the convertible cars and news cameras. And everybody knew somebody in the procession. It seemed that was more exciting than the runner himself because, at times, the lead runner wasn't Bermudian, and nobody knew who he was, so the crowd sang out to the officials instead. It usually wasn't until the lead runners passed that they recognised people they knew.

For the next hour and a half, there were shouts of encouragement and applause from the spectators as each runner or group of runners struggled over the hill and past the 'Heron Bay Posse', as they referred to themselves. Although they were usually full of encouragement, they could also be cruel in their remarks to the runners. Sundae was by far the worst.

"Hey Mitzi, look at your old neighbour in the hot pink shorts. What she tryin'?" Sundae had started.

"At least she's trying, Sundae. It's more than you and I can say."

"What's with that H.I.B.?" she asked.

"What the heck is H.I.B.?" Melba asked.

"Hair I Bought," Sundae and Ebone´ answered together, referring to the woman's weave. The crowd laughed.

"Come on, Al!" somebody shouted.

"Hang in there number forty-seven!"

"Don't give up yet, Sammy, you got a long way to go!"

"Want some water, Albert?" They always filled up cups with water either to pass to or throw on the runners.

"Oh, Sundae, look at Roddy, he looks good," Crystal said.

Sundae stood up to look. "You sure it's him...? Oh yes, it is. I thought he was..." She lowered her voice. "Freedom impaired."

"Got out a month ago," Crystal said, still eating her mango.

"Man, I am losing it. But then again, he ain't important. He's no good, actually. Got locked up for not paying child support. He has five children from three different women and ain't paid a penny for none of 'em."

"That's damn ridiculous. Why don't some of these men just jerk off overboard and make jellyfish instead of babies?" Crystal asked.

"Crystal!" Mitzi looked around to see who had heard her. Raoul turned around and shook his head as Crystal put her hand over her mouth.

The runners were coming in packs now, and Mitzi wondered how Maliq was doing. Again, she hoped he was okay and couldn't wait for her friends to see him.

"Mitzi, look at your client, Mrs. Wilson. Want some water, Mrs. Wilson?" Sundae was almost standing out in the road. Mrs. Wilson smiled and took a cup of water as she ran by.

Someone on the wall was passing around popcorn. RJ came running to Crystal and very excitedly asked her if he could run with the runners as far as the corner at Scenic Heights and run back.

"No, honey, you can't do that."

"Why not?" He looked disappointed.

"You're too little, RJ."

"No I'm not. I'm big and I'm strong, mama."

"I don't care if you can leap tall buildings in a single bound, RJ. You're not running anywhere. Now that's that." He started to cry and stamp his feet. Crystal gave him a look that stopped him mid-stamp. "Thank you. Now please sit down and behave."

"Sundae, isn't that one of your clients?" Mitzi asked, pointing to a female runner.

"Used to be," Sundae said. " 'Til she decided to put those silly twists in her hair. I hate 'em. She looks like a Chia Pet... hey! Don't throw water on her head! Chi, chi, chi, chia," Sundae sang. Their 'friends on the wall' thought she was hilarious.

"Girl, give these people a break," Raoul said, still laughing.

"Hey, they want to run in the twenty-fourth of May marathon, they should be prepared for the comments. I live for this day!" She was having a ball. And even though Ebone´ wasn't saying much, she seemed to be enjoying herself, too.

"Hey, look at Mike. Now tell me why he has to wear that ridiculous outfit," Sundae said, while clapping.

"He's a total jackass," Crystal said, shaking her head.

"He certainly is," Sundae agreed. "He's gotta be two people, 'cause he's too stupid to be one."

"Looking good, Maliq!" someone in the distance shouted, and Mitzi turned to see him running toward them.

"Mitzi, here comes Maliq!" Sundae was shouting. Mitzi got up and got a cup of water.

"What's his number?" Crystal asked, dying to see who he was.

"I can't see that - he's in black shorts." Mitzi was smiling. Maliq looked good as he ran closer to where she was standing. He smiled when he spotted her. "Want some water?" She asked him.

"No thanks, I'm fine." He winked at her and kept running.

"He certainly is fine," Crystal whispered so Raoul wouldn't hear her. Mitzi sat back down. "He has a body by God - not that it matters, but I just thought I'd mention that." They both laughed.

"Saw your sweetie?" Sundae asked. "He looks good, Mitzi." And he did. He looked like he had just started the race. This was the first time Mitzi had seen his legs, and they were thick and firm - and covered in sweat. He had gotten a haircut yesterday, and he looked so... masculine. So good.

"He's not my sweetie, Sundae," Mitzi said. "We're friends."

"Right, right," Sundae said, nodding.

"If I were you, I would upgrade the status of that friendship," Melba said. "And quick."

"I'm workin' on it."

"That a girl," Crystal said.

"My dear Crystal, look at how much weight Randy has lost. He's not sick, is he?" Sundae asked, referring to a runner.

"I don't think so. He's just been training a lot. He does look a tad bony, though. And his girlfriend has gained about a hundred pounds," Crystal said, exaggerating.

"Who?" Sundae's radar was on full alert.

"Miranda."

"Oh I know, I saw her," Sundae said. "I'd like to see *them* in bed. Must be like giving a whale a Tic Tac."

"Sundae, you're so crude. Don't you have somewhere else to go?" Melba asked, laughing and shaking her head. "Where is this 'Tyrone' person?"

"Working. Hang in there, Robert!!" She didn't miss a beat.

When they figured the majority of the runners had gone by, they all packed up and agreed to meet across from the Bank of Butterfield on Front Street to watch the parade at one o'clock.

Maliq had asked Mitzi to pick him up at Bernard Park after the race, and she hoped he wouldn't be waiting too long for her because she had his clothes. She took Ebone´ to her sister's house and went to the park. This was kind of like deja vu - she had met Darren at Bernard Park last year. *Lord, please don't let history repeat itself,* she thought as she parked her car. She spotted Maliq immediately. He was talking to another runner and looked like he hadn't long finished the race - he was still sweating. He broke into a big grin when he saw her, dimples in full effect.

"Hey, thanks for coming," he said, touching her shoulder.

"I had no choice," Mitzi said, smiling. "I have your clothes, remember?" She gave him his duffel bag.

"I really appreciate your doing this for me. I hope I didn't inconvenience you or pull you away from your friends." He was putting his jacket on.

She shook his arm. "I told you already, it's no problem. And I'm meeting those lot later, down at Front Street to watch the parade." She paused. "What are you doin' later?"

He shrugged his shoulders. "I usually go home, take a shower and rest for a bit then go town to watch the parade." He was staring at her and smiling. She smiled back.

"By the way, how did you make out in the race?"

"I finished in an hour and twenty-nine minutes." He looked humble.

Mitzi's eyes widened. "Get out of here! That's very good." She turned her head to the side and looked at him. "You looked good coming past Heron Bay."

That was for you, baby. "Thanks, I felt pretty good up there, I felt good all the way, actually." *That's because I knew I would be seeing you after the race, you sweet thing.*

"Congratulations. You must be proud of yourself." She looked him in the eye. "I'm proud of you."

He smiled. "Tell me something, when someone is proud of someone else... don't they usually... give them a hug... or something?"

Mitzi laughed. "You're right. I would be remiss if I didn't *at least* give you a hug. You do deserve it today." She put her arms around his waist, and he put his around her shoulders. They held each other for a few seconds longer than either of them expected to. *Damn, girl, don't do this to me,* Maliq thought, and when Mitzi finally pulled away, he looked a little sheepish.

"I'm sorry, I know I'm a little wet." He lifted his arm and jokingly smelled his underarm. "And I hope my body odour wasn't too offensive." They both laughed.

"I didn't notice." Mitzi was staring at him and smiling. She really felt good being with him, and it had felt real good having his arms around her.

The parade started well after two o'clock, and Mitzi, Crystal, Sundae, Ebone´ and Melba had been sitting on Front Street since one o'clock. It was a sunny, 'Bermudaful', breezy day, and Front Street was packed. They were sitting on lawn chairs under two umbrellas. Crystal had taken her children to the beach and left them with her mother, who was having a picnic with her family, and Raoul had gone out on a boat with some of his friends. Crystal was relieved to be child and husband 'free' for the day. Between them, they had all cooked chicken, peas and rice, potato salad and coleslaw and had bought breezers, beer and drink - they were prepared for a good time. For the most part, the parade was pretty. It could have done without a few floats, though.

"The purpose of that entry escapes me," Melba said, referring to a truck full of half-naked women and beer drinking men, dancing - just dancing to very loud music. No decorations, no theme, no meaning. There seemed to be a lot of that lately, and it spoiled an otherwise beautiful parade.

"I know, it's really unnecessary," Crystal said, looking disgusted and eating watermelon. "Look at that big bellied bas..." Mitzi covered her mouth because she knew what was coming. "Well, he shouldn't go around without a shirt on," Crystal said, talking about a man on the truck who looked like he was six months pregnant.

"Give these folks a Bermuda Day, and all sense of pride is forgotten," Melba said, lighting a cigarette.

"I agree," Sundae said. "They should all be as classy as you and smoke cigarettes on Front Street." Melba cut her eyes, and Mitzi and Crystal laughed. Ebone´ was sucking beer from a bottle and paying no attention to them. Shortly after the parade began, Maliq and his friend Terry found them and sat in front of them - Maliq on the cooler the two of them had brought and which was full of beer, soda and water - and Terry on the sidewalk. Mitzi introduced her friends to Maliq, and he introduced Terry.

The day was absolutely wonderful. By the time the parade was almost over, they all had laughed so much Crystal was wiping tears from her eyes, Sundae had a headache, and even Melba was slapping her thighs and laughing, and Ebone´ had fully taken part in the joking and teasing that Mitzi and her friends always indulged in whenever they got together. She had even looked at Mitzi and burst into laughter when Ricky walked past them and stuck his middle finger up to her. When the parade was over and Sundae and Crystal had run off to follow the Gombeys, Maliq and Terry helped Mitzi, Ebone´ and Melba pack up. When Melba went to get her car from Reid Street, Maliq asked Mitzi if she and Ebone´ wanted to go to his house for a barbecue.

"You wanna go, Ebone´?" Mitzi asked hopefully. Terry smiled at Ebone´. She shrugged her shoulders.

"Sure, but I have to leave for work no later than seven." It was five o'clock.

"Well, we better get going," Terry said, grabbing an umbrella as Melba drove up and opened the trunk of her car. Just as they finished piling everything in the car, Crystal and Sundae came back out of breath.

"You lot are just in time to help us," Melba said sarcastically, putting the last of their things in her car.

"Glad to be of service, sister," Sundae said, laughing.

"Crystal, what time do you have to pick those children up?" Mitzi asked.

"I have children?" Crystal asked, taking a chicken leg from a bag in the car. Mitzi looked at her and shook her head. Crystal laughed. "Oh, I'm havin' such a good time, I forgot I had 'em." She got serious. "Do I have a husband, too?" She laughed again. Maliq thought she was funny. He had told Mitzi he liked her friends and felt comfortable around them. He was enjoying his day. He also told her she looked like a beautiful African princess.

"Take Crystal home, Melba, and don't give her any more to drink," Sundae said.

"I know," Crystal said, devouring the chicken leg. "Breezers and sun are a lethal combination... oh Lord! My mama's gonna think I'm an unfit mother if she knows I've had a few drinks. One drink and she thinks a person is an alcoholic."

"Just don't talk, Crystal. She'll never know," Mitzi said.

"Come on, Mitzi," Sundae said. "Crystal not talk? Some things are impossible."

"Where you lot going now?" Crystal asked.

"I have to give Tyrone a lift work," Sundae said.

"Sundae, does this Tyrone really exist?" Melba asked. "Because I have yet to meet him."

"You'll meet him, in time," Sundae said.

"Aren't you a little old for imaginary friends, Sundae?" Crystal asked. Sundae sucked her teeth and cut her eyes. "Where you goin', Mitzi?"

"Ebone' and I are going up Maliq's house for a while." Crystal smiled and looked at Maliq. He smiled back. Ebone' and Terry were having a conversation of their own. Crystal nodded in their direction.

"Is Terry going, too?"

"Yes, he is. Now, I'll call you later." She pushed Crystal in the direction of Melba's car. She knew she would start asking a lot of questions.

"So, Ebone', what do you do that has you working on a Bermuda Day evening?" Terry asked. The four of them were sitting in Maliq's yard, drinking rum swizzle. Maliq had chicken and steak on the barbecue.

"I'm a waitress," Ebone' said a bit shyly. She had become slightly introverted in the past couple of weeks, and there were still times when she would go into a shell and become withdrawn.

"You should have told your boss you wanted the night off." Terry seemed to be really interested in Ebone'. He also seemed harmless and sweet. Mitzi would have to find out what he was about from Maliq. She knew he would be straight-up with her.

"I just went back to work this week. I've been off for a while."

"Well, I'm sorry you have to leave early," Terry said, crossing his ankle over his knee and holding it. "We'll have to get together on a night when you don't have to rush off to work." Maliq went to check the meat.

"Mitzi, can you help me please?" he called out to her.

"I thought you were the consummate chef." She stood beside him while he turned the chicken.

"I just wanted to give those two a little time to themselves." He looked at her slyly and when their eyes met this time, neither of them looked away uncomfortably, as they had been doing the few times they had been together. Maliq spoke in a soft, yet very masculine voice. "Did I tell you that you look beautiful today?" She had on a dark green and beige cotton, ethnic print, ankle-length wrap skirt, matching off-the-shoulder top which barely covered her navel and beige sandals. Her hair was braided again and partially wrapped in the same material as her outfit. She did look beautiful.

"Yes, I think you have told me once or twice." She paused and smiled. "Did I tell you how good *you* looked running - your body glistening with sweat?"

She was getting brazen, but Maliq had made her feel so comfortable over the past few days. They had had a very open talk about life and what they wanted out of it while they walked on the beach and then at his house on Sunday. They discovered that they were basically on the same wavelength - so to speak. He told her he was looking for a strong, independent, proud, black soul mate to spend time with. She felt as he did. They had a lot in common. However, during the conversation it was never actually spoken that either of them wanted to start a relationship with each other, so consequently, both of them felt the same confusion at the end of the day, but Maliq knew that was exactly what he wanted, and so did Mitzi. Today they all had laughed and talked so much nonsense at the parade that Mitzi felt like they were old friends, and she could let her hair and her guard down a bit.

"My body was glistening with sweat? You were looking at my body?" he asked, faking surprise.

She laughed then looked in his eyes. "I think every woman in Bermuda was looking at your body." As she spoke, a bead of perspiration ran between her breasts, and her top lip was wet. Maliq stared at her and thought she was the epitome` of pure feminine sexuality.

"Nah, I didn't notice anybody looking at me," he said as modest as always. "Nobody would look at a big fella like me." He winked at her. They stared at each other again silently and sent an unspoken message which said, *I want you and I'm going to have you.* They were both oblivious to everything around them for a minute, each lost in similar thoughts.

"Maliq?"

"Huh?"

"You're burning the chicken." He turned quickly to look at the grill.

"This chicken's not burning."

"Oh I'm sorry, I thought it was," she said, dark brown eyes penetrating his. *It must be me,* she thought. He closed his eyes briefly and smiled.

"Dinner is served," he said, ending the moment. He did that often, and Mitzi wondered if it was intentional or he was just shy.

After dinner, which also included pasta salad, tossed salad and corn on the cob, Mitzi and Maliq took the leftover food into the kitchen and once again left Terry and Ebone´ out in the yard alone.

"Are you leaving when Ebone´ goes?" Maliq asked Mitzi as she put the salad in the fridge.

"Do you want me to?" she asked, hoping like hell he wanted her to stay.

"You really don't need me to answer that, do you?"

"I don't take anything for granted."

"The only person I want to leave when Ebone´ does is Terry."

"You can't kick him out."

"He's my boy, so I can kick him out."

"Mitzi, Maliq, I hate to eat and run, but I have to make time," Ebone´ said, coming into the house with Terry behind her.

"I'm sorry you have to leave, Ebone´, but thanks for coming," Maliq said, meeting them in the living room. Mitzi prayed she would thank Maliq. She was still a little ungrateful.

"Maybe we can get together again sometime," Terry said. "I'd like to get to know you, Ebone´."

"Sure, that sounds all right. Thanks, Maliq." Mitzi smiled. It was a start. "I'll talk to you later, Mitzi. See you, Terry." Mitzi walked her to the door.

"You okay?" she whispered.

Ebone´ smiled. "Yeah, I'm all right. Terry's a trip, girl - a nice guy - but a trip. I'll tell you about him later."

Mitzi, Maliq and Terry went back outside, got something to drink and sat in the yard. The sun was still shining, and it was still hot.

"I like your friend, Mitzi, but she seems a little... distant and... cold," Terry said.

"You'll have to ease her up," Mitzi said in Ebone´'s defense. "Her mama just died about two weeks ago, and she took it real hard."

"Oh man, that's why she was kind of stand-offish. She was talking to me and being polite, but I could sense something was wrong."

"You don't even know the sister, Terry, so how could you be sayin' you *sense* something was wrong?" Maliq laughed.

"I am very sensitive to a woman's moods," Terry said, sounding sure of himself.

"Right. I know all about it. Now, wasn't there somewhere you had to be right about now?" Maliq said, looking at his watch. Mitzi smiled.

Terry held his arms open. "Oh, it's like that. You're kickin' me to the curb?"

"You got it, papa." Terry looked at Mitzi. She smiled and shrugged her shoulders. He stood and took his keys from the table.

"Okay. I can get to that. If I had a pretty sister sittin' in my yard, I wouldn't want your ugly, black a... behind blocking either. Later man." He held his fist out in the 'touch me' gesture, and Maliq 'touched' him. "Nice meeting you, Mitzi."

"And you, Terry." Mitzi smiled.

"He really likes Ebone'," Maliq said.

"What's he about?"

"He's cool. We've been tight for a while, and he's my boy, but he's a little narcissistic - actually he's *really* into himself."

"Didn't appear to be."

"Get to know him."

"I don't know what Ebone' thinks about him other than that 'he's a trip', but she doesn't need any headaches or heartaches right now."

"She seems... deep." He touched Mitzi's hand. Her heart literally skipped a beat. "Nothing like you. You're open and... approachable and... sweet."

Mitzi smiled. "Ebone' can be sweet, too, she's just got a lot goin' on right now."

"Far be it from me to judge anyone, but I just can't see the nexus between you two."

She sighed. "We've been friends for over twenty years and even though we've remained friends, our lives took us in different paths for a while. She had to endure a few more hardships than I did, and they kind of dictated what her personality is today." She rested her empty glass on the ground. "She's a diamond in the rough really, and I have hope for her. The story's too long to get into, but she's working on taking charge of her life."

"You hold her up, don't you?" Maliq admired her defense of her friend.

Mitzi nodded. "I try. She tests our friendship from time to time, but - as you would say - she's my girl, and I hang in with her."

"I guess that's what true friendship's all about," Maliq said, and Mitzi nodded. He now held her hand. "You think we could have a... true friendship?" Mitzi looked at him. She didn't know if he was serious or not. "I don't want to be forward, but I also don't want to lose out. I would love to share my life with a lady like you." Mitzi stared at her hand in his. *Come on Maliq, don't do this, we only met two weeks ago. So what? Why does everything have to be measured in time?*

She finally spoke. "Is that all you want in your life? A friend." She wanted to find out where this was going.

"I believe friendship is the most important element in any relationship, Mitzi. You can build anything on friendship."

She liked where this was going. "True." She was sitting in a chaise lounge with her ankles crossed, exposing a little leg. Very little. He was sitting on the ground with one leg stretched under the chaise and the other bent. Gerald Albright was coming through the speaker he had put in the yard.

"I like you, Mitzi. A lot." He looked in her eyes and again noted how beautiful they were. "True, we only met a couple of weeks ago, but in the little time we've spent together, you've proven to be a very intelligent, strong, open, honest, independent, warm... smart..." He was looking for a few more adjectives. "Funny, straight-up, industrious... beautiful sister." He smiled, and Mitzi laughed. Usually if a man said something like that to her, she would think he was full of it, but it was the *way* Maliq said it.

"And you have a way with words," she said, feeling better and better about him. Actually, she felt damn good about him.

He looked concerned. "I meant every word, lady," he said. "Let me tell you something, Mitzi. My aspirations are great, my dreams many and my demands few, and to quote Whitney Houston, 'What's the sense in trying hard to find your dreams without someone to share them with?'"

"You must tell me about these dreams and aspirations you want to share with someone."

"Not just someone..."

"Daddy!! Oh, there you are." A young girl wearing a skirt too short and who was obviously Maliq's daughter, rounded the hedge with a rough-looking teenage boy trailing behind her. "I've been knockin' on your door for a good ten minutes." She looked at Mitzi. "Hi. No wonder you ain't had no time for me lately, you got new company. What happened to Marilyn or whatever she was named?" She plopped in a chair and stared at Mitzi. Mitzi stared back in shock.

"Maliqa, this is Ms. Robinson," Maliq said, obviously unmoved by this child's obnoxious behaviour.

"It's Mitzi," Mitzi said.

"Oh, I was wonderin' 'cause I don't think it would be about no 'Ms. Robinson'. This is 'G'. 'G', this is my daddy, Maliq." Mitzi was appalled by this brat who had Maliq's dimples.

"Hey, what's up, Money?" the boy asked Maliq. Maliq looked at Mitzi and shook his head. She turned away.

"Daddy, could we lot have a beer?" Maliqa asked. Mitzi hated made-up names, and she didn't particularly like this girl's attitude.

" 'Liqa, you know I'm not giving you any beer," Maliq said, trying to sound authoritative. He looked at 'G' as if to say, *you neither*. 'G' stood with his arms folded and looked like he wanted to kill someone.

"Mama lets me drink 'em."

"That's her. This is my house..."

"Well, what about some money? You have twenty dollars?" Maliq immediately reached in his pocket and gave her the money.

"Thanks." She kissed him. "Now, I'm outta here." She stood up. "Let's go, 'G'."

"Hey, don't be racin' me, right?" Maliqa playfully hit him on the arm, and he glared at her. Maliq stood, and the boy looked at him.

"Check you later, Daddy," Maliqa sang out as she ran off, followed by her gangster boyfriend.

"See you later, Boo. Be careful on that bike. Nice meeting you... what's your real name?"

"Gerald," the boy said with his back to Maliq. "Check you."

Maliq sat in the chair vacated by his daughter and shook his head. "These young men today are so disrespectful." Mitzi wanted to tell him that his daughter was no better, but she didn't think it was her place. Maliqa appeared to be a pert, pushy, obnoxious, spoiled child - nothing like her daddy. Mitzi couldn't believe that Maliq allowed her to be so abrupt. Furthermore, she had interrupted a crucial conversation.

"What you think of my daughter?" He asked.

You really don't wanna know. "Um, she... looks just like you." She didn't want to lie. Or hurt his feelings.

They sat in the yard and talked until well after the sun went down and the moon came up. Maliq had picked the conversation up where he'd left off, asking if he could spend more time with her and take her out because he really wanted to get to know her better. She told him that she had no one else in her life and would love to spend more time with him and get to know him as well. At two thirty in the morning, after sitting very comfortably in the yard, she decided she should leave, especially since they both had to be at work by eight thirty. Maliq walked her to her car. She leaned against the driver's door and faced him.

"Thanks for a nice night," she said and yawned. He frowned and she smiled. "I'm sorry, that's no reflection on you."

"Thanks." He smiled. "I was worried for a second there." He got serious again. "Thank you for helping me this morning - or yesterday morning - taking me up Somerset and being my... cheerleader. That was sweet; I appreciate it." He stood closer to her and held both her hands. "Mitzi, I don't know what's going to happen between us - I know what I *want* to happen and hopefully it will, but I just want you to know that I don't believe in playing games with people, especially women."

"I hope not, 'cause I'm a little too old to play games or have anyone play them with me." They stared in each other's eyes. They could see clearly under the moon.

"Then we're in sync," he said.

She nodded. "I'll talk to you later," she said, still looking at him.

"Tomorrow?" Maliq asked. He didn't want to take anything for granted either.

She nodded and smiled. "I hope so." He leaned closer and stopped. They were so close they could feel each other's breath. Then he kissed her cheek.

"I hope that wasn't too forward," he said shyly. She shook her head. *You could have shoved your tongue down my throat, and it wouldn't have been too forward.* "Would you do me a favour?" he asked.

"Sure." Mitzi unlocked the car and opened the door.

"Call me when you get home, so I'll know you got there safely."

"Gladly." She got in the car, and he closed the door.

It took Mitzi ten minutes to get home, and when she picked up the phone, she still had her bag over her shoulder. She couldn't wait to hear his voice again. She wanted more than a friendship with Maliq Simmons. Of that, she was sure.

As soon as Mitzi left, Maliq ran through the shower, rushing so as not to miss her call. He had just gotten in bed in only a pair of jockeys when the phone rang. It was like music to his ears, and he smiled. He didn't want his excitement to be too obvious, so he let it ring one and a half times. When they hung up a minute later, it was almost three o'clock. Maliq had to get up in three hours and knew he would be tired, but it didn't matter. Mitzi Robinson was going to be his soul mate. Of that, he would make sure.

CHAPTER SIXTEEN
Thursday

Even though Mitzi had been expecting Maliq's call, she was still excited to hear his voice. She had already called him this morning, and he had called her after lunch. They had talked on the phone three times yesterday, and the same thing had happened today.

"Hi sweetheart, how was your day?" Maliq asked in his sensuous, deep voice. Mitzi had been to the gym for the first time in weeks and had just gotten out of the shower. She was sitting on her bed in a tee shirt and underpants, rubbing lotion on her legs.

"It was fine. I wasn't real busy again today which was good because I had to take an hour off to go to counseling with Ebone´."

"How you make out?" Maliq was sitting on his couch, watching TV and reading the *Royal Gazette*. He wished she were beside him. He should have asked her to come after work.

"All right. It was interesting and eye opening. I'm learning how to deal with her while she's going through this period. I want to go back for a few more sessions."

"Good things are going to happen to you, Mitzi."

She smiled. "They already are."

"I was sitting at my desk today, thinking the same thing about myself."

"Really?" She was still smiling.

"Really."

"That's nice to hear."

"It's even nicer to feel." They were both silent for a minute, each reflecting on their own new feelings and emotions.

"What are you doing?" he asked.

"I just got out of the shower."

Maliq smiled and wondered if she needed him to dry her back. He would never say it aloud. Yet. "Ready for your bed?"

"Yep. I'm really tired tonight." It was time for her period again, and she was always tired around this time.

"You should be tired after that guy kept you up 'til three the other morning."

She laughed. "You're right. I better not let that happen again."

He laughed. "I hope you're joking."

"I am."

"Are you doing anything tomorrow night?"

"I was thinking about going movies."

"Can I take you to see Speed? It's up at Neptune Theatre."

"Sure, I'd love to go with you."

"Would you mind if Terry comes?"

Mitzi was a little surprised and disappointed. Yes, she did mind if Terry came. Why did he have to tag along? "Um..."

"He wants to invite Ebone´."

"Oh, okay." *Now, that's different.*

Maliq laughed. "I could imagine what you were thinking. 'Why his friend gotta be going out with us?' " He teased her and laughed again.

"No, I wasn't thinking that." She tried to sound convincing but failed and started laughing, too.

"Sure, sure. Tell me anything. Would you like to go to the early movie then to dinner at Somerset Country Squire?"

"Sure, I love Country Squire." Mitzi hoped she wouldn't finish work too late. She would work something out.

"Can I give Terry your number so he can call Ebone´?"

"Yeah, she's not here right now, but tell him to call her about ten thirty or eleven."

"You think she'll go?"

"I hope so. I'll convince her."

"I'm looking forward to seeing you. The anticipation will help my day go faster tomorrow."

"Thanks. That's sweet." She paused. "I can't wait to see you either."

Then why don't you come down here now? he wanted to say, but he didn't want to push it.

CHAPTER SEVENTEEN
Friday

Mitzi was disappointed. The double date had been canceled. Ebone´ had to work and couldn't make it, so she and Maliq decided to go alone, but then his father had been taken to King Edward with a suspected heart attack. Maliq had called her at four fifteen to tell her he was leaving work to go to the hospital. It turned out that Mr. Simmons had a severe case of indigestion. By the time Maliq left the hospital, it was after nine o'clock, so they all decided to go out on Saturday night. Mitzi had stopped by her mama's house on the way home to wish Macky a happy eighteenth birthday. Her mama wasn't home, but it was quite evident that Macky was even before she saw him because the smell of marijuana hit her as soon as she reached his bedroom. When Macky opened his door, she couldn't see past the smoke. When she'd asked him what in the world he thought he was doing, he told her he and his 'boys' were "just sitting around, smoking blunts." He told her his mama told him that she would rather he smoke in the house than let the police catch him out in public. Two of his 'boys' sat on the floor and looked at her like she had no right to be there asking questions. Mitzi was amazed at their total disrespect and disregard for her mother's home. She felt like killing Macky on the spot. He obviously needed to be taken out of his misery. She really needed to talk to her mama about this. And this time there would be no shouting. No arguing. They had to sit down and sort it out. This was not supposed to be happening in this family. Macky was going to hell in a handbasket.

Mitzi had gotten up early on Saturday morning - as usual - even though she felt the dull throbbing of cramp in her stomach. She took a couple of Advil and ate some breakfast. She didn't have time to exercise or clean her house because she had promised Crystal she would help her move. Granny was spending the weekend at her Aunt Roberta's house in St. David's so she didn't have to worry about doing her hair. She was at Crystal's house at seven o'clock, and Melba, one of Crystal's cousins and a few of Raoul's friends had come to help also. They had so many things to move and made so many trips up and down the country that by the end of the day, everybody was exhausted. They did all that was humanly possible and promised to come back on Sunday and finish.

"How do you feel about going out with Terry?" Mitzi asked Ebone'. She still had cramp.

Ebone' shrugged. "Not half as excited as you feel about going out with Maliq." Mitzi smiled. They were sitting at the kitchen counter, and she was painting her nails. Ebone' was looking through the latest Ebony magazine. It was four thirty, and Maliq and Terry were picking them up in two hours. Mitzi's clothes were ironed, and she just had to shower. Ebone' had been home about fifteen minutes and hadn't begun to get ready yet.

"Those guys are coming for us in two hours, see?" Mitzi blew her nails.

"Mmn. I know." Ebone' sighed. "I regret sayin' I would go now."

"Why?" Mitzi hoped she wasn't going to be in a bad mood tonight. The outing should do her a world of good. She didn't have to have a relationship with Terry, it was just movies and dinner.

Ebone' closed the magazine. " 'Cause I'm nervous."

"You, Ebone'?" Mitzi was surprised. Ebone' had never been nervous around a man. "Why?"

She sighed again. "Because, Terry's... strange. Remember the other day, I told you he was a trip?"

"Yeah."

"Well, he seems like a real nice guy, but he's self-centered. He talks about himself a lot, but he's... sophisticated. I don't know what to talk about with him."

"Don't worry about it. Maliq and I will be there - just go with the flow. Let him do the talking at first and just comment or answer the best way you can."

"That's easy for you to say, you're used to going out with intelligent men, and you can hold a decent conversation."

"Look, we probably won't talk about anything deep 'cause everybody's gonna be trying to get to know each other."

"Suppose he starts talking about world news or something I don't know about?"

Mitzi laughed. "I'll bail you out. Don't worry 'bout it. But let this be a lesson - at least try to have a little knowledge about world news for future dates with whomever."

Ebone´ rolled her eyes and shook her head. "I hope I don't make a fool out of myself."

"You won't. Trust me. Just be yourself." Mitzi was pleased to know that she at least cared about something like this. "Tell me something, usually when you go out with a guy, what do you all talk about?"

"Him. Sometimes me."

Mitzi frowned. "That's it?"

Ebone´ shrugged. "What else is there to really talk about?"

Mitzi shook her head. "We'll have to work on that later. But I wanna talk a little personal for a minute."

"Oh, Lord." Ebone´ crossed her legs and waited.

"Come on now, this is for real, and I don't want you to take any of this as a personal attack, right?"

"I won't. Go 'head."

"How serious are you with your personal hygiene?"

Ebone´ frowned. "My what?"

"Personal hygiene. Do you douche?"

"Uh, uh. I don't know nothin' 'bout all that."

"Are you serious?" Mitzi didn't want to make her feel uncomfortable or insult her.

"Nobody ever told me nothing about how to do all that. And anyway, I heard it's not good for you."

"I don't know about that, but I'm sure it doesn't do any harm."

"How often am I s'posed to do it?"

"Well, since you think it's not good for you, at least douche after your period."

"When do you... douche?" She said it like it was a bad word.

Mitzi shrugged. "Whenever I don't feel... clean. And definitely after my period."

"Don't you have to mix all this stuff together? I don't have time for all that."

Mitzi waved her hand. "Come up in the nineties, sister. They have ready to use douches, and they even have suppositories. That's what I use - they're quick and easy. We'll have to get you some this weekend."

"What else, Ms. Doctor?"

"Okay, next thing. What about shaving?"

"What about it? It's for men."

Mitzi smiled. Your legs are a bit hairy - I know you don't shave them, but what about your underarms?"

"I don't shave them either."

"Honest?" Mitzi's eyes widened.

"Honest. The men I've been with like hairy women. Especially Ricky."

Mitzi stared at her and shook her head vigorously. "No, Ebone´. Men like Ricky don't know anything about femininity, and they sure don't know 'bout hygiene."

"I thought hairy was s'posed to be sexy."

"Some men think hairy legs are sexy, but a man with class does not want to be looking at a thick bush under a woman's arms."

"I've never shaved my armpits."

"Well, we need to do a little makeover."

"Could we?" She lit up.

"Sure. I have to set you up, sister - for the new Ebone´."

"Hey, what do you think about a woman with hair on her chest?"

Mitzi opened her mouth and stuck her index finger in it. "Please don't tell me you have hair on your chest, Ebone´."

She shook her head. "No, but I've seen women with hairy chests."

"That is the ultimate in tackiness." Mitzi looked at the clock. "We don't have time for a makeover now, but shave your underarms. Cut the hair short first, then shave it. Get a suppository from my bathroom drawer, and I'll do your makeup later."

"Why can't I do my own makeup?"

" 'Cause you put on enough to last a week."

Maliq and Terry arrived at six twenty-five in separate cars. Mitzi had just finished Ebone´'s makeup when the door bell rang.

"Oh my God, I'm shaking," Ebone´, said, examining her face in the mirror. She liked the job Mitzi had done.

"Calm down, for goodness sake," Mitzi said, opening the door. Maliq and Terry both had roses for their dates. Mitzi thought it was cute. Ebone´ was a little embarrassed. She had probably never gotten flowers from a man before.

"You ladies look absolutely beautiful," Maliq said as they walked to the cars. Mitzi was wearing white palazzo pants, a long white top and casual gold sandals. Her jewelry was gold, and she had a tiny gold bag crossed over her chest. She had loaned Ebone´ her black and white ethnic print top which she wore with black knee-length shorts and black slip-on shoes. She wore silver accessories and carried Mitzi's black draw-string bag. Her makeup looked natural, and she had 'S' curled her hair. Gone was the hair that had been under her arms for twenty years, and she had douched for the first time in just as long. Mitzi told her that even though she wasn't going to bed with Terry tonight - she hoped not, anyway - and nobody but she would know about her new hygiene practice, she would feel better about herself.

"You're kinda quiet, you okay?" Maliq asked, looking at Mitzi as he drove. Ebone' and Terry drove behind them.

"I'm sorry, I didn't realize I was being so quiet." The top of the car was down and the breeze felt good, but Mitzi's cramp was getting worse. This wasn't a good time for her period to come on. She wondered if she should mention the cramp to Maliq. Why not? He was understanding. "I don't want to spoil anybody's night, but I have a little stomach cramp." She looked at him to see if he understood exactly what she meant. He did.

"I'm sorry. If you'd rather go back home..."

"No, it's not that bad. I can make it through the night."

"You always... suffer?" He looked a little uncomfortable, but concerned.

She shook her head. "Just these last couple of months. I don't know what's going on - I'm getting old I guess."

"Maybe somebody's trying to tell you something - like it's time for a baby." He smiled and kept his head straight.

She smiled, too. "I don't know 'bout all of that."

He frowned. "You don't want children?"

"Oh, definitely. But I just haven't given it much thought. I think I'm afraid to be someone's mother."

"Why?"

She waved to Crystal's mother, who was driving in the opposite direction. "Being a parent is a big responsibility and one I don't want to fail at."

He was amazed. "I think... I know you'd be an exceptional mother. You have so much to offer a child. You have wisdom, knowledge, values, and I'm certain you have a lot of love to offer."

I have a lot of love to offer you, too - you wait and see. "Thank you. You're very kind. How about you? You want more children?"

He nodded. "Definitely. I've wanted more children for a while, but I just haven't found the woman I want to be their mother." *Until now.*

Halfway through the movie, Maliq reached over and held Mitzi's hand, then looked at her to get her reaction. She looked at him and gently squeezed his hand. He smiled. Out of the corner of her eye, Mitzi saw Terry put his arm around Ebone´'s shoulder. Ebone´ stared at the screen. While the characters in the movie became attracted to each other, Maliq caressed and squeezed Mitzi's hand. At one point she closed her eyes and smiled. It had been quite some time since she had felt this good being with a man. She hoped it would last.

They arrived at Country Squire at nine thirty - Maliq had made reservations in his name - and sat in the cozy room at the back of the restaurant. There was only one other party in the room, and when they left, Maliq dimmed the lights. When the maitre d' asked who had turned the lights down, they all acted dumb and laughed when he left. They ate fish, drank wine and talked about the movie for a while until Terry started talking about himself. Ebone´ was quiet and eventually looked at Mitzi and rolled her eyes. Maliq saw her, laughed and changed the subject. Terry never caught on. As the night wore on, Mitzi's cramp got worse, and she really wanted to go home and get in bed but didn't want to break up the party. When she and Ebone´ escaped to the ladies room, Ebone´ told her she was ready to go.

"You're not having a good time?" Mitzi asked, powdering her face.

"Not really. To be honest, I'm tired of going out with self-centered men, which is exactly what Terry is. I'm just as important as he is, so I should be able to at least say a few words." She had obviously learned a thing or two in counseling, and Mitzi was proud of her.

"Well, let's stick the evening out, then you don't have to go out with him anymore."

"You got that right. You and Maliq seem like you're havin' a good time."

"I'd be having a better time if I didn't have this stupid cramp. And the wine's not helping any."

Ebone´ sighed. "Come on, let's go and get this over with." She swung the straw bag over her shoulder.

Mitzi laughed. "It's not that bad, Ebone´."

"It's worse than that." Ebone´ was out the door. Mitzi did think Terry was a narcissist, but not an intolerable one, and thought Ebone´ was exaggerating a bit. But if she didn't like him, it was her life. At least she had given it a chance.

Once they were back at the table, Maliq asked Mitzi how she was feeling, and when she told him she didn't feel well at all, he insisted that they leave so she could go home and rest. He and Terry argued over who was paying the check and finally settled on splitting it. Mitzi didn't talk much on the drive home. She leaned her head back and closed her eyes but still tried to be sociable. As they passed Granaway Heights, Maliq patted her knee and told her they were almost there. Terry and Ebone´ had been in front of them but were now nowhere in sight. As they drove in Mitzi's yard, Terry was driving out. Ebone´ must have jumped out while the car was still moving. Mitzi and Maliq both laughed after Terry drove past and waved.

"Guess that didn't go too well," Mitzi said as Maliq cut the car out.

"I hope Ebone´ doesn't hold it against me," he said smiling.

"Nah, she won't."

"Can I walk you inside?"

"Sure."

Maliq would have loved to help Mitzi get undressed, get ready for bed and make her some hot tea, but he knew that couldn't happen. Yet. He felt sorry for her - he could see she was feeling bad - but she was putting up a good front. She was such a lady. "Can I do anything for you before I go?"

She shook her head and leaned against the living room wall. "No thanks. I just need to take some Advil, get a shower and get in my bed." She tried to smile.

Maliq gently pulled her away from the wall and held her. She lay her head on his chest and hugged him back. He smelled so good. She wanted to stand just like that all night. It was nice to be in a man's arms while she was in pain. But not just any man. A man she really liked. A man she thought she could love. A man she believed she wanted to be in love with.

"I hope I didn't ruin your evening," she said, still holding on to him.

"Are you serious?" He slowly pushed her away from him and held by her shoulders. "Mitzi, I had a damn good time with you tonight, as usual. It's not your fault you have cramp. It happens."

"Thanks for understanding," she said.

"Hey, it's not like we aren't going out again." *I have a lot of plans for you, baby.*

"That's true." *I have big plans for you, honey.*

"Where's your Advil?"

"In the cabinet beside the fridge." He went into the kitchen, got her two Advil and a glass of water. Then he put the kettle on and made her a cup of tea while she sat on the couch.

When he got home, Maliq called to see how Mitzi was feeling. She was in bed and feeling a bit better after the pain killers, tea and a hot shower. And, of course, the fact that he had held her and kissed her softly on her lips before leaving had a lot to do with her improved health.

Mitzi felt absolutely horrible on Sunday morning. The cramp was worse, and her period had come on full blast. At nine o'clock, she was still in bed, curled up in a ball. She had promised Crystal that she would come back and help her again today, but she had to call her and tell her there was no way she could make it.

"You'd better call your doctor and get yourself checked, girl. This is happenin' a bit too often," Crystal told her.

"I called, he's gone on a three-week trip to South Africa."

"He has? My dear, that must have set him back a couple of hysterectomies, innit?"

Mitzi laughed, then groaned. "Crystal, don't make me laugh, girl, my stomach hurts."

"I'm sorry. But you better try to see somebody before your next period. Somethin's wrong with your parts, sister."

"Hold on a minute." Mitzi had a call coming in. A few seconds later she clicked back to Crystal. "Sorry 'bout that."

"Mmn. You need anything?"

"No, that was Maliq. He's gonna bring me some breakfast."

" 'Scuse me. Breakfast in bed?"

"No, it ain't about all that. We went out last night, and he knew I was feeling bad when I got home, so he called to see how I was. He's so sweet, Crystal girl."

"So what's happenin' with you two? Come on, you know I need play by play."

"There's no play to give you. We've seen each other a couple of times, and he and Terry took me and Ebone´ out last night."

"Really? How did Ebone´ and Terry make out?"

"Not good. He's an 'I Doctor'. 'I' this and 'I' that. But Maliq and I had a good time until my cramp got bad."

"Sooo..? What happened at the end of the night?"

"Nothin'."

"Come on, girl!"

"What could happen, Crystal? I had cramp!"

"Well, you might have kissed, at least."

"Oh, we did. Kind of."

"Kind of? Did you kiss or not?"

"Just a little smack on the lips."

"No tongue?!"

"Crystal..!"

"Oh please..."

"No. No tongue. You've been hangin' 'round Sundae too long."

"Look, girl, I'm your best friend."

"And every day you make me so glad you are."

"I'm just tryin' to help, sister."

"Thanks so much. Now, let me get up and try to look halfway decent before Maliq gets here."

"Please do. It's a little early in the relationship to be looking tacky. What you got on?"

"My purple satin pajamas. Should I change?"

"No! You're sick. And that sounds cute."

"Well, I'm going to put a bra on and clean my teeth."

"Why put on a bra?"

Mitzi sucked her teeth and sighed. "Bye Crystal."

"Call me if you need anything."

Mitzi was rubbing moisturizer on her face when Ebone´ knocked on her door.

"Hey, Maliq's here." She smiled. "With breakfast for both of us."

"I'll be right there. How do I look?"

Ebone´ rolled her eyes. "Mitzi, come and get your breakfast." She left, leaving the door open. Mitzi followed her and hoped her pad wasn't showing through her pajamas. She felt behind her to see how long her top hung. It was long enough.

"Mornin', Maliq." He was sitting on the couch.

"Mornin'." He smiled at her. *She's even beautiful bare-faced and sick.* Her eyes looked a bit dark, and he could see she still wasn't feeling well as she sat beside him. "Not feeling any better, are you?"

She shook her head. "Worse actually." Ebone´ took her plate into her room.

"I'm sorry I made you get out of bed."

"I should be sorry for having you drive all the way up here this early."

"It was the least I could do. I feel kind of helpless."

"I'll be all right." Maliq stood up and went into the kitchen. He uncovered a plate full of codfish and potatoes with the works. "I hope you're not tired of eating this."

She smiled. "I'm a Bermudian; I eat codfish and potatoes just about every Sunday." She felt a little weak and held her head.

"Do you eat in your room?" She nodded. "You wanna sit on your bed and eat?"

"Yeah, I don't feel like sitting at the table."

"Well, I'm not staying, but if you want I could... take this in your room for you. If that's okay."

She smiled. "Come on. There's a tray on top of the fridge." He followed her to her room, carrying the tray. Maliq thought her room was as feminine as she was. It was decorated in hunter green and peach and was spotless, like the rest of the house. Mitzi stacked some of her pillows up - she had a bunch of them. Maliq put the tray in front of her.

"Maliq, I really appreciate this, but you didn't have to go through all this trouble..."

"Let me tell you something, Mitzi," he said, stooping beside her. "Last night, I could see you were in pain, and naturally I don't know what you're feeling, but I feel for you, sweetheart. So I'm just trying to do what I can to pamper you and hopefully make you feel better. You deserve it." Their eyes met, and she smiled.

"You're too sweet," she said softly.

He shook his head. "It's not about being sweet. It is my duty as a black man to take care of my sister."

Mitzi closed her eyes and smiled again then she held his hand, looked at him and said nothing. What could she say? He was still crouched beside the bed. She leaned toward him. He didn't move away, so she leaned closer and kissed his lips. He responded but, as Crystal would say, there was no tongue. He stood and held her face, brushing it with his thumb.

"You better eat before that gets cold." Mitzi had gotten so caught up in the moment that she had completely forgotten about the breakfast. "If you need anything else, call me. I'll be home most of the day."

"Thanks, Maliq. And thanks for thinking of Ebone´."

He laughed. "I thought I owed her at least that, to compensate for last night." Mitzi rolled her eyes. "She's not mad at me, is she?"

"Nah. And believe me, if she were, you would've known."

"Take care, beautiful. Hope you feel better."

"I'll try. Talk to you later?"

He winked at her. "You know that."

Mitzi had just put the still half-full plate of food in the fridge - she was in too much pain to eat - and was getting back in her bed when the phone rang. She hoped it was Maliq; she really didn't feel like talking to anyone else. It was Melba. She thought about not answering but changed her mind. She was glad she did. Melba was very upset. Roger had come to her house, persuaded her to let him in and then pulled out a knife and told her he would kill himself in front of her if she tried to make him leave.

"I said, Roger, make my day," Melba recounted the episode. Mitzi couldn't believe her ears. "Then, when I picked up the phone to call the police, the idiot snatched it from me, cut the wire with the knife then started hitting me. Big mistake," she said, her voice trembling with anger.

"What you do, Melba?" Mitzi was shocked.

"What I do? He hit me a ringing slap across my face, so I gave him a hard punch in his."

"My Lord..."

"Then he decided to push me down and get on top of me, and we hooked on the floor."

"You fought him back?"

"Don't ask stupid questions, Mitzi. You know I get the strength of ten men when it comes to fighting."

"Yes, I'm well aware of that."

"Well, I got hold of the knife and sliced his arm. He very quickly got up off me. Blood was running out of his arm, and he was screaming at me, telling me I'm crazy. I know I'm crazy - when some fool messes with me. He asked for it, he got it - and it wasn't a Toyota." Her mouth was going a mile a minute.

"So, did he leave, Melba?"

"No, he stood in my kitchen - blood dripping on my floor - telling me how much he loves me and wants me back and all this bull. I didn't wanna hear it, so I politely asked him to leave the premises several times. Finally, he said he wasn't leaving 'til I at least promised him we could talk. He started coming toward me, all pathetic and I dared his ass to take one more step and Mitzi, I'm telling you, you all would be bringing me cigarettes down Co-Ed." Mitzi didn't doubt that.

"Mel, you don't need this. Why don't he just leave you alone?"

"Well, I don't think he'll ever be back."

"Why not?" Mitzi was scared to listen.

"Because, Mr. 'All of it' then tells me that he isn't going anywhere until I sit down and have a decent conversation with him. And he said it like I had no choice. Then he wrapped his arm with some paper, went out on the porch, lit a joint, sat down and put his feet up on the wall."

"What an idiot!" Mitzi couldn't stand men who acted that way.

"Well, I thought Roger knew me after ten years. But evidently he hasn't been paying attention. I left him alone and put some water in a pot..."

"No Melba..."

"... boiled some rice, calmly walked out on the porch and threw it on him. As we speak, he's at King Edward being treated for burns."

"Melba!"

"Look, enough's enough now! And after they finish treating him the police are waiting to arrest him, 'cause I ran his black backside in."

"Good for you, girl."

"Roger Burchall done barked up the wrong tree this time. Oh, and the police just called me to tell me somebody's coming here to talk to me, *and* Roger had the unmitigated gall to tell them he wants to run me in for assaulting him! Have you ever heard of such?"

"You people belong on 'The Young and The Restless'."

"That's where he's going to wish he were when I'm finished with him. Tomorrow I'm going to get another restraining order against him, for his own good."

"I suggest you do."

"You know, Mitzi, I thought it was going to be real hard being without Roger, but things like this only make me hate him. If there were ever a chance of reconciliation, he has blown it. Never will I go back to him." Mitzi knew she meant it.

Mitzi spent the whole day in bed, only getting up to shower and use the bathroom. She felt terrible. At three o'clock she called Maliq but got no answer. *Didn't he say he would be home today? No, he said he would be home most of the day. Not all men lie,* she told herself. At four thirty he called her to see how she was doing and told her he had cleaned his car for three hours. She didn't mention that she had called him earlier. She told him she didn't think she would be going to work in the morning, and he promised to call and check on her during the day. She thanked him for breakfast once more and hung up. Then she called Ronald to tell him she wouldn't be in tomorrow. He was concerned, as usual, but said he would handle everything. After talking to Ronald, she curled up and tried to sleep.

Mitzi couldn't believe she still had bad cramp after three days. Ebone´ had come in her room after eight to see why she hadn't gotten up for work. When she told her she wasn't going in, Ebone´ actually made her a cup of tea and some toast before leaving for work. After she ate, Mitzi called the doctor's office and got an appointment for June twenty-third - the earliest they could give her. Then she got up, opened the blinds, made her bed and got back in it. Whenever she spent the day in bed - which wasn't often - she had to make it up several times. She couldn't stand the cover to be untidy. Sundae called to see if she needed anything and told her they were busy, but everything was under control. She told her that her clients were concerned and sent their get well wishes. Mitzi was never sick and rarely took time off. Just as she got comfortable to watch the morning talk shows, the phone rang again. It was her mama.

"What you doin' home, honey?"

"I have cramp real bad, Mama."

"I've never known you to have cramp. When did this start?"

"Last month. I don't know what's goin' on. I couldn't get a doctor's appointment until the twenty-third of next month - he's away. Crystal suffers like this all the time - she has endometriosis."

"Endo... who?"

"En-do-me-tri-o-sis, it's like some scar tissue build-up or something around the pelvic area."

"My goodness, that sounds painful."

"Like this cramp I have. It's a nagging pain which increases then subsides. I don't feel it for a while and then all of a sudden it feels like somebody's walking on my stomach. I've had it for three days."

"I think it's time you had a baby, Mitzi."

"I don't know about that, Mama. Mine might turn out like Macky."

"Hmph. You're right. That boy would drive Satan up the wall."

"Mama, how come you let him smoke weed in your house?" The words came out before Mitzi realized it.

"I do what?!"

Oh Lord. "Oh, so he's a liar, too. Mama, I stopped down your house Friday evening and Macky and his little friends were in his room having a little birthday high, okay?"

"I'm gonna kill that child!"

No you're not. "He told me that you said you would rather he smoke in your house than get caught out in the street."

"I didn't even know the child was smoking!"

Sure. "Well, he is. Right in your house. You don't smell it sometimes?"

"No. I've never smelled any smoke except George's cigarette smoke."

"I guess your son really thinks he's a man now that he's eighteen."

Oleeta sucked her teeth. "Girl, I can't be bothered with Macky. I'll just let him have his head 'til he catches himself."

This is where you get off, Mitzi. She shook her head. "How's Tatyana coming along?" she asked cautiously.

"All right, I guess. She's wearing maternity clothes already and hasn't even begun to show yet, silly child."

"Leave her, Mama. She's young."

"Exactly! Too damn young to be having a baby, but I ain't sayin' nothin'."

Thank you. "Now, I'm gonna try and get some rest."

"Okay, honey, I'll call you later on and see how you're percolating." As she hung up, Mitzi wondered why Maliq hadn't called yet. She was sure she would have heard from him by now. Maybe he was busy.

She dozed off until the nagging pain woke her up. It was one forty-five, and Maliq still hadn't called. She was a bit disappointed and got up to take some aspirin. Then she dragged herself to the front door to check the mailbox. The prettiest bunch of flowers was sitting on the doorstep. She must have been in a deep sleep because she hadn't heard the delivery truck. She picked them up, and they were for her. She went back inside - completely forgetting the mail - opened the envelope and read the card. 'Thinking of you. Wish I could ease the pain, but since I can't, hope you feel better soon. Always, Maliq.' Mitzi smiled from ear to ear. Her spirits were lifted immediately. This man had to be on leave from heaven. She called him and felt a little uncomfortable when the receptionist asked who she should tell him was calling. Why did she have to know?

"Hi, beautiful. How you feelin'?" Maliq asked, sounding happy to be talking to her. Or was it her imagination?

"Hi darlin'," she said, smiling. "I feel... so so. Thank you so much for the flowers. They're beautiful."

"That was my attempt at brightening your day."

"It worked."

"I told the people to just leave them on the porch because if you were sleeping, I didn't want them to wake you. That's also why I haven't called you all day."

"Maliq, you are so thoughtful. I appreciate that."

"Anytime, baby. Listen, I was hoping you'd call me before it got too late. I've already taken the liberty of working through lunch so I could knock off early and was hoping I could come and see you."

"I'd be disappointed if you didn't."

"Really?" He sounded surprised.

"Yes, really. I would love to see you."

Maliq rang the door bell shortly after three thirty. Mitzi had gotten another bath and put some clothes on. She didn't want him to see her in the same pajamas, and she certainly didn't want to smell stale. He looked so damn sweet in black linen Bermuda shorts, a white shirt and an African print tie. When she opened the door, he cocked his head to the side and smiled. She smiled back and he passed her a paper bag. "My mama sent this."

"What is it?"

"Homemade soup, in the middle of summer." They both laughed while Mitzi took the soup out of the bag. "And she said you can't have any more until she meets you."

She smiled and nodded. "Fair enough."

"When you wanna meet her?"

"As soon as I feel better."

Maliq stood beside Mitzi, and she noticed his cologne again. "I'd love for her to meet you."

"I'd love to meet her, too. And I love your cologne. What is it?"

It's called 'I'll Get You Tonight', he wanted to say. "C.K. One."

You smell edible. "You smell good."

"Thanks, so do you." He rubbed her arm. "I have something to ask you, and I hope you don't take it the wrong way."

"Only one way to find out."

"My job's sending me to the Bahamas from June eighteenth to the twenty-first for a seminar and... I was wondering if you wanted to go with me." He looked shy.

Mitzi's eyes widened. "The Bahamas?"

He nodded. "Now, I know we haven't known each other that long, but I thought it would be a nice getaway. And, of course, we'll have separate rooms," he said quickly, "if that's what you want," he added just as quickly. Mitzi didn't know what to say. It sounded good, but was this the appropriate thing to do at this juncture? She would have to consult Crystal on this. "You don't have to answer me now."

She smiled. "Are you a mind reader?"

"No. But I know you're a lady. Please understand that I have no ulterior motives or misintentions as far as this trip is concerned. I just thought it would..."

Mitzi put her finger to his lips. "You worry too much."

They both ate some of the soup, then watched 'Oprah', 'The Young and the Restless', and after the news, Maliq left after asking Mitzi again to think about the trip. She promised him she would let him know as soon as possible. They had also agreed that he would take her to meet his family that week. Ebone´ came home as Maliq left.

"You two are really an item, aren't you?" she asked Mitzi, smiling.

"Not exactly."

"You better stop playing hard and just admit that you want the man."

"I do want him, but I just have to take my time. I don't wanna get all caught up, then things don't work out."

"Think positive. Isn't that what you always tell me? And everybody else?"

"Yes, but you don't have to throw it in my face."

Ebone´ rolled her eyes. "I have something to ask you, Mitzi." She put the dishes in the dishwasher. "Would you mind if I gave you my rent week after next? I'm kinda short because of the funeral and the therapist and all."

Mitzi waved her hand. "That's all right. You can give it to me whenever you have it."

"Thanks. What's in this bowl?" She was looking in the fridge.

"Soup. From Maliq's mama."

Ebone´ smiled. "Oh shucks. The man's mama is sending you food? Sounds like a little somethin' somethin' to me."

"He asked me to go away with him next month."

Ebone´ slammed the fridge door and looked at her, smiling. "You goin'?"

"I haven't decided yet."

"Well, don't do it if you don't feel comfortable. Take time and think about it. If you don't go, and he still wants you... good."

Mitzi frowned. "Ebone´?"

CHAPTER EIGHTEEN
Monday Morning

It was all everybody was talking about. O.J. Simpson's ex-wife and a male companion had been stabbed to death outside of her house. Every single client that came into the salon mentioned it, and some even wondered if O.J. himself did it. The place was a-buzz with this latest news. And, of course, it became a race issue. "Why did that fine black man have to marry that little white woman in the first place?" "He should have stayed with the sister he married first." "If they find out he did kill them, this is his pay back." "What's wrong with a black man marrying a white woman?" "She obviously wanted a white man, the man who was killed with her was her white lover."

Even though Mitzi took part in the conversation, her mind was elsewhere. In five days' time, she and Maliq would be on a plane to the romantic Bahamas. A week after he'd invited her, she'd told him she would love to go. He was ecstatic. Of course, she had conferred with Crystal first, who told her to go home and pack immediately.

"I'll call Maliq myself and tell him you're going," Crystal had said, eyes wide.

"Now, all that won't be necessary. But Crystal, suppose this is a mistake? Isn't it a bit early for the man to be buying me a plane ticket and paying for my hotel room? I've barely known him a month. Suppose he expects something in return? I don't wanna feel kept."

"Suppose this...? What if that...? If it ain't broke, don't fix it. Take the man at face value - I told you that before." Mitzi sighed. "Look, you are two mature adults, going on a harmless trip together... to spend time together... sleeping in separate rooms." She rolled her eyes while making the last statement.

"Come on, girl, surely you don't expect us to sleep in the same bed?"

Crystal started humming. Mitzi sucked her teeth. "I don't know why I'm worrying. Maliq has got to be the last gentleman on earth. I mean, we haven't even *really* kissed yet."

"Exactly! So stop worrying. I hardly think that a man who hasn't even let you taste his tongue is going to attack you."

"You are so... common when you want to be."

Crystal ignored her comment. "And if he does try anything - that you don't want - you'll know how to deal with it."

"I need to take lessons from Melba before I go."

"No, please don't do that. You'll have Maliq comin' back in a cedar overcoat if you pay attention to her." They both laughed. "Melba's some girl. What's happenin' with that fool Roger these days anyway?"

"Well, he had to go court after she scalded his behind, and they fined him and bound him over for a year."

"Bound him over? They should have locked him the hell up."

"I guess they felt sorry for him with all those rice scars on his body," Mitzi said seriously. Then she and Crystal looked at each other and hollered.

"That picture must have been worth two million words," Crystal laughed.

"I could see my girl now," Mitzi said, grabbing a pot to imitate what Melba had probably done. "Just calmly taking the pot off the stove and hurling the rice on him."

"I hope she rinsed the starch off with some cold water!" Tears rolled down Crystal's face, as usual, when she laughed.

"It's really not funny, you know," Mitzi said, still smiling.

"The hell it ain't! I don't think 'Uncle Ben' will be messin' with her no more."

"He would be a fool if he did. You know he actually tried to run *her* in for assaulting him?"

"Clown."

Mitzi got serious. "See Crystal, I don't want to be going through all these changes with any man. I don't have the mental energy."

"Um, 'scuse me, Ms. Robinson, but a woman of your intelligence is well aware that all men are not Roger Burchall clones."

"I know that, but you just never know what you could be getting into."

"And you'll never know unless you get into it, so this trip is the perfect start."

"You think so?"

Crystal nodded. "I know so. Do something out of the ordinary, for heaven's sake. Your life is always so planned and... planned."

"All right, I'm going." Crystal clapped. "Now, I know we're not sleeping together but what type of nightwear am I supposed to take?"

"A negligée."

"Come on, Crystal. I have black satin pajamas. Would that be appropriate?"

"Pajamas...?"

"Yeah, you know, pants and the shirt with buttons down the front."

"Oh, that don't sound too bad. He might come to your room before you're dressed in the morning, and you would want to be lookin' decent. Hey, he might walk in his sleep, too, and wander into your room."

Mitzi laughed. "I'm excited, girl. And a little nervous." She paused and sighed. "So tell me again, is it too early for me to be going away with this man?"

Crystal sighed. "How many times are you gonna ask me that damn question?" she asked dramatically. "You're a single woman, he's a single man. You people are adults, you can do what the devil you want."

"I know, but this is completely out of character for me. I feel like I'm running a little low on moral fiber."

"Oh get a grip! Sleep in his bed, you wanna talk to me 'bout low moral fiber. Go and have a good time."

Mitzi finished work early, worked out at the gym for an hour and stopped by her mama's house on the way home. It took all she had to turn her car into the driveway. It had gotten so that she hated going to the house because she never knew what to expect and really didn't have anything to say to Macky. Oleeta and George had just gotten home, and thankfully, Macky wasn't there.

"So George, how's the groom-to-be?" Mitzi asked, smiling.

"Still the same. Your mama's makin' all this fuss about the wedding. If I had my way, we'd be at the registrar at ten and the airport at eleven."

Oleeta put her hands on her hips. "George, you ought to stop lying." He looked at her and smiled. "You're the one who calls me every five minutes, adding a name to the guest list and checking to see if I've thought of this or decided on that..."

"I'm just trying to go along with your program, Honey," he said, hugging and kissing her. Mitzi smiled.

"Now Mama, I can't stay long. I just stopped by to tell you I'm going to the Bahamas this weekend."

"Oh Mitzi, that sounds lovely. You'll love it. The Bahamas are beautiful."

"So I've heard."

"Mind if I ask who you're going with?"

Mitzi smiled. "Remember Maliq? The guy I introduced you to on the plane?"

Oleeta frowned. "You know him, Mitzi?"

"Well, kind of." She knew her mama wouldn't be judgmental in this situation. "Since we met on the plane, we've gone out a few times."

"Hmm. So you like him?"

"Yeah. He's real nice, Mama. I've been meaning to bring him to 'officially' meet you, but we've been really busy. As soon as we come back, I'll bring him up here."

"You don't think this trip is... premature?"

"No. Not really." She looked at George who smiled at her. "At first I wasn't sure, but his job is sending him on business, and he invited me to go. And *he* suggested separate rooms." George left the room.

"Now that was decent of him."

"He's like that, Mama. Very decent. I know you'll like him."

"I remember he had nice manners."

"That wasn't just a front."

"Well, Mitzi, if you're sure this is what you wanna do, then you know best. Have fun and be careful." She smiled at her daughter even though she was a bit doubtful and thought it was too soon for her to be going on a trip with this man.

"Thanks. Now I have to go. I'll talk to you before I leave on Saturday. Want me to bring you back anything?"

"Oh yes, a charm for my bracelet, please. She paused. "You seen your brother lately?"

"Nope."

"Still mad at him?"

Mitzi closed her eyes briefly and smiled. "Mama, you don't get it, do you? I love my brother, but he has to learn responsibility sometime in life, and at eighteen years old, if he hasn't even begun to have a sense of responsibility, then I feel pity, not anger, for him."

Oleeta sighed. "I don't know what to do."

"Can I make one suggestion?" Mitzi asked. Oleeta looked at her with questioning eyes. "Stop baby-sitting and making excuses for him. You're an enabler, Mama."

"I guess in a way I am." Oleeta played with her ring. "I feel like I owe him something..."

Just as Mitzi had thought. "Mama, if you ever owed Macky anything, you've given it to him a thousandfold." She really didn't feel like having this conversation.

"Ever since you told me how he feels about your daddy's death, I just feel like maybe I haven't done enough to make up for his loss."

"Mama, first of all, you weren't responsible for daddy's death, so you owe no one anything. What about the loss you suffered?"

Oleeta sighed again. "I guess you're right. Maybe I need to be a bit firmer with Macky."

"I told you before, don't let him get over you, Mama. You'll regret it. And as far as the baby is concerned, Tatyana and Macky created that baby - no matter what the circumstances - and they are both responsible."

Oleeta shook her head. "I don't even wanna get into that. It upsets me too much."

Good. "We don't have to get into it." They were both silent for a while. Mitzi looked at her watch. "Now, I'm gone. I'll call you later."

Mitzi got home and found a message from Crystal and called her back.

"Girl, I didn't realize you'd be missing my housewarming on Sunday."

"Sorry, but I'd rather be soakin' up the sun in the Bahamas with Maliq than socializing with your 'mo-in-lo'."

Crystal groaned. "If I don't invite her, you think she'd be offended?"

" 'Fraid so, sister."

"Lord, I don't feel like puttin' up with that woman. I must really love Raoul."

"You'll be in my thoughts."

"Yah, right. Like you're gonna have time to be thinking about me and my sorry self."

"You're right; I probably won't even remember your name."

"Thanks. So how you feelin'? Still excited?"

Mitzi sighed. "And nervous."

"I certainly hope you're not planning on changing your mind."

"Oh no, honey, I'm going. Maliq would kill me if I backed out now. He seems so excited, Crystal girl. He calls me every day and reminds me how many days we have left."

"Hey now. That's the type of man you want; one who gets excited about doing things with you and not always the other way around."

"I feel good about this one, girlfriend."

*   *   *   *   *   *

"Deja vu?" Maliq asked, once they were seated and strapped into seats six A and B.

Mitzi smiled. "Almost. Last time we weren't in first class."

Maliq smiled. "I don't want to appear to be showing off, but a first class lady belongs nowhere but in first class."

Mitzi was speechless for a moment and could only smile, but inwardly she was screaming ecstatically. "If someone had told me two months ago that today I would be sitting on a plane next to such a distinguished gentleman - and I mean that in *every* sense of the word - on my way to the Bahamas, I would have thought they were crazy."

"Mitzi, when you sat next to me on the plane a few weeks ago, I never dreamt you would say a second word to me, let alone be on the way to the Bahamas with me today. I'm a lucky man."

"I don't think luck has anything to do with us being here today," Mitzi said after the flight attendant took their drink order. "I think fate is the better word." They smiled at each other - a knowing smile. "Actually Maliq, I had serious doubts about coming with you."

"I know you did, but why?"

"Because this isn't my... style, going on a trip with a man I barely know."

"You've already proven your style, Mitzi. If you're worrying about ruining your reputation, please don't. Two grown people taking a vacation together doesn't make either one of them bad." He held her hand. "We know what we're doing. There is nothing that could - or couldn't - happen on this trip that could change what we already have. We're friends - friends who're trying to get to know each other better." The wine arrived.

Mitzi frowned. "Have you been talking to Crystal?"

Maliq frowned, too. "No, why?"

"Just wondering." They toasted, and he kissed her cheek. "What was that for?"

He looked serious. "Just for being you, baby."

They chatted for a while about what they would do once in the Bahamas. Maliq had arranged for a limo to pick them up at the airport and take them to the Bahamas Princess where, once they checked into separate rooms, they would change and go for an early dinner. He told her that if she wasn't too tired afterward, they could go across the street to the casino and maybe see the Follies show. On Sunday morning they would order a very early room service breakfast, then hit the golf course. Maliq was an avid golfer, and although Mitzi had never set foot on a course, she told him she had always wanted to try, so they decided to get an eight o'clock tee off time. They intended to play it by ear the rest of the day. He was concerned about her being bored on Monday while he was in the seminar, but she knew she would find plenty to do; she never got bored. Monday night it would be all over, and as the food arrived, they both silently wondered what lay ahead of them.

After they ate, they played cards until Mitzi could no longer keep her eyes open. They pushed their seats back, and she covered up with a blanket while he read the latest 'E-Man' magazine. Mitzi wasn't aware of Maliq's lingering, smiling looks at her as she slept. Once again he marveled at her beauty. She was truly a beautiful, black woman.

Mitzi didn't feel so beautiful twenty minutes later when she woke up and realised her mouth was open, and she had been dribbling. She wiped her mouth and glanced at Maliq, hoping he hadn't noticed, but when he broke into his trademark big, dimpled smile, she immediately knew he had. They laughed together, and she covered her face with her hands.

"You're beautiful even when you snore and dribble," he said, still laughing.

A look of horror crossed her face as she yanked her hands away. "Please tell me I wasn't snoring, Maliq..."

He shook his head and smiled. "No honey, you weren't snoring. Just dribbling."

"I am *so* embarrassed." Mitzi sat up straight and adjusted the seat back. "I must have been really tired." She fished her makeup bag from her purse.

Maliq patted her hand. "You don't need to be embarrassed, we're cool like that."

She cut her eyes, took her makeup bag and went to the bathroom where she cleaned her teeth and sprayed her face with aloe mist. She fixed her makeup then went back to her seat after realizing she wasn't really that embarrassed at all. Maliq had made her feel quite comfortable whenever they were together. And, after all, everybody dribbled. At least a little more ice had been broken.

When they arrived - by limo - at the hotel a few hours later, Mitzi got very excited. The place was beautiful, and once they got inside, she felt like a princess in a palace. The lobby was absolutely awesome and so was her room, which was right next to Maliq's. They sat in her room and talked for a few minutes before agreeing to meet for dinner in an hour. Mitzi wore a plain, black, ankle-length tank dress, silver sandals and silver accessories. Maliq wore a black jacket and beige pants and shirt. They truly looked like they belonged together as they walked through the hotel, amidst approving stares from guests mulling about the lobby.

Maliq held her hand as they crossed the street to the restaurant. They were still holding hands as they entered the room, and it felt like the most natural thing in the world to both of them. The maitre d' greeted them politely and sat them in a quiet corner at the window. The relaxed, candlelit ambiance put them both in a romantic mood, and even though they hadn't been intimate yet, they both suddenly felt like throwing all caution to the wind. When Maliq held both Mitzi's hands and stared at her over the slowly flickering candle flame, within moments something transformed them both. Maybe it was the change of scenery and the fact that they were totally alone - they knew no one there. Just touching her hands and looking in her eyes made him feel like taking her right then and there on the table. And Mitzi had to stop herself from begging him to take her back to her room to make love to her. There were definitely deep, unspoken vibes between them, and Maliq hoped that before the trip was over, they could take each other to heights of pure ecstasy. That wasn't the reason he'd invited her to come with him, and nothing would change if they didn't make love, but he was positive that he could love, make love to and be in love with this beautiful creature - exclusively. Mitzi got a bit nervous after a few minutes when they were still holding hands because she wasn't sure exactly what she wanted to happen yet and was afraid that if slightly pressured she wouldn't be able to resist.

Her eyes were so warm and bright and beautiful. They spoke for her, and right now they were telling him that she was as aroused as he was and wanted him. Or was it wishful thinking? Her face was smooth and radiantly brown - perfectly made-up. Just looking at her perfect lips made him want to cover them with his. Her dress was cut just low enough for him to nearly be driven out of his mind by the sight of her chocolate, smooth, taut cleavage. The mole just above her left breast only added to the sensuality she was innocently exuding. He desperately wanted to experience the complete and utter joy he imagined that making love with her could bring. He needed to experience it - if he never experienced anything new again in life.

What's happening to me? he wondered as he seductively narrowed his eyes while staring at her. *I have never felt this excitement about a woman in my life.*

Mitzi simply and innocently stared back into his eyes. Eyes which appeared to undress her - in an unthreatening, unintimidating manner. She sensed his arousal and was enjoying it. She was sure they had lain naked, exhausted after erotic, uninhibited, passionate love-making some time in the past. Or was that what she was imagining now? She wanted to touch the male softness of his face - his smooth, yet masculine skin yearned for her touch. His eyes - dark and seductive - begged for her body - she thought. She hoped. His hands had reduced hers to moisture. *I want this man bad - real bad,* she thought. *This feels right, and I'm positive it is. Well, maybe not positive, but real sure. A little sure? Maybe not. No, it's too soon. I'm old enough to know better!*

The waiter reluctantly interrupted them to take their order.

"You're not hungry?" Maliq asked as he sipped his wine.

"Not really." Mitzi had butterflies and had lost her appetite.

"I'm trying to impress you by wining and dining you, and you order rabbit food?" Maliq pretended to be hurt, and Mitzi smiled.

"I thought if I only ordered a little, we could finish early and have time to do other things..." She said seriously, staring in his eyes. He got serious and stared back - hopeful.

"... like watch the show," she continued, smiling.

Maliq appeared not to have heard her and was still staring at her, willing her to have said what he wanted to hear. Finally Mitzi laughed, for lack of a better way to break his stare.

"You're a wicked woman," he said, smiling.

Mitzi's eyes widened. "Wicked? What did I do?"

He sipped his wine, never taking his eyes off her. "You know exactly what I'm talking about," he said, amazed at the subtle power she was beginning to have over him.

"I have no idea what you're talking about, Maliq."

"I'm sure you don't." *But you will soon.*

An hour later they walked hand in hand across the grass to Princess Towers. As they left the restaurant and Maliq took her hand in his again, it seemed like something that *should* be done. Mitzi looked at him and smiled her approval. He winked at her, and they held on tighter. They entered the casino lobby and were met by giant chandeliers and the sounds of money being won - and lost - as tourists steadily deposited coins into the one-armed bandits.

"Wanna play for a while?" Maliq asked Mitzi.

"Play what?" she asked suggestively and then smiled mischievously.

Maliq shook his head and smiled, too. "You need to stop,
baby," he said, letting go of her hand and sliding his arm
around her waist, prompting her to do the same to him.

Yeah, this is my woman, his gesture said silently to the men
who were obviously admiring Mitzi, who - being her humble
self - was totally oblivious to their admiring stares. After
buying fifty dollars' worth of quarters, they found two empty
stools at a slot machine and commenced to share the bucket of
change, taking turns playing one machine. When Mitzi won
her first 'jackpot' as she called it - which was all of three
dollars - she clapped her hands, threw her head back and
laughed. It made Maliq happy to see her so excited over
something so small. It also made him aware that she wasn't a
difficult woman to make happy. Then and there, he mentally
made that one of his ultimate goals; he would contribute to
whatever happiness she already possessed. His mother had
often told him that men can't make women happy, they can
only enhance their happiness. Maxine Robinson was about to
become one ecstatic woman. If that was what she wanted. He
wondered again how she felt about him. He needed to find out-
soon. They sat like two excited children on Christmas
morning, steadily dropping in quarters, eagerly waiting for
more to spill out. Twenty minutes later, when Mitzi was a
hundred and thirty dollars richer, they headed for the nightclub
to see the Follies show. Maliq again slipped his arm around
Mitzi's waist - guessed it was about a twenty-six - and took her
to their table. He ordered wine for both of them, which arrived
just as the house lights went down and the stage lit up. Mitzi
sat slightly in front of Maliq, and he put his arm around her
shoulder. They toasted to the near end of a beautiful night, and
he silently hoped it would last another few hours. He wouldn't
mind being completely exhausted in the morning if it meant
spending many more hours with this gorgeous woman. The
music started, and Mitzi could have died of embarrassment
when the Follies made their appearance - topless. Topless and

gyrating to a vibrant drum beat. She was as liberal as the next person, but to watch that with a man she didn't really know - but was very much attracted to...? Maliq sat behind her at the table and smiled, aware of her embarrassment. When she took a gulp of her wine then lowered her head and picked at a piece of imaginary fluff on her dress, he gently nudged her. When she slowly turned and looked at him out of the corner of her eye, he smiled and nodded toward the stage. She covered her eyes and laughed.

"I have to go to the ladies room," she said, standing. He stood, too.

"Would you rather we left? We could go..."

"No, no, you already paid. It's okay. I'll be right back." He sat and watched her glide seductively toward the exit. She knew he was watching. Maliq turned back to the show and wondered what Mitzi looked like topless, in his bed, in his arms, wrapped in his body. He knew her body had to be perfect, just as she was. He hoped it wouldn't be too long and he somehow felt, as he sat waiting for her to return, that it wouldn't be. It wasn't lust; he just had to have her - always. They were silently in sync. But was he still just someone she wanted as a friend? Hell, he hoped not. Yes, he wanted to be her friend. And her lover, her love, her man, her confidant, her everything. He looked thoughtfully into his wine glass as he twisted the stem between his fingers. He closed his eyes briefly and smiled inwardly as he let the warmth of his thoughts envelope him. Damn, this felt good! And he hadn't even made love to the woman - she wasn't even near him at that moment. Mitzi smiled when she approached the table and found Maliq staring at his wine glass.

"Too much action up there for you, huh?"

He didn't realise she'd come back. "I didn't want to disrespect you by looking at a bunch of half-naked women."

"Yah, right." She sat in front of him again.

"Ever thought of doing that?" he whispered in her ear.

"Hardly!" she answered quickly. She no longer felt embarrassed, she was just happy to be in his company. The show lasted about an hour, and the whole time, they either held hands or he had his arm around her. Twice he kissed her softly - once on her ear and once on the back of her neck. Both times she had closed her eyes and sighed, inhaling the feeling that went through her body. After the second kiss she turned and looked at him. Their eyes met and held and they looked down at each other's lips, then back in each other's eyes and back to their lips. She leaned toward him involuntarily. He followed suit.

"Would you two care for another drink?" Maliq sucked his teeth, and Mitzi slowly turned to see an obviously 'gay' waiter with a huge, forced smile, standing beside them with a hand on his hip. Mitzi didn't utter a word but slowly shook her head. "Just holler if you do," the waiter sang as he swung off. Mitzi turned back to Maliq, who hadn't taken his eyes off of her.

"I guess he was jealous so he thought he should interrupt us," Maliq said.

"Yeah, jealous of me," Mitzi said. "He probably wants what I have... I mean, he wants who I'm with." She looked sheepish.

Maliq looked serious. "You didn't have to correct yourself." She looked away. He smiled and held her hand.

After the show, they were both exhausted and ready to go to sleep. They walked back to the hotel hand in hand. "Thank you for a beautiful night, Ms. Robinson."

"Thank you for the same, Mr. Simmons. I quite enjoyed that."

"Mmn," Maliq replied, turning to look at her. "The next day and a half can go by as slowly as it wants," he said, holding her hand tighter.

"Indeed. I could get used to this," she said, sounding content.

"Used to what? Being in the Bahamas or being with me?"

"You figure it out," she said as they approached the pool.

He stopped and held both her hands in his. "I figure it to be the latter. Am I being forward?"

"No, you're being very perceptive." She looked at him seriously and again this time, he didn't look away.

"Wanna put your feet in the pool for a while or are you too tired?" Maliq asked, not wanting the night to end yet, even though he was dog-tired and had to be up early. It was after midnight.

"I am tired, but we can sit here for a while. I don't know about putting my feet in the pool, though, I have on this long dress."

"Let me show you how it's done," Maliq said, taking his shoes off. Then he bent over, rolled his pants up to his knees, sat on the edge of the pool and put his legs in. When he looked up at Mitzi, she was laughing and shaking her head.

"You are crazy," she said, taking her sandals off. She pulled her dress up above her knees - grateful that she had used a little extra lotion on them - and joined him. "This feels good, too bad I don't have on my bathing suit."

Maliq looked around. "There's nobody here but us, wear the one God gave you."

"You would like that, wouldn't you?"

"Me? I wouldn't even look. In fact, I would go up to my room," he said, faking seriousness.

Mitzi dipped her fingers in the pool and flicked water in his face. "Liar."

He laughed and hugged her, and they sat like that, talking for half an hour when they both decided it best to call it a night. At Mitzi's door Maliq faced her and put his hands on her shoulders. "You gonna be all right by yourself or do you wanna sleep in the other bed in my room?" She looked at him hard, still holding her sandals in her hand. "Well... I wouldn't want the bogeyman to get you."

"The bogeyman will be in your room. Good night, Maliq." She kissed his cheek, resisting the urge to part his lips with her tongue. He held on to her for a few extra seconds and kissed her softly on her cheek. Mitzi surprised herself then, when she turned her face and let her lips brush his. They both stood still with their eyes closed for a while, and then she moved away.

Damn girl, don't make me rape you! Maliq thought.

"Have a good sleep," she whispered as he opened the door for her.

"How you expect me to...?" He smiled. "I'll call you about six fifteen, is that okay? We can have breakfast in either room and be on the golf course by quarter to eight, okay?"

She smiled. "Okay. I'm looking forward to it. I hope it's a nice day."

"Every day with you is nice," he said seriously.

"Good night, Maliq." He looked like he wanted to kiss her again, and if he did, she would yank his clothes off right here in the hallway. She went into her room, closed the door, and like a child, ran to the phone and dialed Crystal's number. Before it rang, she hung up - realizing it was too late to call her - it was almost two o'clock in Bermuda. Raoul would kill her. Smiling, she turned the TV on and slowly took her dress off and hung it in the closet. She stood in the bathroom in her underwear and cleaned her face and teeth. Feeling like a teenager who had a 'dear diary' entry, she lay across the bed and sighed. Life was so sweet. Regardless of what might be wrong in her life right now - which wasn't much - everything was right at this moment. Mitzi was glad she had thrown her moral concerns aside and come with Maliq. They had only flown to the Bahamas, been to dinner and a show, sat by the pool and talked and had a friendly kiss or two, and she felt complete euphoria. How the hell was she going to feel if and when something else happened? Forget 'if', something *was* going to happen, if she had to make the move herself. She sighed again - deeply. She started to put her pajamas on, then decided it was too warm. She took her bra off and got under the sheet in just her underpants. Laying in bed half-naked, knowing Maliq was next door was too much. "This is driving me crazy," she whispered to herself, grabbing the phone and calling Maliq's room. He answered on the first ring. "I forgot to thank you for tonight," she said, in a voice a little too sexy for even her liking.

"You did thank me, sweetheart," Maliq said in just as sensuous a voice. He was laying in total darkness in only a pair of Bill Blass jockeys, desperately wishing she was beside him. This was pure torture.

The phone rang at six ten. It took Mitzi a few seconds to collect her thoughts and remember where she was. Then she realized it was the dawn of a beautiful new day in the Bahamas.

"It's time for breakfast, baby," Maliq said, voice deep, raspy and sexy.

"Good mornin'," Mitzi whispered sleepily. "It's not there yet, is it?"

"Not yet. What you wanna eat?"

"Just some fruit, cereal and tea, please." She sat up and noticed her bare breasts. She felt funny at first but then smiled. She was 'freeing up'. It dawned on her that today was Father's Day, so she covered her breasts and said a prayer for her daddy and Macky. She got up and was dressed in fifteen minutes. She went next door and knocked on Maliq's door, feeling uneasy when he opened it, dressed in only a pair of silk pajama shorts, his muscular chest in her face.

"This is truly a first," he said, leaning on the door. "A woman actually dressed before me?"

"I can come back..." she didn't know what was appropriate right now. *Damn this is awkward.*

Maliq pulled her in the room. "Come in, girl. "I'll get dressed in the bathroom. Unless you want me to..."

"The bathroom, please," Mitzi said, hitting him with her room card. "And Happy Father's Day."

They were on the golf course at seven forty and played nine holes. They spent the whole two hours laughing - most of the time at nothing. They were so comfortable together. By ten o'clock they were back at the hotel and decided to work out in the gym for an hour and a half. Then they agreed to meet at the pool at noon after showering - separately.

Maliq nearly lost his breath when he looked up from the book he was reading and saw Mitzi standing in front of him in a chocolate brown and gold two-piece bathing suit with a matching sarong. She wore brown sandals with gold shells hanging from them.

"Woman, you are a princess." *And so fine.*

Mitzi had been apprehensive about wearing the two-piece, but hey, she worked hard on her body and was feeling more comfortable around Maliq, so she decided to put it on. "Thank you." He looked good, too, in a navy tank top which had been cut to reveal his tight abs and a multi-coloured pair of boxer trunks. Mitzi spread her towel in the lounge chair next to Maliq, reached in her straw bag, took out a bottle of sun tan oil and handed it to him. "Would you be so kind as to..."

"Oh please, allow me," he jumped up. "On your whole body?" he asked, smiling from ear to ear.

"No!" she snapped. "Just my back, thank you."

He sucked his teeth. "Damn."

"You need help, you know that?" she asked, looking at him over her shoulder.

"I know, but you provoke me."

"Doesn't take much, does it?"

"Nope. So stop it."

"Okay. I'll go and change..." She started to get up, but he pulled her back, brushing her breast by mistake. She glared at him.

"I'm sorry, honey. That wasn't intentional, honest." He looked scared. Joking with her was one thing, but he really didn't want to offend her. And she didn't want him to see her hardened nipples. A simple brush of his hand had aroused her. She looked straight ahead.

"Would you kindly rub some oil on my back?" She turned her head slightly and smiled. "Please?"

"Yes, ma'am."

They sat in the sun for a while, decided it was too hot, put up an umbrella, ordered drinks, sat back and talked. After Maliq finished his beer and she, her pina colada, they swam in the pool. It was ninety-one degrees, and the water felt good. They acted like children in the water. Mitzi had no intention of getting her hair wet, but she didn't want to act too prissy and tell Maliq not to wet it, so by the time they came out half an hour later, it was soaked. She could get it done in the hotel. They sat in their chairs, and Maliq signaled a waiter so they could order lunch.

"So what you doin' on your birthday?" he asked, drying his body.

"My birthday's a whole month away." She was putting her sarong back on.

"I like to plan early. And since I'm planning on being around for your birthday, I thought I would..."

"Oh you are, huh?" Mitzi asked, knowing good and damn well she hoped he would be around.

"Yes, I am," he said, slowly and leaned toward her. "And since I am, I thought we could plan to do something together."

"Like what?" She was rubbing cocoa butter on her face.

"What do you like doing?"

She shrugged. "Just kickin' it with my friends."

"What about a couples' night - a games night or something like that?" he suggested, shrugging. "It's up to you, of course, but we can have it at my house. Or we could have it on my boat."

"You have a boat?"

"Yeah - a twenty-five foot Sea Ray. I call it 'Mystique'."

"Now a party on the boat might be nice," Mitzi said after thinking about it for a minute. "But a couples' night won't really work because only Crystal has a man. Sundae claims she does, but that could change in the next month."

"Well, we can just have a games night. I'll do all the cooking. I'll take care of everything, honey."

They made tentative plans for the party while they ate lunch. They both admitted to needing a nap after eating, and when they got to Maliq's room, he invited her to sleep in the other bed. She thought the idea was harmless enough, so she showered in her room, changed and went back to his room where he had already started to doze off with the TV on. He had showered and changed as well. He opened one eye and gestured to the other bed. Mitzi smiled and lay down on top of the spread. Maliq chuckled with his eyes closed.

"What you laughin' at?" Mitzi asked, smiling.

"I'm laughing at how comical this is. Two adults of the opposite sex, sleeping in the same room in separate beds. Our parents would be proud."

"And we should be, too. By the way, do your parents know that a female is accompanying you to the romantic Bahamas?"

"Uh huh." He smiled. "Why?"

" 'Cause, I still haven't met them yet, and I don't want their first impression of me to be that I'm... loose."

"You worry too much. My parents don't judge people."

"My mama doesn't either. She didn't ask too many questions."

He turned on his back. "Well, since nobody's speculating, we might as well..."

"Turn over and go to sleep, Maliq."

He blew her a kiss. "Is the TV bothering you, 'cause I can't go sleep without it on."

"That's all right, I can go sleep standing up in the middle of a loud party."

"Thanks for the warning."

Mitzi was woken up by a very loud, strange sound. At first she couldn't figure out what the sound was. It was three thirty in the afternoon, and the sun was shining brightly. She looked in the direction of the noise and smiled when she discovered the source. Maliq was stretched on his back, arm out of the bed, mouth open and snoring louder than she had ever heard anyone before. She got up, shoved her arms under his back and attempted to turn him over. As she got him on his side, his outstretched arm wrapped around her hips and by the time she got him fully on his side, he had pulled her onto the bed with him. She let out a small scream, and he slowly opened his eyes and looked at her for a few seconds before they both roared.

"I have you right where I want you. Now what you gonna do?" He asked, trying to sound serious. His arm had moved up around her waist, and her legs were over his. She looked at him seriously, wanting desperately to succumb to the feeling in her loins. She slowly broke away from him and got out of the bed.

"I'm going to clean my teeth," she smiled, walking to the door. "I'll be right back."

"When you come back, can we assume the position we were in a minute ago?"

She stared at him, didn't answer, then left. When she returned, he was flicking through the TV channels with the remote control.

"I wasn't sure if it was safe to come back," she said shyly.

"I'm harmless, baby." He patted the bed. "Come back and sit over here by me." She did so, willingly. After deciding that they both just felt like relaxing for a bit, they sat side by side on the bed, talked, ate nuts, drank the beer and wine they'd ordered from room service and watched TV. Mitzi noticed that the second a commercial came on, Maliq started changing channels. It drove her crazy, but she said nothing. This was his room. After she made an appointment for a day of beauty in the hotel spa for the next day, they had dinner in the Rib Room, a cozy, romantic restaurant in the hotel. She ordered beef ribs, and he ordered chicken and shrimp. She discovered then that he was a vegetarian. He also confirmed Sundae's story about his being raised a Moslem.

"We came up in the Moslem faith, but when the Honorable Elijah Muhammad died, my parents got away from it. My sister Na'imah and my brother Malcolm got back in the faith a few years ago. I never gave up some of the practices, like not eating meat or smoking."

"I guess you had to have at least one vice, huh?" Mitzi asked him as the waiter put a scotch and coke on the table.

He laughed. "Two vices. Guess what the other one is." He sipped his drink.

"I'd rather not."

*   *   *   *   *

"I truly enjoyed my day, sweetheart." Maliq was turning on the lamp in Mitzi's room.

"I did too, honey." She was taking her earrings off. They were new clip-ons and were squeezing her ears. "In fact, I'm enjoying this whole... experience." She smiled at the word, and so did he. As she attempted to walk past him to put the earrings on the dresser, he blocked her and took her in his arms.

I've had enough of this playing around, he thought as he looked in her eyes. She put her arms around his waist. They stared at each other for a moment. "You haven't even begun to experience what I have to offer, baby."

"Maliq..." He put his finger to her lips.

"I'm not just talking about sex, Mitzi. Yes, I would love to make love to you. But right now I want you to be my woman. My lady. I'm tired of beating around the bush. And please, don't think I believe that if you tell me that's what you want too, I'll think we should get in bed immediately. That's not my style."

"How do you know I'm what you want?" She already knew the answer; she felt the same way. For some reason her eyes were filling with tears, and she didn't want them to. Maliq kissed her cheek.

"I know, baby. And you know, too." She closed her eyes and nodded slowly. She knew exactly what he meant - how he felt. When she opened her eyes, a tear rolled from each one. He kissed them both.

"Why you cryin', honey?" He wiped her tears with his thumbs as he held her face in both hands.

"I'm scared, Maliq. I have..."

"There's nothing to be scared of Mitzi. I promise you, I won't hurt you."

She shook her head. "I've been hurt before, and it's not a good feeling."

He put his arms around her shoulders. "I know. I've been there, too. That's why I don't ever want to hurt anyone. Especially you. I don't profess to know you, Mitzi - we just met a month ago. But I've developed a deep closeness to you, simply because of your personality. And I know I want you."

"I feel the same way about you, Maliq." She was whispering.

"I know you do... I'm not bragging, but I know there's some chemistry here."

"Is it chemistry or infatuation? For both of us."

He stood away from her and shook his head. "No, sweetheart, it's real. Let me tell you something..." He led her to the bed where she sat, and he sat on the chair across from her, holding her hands in his. "I've been through every emotion - including happiness - in a relationship, but the happiness was short-lived. All I want now is pure peace of mind. Yes, I've made a few mistakes - made some bad choices - and I have regrets, but I told you, I want a soul mate. Someone to grow with me. I live a simple life, and I don't want to B.S. anybody. I want to be open and honest and genuine and... me."

Mitzi was taking it all in and feeling better by the minute. "I just want to be happy."

"But you know what, baby, you are ultimately responsible for your own happiness. And I promise you that I want to be a part of it. You understand that?"

"Yeah. Makes sense. I guess that by waiting for someone else to make me happy is allowing someone else to define me." She had stopped crying.

"Exactly. And when someone defines you, they eventually confine you."

She smiled. "You're so deep sometimes."

"I don't wanna get too deep and start boring you, but Mitzi, all I'm saying is I have a lot to offer - no money, 'cause right now I'm just a poor black man tryin' to make it - but I want to give my lady what I want for myself."

"That sounds so... perfect. Almost too good to be possible."

"It is possible, honey. I don't wanna sound like I'm building castles in the sky, but..." He stopped and stared at her. "Let's make ourselves happy - together." They stared at each other seriously for a few seconds. Then Maliq smiled. "At least you're not crying anymore.

She covered her face with her hands. "I'm such a baby sometimes. My exterior is much tougher than my interior." She took a tissue from her bag and wiped the mascara that had started to run.

Maliq sat beside her on the bed. "Why were you crying, sweetheart?"

She looked down at the tissue in her hands. He gently turned her face to his. "I like you, Maliq, I truly do and as much as I don't want to admit it, I do want a relationship with you." A slight smile crossed his lips. "But... I just hate starting new relationships. You have to go through this... process. Getting to know each other, what each other likes and dislikes. The different moods and lifestyles, habits and idiosyncrasies... then when you think you have it all figured out, somebody decides it's not what they want, the relationship ends, and you're back to square one again."

Maliq laughed. "I could have said all the things you just said because I've been through all that, too. But I feel differently about us. I could be wrong, but I don't think I am. I have waited a very long time for a woman like you..."

"Like me? What am I like?" she cut him off.

"I've told you over and over - intelligent, successful, educated and, among a number of other things, sweet." He kissed her and let his lips linger on hers. "I want you, Maxine. Be my woman, girl," he said as though he were angry.

She leaned back. "Be your woman? Is that a demand?" she teased.

"Yes, it's what I want. And I'm not givin' up. I don't wanna sound like I'm beggin'..."

"I want you, too, Maliq. I want to be your woman."

"Pardon?"

"You heard me!" She laughed.

"I'm not sure what you..."

She kissed him and this time his mouth covered hers and their tongues met, held, then meshed. They tasted everything they both ever wanted in a soul mate. And they both knew it was for real. When they finally pulled away, Mitzi was crying again. Maliq put his arms around her and gently pushed her back on the bed as they kissed again. This kiss said, "I am yours and you are mine."

*   *   *   *   *

When Maliq left Mitzi's room at six thirty the next morning, albeit reluctantly, she was still asleep. He wrote her a note and softly kissed her cheek. She woke up an hour later and was surprised she hadn't heard him leave. She read his note then called his room. He was getting dressed to meet his group for breakfast. He told her they were scheduled to break for lunch at one, and the two of them made plans to meet.

"Thanks for last night," she said, her voice still heavy with sleep.

"Thanks for what?" he asked, smiling and trying to tie his necktie.

"For understanding that I wasn't ready to be intimate yet."

"I told you, that's not all I want."

"I know. And thanks for keeping your promise to sleep in the other bed."

"I'm a man of my word, baby. You'll learn that soon. But you don't know how hard it was to stay in that bed with you so close. I almost got up and left because the temptation was so strong."

"I must be completely out of my mind, letting you stay in my room all night. Anything could have happened..."

"I'm your man, honey. I'm here to protect you, not harm you."

She smiled. "I must remember that. Now you better go or you'll be late."

He looked at his watch. "You're right. I'll see you at one."

By one o'clock, Mitzi had been to the spa, worked out, sat in the sauna, had her hair done and had gotten a manicure, pedicure and a massage. She looked and felt completely buffed. Maliq only had a forty-five minute break so they ate in the coffee shop, and after buying tee shirts for her 'girls' and the June *Essence* magazine from the gift shop, Mitzi went to her room to call Crystal. She naturally wanted to know if they had 'done it' yet and was disappointed to find out they hadn't. Mitzi told her she was really enjoying herself and was disappointed that the trip was almost over. After she hung up, she turned the radio on, took her magazine out on the balcony, stretched out in the afternoon sun and turned to what she always read first - Susan Taylor's 'In The Spirit'. Susan appeared to be speaking to her when she said, "Much of our ability to experience inner peace and happiness rests with our willingness to accept change. Change is the very essence of life. There is no way to live and not experience it. To resist change is to work against life... When we accept change - and encourage it - we are in the flow of life. There are times when we feel happy and fulfilled because everything in our lives is sweet. Haven't you had those moments you'd like to preserve? It's how I feel today."

And although Mitzi didn't know what was in store for her from here on in, she knew she had to take a chance with Maliq - her gut told her so and Susan Taylor also told her that, "It is difficult to leave behind the familiar past and venture into untraveled territory, so we cling to ideas, habits and people we should let go of...trust God. Trust life... Our lives have cycles, and in order to move from one to another, change must occur." This was the change Mitzi needed. It was time. Hadn't she lain in her bed time after time and asked God to send her a decent man? What did she need - a bolt of lightning to strike her?

At five thirty she was packing - reluctantly - when Maliq knocked on her door. Even though she knew it was him, she stood at the door and asked who it was.

"The man you're going to spend the rest of your life with," he said loudly. She laughed louder and opened the door. They beamed at each other and kissed like they had been apart for a month. And it felt good - damn good to both of them. When they finally were able to pull their lips apart, they decided to have dinner at seven in Mitzi's room. Dinner arrived, complete with candles and wine.

"Ready to go home tomorrow?" Maliq was looking at her over the candle flame.

"No." She looked pensive.

"This time went too quickly, didn't it?" He put his fork down and wiped his mouth.

She looked at him and nodded. "I don't wanna go home," she said as a child would.

He smiled at her innocence. She was a diverse woman, strong and independent one minute, innocent and needing to be cared for the next. "It doesn't end here, you know. This is only the beginning. It's not like this is some illicit affair and when we get home, we have to act like strangers." He took her hand and caressed it. "We can walk off the plane holding hands."

"I know. This just feels so... precious, so new, and I don't want it to end."

"It won't. What we're both feeling right now will only grow, baby. I promise you."

They flew back first class and kissed practically the whole way. They drank champagne and toasted both to their new relationship and the future. This time when Mitzi slept, she slept with her head on Maliq's shoulder and her arm around his waist. When they left the airport, she wanted to go to the salon for a few hours, so he dropped her off and took her bags to his house, after agreeing to pick her up at six. The salon was busy, probably because everybody had gone swimming the day before on the Queen's birthday holiday, and it was Sundae's day off. Ronald filled her in on the previous days' events. Nothing out of the ordinary had happened, not on the job anyway. But there had been major excitement at Crystal's housewarming though, according to Sundae who'd called him that morning. Apparently Crystal and her mother-in-law had a huge argument at the end of the day. Ronald got the whole story - word for word - from Sundae. Mitzi took care of the walk-in clients, and at ten to six she was ready to leave. Maliq came in, and she introduced him as her 'friend' to Ronald and the girls. She left Ronald to lock up and got in the car where Maliq leaned over to kiss her.

"I wanted to do that inside, but I didn't want to... embarrass you." He smiled. It was awkward kissing him in broad daylight in Hamilton, but she liked it.

"Thanks. I'm not sure I'm ready for that yet." They talked about the Simpson/Goldman murders on the way to her mama's house. O.J. had been considered a suspect. Mitzi believed he was the culprit; Maliq didn't think he had anything to do with it. When they arrived at Oleeta's, she was sitting at the kitchen table, going through some papers and looking very distraught.

"Mommy, I'm home," Mitzi sang playfully as she walked in the door with Maliq in tow.

"Hi, honey," Oleeta said, without expression and barely looking up.

"Mama! Aren't you happy to see your daughter?" Mitzi stood beside her now and Maliq stood at the door.

"Of course I am. I'm sorry, sweetie." She stood and hugged Mitzi.

"What's the matter, darlin'?" Mitzi kissed her then stood back to look at her. Something was definitely wrong. Oleeta sat again, leaned back and sighed.

"Good evening, Mrs. Robinson." She hadn't even noticed Maliq until now.

"Oh hi, honey. I'm sorry, I didn't see you."

"What's wrong, Mama?" Mitzi was getting worried.

"Child, you can't even begin to know what's gone on here these last couple of days." She took her glasses off.

"I'll wait for you in the car..."

"No, that's okay... Malcolm, isn't it?"

"Maliq."

"It's nothing personal, Maliq, you can stay. But I might burst into tears in a second..."

"Mama..."

"Macky wrote off my car on Saturday night," she said quickly and in one breath.

Dammit. Don't say anything, Mitzi. "Is he all right?"

Oleeta nodded. "Yeah. He and that child were in the car. Neither of them was hurt, and they examined her and checked the baby at the hospital, and everything seemed okay."

Mitzi sat at the table. Maliq felt a bit uncomfortable and wasn't sure what he should do."How did it happen?" She didn't really want to hear it.

"He and that... girl were arguing, he lost control and struck a wall."

"What's wrong with those two?" Mitzi sighed.

"Not those two - her! She had been home with some type of stomach pain or something, and Macky went up to Tasty Towers with his friends on Saturday night and..."

"Where?" Mitzi frowned.

"Tasty... what you children call it now? On Reid Street... Captain's Ship... Loft."

"Lounge."

"Whatever. Anyway, little Miss Girl didn't like him being out so she traipses her pregnant self down there, sees him talking to a girl and starts an argument with the boy in front of his friends." Mitzi sighed and sucked her teeth. "Exactly. Anyhow, he decided to leave, so she follows him and gets in the car with him. He started to drive her home, and she made him strike the wall." She put her glasses back on.

Mitzi, keep your mouth shut. "Mama, why you blaming her?"

" 'Cause if she had left him alone, it wouldn't have happened. Furthermore, blood's thicker than mud."

Mitzi rolled her eyes. "Well, I'm just glad they're both all right. What are you gonna do about your car?" She stood up to leave. She was seething. Macky was an irresponsible little brat.

"I'll have to buy a new one. You should see it. I don't know how the hell they got out of it alive - divine intervention, I guess, but the car's totaled."

"Mama, I'm sorry to hear about all this, but I have to run. I just stopped by to tell you I'm back and to bring Maliq by..."

Neither of them had noticed that Maliq was no longer in the room. Mitzi and Oleeta walked out to the porch where he was playing with the dog.

"I'm sorry, sweetheart, I haven't been very hospitable."

"I understand, Mrs. Robinson. No problem, I'm sure I'll be back again." He smiled.

"Oh?" she smiled slightly. "So, you guys had a good time, huh?"

Mitzi and Maliq looked at each other and smiled. "It was wonderful, Mama. Oh, I bought your charm." She took a little gold box out of her bag and gave it to her mother. "I'll have to tell you about the trip another day, I'm makin' time right now."

"Okay, honey. Thanks for the charm, it's pretty." She knew Mitzi was dying to say something more about Macky and probably still would.

"You all right, baby?" Maliq patted Mitzi's knee as he drove her home. She looked at him and nodded, smiling a little. She just then realized that she hadn't said a word since she left her mama's house, and they were now at Waterlot Inn. She had the urge to kill Macky. When would it end?

"I'm sorry, honey. I didn't mean to go quiet on you. I could kill my brother. But then again, why blame him? My mama doesn't think anything's his fault."

"I know. But he's her baby, honey. It's hard to believe your baby does anything wrong."

"Especially mamas and their 'baby' boys." She glared at him suspiciously.

He laughed. "It ain't like that in my family. We boys do wrong, my mama goes upside our heads. She doesn't even wanna hear it. I'm still scared of Afeni Simmons."

"Well, that's the whole problem with my mama, she has never put the fear of God in Macky. And he knows good and damn well he wouldn't be acting like this if my daddy were alive."

"Your mama will find out, baby," he said as he turned into her gate. "It might be the hard way and too late, but she'll learn."

Ebone´ had obviously left for work and had left the house spotless. Mitzi found the mail and past two days' newspapers stacked neatly on the dining table. Maliq brought her bags in, and the minute he rested them, they were in each other's arms. They stared at each other and smiled.

"Thank you, sweetheart, for a beautiful trip." Maliq's arms were resting on Mitzi's shoulders, and she had her arms around his waist. Anyone who would have walked in at that moment, would have mistaken them for lovesick teenagers.

"It is I who thank you, Mr. Simmons. It truly was a beautiful trip."

And you didn't even get any. Wait 'til you do, he thought.

I hope I'm doin' the right thing, she thought somewhat cynically as Maliq moved closer to kiss her. They stood and kissed deeply for a good five minutes, and as they did, Maliq moved his hands down to her hips and pulled her closer. She didn't resist. They kissed harder.

"Now baby, I'm going home to get ready for work tomorrow. You comin' with me?"

She shook her head. "No. I have to get ready for tomorrow, too. I want to get an early night." She was tired and felt crampy again. Her period was due on the weekend.

"You are gonna come back to my house sometime soon, right?" They were in the yard.

"Of course. Isn't that what people who are 'going together' do?" she asked playfully.

He shrugged. "I just wanted to know where we were at. But call me before you come next time, okay?" He opened the car door.

Now what the hell does that mean? Mitzi's heart dropped immediately. "Sure. But can I ask why?" *Oh Lord, here comes the disappointment.*

"I want you to let me know when you're coming..." he kissed her. "So my heart will know when to get happy." He got in the car. "Talk to you later, honey." He smiled, knowing he had messed with her.

She sighed with relief and hit his arm. "Goodbye, Maliq. Thanks for everything." She watched him drive out of the yard and went back in the house to call Crystal. There was a dull pain in her stomach.

"Okay, what happened?" Mitzi asked when Crystal answered the phone.

" 'Bout bladdy time you got back. I guess you heard about me and my husband's mother."

"Yeah..."

"Well let me give you the whole story." Crystal then for ten minutes gave Mitzi a detailed account of the events which led to the argument with her mother-in-law. At one point, Mitzi rested the phone down, removed her shirt and picked it up again. Crystal hadn't noticed and was still talking.

"...so to make a long story short..."

"Too late." Mitzi was taking off her pants.

"I know I've been chopsin' so much, I wouldn't even let you get a word in edgewise, innit?"

"That's..."

"So anyhow, then she tells me she didn't appreciate what Sundae said. I was at the end of my rope then."

"What did Sundae say?" Mitzi was getting tired. "And bring it home now, okay? In as few words as possible, please."

"Okay. Everybody was toasting to us and our new house, and Sundae said, 'May the roof never fall in and those beneath it, never fall out'."

Mitzi laughed. "That's cute. Leave it to Sundae."

"Well, mama girlfriend didn't think so. She told me she thinks Sundae is a troublemaker, and she thought her comment was inappropriate - like she was trying to say that me and 'her son' aren't happy and all this B.S. And, of course, Raoul is always 'her son', like he don't have a first name."

"What is her problem?" Mitzi couldn't believe her ears.

"I don't know, but her daughter-in-law blinked. I let her have it. I brought up stuff that happened in the last century..."

"What was Raoul saying?"

"Well, you know him. His loyalties are kind of divided, so he was just telling us to forget about it and it wasn't necessary for us to act like that and blah, blah, blah. Finally he told his mama it was best that she left, and she did."

"Thank God I wasn't there, I would've been upset," Mitzi said, yawning.

"For what? Anyway, Sundae was the only one there. Everybody else was gone by then."

"She wouldn't have left early if someone had paid her. You heard from Mrs. Outerbridge since?" Mitzi turned the TV on and leaned back against her pillows.

"Raoul called her this morning, but I didn't speak to her."

"Is he upset?"

"I guess so. But he apologised to me for her behaviour."

"That's nice. Even though she's his mama, he still knows what she's about."

"He never makes excuses for her. And at least he defends me. He knows she's a bitch, but nobody's actually gonna admit that about their mama. Anyway, enough about Satan's first born. What about you? How was the trip?"

Mitzi closed her eyes. "Wonderful. Absolutely wonderful."

"My girl! Sooo... what happened?" Crystal was getting excited in anticipation of what she thought Mitzi was going to tell her, but when she summed up the trip in two minutes, Crystal was disappointed. "Mitzi, for goodness sake. Did you do the nasty, or what?"

"No. We didn't. But that's not..."

"What the hell are you waitin' for - the second coming?" She laughed at herself. "Never mind, you haven't had the first one yet."

"Crystal, I didn't have to have sex with the man to enjoy the trip, you know."

"Better you than me."

"Anyway, we've decided to let this relationship grow."

"So, he's your man?"

"Uh huh."

"Okay, we're getting somewhere." She paused. "I'm happy for you, sister, if this is what you want."

"It is what I want, Crys. I really like Maliq. He's so... different."

"Well, he better act right, or he'll be hearing from me."

Mitzi's phone beeped. "Now, I'm gone. I have another call." It was Maliq, calling to tell her he was home and that the minute he walked in, his daughter had called and was angry.

"She thought I should have told her I was going away, and I definitely should have let her know that I was going with you."

Mitzi sat up. "Excuse me?" She couldn't believe what she was hearing. "Who is the parent?"

"I know she's out of order, but she's kind of a daddy's girl. And I usually do tell her when I go away." Mitzi said nothing. That spoiled little daddy's girl needed a slap as far as she was concerned, but it wasn't her place to say. Maliq didn't tell Mitzi that his daughter had said she disliked her. "Anyway baby, I just wanted to tell you how much I enjoyed being with you and how much more I'm looking forward to a future with you."

Mitzi smiled. She certainly wasn't going to let that brat spoil her mood. "I feel the same way, Maliq."

"What you doin'?"

"Just lying in my bed. I have cramp again." She also had a headache.

"When is your doctor's appointment?" He was concerned.

"Day after tomorrow." He had remembered that she was going soon.

"Want me to go with you?"

"No, thank you. I'm a big girl. I'll be fine."

*   *   *   *   *

"A lapa what?"

"Laparoscopy. It's just minor, outpatient surgery." Mitzi was talking to her mama from the phone in her office. She was ready to leave for the day. And not a minute too soon. Her stomach really hurt.

"You scared?"

"Nah. It's nothing big. I just want to find out what's going on." He scheduled it for July twelfth."

"I'll write it on my calendar. Let me know if you need me to pick you up."

"Maliq's gonna drop me off and pick me up." Mitzi had called him first.

"Oh, excuse me. Don't need me anymore." She was smiling. "Granny's here. You wanna talk to her?"

"Of course. I haven't seen her for days." Oleeta gave the phone to her mother.

"My dear child, you planning on doing my hair again before the turn of the century?" She would never change.

Mitzi laughed. "Hi, honey. How are you?"

"Who wants to know? 'Cause you're courting now, you don't have time for your old granny."

"That's not true..."

"It better not be, Puddin', 'cause when that 'bye' takes off, I'll still be here."

Mitzi laughed out loud. "Stop it Granny, my stomach hurts already."

"You need a couple of babies, that's your whole problem."

"Bye, Gran." Mitzi had heard that a hundred times.

"I know the truth can be hard to digest. See you later, Puddin'."

"Depending on how I feel this weekend, I'll come and do your hair."

"I won't hold my breath, I'm already on death's door."

Mitzi wasn't able to do anything but stay in bed on the weekend. She was curled up in a ball with the most severe menstrual pain she had ever experienced. She stayed in bed from Friday night until Monday morning. Maliq and Ebone´ waited on her hand and foot. Ebone´ changed her linen and cleaned the house while Maliq cooked. As much as Mitzi was grateful for the treatment, she didn't feel like being bothered with anybody except Maliq. She had been given Donorest for the pain, and it made her sleep a lot. On Sunday evening, after having sat in the chair in her room while she slept all day, Maliq fixed her sheets while she showered. When she came out, he massaged her feet with oil. That was the first time any man had ever done that. Mitzi had a feeling there would be a lot of firsts with her new man.

CHAPTER NINETEEN
Tuesday Morning

"You okay, baby?" Maliq asked Mitzi as they drove out of the hospital parking lot. Mitzi nodded with her eyes closed. She was still groggy, and her navel hurt where it had been cut to have the laparoscopy done. There was a pain a little below her navel, too. They had made two incisions and injected dye through the cut in her navel to check for blockage in her tubes. The doctor had looked through a laparoscope to check for the cause of the pain.

When they arrived at her house, a flower delivery truck was in the yard. Melba and Oleeta had sent her arrangements. Maliq helped her inside and into bed. He turned the ceiling fan on low and put a pitcher of water and a glass on the night table.

"Get some sleep, honey." He kissed her forehead.

"You're leaving?" Mitzi was already drifting off to sleep, but she didn't want him to go. He had taken the day off.

"You want me to?" He held her hand.

She shook her head. "No."

"Then I'll be here when you wake up." He kissed her again. She fell asleep. He watched TV in the living room. He hoped she wouldn't be in too much pain, but if she was, he wanted to be near her. He wished he could get in bed with her and hold her while she slept.

When Ebone' got home at four o'clock, Maliq was in the kitchen, making soup. Even though it was as hot as it got in Bermuda, he didn't think she would want anything heavy to eat

- if at all. Mitzi woke up shortly after, in pain and hungry. Maliq brought her the soup on a tray. She had slept the anaesthetic off and wanted a shower. Maliq called Ebone´ in to help her because she was stiff and sore. He envied Ebone´ because he wanted to take care of Mitzi completely, but of course, he couldn't - yet. By the next morning, she said she felt ninety percent better except for the soreness around her cuts. Maliq had spent the night on the couch and woke her to tell her he was leaving to get ready for work.

"Thanks for being here for me, sweetie."

"You're my woman, honey, that's my job. I'm just sorry I can't stay home with you today."

"I'm fine. Go to work."

"You feel like seein' me this evening?"

"How you expect me to make it through the night without seeing you this evening?"

"I'll be here, baby. You need anything?"

"Just you, honey."

"Then you have all you need already." He kissed her and left.

Mitzi had endometriosis. It was her birthday, and she had gone to work that morning for the first time since going to the hospital. She had gone to the doctor to have the 'staples' removed and for her results. She would be on hormone treatment for a few months, and if that didn't work, she would have to have laser surgery to remove the scar tissue. It wasn't life threatening and very common, so she wasn't upset - the eternal optimist.

After lunch Mitzi walked into her office - which had earlier been decorated with balloons and a 'Happy Birthday' banner - and found three floral arrangements: one from her mama and George, one from Crystal, Raoul and the children and eleven yellow roses from Maliq. His card read, 'Look in the mirror for the twelfth rose. Love ya, Maliq'. She smiled, then laughed out loud. Ronald was arranging them on her desk, and naturally Sundae had followed her in to be pokey.

"Why not red roses?" she asked, taking up the card and reading it.

"Because Sundae..." Mitzi said, snatching the card from her.

"Oh, I know. 'Cause red roses mean love, and you guys haven't reached the love stage yet.

"Figured that out all by yourself, Sundae?" Ronald asked.

"Go ta hell, Ronald," she said, hitting him on his behind as he left the office. "Ooh, nice bumpy." Ronald hit her hand and smiled.

"These are pretty, innit Sundae?" Mitzi asked, smelling the roses.

"All flowers are," Sundae said, smiling.

"I know, but you know what I mean."

"I'm happy for you, Mitzi. I hope this works out for you guys."

Mitzi sat at her desk and sighed thoughtfully. "I do, too, Sundae. I do, too. Now get out so I can call my sweetie." She called Maliq at work, and he sounded busy and harassed when he answered the phone. "Thanks for the flowers, honey."

His demeanour changed as soon as he heard her voice. He leaned back in his chair and smiled. "You're welcome, baby. Did you look in the mirror?"

She laughed. "Not yet. That was so sweet."

"And so are you. How's your birthday been so far?"

"All right. But I got some news from the doctor." She told him what the results were and assured him she wasn't upset.

"Let's hope you don't have to have surgery, but if you do, I'll take care of you."

"Thanks. I know you will."

"So, you haven't told me what you want for dinner tonight." They had decided to spend her birthday alone and have a games night another time.

"Surprise me."

"Okay." *I'll surprise you all right, in more ways than one.* "I have a meeting at two, so I'll be gone for the rest of the day. Wanna come for dinner about seven thirty?"

"I guess I can wait that long to see you."

He smiled. "Call me before you leave home."

"So your heart will know when to get happy?"

"No. So I'll know when to light the candles."

They both laughed. "I'm sure of myself, aren't I?" At one time she would have been embarrassed, but they were past that stage now. She felt connected to Maliq. There were no nagging doubts anymore, just a good, healthy, positive vibe. She felt naturally high and believed Maliq did, too. Time would tell.

"You have every reason to be sure of yourself. This is a sure thing." He looked at his watch. "Now baby, I have to go. I'll see you tonight. Have a good day." He kissed her through the phone, and she kissed him back. The minute she hung up, she missed him. And as he pushed the elevator button on the way to his 'meeting', he wondered what she would do if she knew where he was really going. He felt a bit guilty as he left the building.

*   *   *   *   *

"Surprise!!" What sounded like a thousand voices, shouted as the lights came on in Maliq's living room. Mitzi screamed and backed out of the door. Maliq pulled her back in and hugged and kissed her.

"What the hell...?" Tears welled in her eyes as she looked around the room - which was decorated with balloons, banners and candles - and saw her friends. Crystal and Raoul, Ebone´ and a guy Mitzi didn't know, Sundae and some guy who looked like he didn't want to be there, her mama and George. Ronald and Pearl - who was beginning to show - were sitting on the love seat. Melba was standing alone, but smiling. Five or six other people who Mitzi didn't know, but whom she thought must be related to Maliq, were sitting on the step. She was speechless. Sundae took pictures as Maliq pushed her into the room. No one had ever given her a surprise party before.

"I can't believe you lot did this to me," she whispered, still in shock. A tear rolled down her cheek, but she didn't notice. She was so caught up in her friends, the decorations and the fact that Maliq would do this for her. Then reality set in, and she hit him on his arm. "So this is why I had to call you before I came." She was laughing now. "Mama! I can't believe you didn't tell me! And Sundae, I can't believe you didn't let anything slip!"

"Me either, but one more day and I would have exploded and had a stroke. You know keeping this secret killed me." Everybody laughed as Mitzi began hugging her friends. The people on the steps were Maliq's sister Marshalle and her husband Charles, Na'imah and her boyfriend Sinclair, and his brother Marcus and his wife Atiba. They all hugged her and wished her a happy birthday. Sundae introduced her to the previously elusive Tyrone, and Ebone''s date was a seemingly pleasant guy named Roderick.

Chaka Khan's 'Sweet Thing' was playing. Mitzi walked around the room hugging and kissing everybody. When she reached Crystal, they began screaming, hitting each other's hands and jumping up and down. Then Crystal and Raoul hugged her, hurting the cut on her stomach, but she said nothing.

Finally Maliq pulled her away and put his arms around her. "You feel okay, sweetheart?" he asked seriously.

Mitzi frowned. "Yes, why?"

"I almost changed my mind about having the party after your little surgery because I thought it would be too much for you. If it is, just tell me, and I'll get everybody to leave early."

"No, honey. I'm okay. My stomach's a little sore, but I'll be fine." She got serious. "This is so sweet, Maliq. Thank you. No one has ever done this for me." They kissed softly, ignoring everyone around them.

"You children have company, you know." Oleeta was standing beside them, pretending to be offended. They stopped kissing and laughed.

"Sorry, ma'am," Maliq said, wiping lipstick from his mouth and putting his arm around Mitzi's waist. They all laughed.

"Honey, George and I aren't staying. We just wanted to be here for the surprise and to bring your gift. We don't wanna hang around you lot."

"Thanks for the peas and rice and chicken, Mrs. Robinson," Maliq said, touching Oleeta's arm.

"Anytime, honey. Anything for my daughter." She hugged and kissed them both, and she and George left.

"Dinner is served!" Crystal was standing beside a long table which was covered with a white tablecloth and held all types of food. In the center of the table was a thick, round candle surrounded by orange and white flowers. "Everybody help yourselves."

"Can we bless the food first?" Maliq asked. "I'll do the honours." Grace was said, and the feast began. Maliq brought Mitzi a glass of Perrier in a wine glass. She was still on medication and couldn't drink liquor. By the time they had all finished eating, everybody was laughing, joking and making a lot of noise. When all the food had been cleared from the table, Maliq turned the lights off, and the room glowed with both candlelight and friendship - old and new. Sundae and Crystal brought a colossal orange and white cake from the kitchen. There appeared to be a hundred candles atop it. Everybody gathered around the table and sang 'Happy Birthday', and Mitzi started crying again. Maliq hugged her, and they kissed again - a deep, passionate kiss - while the people they both loved clapped and continued to sing. When they finally pulled their lips apart, Mitzi closed her eyes, made a wish and blew the candles out.

"What did you wish for, baby?" Maliq asked, smiling at his lady lovingly.

"You - it was a retrospective wish." She smiled at him and winked.

Crystal took the cake in the kitchen while everybody else sat back in the living room - some on the floor - with only the candles burning and seventies music playing.

"Maliq, this music is the jam," Sundae said, grooving to The Staples' 'I'll Take You There'.

"I wasn't sure if you'd like this type of music, Sundae."

"Who - her? She's still stuck in the seventies. She probably has an eight-track player at home," Crystal said, coming from the kitchen.

"Of course, she does," Mitzi said. "She still has a big wooden fork and spoon on her kitchen wall."

"And beads separating her living and dining rooms," Crystal continued, sitting between Raoul's legs on the floor and sipping wine.

Maliq's family laughed. They couldn't begin to know what they were in for.

"Damn right I do," Sundae said, unashamedly. "Gimme the seventies any day. Living was a lot more fun then."

"I know that's right," Marcus said. "Somewhere between then and now, life got complicated."

Sundae nodded. "You know what I'm sayin', my brother. Hey, talkin' 'bout the old days, Maliq and Marcus, how 'bout when you guys and Malcolm had that group and used to sing in 'Battle of the Groups'."

"At Rosebank?" Mitzi was surprised. Maliq and Marcus both nodded and laughed. "I didn't know you could sing, Maliq. And I sure don't remember you on stage at 'Battle of the Groups'," Mitzi laughed. "Sing a li'l somethin' for me, honey," she said, sitting beside him on the step.

He winked at her. "Later, baby." They stared at each other for a moment.

"Mmn." Crystal was nudging Raoul and nodding toward them. The whole room went quiet as they all stared at them with collective approval. One or two of them were silently envious. When Mitzi and Maliq realized they had an audience, everybody laughed. Maliq put his arm around her.

"No, she didn't notice me on stage. She was probably out with her big afro boyfriend on his mobylette."

"She was," Ebone' chimed in. "And then they probably left there and went to sit on Nellie's Walk afterwards."

"Oh, if you didn't go and sit on Nellie's Walk after every event, you might as well have stayed home," Marshalle said.

"Uh huh," they all agreed.

"Day or night, Nellie's Walk or City Hall car park was the place," Marcus added.

"Hey, remember what we used to do there during the day?" Maliq asked.

"Count de women who spoke to you," Tyrone - Sundae's date - joined in. He spoke kind of slow and sounded a bit daft.

"Oh yes, that was the order of the day," Marcus agreed.

"And whoever got the most women to speak was the 'baddest'," Raoul added.

"And you had to count de white girls separate from de coloured girls," Tyrone said slowly, laughing.

Coloured? Mitzi looked at Maliq, who frowned and then at Crystal who rolled her eyes. *Where had Sundae found this imbecile?*

"You got it, my man," Marcus laughed, pointing to Tyrone. Was he laughing at or with him?

Crystal sighed loudly. "Would you people please spare me? 'Cause we girls kept track of the amount of men who checked us out, too, thank you." She crossed her legs.

"I don't remember doin' that," Sundae said blankly. All the women in the room glared at her.

"I want to thank you, Sundae, for your never-ending support," Crystal said, cutting her eyes.

"Oops, I'm sorry, I..."

"Next time just flow with it, would you?" Melba asked, shaking her head. She had put on weight and looked a bit untidy.

"You lot know what I thought of the other day?" Mitzi jumped in. Maliq was rubbing the back of her neck, and it felt good. "Who remembers when the vegetable cart came around to houses?"

"I do," came from most of the room. "And the ice cream truck. And the fish man."

"What damn ice cream truck?"

"I never had no ice cream truck in my neighbourhood."

" 'Cause you lived in a rough neighbourhood. You all would have probably stolen the ice cream."

"The fish man and the vegetable cart still come to my neighbourhood."

"How 'bout that man who used to pick up and deliver the dry-cleaning."

"Oh, I forgot about that."

"I clearly remember. He came in that van with the side sliding door."

"That was back when the buses and Telco trucks were green."

"And the police cars were black and white." Every person in the room recalled something from the past.

"Remember the five o'clock siren?"

"Honey, hush! I forgot all about that. Now that was happenin' when the buses left from Reid Street, out there by the Cabinet building."

"Are we getting old, or what?" Mitzi asked, shaking her head.

"Speak for yourself, birthday girl," Crystal said. "I'm still a spring chicken."

"Do you know I just found out from Mrs. Simmons this week that the siren was located up Mount Hill somewhere near where she used to live," Atiba added. She hadn't said much.

"Mount Hill? I thought it was up top of Telco on Washington Street."

"I thought it was at the fire station."

And so it went for the next half hour until it was time for dessert. Crystal, Melba, Sundae and Na'imah went in the kitchen to get the cake and ice cream while the others watched Mitzi open her gifts.

"Sundae, where in hell did you find that boy?" Crystal started the minute they were out of the others' earshot.

Sundae sucked her teeth. "I don' know. He's kinda dopey, innit?"

"Kind of?" Melba was almost shouting. "That's an understatement. He's as simple as simple gets. Is that the best you can do, Sundae?"

"As a matter of fact, yes, that is the best I can do at the moment." Sundae suddenly got defensive. "And might I add, I'm doing a tad bit better than you are, Melba the 'manless' woman."

Na'imah looked like she wasn't sure if she should stay or not, and Crystal noticed. "Don't worry about these two, honey, tomorrow they'll be having lunch together."

"Like hell," Sundae said, scooping ice cream into bowls as Crystal cut the cake.

"You *can* do better, though, Sundae," Crystal continued.

"And it's not only that he's dopey," Melba said. "He speaks badly."

"Actually, he damn-well talks stupid," Crystal said bluntly. "We haven't been coloured people for decades."

Sundae sighed. "Well, I guess I kinda have patience with him because as you know, I haven't always spoken properly either."

"You Sundae? No!" Crystal faked surprise.

Sundae sighed again, cut her eyes at Crystal and continued. "So I feel kinda sorry for him... like he needs me."

"Sundae, for heaven's sake, the boy is not your responsibility," Crystal said, licking icing from her fingers.

"I know he's not. And he does embarrass me - you know - the way he acts." Sundae started to smile. "But he's good between the sheets."

Na'imah shook her head.

"Oh Sundae, please," Melba said, looking disgusted. "Don't make me bring up my food."

"You gave that dweeb some, Sundae?" Crystal asked.

"Hey, I can look past certain faults when we're gettin' busy."

"Sundae, I don't care how good a man is in bed, I believe if he isn't gainfully employed and can't put a proper sentence together, then you shouldn't even lie down beside him, let alone under him."

"He *does* work, Melba." Sundae was defensive again.

"Whatever, Sundae. But he's daft! And why does he smell like Limacol?"

"Limacol? He smells like the essence of whore-blossom, if you ask me," Crystal said, ready to take the cake out to the living room.

"Look, I'll worry 'bout that later. Tonight, I just wanna enjoy myself," Sundae said.

They left the kitchen and took the cake into the candlelit living room. After eating cake, ice cream and fresh fruit, the gathering turned into a real 'jam'. The music was turned up, and they all danced accordingly to 'Flashlight', 'Rock the Boat', 'Jammin'', 'Second Time Around' and when Cheryl Lynn's 'To Be Real' came on, Mitzi, Crystal and Sundae took spoons from the table and used them like microphones. Their 'audience' laughed, with Maliq being the loudest. He was a little surprised at Mitzi and shook his head in amusement when she looked at him. He winked at her with approval, and their eyes held. Mitzi felt as comfortable then as she did around people she had known for years. Maliq was definitely the one. She could be herself around him because he was so easygoing and down to earth. There was no need for a facade when she was with or around him. She looked at his family, and they were clapping the trio on. Mitzi had actually shocked herself. And she hadn't even been drinking. At that moment she was happy - carefree. Life was as good as it had ever been, and she honestly believed it would only get better with Maliq - her soul mate. When the song ended, they bowed to applause, and Sundae continued singing Natalie Cole's 'Our Love'. Tyrone had fallen asleep in the middle of the party. Sundae was too busy enjoying herself to care.

"You girls are sick," Maliq laughed as Mitzi sat beside him.

"We're childish, innit?" She knew he didn't really think so.

Maliq got serious. "No baby, not childish. Sick!" They both laughed, and when they stopped, he kissed her hard on her lips, parting them with his tongue. She responded in kind. "Don't change, honey." His lips were still on hers.

"I don't intend to," she answered, reluctantly pulling away and looking in his eyes, which were smiling.

"Hey Mitzi, remember this cut from that Cup Match up Somerset - when was it, nineteen seventy-eight, seventy-nine?" Crystal asked. 'Boogie Oogie Oogie' was playing.

"Takes me back to that partly finished house overlooking Somerset Cricket Club every time I hear it," Mitzi answered, turning away from Maliq.

"You girls were there? I was, too," Maliq said, getting up to get another drink. "Mitzi, I think you and I were destined to meet. It seems we've been a few of the same places in the past."

"I know you were destined to meet," Sundae said, shaking Tyrone awake. "The way you both keep suckin' on each other's faces." She glared at Tyrone who looked vacant.

"You mean like this?" Maliq asked, kissing Mitzi as he sat beside her again. Everybody groaned in mock annoyance.

Ebone´ and Roderick were the first to leave at one o'clock. Mitzi, Maliq, Crystal, Raoul, Marcus and Atiba were still sitting on the floor, drinking and talking about old times. They all made plans to go to the County game later that day. Marcus and Atiba had a spot reserved at 'Seabreeze' in Bailey's Bay and invited the other four to join them. After deciding what everybody would bring, Marcus thought it best to leave because he intended to be at the field by eight o'clock.

"Invite those other lot, too," Atiba said to Mitzi. "We have a big camp."

"Sundae has to work, but she'll probably come when she knocks off. I'll tell Ebone´ and Melba." They were all standing at the door. "Thanks, you guys, this was so sweet," Mitzi said as she hugged them all.

"Need a lift home, Mitzi?" Raoul asked, smiling and knocking Crystal.

Crystal knocked him back. "No, she doesn't." Mitzi smiled, and Maliq put his arm around her. It felt so good.

"I'll see to it that she gets home, man. Thanks." Maliq smiled mischievously, and the last guests left. He closed the door, leaned against it and pulled Mitzi in his arms. Without saying a word, they kissed yet again. If they had held each other any closer, they would have been inside one another.

"Thank you, honey. I really appreciate everything you did for my birthday," Mitzi said, her face in his chest.

"Anything for you, baby. Did you enjoy yourself?" He led her to the couch. The candles were still lit and the lights still off. Smokey Robinson was singing, 'Quiet Storm'. Maliq sat at the end of the couch and put one leg up, leaving a space for Mitzi to sit between his legs. She took her sandals off and joined him. He softly kissed the back of her neck while his arms were around her waist. She closed her eyes and smiled. Neither one spoke for a long time. He continued kissing her while Roberta Flack and Donny Hathaway sang, 'The Closer I Get to You'.

Is this a plan? Mitzi wondered. *Are these sexually suggestive songs intended to send some type of message to me?' If they are, they're working. I want this man. Now.* She closed her eyes tighter and flinched as Maliq touched the center of her femininity, simply by having his tongue on her neck. *Please don't stop,* she thought, but didn't have the nerve to say. And seconds later he stopped. She turned to look at him, but his eyes were closed and his expression blank. When she turned away, he opened his eyes and smiled. He was teasing her. At first he wasn't sure how far he should go, but now he knew she wanted him. She was clearly becoming aroused. He exhaled deeply against her neck, and she stiffened. The Isleys were singing, 'You're All I Need'.

I'm gonna make sure you want me and let you make the first move, baby, he thought as she took one of his hands in hers. Their hands were on her thigh. He lifted his foot from the floor and crossed his ankle over hers, making their hands move closer to her crotch. Mitzi let out a low, involuntary moan. Maliq smiled behind her. She squeezed his hand. He squeezed hers back. Then he took his free arm and loosely put it around her neck, brushing her breasts as he did. Her nipples immediately hardened, and she groaned again. Mitzi was more aroused than she had ever been.

When Keith Washington started singing, 'Tonight's the Night', she took the hand that was resting on her shoulder and gently moved it to her breast - without shame. What the hell? This man - her man - was driving her crazy, and she was damn-near on the brink of orgasm from anticipation alone. Maliq gently caressed one breast then the other. Mitzi was wearing a zip-front body suit and only a thin bra underneath so in her sexually heightened mind, she could feel his flesh against hers. With each movement of his hand, the moisture between her thighs increased. She pushed back against his body while Eugene Wild sang, 'Don't Say No Tonight'.

Don't worry, ain't nobody sayin' no tonight!

The lyrics were timed too perfectly. It had been planned. Maliq started kissing her neck again, and at the same time Mitzi felt his male stiffness against her back. She reached back and rubbed his hardness while her eyes were still closed. He had stopped playing with her breasts and just held her as he moved his tongue across her shoulders. Her nipples got harder, needing to be touched again. When she could take it no more, she stood and pulled Maliq away from the arm of the couch, making his feet rest on the floor, then she straddled him. She wanted nothing right now, other than for him to make love to her. And if he wasn't going to make the first move, then she would have to take matters into her own hands - so to speak. She put her hands behind his head and pulled him to her, pushing her tongue inside his mouth as she pushed her crotch against his.

"What you want, baby?" he whispered, teasing her again and licking her chest.

She sucked her teeth impatiently. "You know what I want, Maliq," she whispered harshly. She kissed him again. He was caressing her butt.

"Tell me, baby," he urged.

"I want you, honey." She was moaning again.

"You have me, sweetheart. I'm right here." He pulled her harder into his groin.

"Don't do this to me, baby... I need you, Maliq. I need you in me," she moaned. "Make love to me, baby...please." This was the first time she'd ever begged a man for sex, but this was dignified begging. She knew he wouldn't think any less of her for the way she was behaving. He was provoking her. It suddenly dawned on her that he knew exactly what he was doing and was sure he was loving every minute. But so was she. This was beautiful. When Major Harris and Maliq started singing, 'Love Won't Let Me Wait', Mitzi thought she would scream. Instead, she let her head fall back and closed her eyes while Maliq licked her neck.

"The time is right..." he sang.

"Yes baby, it is."

"Please tell me yes..."

"Yes Maliq, please."

"Love won't let me wait... He pulled her zipper down, exposing her cleavage.

"... turn down the lights... Spend the night in wonderland..."

"Move a little closer..." he sang in her ear while simultaneously licking her neck and taking her clothes off. "Listen girl..." It was difficult to tell whether the moaning he heard next was the song or Mitzi.

"... I need your love so desperately... When I make love to you, we'll explode in ecstasy, love won't let me wait..."

By the time the song ended and Bloodstone was singing 'Natural High', Mitzi was completely naked and feverently tearing Maliq's clothes off while sucking his chest. Once naked, he lifted her from the couch and lay her on the floor in front of the fish tank. The room still glowed with candlelight, and the sheer curtains at the French doors blew gently in the north breeze.

"I'll be right back, baby. Don't go anywhere." Mitzi wanted to cry. How much longer did she have to wait? Thirty seconds later he was back with a towel. He had also put on a condom. "You sure this is what you wanna do?" He asked as he lay beside her, his erection calling her. She sucked her teeth again, pushed him back on the towel and straddled him again. This time, she made sure he knew what she wanted. She lost her breath as they consummated their relationship.

"I'm positive this is what I want," she whispered while she made love to him, slowly at first, the intensity increasing, creating pure ecstasy. Mitzi opened herself completely to Maliq, and he, in turn, did all in his power to ensure her satisfaction. They reached sexual heights which many only fantasize about and few achieve. They climaxed together the first time and then each experienced separate orgasms over and over. They moved from the floor to the step, to the kitchen table and finally ended up on his waterbed.

Roberta Flack was singing, 'If I Were Your Woman' in the distance. The ceiling fan was turning slowly. "Turn the light off, honey," Mitzi whispered as Maliq lay on top of her, his body covered in sweat.

"No baby, I need to see the beautiful body that's getting me high like this," he whispered back, kissing her. Then he kissed every part of her body, starting from her lips and ending up at her feet. The light stayed on for quite a while.

Mitzi woke up when she heard Maliq get up and go to the bathroom. She lay still and pretended to be asleep when he got back in bed. He kissed her softly on the cheek. Usually as soon as she was awake, she would pray, but this morning she thought it inappropriate to pray while lying buck naked next to a man whom she had fornicated with all night. She would pray once she was dressed. But now that posed a problem. She had nothing to put on except the clothes she'd had on the night before. What happened next? It had been a while since she had spent the night at a man's house. Quite a while. Did she go right in the shower and then put on the same clothes? She felt awkward. She also 'felt' Maliq staring at her. She opened one eye to find him propped up on one elbow, looking at her and smiling. She smiled back and hoped her face was clean. He had had the opportunity to check his while in the bathroom.

She turned away and said, "Good morning."

Maliq laughed. "Mornin' baby. Our breath probably smells the same so don't worry about it. Gimme a kiss." They kissed - without tongue - then he got up again, wearing his nakedness with pride and opened the closet. He pulled a black silk robe from behind the door and gave it to her. "If you want, you can put this on and look in the closet in the bathroom for a wash cloth and towel. There're a couple of new toothbrushes in there too. Or, you can stay right here just the way you are." She was already putting on the robe.

"What you want me to do with the toothbrush after I'm finished with it?" She was heading for the bathroom.

"Put it in the holder, next to mine. You'll need it again." He smiled. She stood in the middle of the room while they stared at each other. A mutual stare that said, "Thank you."

When she returned, he was standing at the window in black silk boxers. The bed was made. He took her in his arms and kissed her. "Is it too early to tell you I love you, Mitzi?"

"Do you?"

"Yes," he whispered. "Something as beautiful as this has to be love."

*   *   *   *   *

"You always take advantage of men like that?" Maliq asked, putting toast in front of Mitzi who was sitting at the table. He had given her a piggyback to the kitchen.

"Excuse me?" She looked surprised and slightly confused.

Maliq smiled. "You attacked me last night, lady. I'm surprised at you." He was teasing her again.

"I attacked you? What about what you did to me?"

"Let the record clearly show that you, Maxine Robinson, made the first move." They both laughed. "It must have been all that alcohol you drank... oh, I forgot, you didn't drink, did you? You were in total control of yourself last night, weren't you?" He grinned and sat across from her.

"You... are a wicked man, Maliq Simmons," she said slowly, squinting her eyes. She wasn't the least bit ashamed or embarrassed. Her birthday had been absolutely beautiful, especially the culmination. "And can you please tell me the reason for those songs?"

"Subliminal messages, baby," he said, biting a piece of toast.

"Think you're smart, don't you?"

"A pure genius is what I am. Worked, didn't they?"

"Look out for the payback, honey. Two can play that game."

"Punish me, baby."

They finally reached 'Seabreeze' at eleven. Marcus and Atiba had a perfect camp, on the field. Crystal and Raoul were there already. Mitzi had called Ebone´, Sundae and Melba to invite them before leaving Maliq's house. He had given her shorts, a tee shirt and a pair of his jockey's to wear home where she quickly changed. They had a cooler with beer, breezers and soda, as well as fresh fruit and chicken, all left over from the party. Ebone´ would be coming after one, and Melba and Sundae would get there after five.

"Where the hell you been all mornin'?" Crystal asked softly as Mitzi opened her lawn chair next to hers. Maliq put his next to Mitzi's. "I called your house from eight thirty 'til I left home at ten."

"Don't worry 'bout all that," Mitzi said, hitting Crystal on her arm.

"Crystal's eyes widened. Maliq was at the cooler. "You spent the night?!" Crystal whispered in disbelief. She didn't wait for an answer. " 'Bout bladdy time! What happened?!"

"All I'm saying is, he likes my tattoo."

"He saw the tattoo?!" Mitzi had a heart shaped tattoo on her leg where it met her torso. She had gotten it after losing a bet in college. "You go all out when you do something, don't you? I mean, it takes you a while but look out when you do..."

"Ssh, Crystal, I don't want him to think I'm like an excited teenager who just lost her cherry."

"It probably had grown back after all this time."

"You enjoy yourself last night, Crystal?" Maliq asked, sitting next to Mitzi and giving her a soda.

"Maliq, Raoul and I were saying this morning that it's been years since we've enjoyed a good old house party as much as we did last night. The food, the conversation, the music..."

"Yes, the music seemed to have affected a few people last night," Maliq said, staring at Mitzi and smiling slyly. She playfully cut her eyes at him. The two of them spent most of the day staring and smiling at each other. They might as well have worn signs that read, 'We made love for the first time last night'.

They all had just started eating when Ebone' showed up with Roderick. Mitzi hoped this one would last. Roderick seemed like a really nice, humble person, and Ebone' was a totally different person. She was still in therapy, and he occasionally went with her.

"After all that food I ate last night, I think I'm just having fruit today," Atiba said.

"Poor you," Crystal said, piling food on her plate. "It's a new day, honey." Naturally, she ate the most. After lunch the game got slow, and Raoul and Crystal wanted to play Crown and Anchor. "Anybody else feel lucky?" Raoul asked.

Maliq and Mitzi decided to go with them. "Coming Ebone'? Roderick?" Mitzi asked.

"No, I'm tryin' to stay out of the sun," Ebone' said. Roderick was quite content to stay with her while drinking a beer and watching the game.

"Why? The sun making you feel sick?" Mitzi was putting on lipstick.

"No, I just don't wanna get any darker." Mitzi frowned but said nothing.

An hour later the gamblers returned, all of them - except Mitzi - poorer than when they left. Maliqa was sitting in Mitzi's chair, talking to her Uncle Marcus. She stopped abruptly when she saw her daddy and Mitzi.

"It's about time you got back," she said rudely. Mitzi took a deep breath. She was in no mood for this brat. Crystal's eyes widened, and she looked at Mitzi as if she were in shock.

"Hi sweetie," Maliq said - to Mitzi's annoyance. "I haven't seen you for..."

"That's probably 'cause you ran off on a trip with your girlfriend and never said a word to your daughter."

Mitzi just stared at her, too angry to speak. Crystal cleared her throat and sat down, staring at the girl, who never acknowledged anyone but her father.

"And you are...?" Crystal asked firmly. Maliqa ignored her.

"This is my daughter, Maliqa. These are Mitzi's and my friends, honey," Maliq said, looking slightly embarrassed.

"How come you didn't call me to see if I wanted to sit in your camp today?" Everybody was looking at her.

"What's your problem, girl?" Marcus demanded.

"Leave her, Marcus," Maliq said, smiling. "You know how she gets sometimes..."

Marcus ignored him. "You're getting too old to be carrying on like this, Maliqa. Have some respect, girl."

"For who? Her?" she asked, referring to Mitzi.

"She's your father's lady, Maliqa," Atiba said softly.

Maliqa sucked her teeth. "She's the reason I don't get to see my daddy no more," she whined, sounding like a five year-old.

Mitzi had had enough. "Let me tell you something, little girl," she said, calmly but firmly.

Maliqa stood to face her. "Little girl?! I don't think..." Maliq grabbed his daughter's arm gently.

"Come on, Boo, what's the matter? Come talk to me." He put his arm around her and led her away from the others.

Marcus was the first to speak. "That li'l girl needed a cut ass years ago."

"I could do it for her now. What's her problem?" Crystal asked, clearly annoyed.

"Everybody always thought she was cute," Marcus continued, shelling peanuts. "But far as I'm concerned, she stopped being cute a long time ago."

"She's a little bitch... sorry Marcus, I know she's your niece."

Marcus shrugged indifferently.

"I don't know why she dislikes me," Mitzi said, still angry.

"Oh, it's not you," Marcus said, mouth full of peanuts.

"She's always treated Maliq's female friends like that," Atiba added.

"Jealous li'l heifer, ain't she?" Crystal asked.

Raoul knocked her. "That's enough. You keep out."

"I have never, in the short time I have known Maliq, tried to keep him from her. And it's not like she calls or comes to see him."

"Girl, don't pay her any mind," Atiba said.

Maliq motioned for Mitzi to join them. Maliqa said, "I'm sorry for the way I treated you." She hardly looked sincere.

"Why do you treat me like that? You don't even know me."

Maliqa shrugged her shoulders. "I just don't like nobody comin' between me and my daddy. I..."

"I haven't come between you and your daddy, Maliqa. You're not a little girl, you have your friends and your life. And your daddy's there whenever you *decide* to call or come to see him."

Maliqa glared at her then him. "What that s'posed to mean?" Maliq was just listening. Mitzi wished he would say something.

"It means that you only seem to remember that you have a daddy when I'm around."

"That's not true," she said, annoyed.

"Whatever," Mitzi said. "But just know that I care about your father, and I do intend to spend a lot of time with him, but I don't ever intend to try to *keep* him from you. I would like for us to be friends. We both care about the same man, and we're not children so I don't see why we simply can't get along." Maliqa sighed and didn't reply. Mitzi sucked her teeth. "Look Maliq, this child is none of my company, and I refuse to stand here trying to make conversation while she's ignoring me." She turned to walk away.

"Maliqa, all this isn't necessary." Maliq had finally spoken.

"I'm sorry." She sounded a little sincere.

"Really?" Mitzi asked sarcastically.

"Yes, really. I'm sorry for the way I've treated you." She spoke softly. "I guess I'm just jealous."

"There's no need to be. I'm not a threat." Mitzi was still pissed off with her and walked away.

"I hope you got her..." Crystal started.

"Anybody want a drink?" Raoul cut her off.

"You okay, baby?" Maliq had returned, minus the brat.

Mitzi smiled. "I'm fine." She couldn't be angry with him. "Where is she?" She really didn't care.

"She went to meet her friends. I really apologise for her behaviour," he said, putting his arm around her shoulder. He looked so good. And sincere.

Mitzi looked at him. "Don't worry about it. Hopefully time will work things out. She'll need me before I need her."

CHAPTER TWENTY

"I need to talk to you, Mitzi," Maliqa said. "Do you have a minute?" She leaned against Maliq's front door.

"Now Maliqa, don't start..." Maliq was pleading with her.

"I'm not startin' anything, Daddy." She sat on the edge of a chair and wasn't her usual harsh self.

Mitzi and Maliq were watching TV. He had been lying on the couch with his head in her lap until the doorbell rang. Mitzi's face fell when she opened the door to find Maliqa standing on the other side. She had been having a very nice day - until now - having spent the night at Maliq's, as she now often did. They had spent the better part of the morning making love before she had gone to wash her granny's hair. Then she had stopped home to clean and came back to relax with her man. The last thing she felt like right now was putting up with this child.

"What's up, Maliqa?" Mitzi asked.

"It's... kinda personal."

Mitzi got up. "Come in here," she said, heading for Maliq's room. *What could she want to talk to me about?* Mitzi wondered as she closed the door.

"I'm sure you're wondering why I wanna talk to you," she said, putting emphasis on 'you'. Mitzi just looked at her while they both sat on the bed. "I don't know if my daddy told you, but me and my mama don't really get along."

Surprise, surprise.

"I can usually talk to my daddy about anything, but this is a female thing."

"And you want to talk to me?" Mitzi was stunned.

Maliqa looked at her sheepishly. "I really need to talk, and I thought this would be a good way for us to... be friends."

Oh, you need me now. "I guess so."

Maliqa sighed. "My mama wants to put me on the pill now." She looked at Mitzi for her reaction.

"You're seventeen, Maliqa. I guess this is as good a time as any. Are you having sex?" She nodded with her head down. "So what's the problem?"

She looked up. "I don't wanna go on the pill."

"Well, tell your mama..."

"I wanna have a baby," she said slowly and softly.

Mitzi's eyes widened. "Why?" *What the heck is wrong with these children?*

Maliqa shrugged. " 'Cause I don't have any brothers or sisters, so I'm not gonna have nieces or nephews. My mama and her husband are never home, my daddy has you... I just want a baby so I can have somebody to love and spend time with."

"Maliqa, those are not good reasons for a seventeen year-old to have a baby. A baby is a big responsibility."

Is this deja vu, or what? Mitzi sighed. "You're young, don't you have friends?"

She nodded. "Yes, but some of them have babies."

"You feel left out?"

"Sort of."

"Well, maybe what you should do is take one of your friends' babies home for a weekend and see just how much of your time he demands."

"I could handle it." She was such a different person now, here in the confines of the bedroom with no one around for her to show off for.

"Sure, you could handle it - for a weekend. You're a mother for life."

"Not all the time. My mama stopped being a mother a while back."

"Have you stopped to think that's because she became one when she was younger than you are now? She didn't have the chance to enjoy her teenage years." Maliqa looked as though something had clicked.

"Do you want to treat your child the same way she's treating you?"

She sighed again as if she had the weight of the world on her shoulders. "I guess not. I never thought of it like that." She stood.

"Don't do it, Maliqa. You'll regret it, and you'll resent your child."

"Are you saying my mama resents me?"

"I don't know your mama, so I can't say that. But it happens sometimes. Why don't you ask her how she feels about you? It might make things a little clearer."

She looked Mitzi in the eye. "I'll do that the next time she comes home." She started toward the door. Mitzi felt sorry for her. She acted the way she did because she needed attention from her mother and got too much from her father.

"Maliqa?" She turned around. "What does your boyfriend think?"

She smiled and cocked her head to the side. "I don't exactly have one anymore."

"Well, how were you plannin' on...? Never mind, I don't even want to know."

"Promise you won't tell my daddy what we talked about?"

"I promise."

*   *   *   *   *

"So, what did my daughter want to talk about?" Mitzi was putting on her makeup. They were getting ready to meet Crystal, Raoul, Melba and Sundae for dinner at Whaler Inn. Maliq sat in the chair.

"It was a girl thing. I promised her I wouldn't tell you."

"She surprised me."

"No more than she surprised me."

"Thanks for listening to her."

"Happy?" She smiled at him. He smiled back.

"Yeah." He reached out and squeezed her butt. She wasn't wearing underpants and was instantly aroused.

"Don't start something you can't finish."

"You wanna see me finish?" He stood. She backed away playfully.

"No, nympho. We have to leave now."

"Yeah, you're backin' down now."

"Yes, but there's always later." She stood in his face now, and he kissed her softly on her lips. They stood face to face for a few seconds.

"Don't forget you said that," he said, their lips brushing as they spoke.

"Are we ever not going to make love?" Mitzi wanted to know. They had made love just about every day - several times a day - since the first time on her birthday.

"I hope not, baby," Maliq answered, softly. "Why?"

Mitzi shrugged her shoulders. "Because, I just don't want sex to be the basis of our relationship."

Maliq smiled and shook his head. "You worry too much, girl."

"I know..."

"We're adults, Mitzi. We know what we want. And what we're doing." He held her shoulders. "We're experiencing something beautiful and new right now." He got serious. "Do you feel like I'm taking advantage or you?"

"No," she said softly.

"Do you think you're taking advantage of me?" He was still serious. She smiled, then he did, too.

"No, but I'm sure you wouldn't complain."

"I love you, honey. I want a relationship with you. I want us to be together and grow together, and if we both want to make love every day, then hey..." He shrugged. "So be it. I won't ever force you to do anything you don't want to do, and if ever you think I'm trying, I know you'll stop me."

She kissed him. "Let's go so we can hurry back." She winked at him, sprayed some 'Narcisse' and led him from her room.

"And tomorrow, I'll get the blame," he mumbled sarcastically.

They nearly bumped into Ebone´ in the hallway. She was running for the door. "I thought you'd long gone," Mitzi said, looking at her watch.

"I should have been," Ebone´ said, grabbing her helmet. "But Roderick and I were out on a boat all day." She was smiling, something she did a lot lately.

" 'Scuse me," Mitzi said, smiling, too. "You want me to call Wendell?"

"I already did. Check you guys later." She ran out of the house.

Mitzi shook her head. "I don't know what's happening to her, but let's pray it doesn't end."

Crystal and Raoul were already sitting at the bar, talking to the barmaid and maitre d'. Mitzi was surprised to see Crystal without makeup.

"Sundae called me just before I left home. Something happened, and she can't make it," Crystal said, sipping her drink. "And Melba's son had an accident, broke his leg and has a concussion. She left to fly up to him this afternoon, so it's just us four." Mitzi and Maliq joined them at the bar.

"What? Why didn't Melba call me?"

"Didn't have time. She only had two hours to catch the plane. I just happened to be at her job when the school called. Maliq ordered a round of drinks for everybody.

"Is Melvin gonna be all right?"

"Crystal shrugged. "They didn't tell her too much, but it's not life threatening."

Maliq handed Mitzi a glass of wine. "Thank God for that. What's the deal with Sundae?"

Crystal waved her hand. "Who knows? You know her, always got a crisis. She'll call one of us later."

The captain arrived to seat them outside where they ate from the buffet until they could eat no more. It was still very warm, but a nice breeze blew under the umbrella. They could see the beach below which was crowded with tourists - probably Southampton Princess hotel guests.

"So how you like your friend without makeup, Mitzi?" Raoul asked, caressing his wife's arm.

"I'm glad you asked," Mitzi said. "What's with this bare-faced look, sister? Did Fashion Fair go out of business?"

Crystal took a mirror from her bag and checked her face. "No, I just felt like takin' a break from all that mess. And furthermore," she said, putting the mirror back, "why paint the peacock?" They all laughed except Raoul who made a face at her.

When they left Whaler Inn, they stopped at Cafe Lido for a few drinks. Mitzi and Crystal immediately went to the ladies room.

"Do I have V.P.L., Mitzi?" Crystal asked, checking for a visible panty line.

Mitzi looked. "No. And I know I don't"

"How you know? Lemme see." Crystal pulled her by her arm.

"I know I don't 'cause I'm not wearin' underwear."

Crystal's mouth fell open. " 'Miss Manners' ain't got no drawers on?"

"No bra either." Mitzi was smiling.

Crystal was shocked. "I never thought I'd see the day..."

Mitzi stopped smiling. "I do feel a bit funny, though. I've never done this before. I don't know what's happenin' to me. I feel a little... morally bankrupt."

"Oh for Jesus' sake... Does Maliq know?"

Mitzi nodded. "He was at the house when I got dressed."

"Oh girl, so when you walked off to the bathroom, he was staring right through your clothes." Mitzi winked, swung around and sashayed out of the ladies room.

Crystal followed her. "Talk about keepin' your man interested... I have *got* to try this."

*　　*　　*　　*　　*

"Sundae, are you out of your damn mind?!" Crystal, Mitzi and Sundae were on conference call.

"The clap?! You haven't been going with that boy but a minute, and you were scr..." Crystal stopped and sighed. "...having unprotected sex?! What the hell is wrong with you?!"

"Take it easy, Crystal." Mitzi was as annoyed as Crystal was, but as usual, she was the calm one. Sundae said nothing.

"Sundae, obviously what you do is your business, but come on now, you're grown. Surely you know better. This could have been AIDS," Mitzi said, calmly.

"It's not too late," Crystal started again. "How does she know she hasn't gotten AIDS from that empty headed dork?"

"You don't have to attack him like that, Crystal," Sundae finally spoke.

"I don't? He bladdy well knew he had some germy disease, and he wasn't man enough to..."

"It's too late now, Crystal. Sundae, did you get a prescription from the doctor?"

"Yeah," she said meekly. "And he gave me an AIDS test. I have to wait a while for the results."

"You'll be okay," Mitzi said, failing in her attempt to sound convincing.

"Sundae, please..." Crystal said, sounding a little calmer.

"Anyway," Mitzi cut her off. "We'll be here for you. Right, Crystal?"

"Yah, I'll be here to drive her to St. Brendan's. She needs her head examined, that's what she needs."

"Don't worry 'bout her, Sundae," Mitzi said.

"Sundae, I don't mean to be harsh, but you need to exercise better judgment," Crystal said. Sundae sighed again, and this time they both felt sorry for her.

"I don't feel like talkin' 'bout it any more." Sundae sounded very distraught.

"So, what's the deal with you two now?" Crystal asked, ignoring her comment.

"There is no 'we two'. I broke up with him."

"Thank God. Dopey, nasty frigger."

"Anyhow, I'm going to my bed. I'll talk to you lot later."
Sundae hung up.

"Every day I realize just how much I don't need children; I
have Sundae," Mitzi said to Crystal.

"Hold on, Mitzi, somebody's calling me." Crystal clicked
over, answered the call and came right back. "Mitzi, Melba's
on the line."

"Hey girl, you back home?"

Melba sighed. "Yeah, I got back yesterday."

"Yesterday?!" Both Mitzi and Crystal asked at the same
time. "Why are you just calling us?" Crystal demanded.

"I've been busy since I got back."

"How's Mel doin'?"

"Oh, much better. He'll have the cast on his leg for a while
obviously, but they did a CAT scan, and his head is fine."

"That's a relief," Mitzi said. "Is Tony going up?"

"He went with me."

"Oh?" Crystal's ears perked up.

"Yes," Melba said slowly, smiling.

"Did he come back with you, too?" Crystal asked.

"Yes. And your point...?"

"None. By the way, where did you two stay while you were
out there?"

"At a Howard Johnson near the hospital."

"Let me help you, Crystal." Mitzi interrupted. "Melba, did
you have two rooms or one? If you had one, did you sleep in
one bed or two? If you slept in one bed, did you do it? If you
didn't do it out there, do you plan to do it sometime in the near
future?"

"Are you finished?" Melba asked, both she and Crystal
laughing.

"Hey, I don't wanna know all this stuff, those are the things
Crystal wants to ask you."

"Well, since you two have to know, we stayed in separate
rooms in the same hotel. And when Melvin got out of the

hospital, we all stayed in the same room for one night, then Tony and I flew home yesterday."

"That doesn't sound too bad..."

"And... last night, he cooked dinner for me."

"Hey now," Mitzi said.

"That's what I'm talkin' 'bout," Crystal added. "No wonder you didn't have time for your girls."

Melba laughed and sounded more happy and relaxed than she had in a while.

"You two gonna get back together, Melba?" Crystal asked seriously.

"I didn't say that."

"I know, but what do you think?"

"Look, I'm not thinking about anything right now. Que sera sera."

Mitzi and Crystal filled Melba in on Sundae's dilemma, and surprisingly she was a little sympathetic. It was something how a new love interest could change a person. Then they made plans for Cup Match. It was going to be in Somerset this year, and Maliq had invited them to go up to the game on his boat. Melba said she would invite Tony.

* * * * *

"And don't be late tomorrow, Sundae," Crystal complained.

It was the end of the first day of Cup Match. They were all getting off the boat at Jews Bay, which was where Maliq kept it. It was early dusk, and Maliq, Raoul, Tony, Roderick and Marcus were unloading coolers from 'Mystique'. Mitzi, Crystal, Sundae, Ebone´ Melba and Atiba were loading things into their cars. They had set off from the dock at seven that morning and by eight had their camp at Somerset Cricket Club fully set up. Everybody was child-free, and they had had a ball. At lunchtime, they all ate in the camp and during tea break, Mitzi and Maliq had walked around, visiting friends. Crystal and Raoul had won three hundred dollars playing Crown and Anchor, while Melba and Tony had lost God knew how much. Marcus and Roderick had gone to check on the boat while the remaining few had stayed at the camp, listening to Soca, eating junk food and having cocktails. As soon as stumps were drawn, they all packed up and left the field.

"I couldn't help being late this morning, girl," Sundae answered Crystal. "I told you already..."

"Whatever," Crystal held her hand up to cut Sundae off. "Tomorrow we have to move early. You know how many people come out on the second day."

"The boat leaves at seven tomorrow morning, Sundae," Mitzi said, trying to be stern.

"I'll be here at six thirty," Sundae insisted, putting the last bag in Crystal's trunk.

Mitzi and Maliq took the boat back out to anchor it, and by the time they did, the sun had set and the moon had lit the clear, tranquil water.

"Have a good day, baby?" Maliq asked Mitzi as they stood on the boat, his arms around her waist as he stood behind her. Despite the humid air, it felt good to be in his arms.

"I sure did," Mitzi smiled and put her hands over his. "You?"

"All my days with you are good." He kissed the back of her neck. It was a little sticky, but he didn't care.

"I feel the same way, sweetie," she said, flinching from the feeling of his tongue on her skin.

"Why don't you take your top off?" He knew she had her bathing suit on under her net top and shorts.

She looked at him suspiciously. "Why?"

"So you won't feel the heat."

"Who told you I feel the heat?" She knew where he was going.

"Nobody had to tell me. I know I make you... hot," he said, breathing in her ear as he did. She turned to face him, put her arms around his neck and kissed him. He pulled her top over her head and threw it on the floor of the boat. Her bathing suit followed shortly after, and as the moon shone on only their moist, naked bodies, they spread a sheet at their feet and made love on it until they fell asleep. Sometime during the night, they went into the cabin, made love once again and went back to sleep.

Maliq woke Mitzi up at five thirty, and they both laughed. "How the heck did we end up sleeping on the boat?" They were both dressing, having slept naked.

"I didn't have the chance to get off the boat. You were all over me all night," Maliq teased.

She hit his firm, bare chest with her shorts just before putting them on. "And you couldn't escape? Is that it?" she asked as he pulled her in his arms.

"Kiss me, baby." he whispered.

"I haven't cleaned my teeth yet." She tried to pull away.

"So what?" He held on. "I haven't either, but we're in love so it doesn't matter," he said, as his tongue pushed her lips apart. As Mitzi closed her eyes and responded, she realised that that was the first time Maliq had ever said anything about them being in love. She had never said it either - not even to herself. But as she stood in his arms under the early morning sky, she knew she was.

*   *   *   *   *

"What time did you guys get home last night?" Crystal asked Mitzi as they loaded the boat. "We slept on the boat," Mitzi answered. Maliq winked at her. Crystal's face lit up.

"You two are nasty." Crystal was smiling.

"If they're so nasty, why are you smiling?" Raoul asked.

Crystal sucked her teeth and laughed. "Because, nasty ain't necessarily a bad thing."

"Who's nasty?" Sundae wanted to know. They hadn't even seen her coming.

"Don't worry 'bout who's nasty," Crystal said, looking at her watch. "Who the hell's late?"

Sundae grabbed Crystal's arms. "Girl, I bet you I'd push you overboard."

Crystal got serious. "Don't mess around, Sundae girl. You know I can't swim."

"You still can't swim, Crystal?" Mitzi asked, surprised. Raoul rolled his eyes.

"You're a Bermudian, and you can't swim?" Sundae asked.

"So what? I've had two babies; doesn't make me a gynecologist. What's your point?" Maliq laughed - he thought Crystal was *so* funny.

"Sundae please, do everybody a favour. Don't let this woman go overboard, 'cause I'll have to jump in after her, and she'll drown the both of us."

"All those bathin' suits you have..." Sundae had to keep it going.

"I'm a poser, Sundae. I pose, okay? Now leave me the hell alone!" She hit Sundae with a towel.

Mitzi looked at her watch as the rest of the crew arrived all at the same time. Within half an hour they were on their way to Somerset.

As expected, there was a bigger crowd than the first day, but there still didn't appear to be as many people as usual. The first day had belonged to Somerset - they had declared at two hundred forty-seven for four, then took three St. George's wickets in the last twenty minutes of the day. They arrived at the Club this morning to find spectators tidying up camps, restocking coolers and laying out food. Soca music played in the distance, and everybody was in a festive mood. Cup Match usually brought out the best in everybody - until some of them had a bit too much to drink. A guy who looked like he had spent the night sleeping next to their camp was now sitting up, looking as if he were trying to figure out where and who he was. Maliq gave him a cup of water which he immediately poured over his head. Their 'neighbours' arrived shortly after they did, and the 'Somerset/St. George's' arguments began. By the time the game started, the camp was settled - Crystal was eating, of course - and ready for whatever the day would bring. It brought a lot of heat. It was unbearably hot - ninety degrees - but the exciting game took everyone's attention to the field. The St. George's captain promised he was going for a win, and that he did. St. George's six wicket victory over

Somerset, albeit away from home, sparked a major celebration - a carnival atmosphere. When it was clearly evident that St. George's would take the cup back to the East End, their loyal supporters - including Raoul, Crystal and Sundae - lined the boundary, and on the winning 'knock', hundreds converged on Somerset Cricket Club field. St. George's had won in Somerset, for the third time in just over ten years.

Mitzi and her 'crew' began packing up the camp as soon as the game ended and left immediately after the presentation. With spirits high, they headed back to the boat. They still had enough food and drink left to feed a nation.

"Thank God I'm not opening the shop tomorrow," Mitzi said. They were anchoring at Castle Island, where they planned on barbecuing. As soon as Marcus cut the engine out, Roderick, Tony and Atiba jumped in the water. It was eight o'clock and still light. Ebone´ and Marcus followed the others overboard. Maliq started the gas grill then took off his shirt, ready to dive off the edge of the boat. The water looked like glass. A few minutes later only Crystal was left on the boat, so she started cooking. Mitzi was the first one out of the water as dusk fell.

"It's not about swimming in the dark," she said, drying herself.

Crystal looked in the water. "All that noise those lot are making would scare any creature away."

Shortly after, Ebone´ got back on the boat and wrapped herself in a towel. "It's getting too dark for me, too. But then, as dark as I am, no sea creature would see me anyway."

"You're right," Crystal said without thinking. Ebone´'s expression changed. "I'm sorry, Ebone´, I didn't say that to offend you. I just meant..."

"Don't worry 'bout it. I'm used to it." She dried herself.

Crystal looked at Mitzi who raised her eyebrows. "Does your dark skin bother you, Ebone´?" Crystal asked, feeling bad.

Ebone´ shrugged. "Sometimes."

"Why?"

"I don't know. It always has. I guess it goes back to when I was in school. The 'yella' skinned girls with good hair always got treated better than us with dark skin. The only thing that got me through was my good hair."

Crystal knew fair-well what Ebone´ meant. She wasn't exactly dark, compared to Ebone´, but she had dark brown skin and had been teased in school, too. Being short hadn't been easy either. "You do know that there's no such thing as 'good' hair anymore, right?"

"Yours is good," Ebone´ said to Crystal. The texture of Crystal's hair had saved her from severe teasing, too, but she still didn't subscribe to the 'good' hair notion.

"Ebone´, that 'dark skin makes you inferior' theory went out a long time ago."

"I know, but sometimes people stare at me - I know they're looking at my complexion - and I feel uncomfortable."

"Maybe they're staring at you 'cause you're a beautiful black woman," Crystal said, trying to reassure her.

"The colour of your skin has never bothered you, Crystal?" Ebone´ asked, getting dressed.

"When I was small, and I don't know if you lot ever notice this, but some people seem to lighten up as they get older. If you look at pictures of me when I was Zindzi's age, I was almost navy blue..."

"I know what you mean, but I think we just spent more time outdoors in the sun when we were young. Now we're inside working," Mitzi explained.

"Never thought of that," Crystal continued. "But anyway, as I got older, I realized that my complexion didn't make me. I still would have been just as I am, whatever the colour of my skin."

"Unfortunately," Mitzi mumbled.

Crystal cut her eyes at her and continued. "I am at peace with my blackness, and Ebone´, you should be, too."

"I guess you're right," Ebone´ said as the others climbed on the boat one by one. "I know now that I'm a *decent* person, no matter what I look like," she said, smiling as Roderick wrapped his wet arms around her and kissed her. Mitzi realized then that Ebone´ was going to be all right.

They all ate then stayed on the boat listening to music and talking until one o'clock in the morning. They finished the 'dark skin - light skin; good hair - bad hair' discussion then talked about everything - 'mama's boys', fetishes, racial prejudice, infidelity and, of course, sex.

* * * * *

"I'm nervous, Maliq," Mitzi said as they drove to Albouy's Point. It was his parents' fortieth anniversary, and his whole family was going out on 'Mystique'. Marcus was bringing the boat down. Mitzi had styled a wedding party at the salon, and Maliq had picked her up.

"There's no reason to be nervous, honey. My family will love you. You already know some of them."

"I know, but the thought of being with all of them together intimidates me."

"The ever confident Mitzi Robinson is intimidated by something?" Maliq frowned.

"I know, scary, isn't it?" Mitzi checked her makeup. Her hair was piled on top of her head, and she had changed into a white shorts outfit. She had her one-piece bathing suit on underneath. She didn't think it was appropriate to wear a bikini this evening.

"They'll think you're cute, anyway," Maliq said, smiling as they parked in front of the bank. They were the last ones to arrive except for Malcolm whom they didn't expect to show up anyway. Maliq's family welcomed her warmly. Maliqa was happy to see her and was excited to introduce her to her cousins as her daddy's girlfriend. Within minutes she felt as if she had known them forever, and Maliq left her to talk to his sister and sister-in-law. They stopped at Paradise Lake where the kids promptly jumped overboard, and the adults laid out a huge 'spread' for dinner.

"Remember what we were doing about a week ago in this same spot?" Maliq whispered in Mitzi's ear. She looked

down, and her mouth fell open. They were standing in the
same spot they had made love on the first night of Cup Match.

"Boy, your mama's right there!" Mitzi whispered loudly.

"And you just gave yourself away. We could have been
dancing right here for all she knew." Mitzi laughed and shook
her head.

"I'm trying to make an impression here, do you mind?" She
was trying to be serious, and he kissed the back of her neck.
After dinner the Simmons children presented their parents with
their gift which was two huge portraits, one, of all the children
- including Malcolm - and the other, of all thirteen grandchildren. Then Maliq and Na'imah sang Diana Ross' 'Best
Years of My Life' and 'Endless Love' to their parents. Just as
they finished, Malcolm pulled up beside them in a friend's
boat. Mrs. Simmons cried while she danced with her husband.
Then everybody started crying - the women anyway - when
Na'imah's boyfriend Sinclair, asked Mr. Simmons if he could
marry his daughter. Then he pulled out a ring, got on his knee
and proposed. She promptly agreed to be his wife. While
Na'imah showed her ring to the women, the men took Sinclair
aside and warned him of the consequences of messing with a
Simmons sister. The grandchildren couldn't care less, and all
jumped back into the water.

CHAPTER
TWENTY-ONE

Lord, I can't wait for this wedding to be over, Mitzi thought as her mama rambled on and on about it on the phone.

"Everything will fall into place, Mama," Mitzi assured her. She wasn't really in the mood to talk to anybody; she had a strange pain in her stomach. Not as bad as cramps, but it hurt. She was trying to wash her granny's hair and hold the phone between her shoulder and ear.

"Let me speak to her," Granny said as Mitzi wrapped a towel around her head. She took the phone from Mitzi.

"Oleeta? Why are you acting like a virgin bride? You've done this before." She paused. "Nervous for what? On the day of the wedding, get dressed, go church, say 'I do' and go 'long 'bout your business." She listened again. "Well, whatever's not ready, too bad. How the devil you gonna act when Belinda... Oleeta... Roberta..." she sucked her teeth, "...this child gets married?" She asked, trying to remember Mitzi's name.

"Mitzi," she reminded her.

"Whoever," Granny said, waving her hand.

"Just take it one day at a time. Now, Mitzi can't talk, she has to finish my hair."

"Tell her I'll..." Oleeta started to say. Granny hung up.

"You don't worry about too much, do you Gran?"

"Puddin', let me tell you something. Ever since the day your Uncle Robert left here on a boat to go fishing and never came back, I realized that few things in life are guaranteed. My boy went fishing three, four times a week, every week for about ten years. Left the same time in the morning and came back the same time in the evening - like clockwork. One day he left, but he never came back." After fifteen years, talking about it still made her sad. She didn't cry anymore, but she still felt it.

"You miss him, don't you, Granny?" Mitzi was rolling her hair.

"When your child goes before you, it leaves a hole in your heart that is never filled."

"What you think happened to him?" Mitzi knew her granny needed to talk about it from time to time.

"They never found the boat or the two bodies, but I know in my heart he's dead."

"How do you know?"

"A mother knows when her child has stopped breathing, stopped *being*. I don't believe he died right away, but I woke up about four o'clock one morning about nine days later and knew he was dead."

"They never ever found any signs?" Mitzi was sixteen at the time and remembered the incident.

Granny shook her head. "They disappeared without a trace. The other boy's mother called me one day, talkin' 'bout they must have had it planned and ran off to another country."

"You don't think that could have happened?"

She shook her head again. "They were in an eighteen-foot boat. Now they could have arranged to be picked up by a bigger boat, but..." she sighed. "My Robert would never have let me suffer like that. I didn't bring him up that way. And furthermore, what reason did he have to run? I mean, he could have been mixed up in drugs or something illegal, but he would have contacted me some way. He wouldn't have let me suffer. My boy died out there." She sounded so sad.

"It's still hard, isn't it, honey?" Mitzi asked, rubbing her granny's shoulder.

"Not as hard as it used to be," Granny answered, blowing her nose. "But I'll tell you, all I'm sure of now, is that the sun will rise and set every day. Nothing else."

"You can also be sure that I love you, Granny." Mitzi tied the net over her rollers and kissed her.

"I don't know 'bout that either. Ever since that new 'bye' came along..." She stood and smiled at her granddaughter. She was joking with her. Maliq appeared to be decent, and Mitzi seemed happy.

"So when you two gonna stop shackin' up? Your mama's finally gonna be made an honest woman."

"We're not shackin' up. He has his house and I..."

She hit Mitzi playfully with a towel. "You know what I mean. You both wake up in your own beds every morning?" Mitzi smiled. "I thought not. You children think I came down in the last shower of rain."

"We don't need to get married yet. We haven't been going together that long."

"You're doing what married people do, so what's the difference?"

*   *   *   *   *

It was nearly the end of August, and the summer had been quite eventful so far. Oleeta was more of a nervous wreck with less than three weeks to go before the wedding. Mitzi had thrown a surprise Sunday morning breakfast shower for her at her aunt's house. She didn't need any gifts, but her aunts and their friends all wanted to have a little 'hen' party before the big day. And because she didn't need household gifts, they all bought her lingerie, some of which embarrassed Mitzi. Oleeta loved it.

"George is gonna know I'm his wife when I put these little numbers on," she had said, causing Mitzi to roll her eyes.

Tatyana's friends had had a shower for her, too. Mitzi had gone, but her mama only sent a gift, saying she was too busy. Macky hadn't bothered to show up. He and Tatyana had grown farther apart. It was a sad situation, but Mitzi still refused to hold her totally responsible. She was very disappointed in Macky.

On Saturday Mitzi worked until one o'clock then joined Maliq, Crystal and Raoul at the last County game. Marcus and

Atiba were away. Maliq had taken the barbecue and cooked steak, chicken and corn on the cob, right in the camp. Mitzi and Maliq had walked around the field, had their picture taken by a gray-haired man - whom neither of them knew - bought snowballs and finally left the field at nine o'clock.

Today, August twenty-ninth, was Maliq's birthday, and he and Mitzi had taken the day off. It was quarter to seven in the morning, and someone was ringing the doorbell.

"This can't be happenin'," Maliq said, in his morning voice. "Who the hell is that at this hour?"

He reluctantly released Mitzi who had been lying in his arms. The air conditioner and ceiling fan were on, and the early morning sun was threatening to steal the coolness they had been enjoying all night. Maliq pulled on a pair of shorts and went to the door. Mitzi automatically moved over to his side of the bed and inhaled the scent from his pillow. She had never before been so content. Maliq was back within minutes.

"I'm sorry, baby, but you have to get dressed." Mitzi frowned, and he smiled. "Maliqa's here with breakfast for us." He put on a tee shirt and went into the bathroom to clean his teeth. Mitzi joined him and when they were both decent, they went into the dining room and found the table set and a huge breakfast spread out, complete with a rose.

"I'm sorry to disturb you this early, Mitzi, but I wanted to catch you guys before you went anywhere." Maliqa smiled and lit a candle.

"Maliqa, this is a surprise," Mitzi said as she looked around at the pancakes, bacon, scrambled eggs, muffins, juice, champagne and tea. Maliq hugged his daughter and Mitzi no longer looked at her as the spoiled brat she had been when they first met.

"I'm not stayin' - my friend's waitin' for me. I just wanted to bring you breakfast and wish you a Happy Birthday, Daddy." She grabbed her keys, kissed Maliq, hugged Mitzi and left.

"Happy Birthday, sweetie," Mitzi said, kissing Maliq and taking off the wrap she had on over her nightie.

"Thank you, but I would be happier if you took this off, too," he said, pulling on her strap.

"Later. We have to eat now."

After breakfast they showered together, dressed and left home at eight o'clock. They had decided to tour the island all day, doing whatever they wanted. The sun was shining a bright eighty degrees as they drove straight down to St. George's via South Shore Road. They began their tour at Fort St. Catherine, where they took pictures of the beautiful old scenery and each other. From there they stopped at King's Square, taking pictures in the stocks. They left the old town and stopped for a few minutes at Lovers Lake, which was at Ferry Reach. Mitzi had never even heard of it before.

"So, this is where you've brought countless women before me." She smiled as he held her hand.

"But the only memory I'll ever retain is being here with you." He winked then took her picture. She laughed just as he did - her happiness captured.

They turned into St. David's and drove to the lighthouse. Mitzi was afraid of heights, but she bravely climbed the stairs, where she clung desperately to Maliq. He held her in his arms. They didn't even notice the tourists taking their picture. Then they stopped at Black Horse for lunch and drinks. There they sat outdoors and enjoyed the warm breeze blowing under an umbrella. Mitzi pushed her shades up on her head and patted her face with a tissue while Maliq ordered drinks for them. She ordered a seafood platter, he ordered a fish dinner, and by the time they finished eating, they were both so full, they just wanted to lie down and sleep. But as they drove along the causeway with the top down, they were re-vitalized and ready to continue. They stopped briefly at Crystal and Lemington Caves and the Bird Sanctuary at Spittal Pond. They took more pictures at Gibbons' Gardens and stopped to rest at Botanical Gardens. Maliq took a beach towel from the trunk of the car and spread it under a tree. They drank water and ate fruit from the cooler which was in the back of the car. From Botanical Gardens, they drove up to Fort Hamilton, sat on a bench and looked out at the city. The view was absolutely breathtaking. As they drove down King Street, they spotted Marcus and

Atiba. Maliq convinced Marcus to follow them to the ferry terminal so he and Mitzi could catch the ferry to Darrell's Wharf. Marcus could then take Maliq's car and park it at Darrell's Wharf. They ran to catch the boat as it prepared to pull out and were out of breath and laughing as they found seats in the sun. Mitzi took sun tan oil from her bag, and Maliq was more than happy to rub it on her legs and back. They stretched out in the summer air while the ferry cut through the glass-like water.

The ferry ride ended too soon, and they were back in the car, headed for Warwick Long Bay. There they put the umbrella up on the beach, spread a sheet, undressed and ran for the ocean. Mitzi reached the water's edge first with Maliq right behind her. He grabbed her around her waist, lifted her over the tide and pulled her through a wave with him. She squealed as the warm water covered her body. She had on a new two piece bathing suit - a cute little number she had bought just for this occasion. Maliq held on to her waist and kissed her. The beach was crowded, but mainly with tourists, so they didn't care that they were acting like teenagers.

"Remember the last time we were on this beach," he asked, referring to the first time they ran together.

"You mean, the time I left you behind?"

"No, I mean the time you had to fake an injury because..." She pushed him underwater.

They left the beach an hour later, and Mitzi was surprised they weren't tired; it was seven thirty. They had been going for nearly twelve hours. They drove westward, stopped at Fort Scaur - where they walked around for a while - then drove up to Dockyard. On the way out of Somerset, they stopped at Loyalty Inn for a few drinks and some mussel pie. By the time they left Loyalty, it was dark and they drove to Long Bay and spread the sheet on the beach.

"Have you enjoyed your birthday, honey?" Mitzi sat between Maliq's legs and pulled her top over her head. He rubbed her back.

"Are you tellin' me my birthday's over?" He was feeling 'nice'.

"I didn't say that. I'm just wondering if you've enjoyed it so far." She took both their shoes off.

"I've been with you all day, of course I've enjoyed it," he whispered. "I don't want to sound patronizing, but I have never celebrated any birthday like this one." He kissed her neck between words. "I've needed you for a long time, Mitzi."

"Needed or wanted?" She looked up at the stars as she enjoyed his soft, wet flesh against hers.

"Needed." Anybody can get what they want but not always do we get what we need." He sucked her neck. She closed her eyes and didn't open them again until they had both climaxed, on the beach under the stars.

"Do you realize we could get arrested for this?" Mitzi whispered, pulling her shorts on.

"You just finished making love in the middle of a public beach, and now you're whispering?"

"I can't believe the things you make me do," she said, putting her shoes on.

"How can I *make* a grown woman do something against her will? I'm not that sharp."

"You should be ashamed of yourself."

"I'll leave that to you - all that noise you made a few minutes ago..." He was smiling, enjoying the effects of both the liquor and the sex. She hit him with a towel.

"I'm so embarrassed. Was I really that loud?"

"Scared the fish away."

She covered her face in mock shame. He held her. "But when two people are as much in love as we are, that doesn't matter. Nothing does, except our love for each other."

Maliq had once before spoken about them being in love, and she had wondered if it was just something he thought he should say. But as she stood here in his arms in the warm August night after having made passionate love only moments before, she realized that there was no other possible way to describe this feeling, this 'oneness' with this man she had known for three short months. Never before had she felt this peace, this unadulterated satisfaction, this contentment, this ability to be herself,

to be true and open and honest - without effort. Without
pretense. Yes, she knew that God had put her heart in Maliq's
hand. She could discard her long-time belief that two people
had to spend years together before love was even discussed.
She had no idea when he had actually fallen in love with her,
but she knew at this very moment that she was definitely in
love with him - and had been her whole life; she had just been
waiting for him to show up.

"I love you, baby," he whispered.

"I know. I love you, too."

When they reached his house, there were three cars in his
yard. Mitzi recognised Marcus' car. He, Terry and two guys
whom she didn't know, were all sitting in the back yard. They
had come to have a 'few' with Maliq on his birthday and were
prepared to wait as long as they had to for him to come home.

"You're not disappointed, are you, honey?" They were in
the shower. His brother and friends were in the living room,
starting the 'set'.

"Of course not. We've been together the whole day." She
put her arms around his waist as they stood under the cool
water. "I had big plans for you tonight, but..." She was teasing
him. "... If you want to spend the night with a bunch of hairy
men..." Maliq opened the shower curtain and started to get out.
"Where you going?"

"To tell those brothers to get out of my house."

She pulled him back and laughed. "No, I'll go home and
leave you to end your day with the boys." She kissed him.
"I'll see you tomorrow." She knew she didn't have to ask if
she would see him tomorrow. They were in love; she knew he
wanted to see her, too.

CHAPTER TWENTY-TWO

"Maliq, I'm talkin' to you." Mitzi was sitting on the edge of his bed, trying to have a conversation with him while he watched baseball on TV.

"I hear you, honey... damn!" He shouted at the TV.

Mitzi sighed. She was getting annoyed. "Well, what did I say?"

Maliq continued to look at the TV. "You... said something about... the wedding... man hit the ball!"

She sucked her teeth. "What did I say about the wedding?"

"Huh? You said you can't believe it's here already." He finally looked at her. "Didn't you?"

"I'm getting tired of this now. This is the third night in a row you've treated me like this." She stood.

"Treated you like what?" His eyes were glued to the game.

Mitzi put her sandals on. "Like I'm not even here. Why are you ignoring me?"

"Mitzi, I'm right here. I'm watching the game. All you have to do is take your clothes off, lie down beside me and get comfortable. You can put the lamp on and read if you don't wanna watch the game, but I do."

She sucked her teeth. "Then watch it by yourself." She started to leave.

"Mitzi... this isn't called for, baby." He patted the pillow beside him. "Come lie down with me; the game's almost over - another half hour. Then I'll get up and make you somethin' nice..."

She stared at him for a minute. The sight of him in nothing but jockeys did nothing for her - she was mad. *I must have*

P.M.S. "Good-bye Maliq. I can go home and be ignored."
She headed for the door and waited for him to call her back.
This time she would give in.

"Good-bye, Mitzi." He didn't even look at her.

She hesitated for a split second but kept walking. *Good-bye
Mitzi?* Her plan had back-fired! *I can't go back now.* She
grabbed her keys from the kitchen table, knowing that by the
time she reached the door, he would be there to stop her from
leaving. She was opening the car door now. *Where is he? Is
he really gonna let me leave?* She was halfway home when
she realized that maybe she was acting like a spoiled, P.M.S.-
having, brat. Her mama's wedding was the next day, and she
had spent half the evening with her aunts, decorating the hall
and doing last minute things. When she got to Maliq's house,
he was in bed with the air conditioner on, drinking a cold beer,
eating popcorn and watching the game - minding his own
business. He hadn't expected her at all because he thought she
would be busy helping her mother. So he had planned to spend
the night alone. He had been pleasantly surprised when she
showed up, but he still wanted to watch the game and didn't
think that was too much to ask.

"He didn't ask me to leave," she told herself. "And there
were things I could have done while he watched TV. At least
we would have been together. She went home where she found
Ebone´ and Roderick playing cards and laughing loud enough
for the whole neighbourhood to hear. Her mood lifted as soon
as she saw how happy Ebone´ was. She had changed drastically over the past couple of months. Even her complexion
had gone from dull and ashy to vibrant and glowing. She wore
very little makeup these days. She had also been taking night
classes at Bermuda College, had given up smoking and
exercised regularly with Roderick.

"Guess what, Mitzi!" She shouted, throwing her trump card
on the table.

Mitzi was laughing because Ebone´ was. "What?"

"I got a new job! I start next week!"

Mitzi's mouth fell open. "You're leaving Wendell's?"
Mitzi hadn't realized she'd been looking for a new job.

"Not altogether. I got a job as a receptionist at an Exempt company, and I'll still work for Wendell three or four nights a week." She was beaming. Mitzi hugged her, and they squealed like school girls.

"Ebone', I am so proud of you." Mitzi kissed her, and that ended the moment.

Ebone' pulled away from her, still laughing. "Okay, don't tear it now," she said, wiping the kiss from her face. "It's not about all that mushy stuff."

Mitzi sucked her teeth. "Don't be so silly, girl." Roderick laughed at them. He was proud of Ebone', too. They had gotten really close, and he cared about her a lot. She had put a lot of effort into bettering her life. She still had a little way to go, but she was almost there.

Mitzi took a shower and thought about how silly she had acted at Maliq's house. She pulled a pair of shorts and a tank top from her drawer. "I need to go back and apologise to him," she said aloud while rubbing lotion on her body. Then she put the clothes back in her drawer, took her black, silk kimono from behind the bathroom door, put it on over her naked body, slipped into a pair of sandals, got in her car and prayed she didn't get a flat or have an accident. Her prayers were answered. She let herself in with the key Maliq had put on her key ring several weeks before. He was still in his bedroom, and she could hear the TV. He had been half asleep when she walked in the room but turned on the lamp when he saw her. He looked surprised as she stood beside the bed.

"You drove here in your robe?" He asked. She just smiled.

He pulled her to him as he sat up in the bed. Then he pulled the tie of her kimono and got the shock of his life. It slowly fell open, first exposing her dark brown, firm breasts. He became aroused as her taut stomach was revealed. This woman knew how to keep her man happy. His eyes traveled from her deep navel down to the top of her hair. He pulled the silk material from her shoulders and let the garment fall to her now bare feet.

"I'm sorry..." He stood and silenced her with his warm tongue. He held her soft skin in the palms of his hands and pulled her closer to his heaving body. She kissed his chest. "You're not mad at me?" She slowly ran her tongue from his chest to his ear.

"For what, baby?" he whispered.

"For the way I acted earlier." They stood - their flesh together. Maliq still had his jockeys on.

"You're entitled to go off every once in a while; you're a woman." She smiled, and he gently pushed her away from him. She moved reluctantly. He held her shoulders and studied her nakedness. His eyes lingered on her breasts and were half-closed as if the sight of her was making him intoxicated. "Look at you. How could any man in his right mind ever be mad at you?"

"I didn't have to carry on like that."

"Like what?" he asked, lifting her and laying her face-down on his bed. "I don't know what you're talkin' about." The scent of his pillow seduced her - it was a scent synonymous with his 'man-ness', his body, his being. Maliq opened the night stand drawer, took out a small bottle of 'White Musk' massage oil and poured it along her spine. She sighed in the pillow which she held as if it were him. He worked the oil into her flesh with familiar fingers that were partly responsible for the indescribable pleasure she had experienced over the last few months.

"Are you still mad at me?" Maliq took off his undershorts and straddled her. He continued to massage her flesh as she moaned.

"I... don't know... what you're talking about..." She struggled to get the words out as she lay beneath her man. Times like this assured her that all of the details - both major and minor - that were a part of her everyday existence, all the things which demanded her attention - life's subtle uncertainties - didn't have to be omnipresent. It wasn't just the sex, but the fact that there was another human being with whom she could be this vulnerable. What Mitzi Robinson felt for Maliq Simmons came from the depths of her soul. And if he didn't feel the same way for her, that was okay. She had found a home for her soul.

CHAPTER TWENTY-THREE

Oleeta looked twenty years younger in her wedding dress, which was a peach ankle length gown. She wore a matching headpiece and ivory, iridescent shoes. She carried a single calla lily. Mitzi was her mother's maid of honour, Aunt Roberta and Aunt Bey were her bridesmaids. They had all gone in to Mitzi's salon to have their hair done by Sundae, and Crystal had done their makeup. She had done a beautiful job, including covering the hickey on Mitzi's neck. She hated hickeys but had smiled when she saw the vestiges of her and Maliq's love-making in the mirror that morning. Sundae had pointed out how tacky it would be for her to walk down the aisle at her mother's wedding with "evidence of having done the nasty". Maliq had woken her up at eight with breakfast in bed. He had served it on a tray, complete with a flower from the garden and a note written on her napkin, which read, 'Thanks for last night. I love you.' She had wanted to make love again before she left, but Macky had called to complain about the way his suit fit and needed her to come and look at it. As much as she was mad with him, she went because she wanted everything to be perfect for her mother.

They were standing by Aunt Bey's pool, taking pictures as the horses and carriages pulled up. Mitzi wore a deeper peach knee-length dress, while Bey and Roberta wore orange dresses in the same style. They carried imported tulips - Oleeta's favourite flower. Macky and Frankie wore off-white suits with accessories matching Oleeta's. Granny wore a cream coloured skirt suit and grumbled about having to sit behind a smelly horse.

They arrived at the Cathedral at ten to six, to the ringing of the bell, and at six o'clock the procession started. Uncle Frankie had escorted his mother to her seat moments before, and as soon as the wedding march began, Mitzi's eyes welled up. She had a lot of reasons to be happy, but today her happiness was for the mother she loved - despite their differences - and the man who was about to become her step-father. Maliq was the first person she saw in church, and a tear rolled down her cheek as she smiled at him - another reason for her happiness. He smiled back and winked at her. Crystal and Sundae were beside him, and naturally Crystal started crying, too. George also winked at Mitzi as she reached the altar. His son was his best man, and his brother and a friend were groomsmen. More tears flowed as her mama walked toward them on Macky's arm.

There had been a time when Mitzi thought she would feel betrayed if her mama remarried after her daddy died. But today there were no feelings of betrayal. The father Mitzi knew, would have wanted his widow to go on with her life with someone who would be good to her and make her happy. Oleeta knew it, too. Mitzi and Macky had talked a few days before, and he had confessed that he was looking forward to George's being his step-daddy and moving in with them. She looked at her granny who was wiping her eyes. She would never admit to crying, though. Oleeta stopped and kissed Mitzi before Macky handed her to Frankie to give her away. Macky wasn't old enough to do it.

Oleeta cried softly as she said her vows, which meant she was happy. George held her hand and smiled at her throughout the ceremony. They were a beautiful couple. Following the ceremony, they went - by cars - to Hamilton Princess to take pictures. Then the horses took them to the reception. Granny and George's father joined Mitzi and George's son in their carriage, the new Mr. and Mrs. Bean traveled by themselves, and the rest of the party was in the last carriage. About a hundred guests greeted them at P.C.C., where the hall was filled with flowers, candles and balloons. Ten tables were tastefully decorated with flowers and baskets of fruit while the head table was adorned with candles surrounded by elegant floral arrangements. The sun was setting as the minister blessed the food and guests were invited to eat. There was a bar at either end of the hall, with the food spread strategically throughout the room to avoid lines. Maliq sat at a table with Crystal, Sundae, her sister Laverne, Ebone´, Roderick, Melba and Tony. Everybody had been surprised to see the two of them together. When the picture taking was finished, Mitzi left the head table and joined them. Maliq stood as she approached the table and kissed her.

"You look beautiful, baby," he said, holding her hand.

"Thank you, honey. You look like a million yourself."

"Good evening, Mitzi," Crystal and Sundae said together.

Mitzi and Maliq laughed. She had unintentionally ignored her friends while she talked to her sweetheart.

"Oh, I'm sorry my darlin's." She put her arms around both their shoulders. Crystal pulled away.

"No see, 'cause your man's here and you have on a halfway decent press..." Sundae held her hand up to Mitzi's face.

Mitzi stood back. "It's not that. I was just too busy lookin' good." She winked her eye at Maliq. He was practically mesmerised by her beauty. Ebone´, Roderick and Laverne got up to get some food, and Mitzi sat beside Maliq. "Crystal, where's Raoul?" she asked.

Crystal cut her eyes, and Sundae laughed. "She left her groceries home," Sundae said, referring to Raoul, and knocking Melba who was deep in conversation with Tony.

"I'm sleepin' with the enemy right now, Mitzi," Crystal said, sipping her drink. Maliq looked at Mitzi and frowned.

"That means she's not speaking to Raoul."

Maliq threw his head back and laughed. "You girls are a trip!"

"What about you, Sundae - couldn't find a date?" Mitzi asked.

"Nope. I had a few prospects, but I turned 'em down."

"Turned 'em down? Sundae, you better take what you can get. You don't particularly have a wide margin for error - you can't afford to be choosey," Melba said. Sundae stuck her tongue out at her.

"Now this conversation's takin' a turn," Maliq said, standing. "I'd better go to the bar before I have to duck a glass or something."

Tony stood, too. "I heard that. Let's have one, man." They headed for the bar and were hardly out of earshot when the gossip kicked in.

"Melba, what the hell is going on? One minute you're a damn recluse, the next, you're out with your 'ex'," Sundae started. "What's the deal with that - when did you two get back together?"

"Don't worry about all that," Melba said, lighting a cigarette. "And we're not really back together - yet." She exhaled and smiled.

"Incidentally Melba, you couldn't find a better dress than that for your courting debut?" Crystal asked. "Where you get that li'l 'do' - 'Maria Benns'?" Sundae laughed and choked on her drink.

"Look who's talkin', Crystal. Where yours come from - 'Whores Are Us'?"

"What's wrong with this dress?" Crystal asked, crossing her leg and exposing a lot of it.

"What's wrong with it? People can see what you're thinking in that thing."

"Yes, but nobody knows what the hell you were thinkin' when you bought this," Sundae said, pulling at the fabric. Melba knocked her hand away. "And lose some weight."

Melba cut her eyes. "Jealousy is a very ugly thing."

"And so are you, Melba - in that dress." Sundae loved to pay her back.

"And not to mention you, Sundae - are you trying to achieve a little cleavage?" Melba didn't like to lose.

Sundae sat up straight and looked at her breasts. "Yeah, I have on a push-up bra, is it workin'?"

"No," Mitzi said. "If you blink, you'll miss those things."

"Since Sundae brought it up, what's with the weight gain, Melba?" Crystal asked.

"Look, only dogs like bones, okay?" Melba shot back.

"Well, we can safely say that you don't have to worry about any dogs barking around you," Sundae said, smiling. Melba turned her back.

There was loud cheering coming from the dance floor. Mitzi's granny and George's daddy were doing the 'off-time'. Mitzi stood to watch and caught Maliq's eye as he stood across the room, watching too. The smile remained on his face as did hers. She waved to him, and he blew her a kiss.

"Mitzi, you didn't tell me your nana was coming," Crystal said. Nana had come from Florida and was sitting at a table, laughing and clapping her counterpart on.

"We didn't know. She surprised us. Doesn't she look good?"

Crystal nodded. "She hasn't aged."

"She sure hasn't. She's eighty-six, you know? That lady defies mortality... hey, look at Mrs. Seymour, putting food in foil! How can people do that?" Mitzi was annoyed. Crystal's mouth hung open in awe.

A man dressed in a pale blue suit - which was about two sizes too small - approached the table. "Oh Lord," Crystal said, holding her head. "Not today."

"Hi girls," the man said, leaning on the back of Sundae's chair. They tried to ignore him.

"You sweet, young things look like you need some company over here." He patted Sundae's back.

She turned around. "Hey, don't do that ace-boy," she said.

"Shouldn't you be somewhere baying at the moon?" Crystal asked.

He laughed and smoothed his mustache, hardly offended. "I was standing over there, watching you beautiful specimens and thought you all might need a little..." he cleared his throat, "... male company."

"Trust me when I tell you that you have completely mis-assessed the situation at this table," Melba said, blowing smoke in his face.

He waved the smoke away and smiled. "Perhaps ah... you fine creatures don't know who I am."

"Not a clue," Mitzi said. She didn't want to be too rude to him; he was probably one of George's relatives.

"Allow me then, to tell you about myself. I'm sure at least one of you will want me by the time I'm finished."

"Go ahead," Crystal said. "Every ass loves to hear himself bray. We wouldn't want to stop *you*."

This man was obviously drunk. He stumbled around to face Sundae and touched her hand. "So, where you been all my life, beautiful?"

"Hidin' from your ugly ass. And if you don't take your hand off mine, I'll kill you."

"I really don't think these ladies want you bothering them, papa." Maliq pushed himself between Sundae and the 'lovely', who straightened up and stuck his chest out. Maliq wasn't moved. The man straightened his jacket, cleared his throat and looked around the table.

"What - have I missed something...?"

"Just a few decades of fashion," Crystal said, looking down at his shoes.

"I thought you girls were lonely... this guy is with you?"

"Yah, so it's time for you to move." Maliq was getting serious.

"Damn man, all this leg is yours?" Tony grabbed his arm and shoved him away from the table as they all laughed.

"Now, which one of you sisters gave the brother a phone number?" Maliq asked.

"Crystal probably did since she's not speaking to me." Raoul had arrived.

Crystal looked up and cut her eyes at him. He bent down and kissed her. She tried to stay angry, but she blushed, pushing him away.

Maliq pulled Mitzi by her arm. "Come have a picture taken with me, sweetness. Or are you saving yourself for your friend?" he asked, looking in the direction of the 'devil in the blue suit', who was staring at them with a frilly-edged toothpick stuck between his wet, sloppy lips.

Mitzi cut her eyes. "I would love to take a picture with you, sweetie."

"Mitzi, get that shine off your face before you go posing for any pictures," Crystal said, taking Mitzi's face powder from her bag.

After the wedding Crystal and Raoul invited them all to their house. They sat on their patio in the still warm September air and drank wine.

"That was a beautiful wedding, Mitzi, you cry baby," Crystal said.

Oleeta had thrown her bouquet moments before she left, and Mitzi had caught it. She and her mama had both cried as they hugged. Out of the corner of her eye, she had seen Macky wiping tears away as George first shook his hand, then hugged him.

"I know, I'm such a sap. And so are you - you cried right along with me. The wedding was so beautiful. My mama was such a happy bride."

"Just like you'll be one day," Maliq whispered in her ear. She was sitting between his legs on a chaise and turned to face him, smiling - her eyes bright.

"I thought you were supposed to take your granny home, Mitzi," Sundae said, sitting alone. It didn't seem to bother her.

"Girl, she told me not to worry about her. Mr. Bean took her home."

" 'Scuse me," Melba and Sundae said together.

"Well, it's almost the end of summer already," Crystal sighed.

"Can you believe it?" Melba asked. She too, was sitting in a chaise with Tony, as Crystal was with Raoul. Tony had his arms around Melba's shoulders, and she was stroking his hand.

She didn't seem as uptight as she normally did. Getting rid of Roger was the best thing she could have done. Tony was so much more pleasant and friendly than Roger was.

"How come Ebone´ didn't come up here?" Raoul asked.

"Roderick's family is having an end of summer barbecue tonight, so they went to that."

"Mitzi, I can't get over how much she's changed," Melba said.

Mitzi nodded. "She certainly has come a long way."

"And in a matter of months," Crystal added.

"You know, a lot has happened to all our lives this summer," Mitzi said.

"Damn right," Sundae said, reflecting. "Lord knows I've been through the wringer myself."

"But you're a better person for it, Sundae," Crystal said.

"She is?" Melba joked.

Sundae cut her eyes at her. "I truly am a better person. I mean, I don't wanna bring up the fact that you girls are sitting here, wrapped in your men's arms and all, and I am damn-well by myself, but hey... I'd rather be alone and jealous, than with some idiot and unhappy. I can do bad all by myself." She looked as though she truly understood that.

"My girl," Crystal said, getting up and hugging her.

"Oh get away from me Crystal, you phony bitch," she said, not attempting to return the hug.

Crystal sucked her teeth. "I care about you, simple. And don't worry, we lot's gonna hook you up with a decent, clean brother."

"Like who? That winner in the blue suit at the wedding?" Everybody laughed.

"I won't let 'em do that to you, Sundae honey," Maliq said. "I'll set you up. Just tell me when."

She leaned forward and whispered to him. "What you doin' when you leave here? We could start tonight." Maliq smiled and shook his head.

"Poor you," Crystal said.

"Life really is strange," Mitzi continued thoughtfully. "It seems like ages ago that Ebone´ went through that mess. Just a few months ago I didn't know what was gonna happen to her. I mean, we always complain about being on the edge when things happen, but my girl was over the edge."

"I don't think I could have survived the things she has," Crystal said.

"A lot of people wouldn't have survived, but we all possess an inner strength - like a back-up - and I guess she used hers. Look at her now..."

"A new person," Melba added.

"In every way." Sundae said. "Appearance, attitude, decent fella."

"That's a strong black woman," Tony said.

Melba smiled and shook her head. "I'll never forget the summer I've had."

"Who the hell *could* forget that?" Crystal asked.

"I think I went to hell and back," Melba continued. "Damn, why do we have to go through so much in life? But just when I thought I couldn't take anymore..."

"I came back," Tony said, humbly smiling.

"Something like that." Of course, she couldn't give him full credit. She turned to face him though, and their eyes held for a while.

"The important thing is to hold on to all the lessons learned," Mitzi suggested. "Isn't it funny how, no matter how bad things seem - with friends in your life - they always have a way of working out? Just when it gets as dark as you think it could, the stars appear brighter."

"Uh huh," Crystal agreed. "We just always have to remember, the sun will rise and the sun will set every single day. And life goes on - we have to go on with it, even in the face of adversity. God has a hand in everything."

"Like I said, we all had something profound happen to us this summer," Mitzi said. "After all the mess I've been through lately, I would have never even dreamt that I would be sitting here, secure in the arms of my soul mate - emotionally satisfied." She turned around and kissed Maliq.

"Oh pleeeease..." Sundae groaned.

"I must say that meeting you all has definitely changed my life," Maliq said.

Raoul laughed. "You've only just begun, my brother. Trust me, these girls would change Satan's life."

Crystal sucked her teeth. "Raoul, you wouldn't be able to function without me in your life."

"Without all of us, Raoul," Mitzi added.

"That's right, 'cause without us, you might have to eat alone," Sundae said, trying to look innocent. Crystal threw a rolled up napkin at her.

Raoul hugged his wife tightly. "You're right, baby. I wouldn't even wanna think about life without you and the children you've given me. And I would never have been able to afford this house without your support."

"I know that's right," Crystal said jokingly.

The phone rang, and Raoul went to answer it.

"So you two got out of the doghouse fast," Sundae said as soon as he left.

Crystal waved her hand. "Sundae, one day you'll find out that, when you're with the man you belong with, little things don't count. I was mad at Raoul 'cause he was watching TV and waited too long to start getting dressed for the wedding. So, I left him home. But the wedding still went on, didn't it? Nobody heard Mrs. Robinson... Mrs. Bean say she wasn't gonna walk down the aisle because she didn't see Raoul Outerbridge in church."

Mitzi knew exactly what she was talking about. Real love and commitment were about the bigger things in life.

"Telephone, Mitzi." She excused herself and went into the kitchen.

"The world would be a better place if people would only realize that it's useless to worry about things we can't do anything about. What's meant to be, will be," Crystal said.

"And sometimes, no matter what we do, we can't change some things."

Mitzi came back and under the starlit sky and through the glow of the candles, they all could see she had tears in her eyes.

Maliq jumped up. "What's wrong, baby?"

Mitzi closed her eyes and sighed. Then she opened them. "That was Macky... his baby just died." Maliq held her as tears rolled from her eyes.

"I'm sorry, honey." He kissed her.

"It's okay, baby. God knows best."